The Water Lilies *of* Mishipeshu

By Karla Cruise

ISBNs: 978-1-963452-24-2 (pb);
978-1-963452-25-9 (hc);
978-1-963452-26-6 (eBook)

Book Cover Design: Mel Nigro, melnigro.com
Interior Book Design: Inanna Arthen, inannaarthen.com

The maps were generated using OpenStreetMap data in ArcGIS Pro, available under the Open Database License (ODbL). Photos courtesy of The History Museum in South Bend, Indiana. Maps by Erik Sauer.

Though grounded in the landscapes of history, some places and boundaries have been adjusted to fit the needs of the story.

Library of Congress Control Number: 2025910386
First Printing: 2025
Printed in the United States of America

Publisher's Cataloging-in-Publication
(Provided by Cassidy Cataloguing Services, Inc.)
Names: Cruise, Karla A., author.
Title: The water lilies of Mishipeshu / by Karla Cruise.
Description: [Minneapolis, Minnesota] : [History Through Fiction], [2026]
Identifiers: ISBN: 9781963452259 (hardcover) | 9781963452242 (paperback) | 9781963452266 (ebook)
Subjects: LCSH: Manuscripts--Fiction. | Algonquin Indians--Legends--Fiction. | Indians of North America--History--Fiction. | Women graduate students--Fiction. | Cultural property--Preservation--Fiction. | Pharmaceutical industry--Fiction. | Environmental justice--Fiction. | Religious awakening--Fiction. | Visions--Fiction. | LCGFT: Historical fiction. | BISAC: FICTION / Indigenous. | FICTION / Historical / General. | FICTION / Fantasy / Historical.
Classification: LCC: PS3603.R852 W38 2026 | DDC: 813/.6--dc23

To my husband, Ken, for never giving up on me—
and to my sons, Ethan and Erik, for all the magic bits.

At a rending of veils.
It will rise, in a time after times,
After swallowing death and the pit
It will return stainless
For the delivery of this world.
So the river is a god
Knee-deep among reeds, watching men,
Or hung by the heels down the door of a dam
It is a god, and inviolable.
Immortal. And will wash itself of all deaths.

– *River* by Ted Hughes

Acknowledgments

I would like to express my thanks to the Pokagon Potawatomi Band for sharing their knowledge of Neshnabe history and the Potawatomi language; to Brian S Collier, PhD, Director of the American Indian Catholic Schools Network and Faculty for the Alliance for Catholic Education at the University of Notre Dame for his close reading and advice; Travis Childes, archivist and St. Joseph County historian at The History Museum, for sharing his knowledge of local history; Rachel Bohlmann, American History Librarian and Curator who assisted me finding historical records concerning the removal period of the Potawatomi people in the Great Lakes region; Erika Hosselkus, curator of Latin Americana at the University of Notre Dame who provided me with resources on the Spanish in colonial America; Nolan Marciniec, my life-long mentor, who has instilled a great love of literature in the hearts of so many; and, finally, to my husband, Ken Sauer, and my sons, Ethan and Erik, for their great patience, good humor, and countless contributions to this story.

Mishipeshu's World
Lake Michigan
St Joseph River
MIAMI VILLAGE
POTAWATOMI VILLAGE
CAREY MISSION
Sauk Trail
FORT ST. JOSEPH
N
W
E
S
NOTRE DAME DU LAC
NAVARRE'S CABIN
SANCTUARY OF THE DEAD
Portage
MISHIPESHU'S CAVE
Kankakee River
Grand Kankakee Marsh

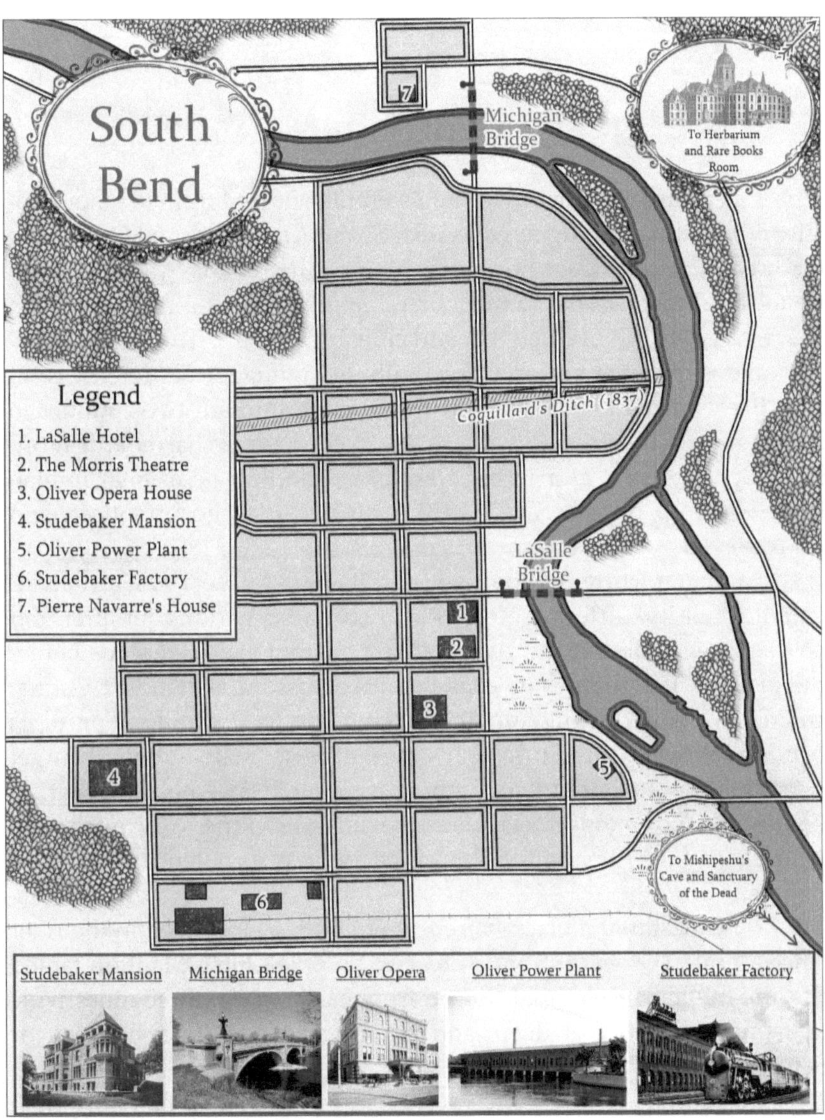

South Bend
Legend
1. LaSalle Hotel
2. The Morris Theatre
3. Oliver Opera House
4. Studebaker Mansion
5. Oliver Power Plant
6. Studebaker Factory
7. Pierre Navarre's House
Michigan Bridge
To Herbarium and Rare Books Room
Coquillard's Ditch (1837)
LaSalle Bridge
To Mishipeshu's Cave and Sanctuary of the Dead
Studebaker Mansion
Michigan Bridge
Oliver Opera
Oliver Power Plant
Studebaker Factory

PROLOGUE

Once the waters of the Senathëwen Zibé flowed from the mouth of Gitche Manitou, the Algonquin Great Spirit. And it was by Her will the birch bark canoes swept northwest each spring to Lake Michigan then on to the distant Straits of Mackinaw, returning south in the fall with woven baskets full of dried fish and crab apples.

Now, the waters simply flow without mythological pretense from Baw Beese Lake in Hillsdale, Michigan, south through two counties in Indiana, then unexpectedly north again through orchards and farmland. Spear-points, gun parts, glass beads and an occasional human bone wash up on the river's banks. Mostly, they go unnoticed and un-retrieved.

Satellite pictures of the river and its banks reveal modern civilization in all its Cartesian glory: Pizza Hut after parking lot after golf course after mall. Yet the river's shape has not changed since before the glaciers. It continues its snake dance across the flatlands, twisting, coiling, widening, regressing, then continuing for 250 miles. For all its bends and twists, the St. Joseph's current is so swift nothing can get a foothold on the bottom. Everything is swept away—bottles, crayfish, bodies, silt. No change in elevation explains its swiftness; the uncharted landscape of the river bottom causes mysterious turbulence at its lower depths.

Mishipeshu, the black-haired river goddess, has lived in the river since Manitou carved it from a great ocean of ice. First, Manitou tamed the Great Illinois River that flowed from east to west, three miles wide and one hundred feet deep, and from that the St. Joseph River, or Senathëwen Zibé, was created.

Mishipeshu's sister, Meskwake, was lost during that turbulent time. Manitou told her that a time would come when the rivers would rise and she would be reunited with her sister, but how long must she wait?

The first two-leggeds brought Mishipeshu gifts and revered her.

She watched them when they entered the river. Some were clumsy and oddly shaped; others, beautiful. Their legs and arms were strong yet soft beneath her caresses. She discovered they could not live long in water. They thrashed violently, became still, then the water would loosen the flesh from their bones. They were poor naked creatures with neither pelt nor fish's tail.

Mishipeshu swims with the river's swift current and, when she wishes, dives down to the sandy bottom where black leaves and rotten tree limbs decay. Lying on her back, she watches leaves drop on the surface, pale green in springtime, golden in fall. Animals come to the river to drink: the tranquil face of a doe, the impatient muzzle of a black bear, the rhythmic cat-lap of the cougar. She sees the small fish dart through the tall, green, undulating grass and the blackened skeletons of trees holding up their arms in the tessellated sunlight.

Canoes have sliced through the blue dome above her. She's seen the slow-moving rectangles of flatboats with long poles descending, and a large wooden fishtail cutting through the water behind. The paddle-boat's rhythmic rumble came next followed by the high-pitched whine of motors that made her ears ring.

Something, somewhere had gone quite wrong of late. What was taken did not equal what was given; what was said was more than what was heard. True, night still followed day, and day night, but somewhere a stone had shifted beneath a mountain range, or a raindrop that should have joined a river flowing east went west instead.

Whatever had happened, Manitou would set things right. A firestorm would scour the Earth. Smoke would veil the sky. And rain, the sacred tears of the gentle seas, would quiet the great confusion in a general hush.

That's how the story would end. But it began quite simply: there was a river, a journey, and an unforeseen death.

Chapter 1

Father Marquette's Last Journey

~ 1675 ~

On the portage between the Theatiki and Senathëwen Zibé, Father Jacques Marquette stumbled on a tree root, fell, and could not stand. The two Illinois Indians traveling with him set off into the woods with their hatchets and returned with saplings to make a sling to carry him.

While they worked, Father Marquette looked up into the canopy of basswoods and sycamore, and, in his fevered state, he saw again the snow that blew like a bridal veil across the roof of the crude hut they'd built last winter not far from Lake Michigan.

The sickness he'd thought had left him had returned. He remembered the long nights with his knees drawn up to his chest whispering the rosary, bead by bead, prayer by prayer. He remembered the excruciating trips to the outhouse—when he could make it that far—and the humiliating stench when he could not.

St. Ignatius suffered, and God spoke to him through his suffering; but Father Marquette's pain seemed to him without purpose. He reviewed the past year's events with a growing sense of injustice. Why had they waited until November to leave the mission at St. Ignace and head south? If they had left earlier, they could have avoided the snowstorms and bitter cold that brought his illness back and kept them stranded on the western shore of Lac des Illinois watching the surf turn gray beneath the winter sky. The few deer they'd found and killed had been too lean to furnish more than a few bellyfulls of meat.

His health had returned with the arrival of spring, and, as soon as the waterways were navigable, they continued south. He celebrated Easter, as he had long wished, among the Illinois. He remembered how he had stood above them on a great rock promontory and preached about his God in heaven who had triumphed over death. He remembered the hundreds of Illinois Indians sitting on bear skins, listening quietly, reverently, as the colorful, French-made devotional banners fluttered in the first sun-warmed breezes of spring.

But two days after Easter his stomach pain and bloody diarrhea returned with such debilitating violence that he knew he was dying. His two Illinois companions, brothers, who had accompanied him from the St. Ignace mission hurriedly prepared to make the journey back north.

Dying the death of a martyr was the fate Father Marquette had anticipated and embraced. But being carried off so prematurely just as his great work was beginning could not be part of any divine plan. Happenstance and poor planning had reduced him to this state, he reflected, not God's will.

Now, it was four days into their journey north through Illinois country. He lay on a buffalo hide beside the path, digging his fingers into the thick, bristly hair and breathing in its comforting, faintly musky scent. He could hear his companions talking in their native language as they checked the condition of their hunting gear.

"Deer are long gone before you pull the trigger," said Gekéndasot, the older and bulkier of the two. "They smell the smoke and the powder. And you have to find a tree that has the right height, shape, and strength to steady the barrel. The powder has to be kept dry too. How are you supposed to do that when you're hunting ducks in a swamp?"

"All this is true. But I'd rather have a gun to kill a bear," Akwandwė said, cocking his head to one side and raising his brows as he re-tied a bit of sinew on an arrow.

"That's a dishonorable way to kill a bear."

"I knew you would say that," said Akwandwė, leaning forward and rubbing the end of his sharply chiseled nose with enthusiasm. "See, brother, how you're no longer talking about the most effective way to hunt. You *were* talking about practical matters—the smell, the weight, the problem of keeping the powder dry. Now you're talking about something quite different: what is the most *honorable* way to hunt and kill a bear."

Gekéndasot sat back on his heels and sighed. "You can make any conversation tedious, brother."

"But, you see my point, don't you?" he said, holding the arrow he was working on for emphasis. "The French would say, 'Why must one know anything more about a bear than is necessary to kill it?'"

"There's more to it than that," said Gekéndasot, shrugging his shoulders and slinging his quiver over his back.

Marquette listened to the brothers' conversation from where he lay. Now that he could understand their language, their thoughts became clear pictures in his mind—battles lost and won, feats of strength, acts of cowardice, deer tracks that disappeared in the snow, bright moons suddenly covered by clouds, and always and everywhere the restless spirits of the dead.

Over the months and years, his purpose in this country had become increasingly muddy. Would he teach Christian charity to the Illinois? The Natives already protected the young and old more effectively than the French. Would he teach them to love strangers? They would rise from their beds in the middle of the night to prepare food for unknown visitors. Would he teach them to love their enemies? Doing so required despising strength and shunning glory. Even after centuries of Christianity, Frenchmen could not do that.

It was clear to him now that furs, gold, and a trade route to the Sea of China had been the real prizes for the French in the New World. Indian souls, a mere afterthought.

He closed his eyes and felt the gnawing pain in his gut. He had refused all the medicines his Native friends had offered. God would cure him, so he could fulfill his higher purpose. But God had other plans, it seemed.

Akwandwė knelt down next to Father Marquette. "Do you feel that you will die here?" Though his question might have sounded brutal to a tribe member, Marquette understood that Akwandwė did not want to trouble his friend with verbal ornament.

"Not here, but I will die someplace soon. Can you carry me further north, a little closer to St. Ignace? I want to see its white steeple one last time." Akwandwė's silent, steady gaze revealed doubt that he would last that long.

At a lake they'd passed by, Marquette had cupped the water to his lips to drink. When the ripples cleared, he saw his emaciated face reflected on the surface. He turned away, appalled and frightened by the transformation. He was only thirty-seven.

Marquette looked a little wildly at Akwandwė. "Do you have the water lily potion you told me of? The one you said brings visions and ends pain?" The lily medicine was a secret of the Medéwewen, and the brothers had sworn not to share its secrets with those outside the tribe. But the elixir was brought, and the priest took it gratefully.

Marquette lay his head back on the rushes. He could feel the will that had kept him moving forward through this wilderness for nine years deserting him. He drifted into a dream.

Dressed from head to foot in an outlandish patchwork costume of animal pelts, beaver, rabbit, muskrat, fox, and bear, Father Allouez, the Vicar General of Quebec, sat in the canoe's stern. He paddled without seeming to know or care where he was going. He smiled at Father Marquette, and a network of fine lines covered his parchment-like skin.

"Nanobozho so loved the world that he turned bits of his own flesh into raccoons to feed his people. Sky Woman, even with no husband, conceived twin sons and became mother of the Iroquois and the Huron. Holy Mother of God, pray for us. Corn Man, pray for us. Deer Woman, pray for us. Little Thunder, pray for us."

Father Allouez then put his paddle to one side and pulled a silver goblet from somewhere deep inside his furs. He filled it with river water, drank it to the last drop, and wiped his mouth with the back of his hand. "This country gives such pure libations to its children, yet we would have them drink our wine."

Marquette awoke feeling strangely detached from his pain. He lay at the bottom of the birch canoe, rocking gently on the water. His black cassock was wet, and he was alone. Akwandwė and Gekéndasot had tethered the canoe in the water to protect him from scavengers while they were out hunting.

Now that all his plans were thwarted and his driving ambition gone, he could gaze in wonder at the trees and sky. A large red-tailed hawk landed on the edge of the canoe. He strutted and displayed his majestic white and brown speckled breast and wings. Turning his head slightly, the hawk aimed an examining eye at Father Marquette. At this close range, the priest could see all the details his earlier sightings had left ill-defined: the amber-brown eyes flecked with gold; the imperious curved, steel-gray beak; the gossamer inner white feathers that were at this moment gently agitated by the breeze. With great effort, he lifted his enfeebled right arm and made the sign of the cross. A wave of love for the bird washed over him. Adoro te devote, latens deitas.

Akwandwė pushed the loaded canoe into the river, while Father Marquette looked into the deep blue sky. He heard the springtime call of birds he could now identify: the warbler's syncopated song, the melodic piping of the wood thrush, the rusty-hinge call of the blue jay.

None of his Jesuit brothers would be there to record his final moments. No one would know if, at the end, he had praised God or cursed him. He raised his right hand and slowly made the sign of the cross in every direction, encompassing not only his own companions, but also Gitche Manitou, the Great Spirit.

He blessed the whiskered catfish he knew swam somewhere in the watery underworld beneath him, and the deer watching them silently from the distant bank, and the turtles warming themselves on the rocks, and all the souls of the people and animals who had lived or would ever live along this river—all in one final benediction.

The brothers spoke of the need to tell the White men of the lily's power. They knew that there were Medéwewen who would oppose it—but if they could see the relief it brought their Black Robe, some might surely change their minds. They spoke as if he were no longer with them, and that was mostly true.

Droplets of river water fell on the priest's forehead from the paddle, as the brothers discussed the river's name. Saakiiweesiipiiwi was the name the Myaamia had given it—the outlet river. Not very imaginative, they observed. The Potawatomi called it Senathwen Zibe, or 'Difficult River,' and they blamed the river goddess, Mishipeshu, for its turbulence.

But the river wasn't difficult for Father Marquette. Lying on his back at the bottom of the canoe, he was gliding, flying between water and sky. Compelled by a will stronger than his own toward some destination—where exactly, he could not say.

Dawn

The sun was just beginning to rise when the river goddess Mishipeshu swam to the green-glass surface to look for Manitou.

Manitou had warmed a rock by the Old Oak, so her daughter could sit comfortably and comb her long, black hair.

Mishipeshu looked at her reflection in the water and waved her fish's tail gently in the water. "I miss Meskwake. Where do you think she is?"

"She has lost her way."

"If she is lost, Manitou, surely *you* could find her," said Mishipeshu, looking up at her mother whose golden antlers reflected the light of the stars.

"I must stay here so all things remain in balance."

Mishipeshu looked at her reflection in the water as she combed her hair, "Then *I* must find her."

"Meskwake isn't lost somewhere; she's lost in some time." Light rippled through Manitou's robes. "Your sister has fallen into the world of men, where days and nights have a geometry that is not ours. Be patient, my child. she will find her way home."

"I am young and have seen little of their world, but what I have seen does not put my heart at ease. Better to fall in with the bulrush, the duckweed, the catfish or the toads! You seem indifferent to my sister's terrible exile."

"Men are flesh, but also dream," said Manitou, caressing her daughter's head.

"You speak with compassion. Why?"

"Mishipeshu, the River nurtures all with its sweet water—the mighty sturgeon, the humble toad, and, yes, man as well. Be patient, my child." Manitou raised her bear paws skyward and rose up into the night.

Mishipeshu stared at the dark point where Manitou had

disappeared, then she dove into the river. She swam against the current to the river's bend and into the cave she had made her home. Long ago, when the river was still filled with ice, she had discovered this underground chamber with walls of golden sandstone.

Here, she rested on a bed of rushes, but she could find no peace. She looked at the treasures she had collected with her sister—nuggets of golden pyrite, clusters of sparkling quartz, a man's large, leather boot—and remembered their joy in finding them. She remembered the tricks they'd played on muskrat. She remembered their laughter.

She swam out of her cave to the river meadow, where fields of pondweed swayed gently in the current. So many tasks called for her attention. Beaver needed help gathering willow branches for his lodge. The muskies needed a bigger gravel bed to lay their eggs. The damselflies needed a roost to dry their gossamer wings. Yet Mishipeshu could think of nothing but her sister.

A bed of water lilies demanded her attention. Muskrat had torn up several plants in his relentless search for pondweed. She dug up the silt and sand to replant them. As she worked, she stuck a thick water lily stem in her mouth. When she chewed it and drank its bitter juice, time's tendrils slowly wound their way around her ankles and tugged. She remembered the lilies' time-traveling powers. If Meskwake was lost in time, surely these water lilies could help find her.

She went to work harvesting the water lilies. She ground the roots into a white paste and from that brewed an elixir: nabagûck. She fashioned twenty vials from river mud and made them transparent with her tears. Each vial she filled with potion.

She would not mention her journeys to Manitou. Despite Manitou's awesome power, she could not feel what it was like to be a sister.

Outside the entrance to her cave in his paddock, Namé, her giant sturgeon, rubbed his scaly belly against the gravel. Tomorrow, she would fasten the pearl-encrusted harness over his upturned snout, drink the elixir, and set off to look for Meskwake.

CHAPTER 2

OF GUNS AND BOTANY

~ 1763 ~

Lieutenant Francis Schlosser worked on his botanical manuscript with far more energy and attention to detail than he had ever expended on his military duties. He had inherited a soldier's life from his father without having any personal affinity for combat, strategy, weapons, or even order. Yet he'd proven duty-driven enough not only to survive in the profession but to succeed. Two years ago, he'd been given command of a regiment of *Royal Americans*, a British infantry unit of mostly Swiss mercenaries. They were responsible for the defense of the wilderness trading post, Fort St. Joseph—a link in the chain of garrisons the British had won from the French during the Seven Years War.

Forest warfare was supposed to be the specialty of Schlosser's regiment, but Schlosser didn't see how musket drills or harsh discipline would make them better prepared. They had enough muskets and ammunition to defend the fort, and their relationship with the natives was mutually beneficial, even friendly. The Lieutenant spent his days collecting plant specimens while the men played games of chance.

On the morning of the attack, Schlosser was doing what he had been doing nearly every morning for the past two years: working on his manuscript. He leaned back from his drawing of a water lily to let the still feeble light from the window fall more directly on his work. This would be his three-hundred-and-fifty-second drawing of a native plant. He had fallen in love with them all—the trillium, Junegrass, larkspur, columbine—and had rendered each with faithful precision.

And it wasn't the plant life alone that had won his heart. He had fallen in love with a half-French, half-Bodwéwadmi woman, Marguerite. She was a member of the medicine society, the Medéwewen, and knew each plant's healing properties and remedies for every ailment. Elixirs to reduce fevers, powders to thin the blood, roots to purge demons from the soul. She shared with him secrets that had been etched in pictographs on bark and passed down from one generation to the next.

Marguerite's grandfather had been Father Marquette's final companion, Gekéndasot, and she shared his dedication to teach Medéwewen wisdom.

Schlosser was a self-taught botanist. During his military training in Philadelphia and later while stationed at New York's Fort Stanwix, he read whatever he could find on the subject until deep into the night. He had even corresponded with botanists abroad. Schlosser didn't care that he slept on a floor mat filled with lice-infested straw. He didn't care that his rum was strictly rationed. And he was largely indifferent to the flour paste he lived on during the lean winter months. Marguerite and the manuscript filled his days.

Gnêw steered the canoe toward the riverbank as the six Bodwéwadmi warriors traveling with him paddled through a tangle of water lilies.

A field of grass opened before them on the right, and they could see the palisades of Fort St. Joseph beyond. A breeze carried the smell of smoke, pig fat, and corn cakes. One of the men put down his paddle and slipped into the cold water, guiding the canoe through the muck and blackened leaves from last autumn. Three more long canoes followed: two carrying eight men each; the other loaded with a secret cache of flintlocks, tomahawks, and gunpowder concealed beneath a layer of woolen blankets.

Farther south where the banks of the St. Joseph were covered with tightly woven brambles, another four canoes were coming ashore, each carrying eight warriors. Unlike the men now approaching the palisades at Fort St. Joseph, these men wore red and black war paint and carried their weapons openly. They dragged their canoes in the underbrush and made for a trail marker, a white oak hit by lightning several years before. They would wait there for the word that the attack had begun.

Within the fort's timbered walls, the soldiers were beginning their morning routines: cleaning muskets, fetching water, and rekindling fires that had died during the night.

The arthritic cook sat outside the kitchen peeling potatoes, occasionally straightening his spine with a grimace.

Marguerite sat behind the counter inside the fort's trading post. Her dark, wavy hair, escaping at every twist from the single, thick braid that stretched to the small of her back. She'd gotten up early to update the ledger with last week's transactions. As she worked, she could hear the fat, slow-moving cluster flies bump against the small panes of sun-warmed glass.

With her brow furrowed, she toyed with one of her silver cone earrings as she paged through an enormous, leather-bound ledger. Each page gave off a rich, musty scent: *10 beaver pelts, 6 rabbit, 20 lbs. sugar, 3 lbs. tobacco, 2 bushels black walnuts, 2 bouquets dried wormwood, 2 pieces sumac bark, 1 bag devil's bane, 3 seed pods may flower*. The Fort did a healthy trade in herbal remedies.

Jean-Luc Pélissier, a Québecois fur trader, struggled to open the trading post's heavy wooden door that had swollen in the warm, humid spring air. He leaned his shoulder against it, nearly falling into the room when it finally gave way.

Jean-Luc had arrived two days ago with six men in a canoe overloaded with brandy, tobacco, iron pans, and musket balls. The men wore red, knit hats and well-cut woolen breeches, and the Bodwéwadmi women, concealed behind a screen of quaking aspens, had watched them unload their supplies.

After getting their pay at the trading post, the men didn't go to the village, as the women had hoped. Instead, they went directly to the trapper's lodge on the fort's east side, where they drank large quantities of rum. Late in the night, they stumbled down the lodge steps, fanned out into the forest, and dropped to the earth. When dawn's cold light woke them, they returned to the lodge, dead leaves clinging to their backs.

Marguerite didn't look up until Jean-Luc was leaning his short, stocky figure across the counter. His large, hazel eyes framed by long dark lashes made him look like an old boy. His hands were large, his fingernails dirty and broken, and the skin on his hands was suffused with dark purple marbling from years of working in the bitter cold. He smelled strongly of rum, tobacco, and urine.

Usually, he wore a flirtatious smirk when he spoke with her, so it was odd to see him in distress. "You should leave here now, Marguerite." He furrowed his brow and spoke in a soft but urgent voice.

She focused her wide-set, dark eyes on him with a slightly skeptical expression. She was accustomed to dismissing most of what Jean-Luc said.

"Your brother's canoes are full of guns and tomahawks. I've seen them with my own eyes."

She kept her face impassive, unsure how much credit to give his words. "Gnêw has no reason to destroy the fort," she said as she pushed her hair behind her right ear and continued her scrutiny of the ledger.

He leaned further across the counter and whispered with even greater intensity: "Then why are his boats full of weapons?"

"Hunting?" she said, regarding him with the slightest trace of a smile.

The door pushed open and two young Bodwéwadmi men walked in, carrying fox pelts. One was her half-brother, Gnêw, an unusually tall man. His dark eyes were wide-set like his sister's but had none of their gentleness. A momentary silence fell over them; they heard the calls of late-returning sandhill cranes in the distance.

Gnêw nodded at the open door, and Jean-Luc shook his head and left.

"Bozho, Gnêw. I am glad to see you," said Marguerite in their native dialect. Gnêw let several moments pass before answering.

"We're not here to celebrate the arrival of spring."

Marguerite's father had been a kind though irresponsible French voyageur who left when Marguerite was just four. He was too homesick for Montreal and too bored with life in the wilderness. Gnêw's father had been a well-known Bodwéwadmi warrior. He died of smallpox on a journey to visit a southern branch of the tribe.

She had watched Gnêw play many roles as he grew up. First, a clown when he was small, trying to impress his friends with his latest prank; then, a holy man, observing tribal rites with a zealot's fervor; and now the warrior-chief who stood before her.

"So, you're here to kill me?"

Her jeering tone had been unintended. Gnêw looked momentarily unnerved.

"I'm here," he looked at his friend, Zhéték, who stood by the door, "*we're* here to burn this fort and kill all the Zhagnashêk in it."

She gazed into his familiar yet unfamiliar face. His eyes had the same trusting, tender look they had had in childhood, yet they now peered at her from behind a hostile mask.

"Gnêw, these men aren't your enemy. They're farmers, traders, blacksmiths. They're not even Zhagnashêk. They're mercenaries— mountain people from far away." Marguerite had worked at the fort for two years now and was well aware of differences among the White men.

"Why should I care where they're from?" he said, after a brief silence. "They don't belong here. They might not be Zhagnashêk, but they're paid by them. If they're not warriors, then they insult us by thinking we're such an insignificant threat they can man their forts with babies and pig farmers. Let them discover their mistake."

He stood on the other side of the counter from her and grabbed a knife from a shelf on the wall. He examined the stitching on its leather sheath.

"You think they'll love you in the village if you burn this place down? Bodwéwadmi, Wea, and Myaamia trade pelts, buy grain here. I buy *our* mother pans, blankets, medicine. Taking this fort will not make you a hero."

Gnêw examined her coolly. "In the village, they don't think beyond their own fire pits. They don't see what's happening in the world." He said this a bit self-consciously. He had stolen these lines from a speech by the revered warrior Chief Pontiac, who had just begun an armed rebellion against Zhagnashêk in the north and to the east.

Gnêw stared at Marguerite for several seconds, growing more comfortable with this new mask of indifference. "It saddens me to see what you've become. They've bought you with their frying pans, blankets, bags of sugar," he said, gesturing to the shelves piled high with goods. "When the time comes, you and this whole village will be herded west like buffalo. But I," he touched his chest, "will fight. I will not be pushed over the Mchëzibe and into the lands of strangers. The spirits of our dead will not be satisfied that we have pots and pans. They will lie quietly only when the enemy's blood is spilled."

Marguerite realized that this speech was for Zhétêk's sake as well as her own. She had underestimated her brother's political ambitions. She forced herself to take several breaths before answering. "Killing these men"—she pointed her chin in the direction of the fort's enclosure, speaking now with a tremor in her voice— "won't stop Zhagnashêk from moving in. Once you spill blood here, they'll want vengeance. And, then, just like you, they won't make any distinction among peoples. They won't care if they kill Myaamia, Bodwéwadmi, Ojibwe, or Nadwék."

"Zhagnashêk treat us like a conquered people. But we were just… asleep. Unfortunately for Lieutenant Schlosser, we're awake now—awake and united."

He buckled the knife he'd been examining into its leather sheath and tossed it to Zhétêk who was still waiting by the door. He threw it too far, and it landed in a corner. She could see that Gnêw was embarrassed;

anything clumsy disturbed his rigid choreography of aggression. Now, she understood—his course of action was fixed.

"*He'll* be worth nothing to you dead. You can ransom him." Her voice was ragged with emotion as she tried to sound as if she were arguing from a position of strength, rather than pleading. Francis was a big man, but cerebral and disinclined to swift action. She pictured his massive head, coarse light hair, and comical pince-nez perched on his nose. Taking down a man like Schlosser would seem vaguely dishonorable to her brother—like slaughtering a cow.

"Make him come out and talk to us, and make sure he brings no weapons. Tell him Bodwéwadmi warriors have stopped by to wish him good morning."

"You'll ransom him, then?"

For a moment, his eyes drew his sister close, but then the hostile mask returned. "I'll make no promises," he said, surveying the shelves of hardware and blankets.

Marguerite, breathless, grabbed her cloak, wrapped it tightly about her thin shoulders, and moved swiftly to the door. Her actions were decisive, but she had no plan. Her heart and head were in chaos. She fought with the swollen door, until Zhététk assisted her by giving it a powerful kick at the sticking point.

"Don't warn the men, or Schlosser will pay for it," her brother added.

She crossed the open courtyard on the planks that spanned the drying mud. Four soldiers sat outside the barracks on logs, playing cards in the long-awaited sunshine. They had seen the Bodwéwadmi arrive and thought nothing of it. Gnêw and his men frequently brought furs and medicinal herbs to the trading house. They tipped their hats as Marguerite walked by.

"Good morning," she said.

A mangy mutt whined and wagged his tail furiously, trying to get the men to throw the stick he had just placed within their reach. She could hear the blacksmith's hammer strike the anvil rhythmically.

She reached Schlosser's squat, one-story wooden cabin where he spent most of his time. Shingles were missing on the roof where a large tree limb had fallen during a windstorm last year; the front porch boards were rotten. Maintenance tasks went undone so that he could focus every free moment on the manuscript. She went around to the back door, where he'd placed a flat river rock to serve as a step. She knocked.

"Come in!" he yelled in a gruff, slightly impatient voice.

She entered the dark room and saw his large back sheathed in the white cotton of his shirt. He was leaning over his writing table beneath a window, drawing. She could hear the ticking of his wooden clock, sounding as warm and resonant as a heartbeat. It was one of the few things he had brought with him from his world—the world of brick houses, cobblestone streets, and horse-drawn carriages.

"I've got the petal shapes right, but the roots are wrong. What's not right here?" he asked.

She stood next to him and stared at his drawing, not knowing exactly how to begin. He took her hand in his and pressed it to his lips, as if deriving secret sustenance from her skin. She put her fingers into his thick, light-brown hair but suddenly imagined blood and a sharpened blade.

"Gnêw's here with his men. He says he's going to burn the fort and kill the soldiers," she said breathlessly.

Schlosser turned to look at her, his face blank with shock. "Why?"

"I don't know. I don't…" Then her brother's anger rose up in her own breast, and she finally felt what she did not want to feel. "They want all of you gone. They're sick of being treated like children. They want the British out."

"They're not going to make that happen by burning the fort." Schlosser drew in a deep breath and looked at the floor. "I should have seen this coming." He stood up, looked down at the manuscript, closed it, and awkwardly pawed through the scattered papers on his desk in search of his glasses. They heard a chilling *whoop* followed by shouting.

"Jean-Luc said they have guns," she said in a quiet voice.

They looked directly into one another's eyes, desperation intensifying their closeness.

It was the young man Francis who closed his eyes tightly and embraced Marguerite, but it was Ensign Schlosser who then held her at arm's length and spoke gravely. "Take the manuscript and go to the village. Leave through the backdoor. And for God's sake, make sure no one sees you."

He grabbed his rifle off the wall and lumbered to the front door.

She rushed towards him. "Don't go out there! They'll kill you!"

He froze for a moment, as if reconsidering, but then shook his head and said, "I don't have a choice."

He opened the door and stepped out. A rifle fired, and she ran out after him.

He lay on the porch, a red flower of blood blooming across his white shirt. "Go!" he shouted, his face contorted with pain and anger.

She retreated inside the cabin but then stood motionless. War cries rang out in a shrill staccato, bringing her back to her senses. She took Schlosser's jacket, still warm from his body, and wrapped the manuscript. On the shelf above his desk, she saw the amulet her mother had given her, and she had given to him. It was a lock of Mishipeshu's hair. Gunfire rang out from all directions. She took the amulet, put it between the pages of the manuscript, and hurried out the back door.

There was no one in the narrow alley that ran between Schlosser's cabin and the fort's high wall. The path was overgrown, used only by the fort's two dogs and the raccoons that visited the trash pile outside the kitchen. She slipped through a narrow opening in the palisade and ran into the forest.

Schlosser lay on the porch waiting to die. He thought he'd been shot through the heart and was surprised he was still breathing. He lifted his head slightly and saw his rifle about a foot from his head. He would have to shift his body to reach it.

Men's shouts and cries of pain filled the crystalline spring air. The burly blacksmith with thick, curly hair and three good teeth in his mouth was defending himself with a hot poker but had taken a blow to the head from a tomahawk. As he fell against the forge, he clutched a Jesuit medallion around his neck and whispered the words engraved there: "Clarior sole misere": "You, who are brighter than the sun, pray for us."

Images of his family's farm in the Alps appeared before the eyes of a young recruit while an even younger Bodwéwadmi warrior was inexpertly removing his scalp. The cook had expired immediately after taking a shot at close range to the chest. Three young soldiers hid in the loft of the storage building, listening to the cries of agony of the young Swiss soldier, who had won a belt and a tin cup in a card game the night before.

Two Bodwéwadmi started a fire on the first floor of the storage house.

Schlosser could smell smoke and thought of the gunpowder stored in the trading post. He had almost succeeded in reaching his rifle with his outstretched fingers. He heard the fort's heavy, wooden gate bang open and Bodwéwadmi voices yelling. A new contingent had arrived. His soldiers were definitely outnumbered now.

"What have you done? You idiot!" yelled Mathak, the scarred and sinewy commander of the band of warriors who had arrived from the south. He ran at Gnêw and grabbed him by his fringed leather jacket, shaking him back and forth then pulling him closer to his angry face.

"We needed supplies and hostages! What do *you* do? Set the place on fire and kill everyone." Mathak shot venom from his bloodshot eyes, outlined in black war paint. "Where's the ammunition? The commander?"

Zhéték, who had helped his friends dispatch the cook, the blacksmith, and a soldier unable to assemble his musket in time, crept stealthily up the steps of Schlosser's front porch.

Schlosser had lost a lot of blood—the air felt cold; voices sounded distant.

Zhéték stepped on Schlosser's hand that had just grasped the rifle's barrel. "He's not dead!" Zhéték yelled.

Mathak released Gnêw's jacket as if awakening from an unpleasant dream and joined Zhéték on the porch. They both examined the wounded man. Gnêw joined them on the porch.

Without looking at Gnêw, Mathak growled, "*You'll* make sure he gets to Fort Ponchatrain alive. If we lose him on the way, you can find yourself a new home among the Zhagnashêk."

Flaming arrows released by Mathak's men flew through the air, igniting the wooden shingles of the trading house. Smoke puffed then billowed out the door.

"Call them off!" Mathak yelled, waving his arms above his head. "No fire until we empty the trading post!"

Two Bodwéwadmi warriors hoisted the groaning Schlosser across the back of his horse, while Gnêw looked on. It was only then that he remembered his sister.

Marguerite could see the glint of the river through the trees. She didn't know where she would go. To the White men, she was the enemy; to her own people, a traitor. The fort was the only life she'd known for the past two years.

In a thick patch of underbrush, she saw a canoe, which appeared to be in good condition. Someone must have hidden it last fall and forgot to reclaim it. She worked it free from the brambles, dragged it to the river, and slipped it into the water behind a blind of low-hanging grapevine.

She got in, crouched down, and closed her eyes. She saw Francis open the front door. She heard him fall. Again, he opened the door, and, again, he fell. Time had stopped its normal progression. A different scenario unfolded in her imagination: they were both running through the forest, both paddling the Senathwen Zibe, and they had just entered Michigami's wide, limitless blue waters.

How swiftly everything had disappeared, and none of her potions had given her the power to foresee or to stop it. She closed her eyes tightly and whispered, "Mishipeshu, hear me." She waited; she opened her eyes; nothing happened.

Why would the goddess listen to her? A girl who had betrayed the Medéwewen. But is that what she was? Had it been so wrong to share the goddess's secrets with Francis? If ever a man loved the trees, the flowers, the grasses—everything that grew in Her garden—it was he. Did She not want *all* men to worship her? And hadn't she, Marguerite, sought to awaken that love? When the elusive frost grapes had sought out her fingers, or the deep-rooted, purple liatris had so readily released its grip on the soil, Marguerite had dared to wonder: is the goddess guiding my hand? Only the water lily had resisted her, pulling her down into the mud until, after great effort, she emerged from the water, tuber in hand.

A muskrat, holding a twig in its mouth, twitched its white whiskers and swam to the opposite bank.

Marguerite unwrapped a corner of the leather manuscript and ran her finger along the gold-leaf tracery. Its fate was now tied to her own.

CHAPTER 3

THE SLAVES FROM KASKASKIA

~ 1781 ~

Wéshkebet, like his mother Marguerite, had the power to see through the chaos of objects and unpredictable circumstances to a deeper underlying order. As clearly as he saw the rising sun in the morning, he had seen and understood the signs that pointed to Barbier's death. First, the flood at the mine, and then all the subtle and providential qualities of that late fall afternoon along the Mississippi—the long shadows that disguised his approach, the wind that masked the sound of his footsteps, the tall corn that had circumscribed his master's view.

He had never imagined that he would end up being anyone's slave. A raiding party of Fox had attacked Wéshkebet's village at night. Even as a boy, he was tall, and his legs had extended beyond his sleeping mat in his mother's wigwam. He woke up as a Fox warrior was dragging him by the leg. He was quickly shackled together with five other young men and three girls. They were dragged off while the men of his village were away on their winter hunt. He was marched all the way to Montreal to the slave market where the Fox warriors sold him for two copper pots.

Wéshkebet was amazed by Montreal's great stone buildings, peculiar clothing, and the strange manners of the people. The priests were familiar figures to him, but in Montreal they were accompanied by women priests: Gray Nuns, they were called. The nuns brought them food while they waited on the cobblestones for the slave market to open. Wéshkebet spoke to them in French, the language he had learned from his métis mother. He loved the kindly, pink, wrinkled faces of the Sisters of Charity. Surely, they'd want a tall, fifteen-year-old as a gardener or a jack-of-all-trades. But the Gray Nuns couldn't afford to pay the price the slave traders wanted for him. Priests were poor, and the Gray Nuns were no doubt poorer still.

From the marketplace, he could see frigates with great white billowing sails scudding across the broad St. Lawrence River. The slave traders, dark, silent men, waited with their goods—some Negroes but mostly Natives. The slaves stood on boxes looking out at the horizon. Men in three-cornered hats and women in white bonnets bought fish and haggled for livestock. Sometimes, Wéshkebet would catch them looking at him: some curious, others fearful, a few tentatively compassionate.

When Barbier approached him, the temperature of the air dropped. He was a tall man with a long, straight back. He had thin, pale, earthworm lips, a furrowed brow and shaggy tufts of brown hair at his temples. His eyes were so deeply set in his head, he seemed to be looking out of black pits. He felt Wéshkebet's arm muscles with his damp hands. Wéshkebet recoiled at his touch. He thought he saw scratch marks on Barbier's pale throat. The purchase was made. His new master led him out of the market.

Barbier was a silent, unsociable man, with crude habits. On the way to St. Louis, he made snares for rabbits using his own stringy hair and ate the meat raw. After Wéshkebet revealed his familiarity with the forests around Lake Michigan, Barbier feared that he would run away and always kept him in view, even when Wéshkebet was relieving himself. He watched him with a blank stare. It was like being watched by a dark cave—empty, inscrutable.

A French trader took them down the Illinois in a dugout canoe. Wéshkebet, who was doing most of the paddling, asked to stop so that he could make an offering to the river goddess at a sacred place where her likeness had been painted on the rocks. Barbier, in response, struck him over the head with his flintlock. The French trader who owned the dugout was taken aback but clearly unwilling to anger Barbier further. As Wéshkebet mopped up the blood on his head with his sleeve, the men looked away.

By the time they reached Kaskaskia, the heat of summer was upon them. Clouds of gnats hung above the slow-moving, turbid water. Fields of wheat, corn, and tobacco lined the bank. Women, with a frightening dullness in their eyes, sat on porches at midday fanning themselves.

Without waiting for him to recover from the journey, Barbier brought Wéshkebet to an enormous pit filled with Negro and Native slaves striking their picks into the packed earth again and again. Mountains of orange-brown slag glinted in the sun. Noxious fumes from smelting lead mixed with human sweat and the minty freshness of hummingbird sage.

For the next two years, Wéshkebet worked in the mine, and Barbier took the money. He made enough to buy lumber for a house and a young Negro slave woman. One day, after heavy rains, the mining pit collapsed, and Wéshkebet had to stay in the front yard of Barbier's new log house while some of the mine's buildings were repaired. He was chained to a tree and was thankful to be lying still without too many flies clustering at the open wounds around his shackles. Strong breezes were buffeting the trees, and Barbier nearly lost his hat. Wéshkebet absentmindedly moved the pin that secured one of the rusted manacles about his wrist; it dropped out. Slowly, he released his hand from the cuff. As Barbier disappeared into the rows of corn, Wéshkebet released his other hand.

Not far from where he sat was a wood pile. A section of a tree branch suitable as a club presented itself to him. He grabbed it and walked into the shadow of the shed. The wind blew the corn tassels. Where was his master now? Near the middle of the row? At the end? He entered a row of corn, preparing to meet him face-to-face at any second. Luckily, Barbier had his back to him. Wéshkebet crept up behind him and let the club down hard on his head. He lifted his arm to strike again. But Barbier lay on the ground motionless. Wéshkebet knelt down. Barbier was still breathing. He felt the power of his arm and the weapon so secure in his grip. His master's repugnant face in repose wore a self-contented smirk. That together with the years of cruelty urged him to strike another blow. Yet something stayed his hand. What needed to be done to escape was done, and that was all he cared to do.

He ran to the house to get enough food to survive for several weeks. The Black slave woman, Catherine, stepped back from him in fear when he entered the house. She was pregnant and instinctively put her hand on her belly. He put his finger to his lips.

"Where's Barbier?" she asked in alarm.

"He's in the corn patch." Wéshkebet gestured vaguely toward the still open door.

"Dead?"

"No. Knocked out."

Catherine ran outside. Wéshkebet went to the storage room and quickly gathered together cornmeal, dried meat, and beans. He grabbed Barbier's shotgun.

When he came outside, he heard Catherine screaming. He thought Barbier had come to and grabbed her. He dropped the food and went into the corn patch with Barbier's gun. He found Catherine standing over her master's body with an ax, readying to let it fall for the second, maybe third time. She was splattered with blood. The roosters fluttered and crowed in the yard. Wéshkebet pried her fingers from around the ax's shaft and eventually convinced her to come with him.

All that night and into the next, they kept moving, staying close to the river. Barbier was neither loved nor respected. No one, they hoped, would miss him anytime soon. The owners of the mine would be more likely to miss Wéshkebet first, but the mine wouldn't be back in operation for another week. If they kept moving, they might be in Sauk country by then. Wéshkebet's mother, though half French and Bodwéwadmi, had friends among the Sauk. Whether they'd feel loyal enough to his mother not to turn them over to soldiers or bounty hunters, he didn't know.

Catherine knew what awaited them both if they were caught, and moved as quickly as she could, but, in her condition, she needed to stop every few hours to rest. Catherine didn't talk about their dead master, and Wéshkebet didn't ask her. He saw welts on her arms and could guess the kind of "love" a man like Barbier would be after. Yet despite her long ordeal and the distances they covered each day, she was getting stronger.

A red-tailed hawk followed them wherever they went. When Catherine stopped at a river or a stream for water, it would swoop down and stay close to her while she bathed or collected water. Once, Wéshkebet overheard her talking to the bird.

"Do you know the language of the birds?" he asked her.

"I imagine I understand them sometimes." She smiled and looked at him with her dark, melancholy eyes, then looked away.

There was a bite to the air the morning that they arrived at the Sauk village near Vincennes. Negroes were uncommon in the area, so Catherine was at first an object of great interest. But at her request, the Sauk women braided her hair and dressed her in a wraparound skirt with embroidery, and she blended in enough not to elicit unwanted attention. Wéshkebet was younger than Catherine by five years, but some thought they might be a couple. Others thought Catherine might be Wéshkebet's slave.

Catherine had no family of her own. She'd been born into slavery in Saint-Domingue, and her mother had died of a fever when Catherine was eight. She didn't know who her father was. She didn't remember much about Saint-Domingue but the heat, the iguanas, the mangoes, and the enormous moon that stared into the window of her mud hut at night.

Her aunt had accompanied her to New Orleans where they were separated. She was put on a boat with other slaves and taken north to Kaskaskia where she'd been purchased by a French farming family to work as a domestic. She'd worked long hours, and she'd been lonely, but the people were decent. They moved away and couldn't afford to take her with them, so she'd been sold to Barbier.

The baby arrived during the first snowfall. All went well, and Wéshkebet did not have to use the motherwort he had gathered along the trail. Just as they were beginning to feel as though they had left their pasts behind, word arrived that there were soldiers looking for a Negro woman and a tall Bodwéwadmi man.

Wéshkebet had been planning to return to his native village on the St. Joseph River as soon as possible, and Catherine, who had been accepted by the Sauks, planned to stay. Now, all three would go north. Catherine did not want to leave her baby with the Sauk, even though a mother who had recently lost her own child had begged her to do so.

Wéshkebet thought that if they walked for nine hours a day, they would arrive in his village in a little over two weeks, if all went well. At night, they made a fire and nestled into the furs the Sauks had given them.

They made good progress for a week and a half, but the temperature descended daily. The forests were silent except for their own heavy breathing and the shimmering whisper of icy snowflakes against bare branches.

Once, while they were crossing an empty prairie, they'd seen a solitary bull bison blanketed with snow, his vaporous breath wreathed about his head. He could have charged them. Wéshkebet could have shot him. But they simply looked at each other, the cold making them temporary confederates.

After a week and a half on the trail, Catherine started bleeding again, and the baby wasn't getting enough milk. Their supply of corn-meal and dried meat was running out. If a blizzard came, they wouldn't have enough fat on their bodies to survive.

A blizzard did come. One morning, before the sun rose, a wind blew in from the northwest and continued to pick up force. As they crossed an open field, the cold seared their exposed flesh and the wind pushed them back with so much force, they could scarcely move forward. Eventually, they gave up. They made a small cave in a snow-drift and crawled in. The baby, who was used to sleeping during the day, lulled by the motion and warmth of her mother's body, cried with a new force and bitterness, as if aware of all the wretchedness of her situation. They listened to the tireless wind and the groaning of the massive walnut and oak trees towering above them.

Wéshkebet awoke after a few hours of fitful sleep. All was quiet. Carefully, so as not to dislodge too much snow above their heads, he reached over and lifted the fur from the baby's face. He put his hand next to her tiny nose; he could feel gentle, scarcely perceptible puffs of air.

"Wéshkebet?" Catherine's voice was a whisper.

"Yes?"

"Take the baby and go to your village. I can't go further." She turned her face to him. Her eyes were narrow slits. "I'm finished."

"We've come so far. It's not that much farther."

"I'm too weak." Her hand shaking, she took a bracelet of yellow agate from her wrist. The stones glowed like a summer sunset.

"Take this. Tell her it was a gift from her mother. My mother gave it to me before she died. She said we were kin to a bird god."

She smiled wanly, then continued earnestly, "Do what you can for her."

"I'll come back for you." The words left his mouth before he had considered what he was saying. How could he come back? He scarcely knew where they were.

"There'll be nothing to come back for."

Wéshkebet wriggled out of the snow cave. The sun was setting, the sky was clear. He wrapped the baby in a fur pelt and found a way to keep her close to his chest. He gathered sticks and stuck them at strange angles in the snow. He tried to memorize the position, shape, and type of trees. There wasn't much that was distinctive about the place.

If he stayed, it was clear they'd all die. He would have to move as quickly as possible. Maybe she'd last until he returned, or maybe a pack of hungry wolves would find her. He set off through the woods.

For the first few hours, the baby slept, but then she awoke and sensed that she was no longer nestled against her mother. She cried and rooted frantically against his chest. Wéshkebet's legs ached. Instead of walking upright, his weakened body was pitched forward towards the snow; he was weaving back and forth. His feet were numb.

By afternoon, the St. Joseph River appeared before him. He could smell the fragrance of burning cedar—diaphanous, ghostly, and tears of gratitude welled up in his eyes.

By the light of the full Great Bear Moon that was just rising above the trees, he saw the wigwams of his village. He fell to his knees by a woodpile. Two men who had been out by the fire heard him and helped him to his mother's wigwam.

When he finally awoke, it was well past noon. His mother was wearing the silver cone earrings she had always worn. As they embraced, he felt the bones of her small back. She wiped the tears from her face with the back of her hand and gave him a large bowl of oats with maple water.

Her earrings now matched the silver streaks in her otherwise dark hair. She had always been a small, delicately-built woman, but now her body had retreated even further into her deer skin dress. Someone who did not know her would have thought she was as insubstantial as the wind-borne seed of some meadow flower—a bit of gossamer that could ride a gentle breeze for days. Yet her nature was fixed and fierce. The mild, gentle expression that usually brightened the faded prettiness of her face could, in an instant, change, and one glance could feel like a sharpened, well-hurled tomahawk.

He spooned the sweet, warm oats into his mouth with reverence, and she sat close to him with her hand on his arm. Wabën, his half-brother's wife, nursed the baby by the door.

He told his mother of his enslavement, escape, and the welcome they'd received from the Sauk warrior Nanakibek when he'd mentioned her name. He also told her that he had left the slave woman Cathcrinc behind. When Wabën opened the door flap to leave, Wéshkebet saw that the sun had sunk low in the sky. "I have to go."

His mother looked at him but said nothing. Wéshkebet had forgotten what it felt like to be looked at with love; he never wanted to leave that radiant warmth again. His legs ached, and he still could not feel two of his toes. But then he thought of Catherine lying alone in the cold, trying to purge the last bit of hope from her heart. He put down the bowl of oats.

"The forests are full of soldiers—maybe a hundred. The Spaniards took Fort St. Joseph yesterday."

"The Spaniards? Here?"

"Siggenauk was behind this. He fights for whichever White man pays the most. He presents himself as wgema of any Bodwéwadmi village foolish enough to let him tie up his horse. As soon as he found out the British were storing ammunition at the fort, he told the Spaniards that the English were planning a raid against them in St. Louis." She bit her lower lip. "We don't need another tribe of White men here. We don't need their wars."

"But we do need their guns."

"Gnêw was right. There was a time when we could have defended what was ours."

"That time has passed." He spoke quietly, and with authority, as he laid out his few possessions on the floor.

Marguerite saw that his years in servitude had changed him and felt the guilt of the old before the young—Wéshkebet's world was even more troubled than her own.

"If a hundred or more Spanish soldiers have just arrived here, they've made a very useful north-south path through the snow. If only I could find a horse…" Wéshkebet strapped on his leather boots.

"How far away is the woman you traveled with?" she asked, knitting her brow.

"By horse, I believe I could get there and return before dawn."

The last time Marguerite had seen her son, he'd been flat on his back and snoring. He'd been a pudgy adolescent with skin as smooth as polished soapstone. When the young men of the village brought him into her wigwam the previous night, she had not recognized him at first. Then, as she had studied this strange man as he slept, the hard edge to his jaw, the muscles that defined his arms, legs, and back, she had caught a glimpse of the boy who had been hers: the slight asymmetry of the eyes, the unruly lock of hair that would not lie flat, the scar on his cheek where he'd run into a broken branch. She had watched him the whole night, covering him with the rabbit fur blanket he had loved as a child, adding aromatic cedar to the fire to speed his recovery.

Thank God he didn't have his father's pale skin. Only in his height and poor eyesight was he his father's son. Everyone knew that he wasn't Nokaming's, but he didn't look so different from the other Bodwéwadmi boys.

She was Medéwewen, and her son would be as well; she had taught him about plants, medicine, and magic when he was barely old enough to follow behind her into the forest. After she had departed for the spirit world, he would, she hoped, be the most knowledgeable Medéwewen in the village, and his usefulness would secure his position in the tribe.

The night he'd been taken away from her, she'd known what his fate would be. Bands of Fox had previously descended on villages close by and taken children into slavery. Whatever he'd done to escape, it had been right. Violence justified violence.

"The soldiers will be here shortly. The Spaniards have hired the French to lead them; they know nothing of the North. They've made Pouré, a French trader, their captain. Chevalier, another French trader—maybe a British spy—is their liaison with us. They've promised to bring us half the spoils from the fort as a gift for not defending it," she said.

"Having stolen goods will only make us a target for British retribution," he said.

"I know." She smoothed his hair with her hand. He had his father's widow's peak. "Promise me you'll stay hidden, at least for now."

A ghost of a smile passed across his face. "I promise."

In the center of the village, wood smoke mixed with blowing snow. Children sat by the fire turning the ends of sticks into charcoal to draw pictures on wood. To keep the snow from her eyes, a young woman with black braids pulled a blanket over her head. She poured dry corn kernels from a cloth bag and ground them with a stone pestle. A brown and white dog lay next to her licking its paw.

Red uniforms appeared in the trees that edged the village: everyone scattered. Three Spanish soldiers walked at a leisurely pace to the deserted fire pit, clearly well-pleased by their power to intimidate.

Marguerite came forward to meet the men, and they looked over her diminutive figure, expecting a male wgema.

"Our men are gone on their winter hunt," she said in French.

"Will they be back soon?" a pot-bellied man with toad-like features asked in Bodwéwadmi. His Spanish three-cornered hat was the only article of clothing associating him with the two other soldiers.

"I don't know when they'll be back," she answered in French.

A tall, thin soldier wearing a heavy leather vest over his red waistcoat smoothed his black mustache with his fingers and put his hands on his hips.

The pot-bellied man turned towards him. "This is Captain of the Second Company of militia, Don Eugenio Pouré, and this," pointing to a man with large, frightened eyes, "is second lieutenant Don Carlos Tayon." The bandage on Tayon's arm was red, and his face was pale.

"Enchanté," said Marguerite.

"You forgot to introduce yourself, Chevalier," Pouré said with a smirk. "What are you these days? Merchant? Spy? Friend to the Spanish? English?"

"Let's just say that I am a Friend to Commerce," Chevalier answered, turning his back to Marguerite.

"It seems the woman speaks French, Chevalier. No need to translate." He turned to Marguerite. "This morning, Madam." Pouré had a deep, resonant voice that vibrated pleasantly like a woodwind instrument. "Today, we planted the royal colors of Spain in Fort St. Joseph thereby annexing the domains for his Very Catholic Majesty, the King of Spain, my master. From now on and forever, this post of St. Joseph and its dependencies belongs to Spain." Pouré took a breath, his complexion was florid. Bits of torn and dirty lace stuck out from beneath the red cuffs of his waistcoat. Marguerite recognized his accent as French-Canadian. Instead of the more formal three-cornered hat, he wore a wool knitted one.

"As we promised your wgema…" Again, he looked around the deserted village. "Half of all the goods we found in the fort are yours."

"I'm not sure who you spoke with, gentlemen, but I beg you to keep what you've taken from the fort for yourselves. You've traveled over a hundred leagues in the snow and ice. Your men deserve their plunder, and we don't want it. The British will have a hard time believing we've been neutral if we benefit so handsomely from their defeat."

Pouré wrinkled his nose and squinted at her. "There is absolutely no need for you to worry yourself about our soldiers. All sixty will be rewarded by the King of Spain. They have my word on that. My men will have more than pots and pans and a few bottles of rum. Our orders are to give your people the British goods, and, someone," again, Pouré's eyes darted around the empty village, "told us that you would take them." As if reasoning with a child, Pouré added: "If you're concerned about retribution, you can hide the goods for a while before selling them. The British can't watch everything you do."

"We don't want anything from the fort."

"I don't think you can speak for the entire tribe. In fact, I'll wager they'll be angry when they find out you've refused our generosity."

Chevalier, seeing that this meeting was not going the way he had assured the Spanish commander it would go, touched Marguerite's arm and looked down into her face with a smile that resembled a grimace: "Our generosity is not something you have the power to refuse."

Marguerite wondered how he had managed to maintain so much fat on his body during such an arduous journey.

"Who trades in medicine here?" Pouré asked.

"I trade in medicines," Marguerite said.

Pouré folded his arms over his chest and moved closer to her. "It seems you're a very important person." He smiled indulgently. "Our friend Don Carlos was injured. He's lost a lot of blood and needs medicine. Can you help him? We also need pain killers."

As they spoke, four Spanish soldiers and a despondent-looking horse arrived loaded with grain sacks, copper kettles, and wrapped parcels.

"Your gifts! See? Your people will be very happy." Then, quickly becoming serious, Pouré added, "Do you have anything for our friend here?"

Chevalier looked critically at Pouré, "You can't be serious. He needs a proper doctor. One who can bleed him. These people know nothing about the drawing of corrupt blood."

"A 'proper doctor' is unfortunately not available."

"We'll need supper, of course, too," Chevalier said.

She continued to look at the gifts. "Is the horse a gift as well?" she asked.

The men looked at the horse the Spanish soldiers were in the process of unloading.

"No. We *need* the horse," Chevalier said.

"So," Pouré clapped his hands together, "we'll have supper and those medicines."

Marguerite stopped by the wigwam next to hers and told the women to make dried venison soup and cornmeal porridge for the soldiers.

When she entered her wigwam, she found Wéshkebet dressed. He had taken apart Barbier's gun and was cleaning it. His pack was ready and by the door. He looked up when she came in and noted the anxiety in her face. "Are they causing trouble?"

"No. It's all as I expected."

She opened a chest near the mat where she slept and took out a large manuscript. In the years since the fort had burned, she had transcribed more words of the wiigwaasabak from birch bark scrolls to the manuscript. She opened the large book to the last page with Schlosser's drawing of a water lily. Then, she sat down at the makeshift table, reached into a brown canvas sack, and extracted a handful of brown leaves and water lily seed pods—nabagûck. When the seed pods were crushed, they yielded a white pulpy substance, which she then pounded into a paste.

Wéshkebet had seen what nabagûck could do to those who took it, even a little could cause hallucinations. Anything more than a teaspoon could be lethal. He'd seen full grown men howl like wild beasts and thrash on the floor. He'd seen their eyes roll up into their heads. Some had died.

"Who is this for?"

"For the soldiers?"

"They asked for nabagûck?"

"We need for them to fall into a deep sleep. You need their horse."

Wéshkebet shook his head: "There's too much risk in what you do."

"I have made sleeping potions from nabagûck before."

"I can make my way on foot."

"With so many soldiers around us and a price on your head?"

He lifted a corner of the hide covering the door and peered out. Chevalier's round face was red and slack; his belly protruded from his ill-fitting wool jacket. Don Carlos, a slight man with narrow shoulders, gazed pensively into the fire. Pouré, who had extended his long legs until his boots were nearly in the fire, was telling a story. From time to time, as if to emphasize his point, he'd adjust one of his torn lace cuffs. The women put more wood on the fire, which snapped hungrily and spit sparks.

Wabën appeared in the doorway of their wigwam. "They're asking for the 'medicine woman,'" she said as she went to the infant who was kicking its tiny limbs beneath the fur.

Marguerite put all the medicines she'd prepared into a bag, nodded to Wéshkebet, and went out to the men at the fire. She placed them before Pouré on a flat rock. "The yarrow," she said, "will help stop your friend's bleeding."

Don Carlos raised his large, sorrowful eyes. "Could I have the yarrow now?"

Marguerite showed him how to apply it to his arm.

"I believe you now have everything you asked for," she said.

"You can take your gifts now," Chevalier said. "We'll be on our way soon, after a few buffalo hides."

"I'm afraid we no longer have any buffalo hides, even for ourselves."

"Traded for drink? Pity."

In the glow of the firelight, Marguerite could see the pile of assorted goods taken from the fort; beyond that, stood an underweight mare tied to a tree. The poor creature's ankles looked fragile, but it was otherwise serviceable. She rubbed its ears and the white star on its forehead.

The "gifts" were three small bags of grain, two bolts of broadcloth, an iron skillet, and a bottle of Jamaican rum. A pittance, really. She took the rum and went to the soldiers.

"Our men don't need any more of this." She held up the bottle of rum. "I'm giving it back to you."

"Surely, your men would not want you to give away their rum."

Marguerite shook her head. "Take it, please."

The men were silent. Then Pouré said, "Gentlemen, you heard the lady. We must not lead the savages into temptation."

Chevalier laughed and shook his head.

"Commander, I would like to return to the fort," Don Carlos said with a wan smile.

"A bit of rum might be just what the doctor ordered, Don Carlos," said Pouré.

"I'd rather enjoy a night with a roof over my head," Don Carlos said.

"Don't get too accustomed to it. We leave tomorrow."

"Tomorrow?"

"Orders," said Pouré, seeming to enjoy Don Carlos' look of shock.

"I don't understand. Today we claimed the fort for Spain, and tomorrow we'll abandon it to the English? What was the point?"

"Theater, my friend, a show of strength and determination." Pouré clenched his fist in mock enthusiasm.

"I will not be sharing that news with the men. Good night."

"Good night, Don Carlos. Don Luis and I will be back a little later."

"Yes, tell them not to wait up," Chevalier said, chuckling.

Marguerite still held the bottle. "I don't have glasses, but I have wooden cups."

"Then bring us the wooden cups, woman!" Pouré said gaily. She returned with the cups, which she then filled with rum. She put the jug of rum on the ground next to them and went back to her wigwam.

Wéshkebet had been watching from the doorway. Together, they peered out through a gap in the door flap at Pouré and Chevalier. The two men were laughing over some shared joke and drinking deeply from the cups. Then, their faces became serious. Chevalier dropped his cup and fell toward the fire. Pouré put his hands to his temples and slumped to the ground. The fire crackled.

Marguerite and Wéshkebet left the wigwam to look at the men. Their eyes had rolled up into their heads, leaving only white half-moons visible. Wéshkebet untethered the horse, put the amulet and rosary his mother had given him in a shirt pocket. She stood by the fire, watching him disappear into the black trees.

Wéshkebet dug his heels into the sides of the weary mare to keep her from slowing to a standstill. She was clearly more used to carrying supplies than men.

Warm air had moved in from the south, and an icy fog blew across the trail before him. The snow that had been powder the night before was now hard packed beneath the horse's hooves. He could hear the soldiers' drunken voices at the fort. Someone shouted a question and the others answered and laughed loudly. He could hear singing too, but that was less distinct. The clouds moved northeast, leaving the waning moon riding high and distant in the sky.

He left the trail made by the soldiers' feet to follow a narrow pathway through the woods. In summer, this was a swamp. He'd hunted mallards, teals, and wild geese here. Only in winter when the ground was frozen could it be crossed on horseback. Wooded groves alternated with tangled islands of scrub brush and open glens. A surprised snowy owl flew out of its hiding place, passing just above Wéshkebet's head.

Again, the horse's pace slackened to a ramble and again he pressed his heel into the horse's side. Instead of going faster, the distracted animal lost its footing and stumbled. He hadn't considered the possibility of injuring the horse, failing to find Catherine, *and* making his village the target of Spanish vengeance.

At length, he saw a maple with branches like arms held up to the sky. He was sure he'd seen that tree not long after he'd left Catherine. He remembered that there had been a dip in the land, as deep as he was tall, and then an open meadow followed by a cluster of oaks. Just when he was most in need of its illumination, the moon disappeared behind the clouds.

"Catherine!" he called out into the darkness.

Before him, he saw the familiar oak with a lower branch nearly as thick as the trunk. He recognized the sticks he had arranged at the base. Breathlessly, he jumped down from the horse and pulled the reins toward the tree.

He got down on his knees at their snow cave, which was already becoming hard packed and icy.

"Catherine? It's me, Wéshkebet."

He groped around the inside of their little cave, not seeing anything, but still hoping to feel a warm limb. It was empty. He dug with his hands in the snow then sat back on his heels. Had she left, or had she been dragged?

"Catherine!"

Faint moonlight once again illuminated the woods. A dark spot upon the white snow and canine footprints.

He fed the tired mare some grain and set off on the narrow trail towards home. Somewhere, above his head, a night hawk screeched.

Catherine was walking in the driving rain, jumping over puddles and leaving little footprints in the red dirt.

She'd eaten nothing since yesterday and remembered a grove of mango trees that grew along the beach. She could almost taste the fruits' sweet flesh.

She walked through the tall grass, up a hill, and down onto a rocky beach. Towering black waves crashed and foamed; curtains of rain drifted out to sea.

"Petite fille! Petite fille!"

She looked around. The empty beach stretched ahead and behind her. Seagulls wheeled above.

"Petite fille!" someone repeated more sternly.

An enormous turkey vulture was perched on a piece of driftwood, extending and flapping his great wings, scattering raindrops in all directions. He turned his red, skeleton head towards her. He had round, lash-less eyes.

"No further!" he said.

"Why not?" Catherine asked.

He made no answer but blinked his lash-less eyes.

"You have me confused with someone else. I'm just a little girl trying to find a mango grove."

"I know who you are. Where's the ax?"

Memories rushed back like ice water. She was little Catherine, but she was also that Catherine—the one who needed to run away. She walked with determination toward the forest where the mango trees were bent low with fruit.

"Petite fille!" the vulture squawked.

She heard his great wings flapping behind her, but then the sound grew faint. The vulture had no doubt realized that she was, after all, just a little girl seeking a mango grove.

Suddenly, the great bird descended on her from the heavens, knocking her to the ground and striking her foot, her hand, her head. It snarled and pulled at her flesh. Why does this bird snarl? she wondered. She shielded her face with her arms and ran towards the water.

In the distance, a woman was sitting on a rock, brushing her long black hair. She turned towards Catherine and smiled. "Come, Thunderbird!" she called. Her eyes were as red as coals.

Marguerite looked at the two Spanish soldiers by the fire. Pouré's mouth was open; saliva sparkled at the corner of his lips; and his breath was harsh and labored. Chevalier's back was arched, and he was shaking. She had given them too much nabagûck; they would soon disappear into the spirit world. She had no experience bargaining for the souls of White men. She would need to go to the river. She would need to find Mishipeshu.

Marguerite took a piece of the pulverized water lily seed and put it in her mouth. She closed her eyes.

She heard a dry leaf detach from a twig and fall through the cold air. She could smell the warm fur of a coyote as it approached the river. She could feel a single snowflake sting and burn her hand.

She walked through the snow-covered forest along a dark, narrow path. The path led to the edge of the frozen river and continued beneath the ice. Her beaded moccasins broke through the ice. Her garments grew loose and heavy as they drank the dark water.

Water covered the top of her head and filled her eyes. The path continued along the river bottom; the water deepened. A curious perch with sparkling, silver fins swam past. The water lifted and twisted her hair. Moonlight passed through the ice, scattering ribbons of light across the river bottom.

Ahead, there was a large, flat rock, where a woman sat, her long black hair, a thundercloud above her head.

"I'm not saying *that*, my friend." Pouré was drinking a cup of tea as he sat by a newly rekindled fire.

"What *are* you saying then?"

"Do we agree that Don Carlos is a man inferior to me in every way?"

"Of course!" Chevalier did not enjoy being led by the nose through this one-sided conversation. Pouré had helped him increase his Spanish customers by at least fifty percent, and he needed to remind himself of that. The satisfaction of a sharp word now wasn't worth the loss of all that silver.

"Then explain to me how someone as deficient as Don Carlos landed a position in the Presidio? How is it that he gets to sit on his ass and smoke Cuban cigars all day?"

"Well, my friend," said Chevalier with a smile that showed he was permitting himself a bit of sarcasm, "it's surprising how often 400-pesos-a-year men are mistaken for men who are worth at least 800." Stiff from a night sleeping on the ground, he arched his back and lumbered off into the woods to relieve himself. He continued to talk to Pouré over his shoulder: "Jesus, my head hurts."

"Jamaican rum, my friend."

"Hard to believe that such shit could power the Royal Navy? Give me a glass of Portuguese Madeira any day." Chevalier looked around in the woods. "Where's the horse?"

"Don Carlos probably brought it back to the camp."

"I don't think so. Not with one good arm. Besides, I distinctly remember seeing the horse standing there after Don Carlos left. You don't suppose someone stole it."

"Better not be the case. I don't mind the natives pilfering our flour from time to time, but we need the horses."

"Settle down, gentlemen. Here's your horse," said a short, barrel-chested Bodwéwadmi man who walked with a bit of a swagger. The man casually strolled toward the men leading the horse. "She's not exactly a looker."

"Always a pleasure to see you, Siggenauk. Those red boots are… eye-catching." Pouré smiled broadly.

"My boots are made of the finest British wool, given to me, not so willingly, by a British officer. I heard you gentlemen were enjoying some Jamaican rum last night."

Pouré pulled at his dirty lace cuffs. "Just doing our part to keep the Bodwéwadmi men away from the fire water. Where was the horse?"

"Seems a young Bodwéwadmi man took it for a ride last night."

"Where is the bastard? The horse is the property of the Spanish Crown."

"Pouré, for God's sake, defending the 'Spanish Crown' now, are you? You're nothing but a hired gun. Besides, justice is already done."

"Where is he?"

"I shot him."

Pouré raised his eyebrows. "That's not how I would have handled it and not what the Spanish Crown would have wanted. That's not justice. What sort of 'justice' is that?"

"The time-saving sort. Here's your horse." Siggenauk tried to hand the reins to Pouré, but he gestured to Chevalier who looked annoyed but took the reins anyway.

"It's not a capital offense to take a horse."

"He was an escaped slave—some sort of half-breed."

"You probably could have gotten a reward for him," said Chevalier.

"Not worth my time."

Pouré shook his head and stared at him. "You know, Siggenauk, you're a real bastard."

Siggenauk shrugged. "Bastards win wars. That's why you hired me."

"Well, what's done is done. Time for us to start our journey south. Our glorious conquest has come to an end. Will you be coming south with us?" Pouré looked at Siggenauk.

"No, not now. The weather's not ideal, and I want to rest. I'm not ready for another hundred leagues in snow and ice."

"Listen to that will you, Don Luis? He wants to rest and doesn't fancy the cold." He put his hands on his hips. "That's the kind of life you lead when you're an Indian."

"That's the kind of life you lead when you get paid up front for your services," said Chevalier.

Pouré's mouth dropped open. "They paid *him* up front, but *me* they don't trust?"

"They clearly need me more," Siggenauk said, casually extracting a linen handkerchief from his pocket and blowing his nose loudly.

Pouré stared at him in icy silence.

"We should get going. We've got a lot of territory to cover," said Chevalier. He picked up Pouré's glove that had fallen in the dirt by the fire and handed it to him.

Pouré tugged at his lace cuff and headed purposefully down the trail.

Some of the Bodwéwadmi men had returned to the village from the winter hunt. They carried two dead deer, their legs strapped to poles, to the fire pit to be butchered. The dogs, anticipating the scraps, barked wildly.

Wéshkebet left his mother's wigwam and went up to Siggenauk who was admiring a piece of obsidian he had just bought from a Spanish officer. He held the stone up to the fire, and the facets reflected the light.

"How's your mother?" Siggenauk asked, not looking up from his piece of obsidian.

"She's breathing but not responding. I've given her medicine. Now, we must wait." Wéshkebet rubbed his eyes.

With the soldiers gone, women and children emerged from their wigwams to welcome the men who had come back from the hunt. The customary bustle of the village slowly returned.

Wéshkebet squatted down by the fire next to where Siggenauk sat. He stared dully at the flames.

"My mother misjudged you. She thought you were behind the Spanish attack. She thought your only loyalties were to gold and gunpowder."

"She was right. I do like Spanish gold, and I did want British gunpowder. But she's giving me far too much credit if she thought I was "behind" this attack. I don't imagine myself so powerful that I can *make* the Spanish do something they weren't planning to do themselves. I saw that an attack on the fort was a possible course of action, and I fed them just enough information to make my way appear best. It's that simple."

"That's not simple and neither are the consequences. Now we have the French, the English, *and* the Spanish fighting for our land."

"Listen, Wéshkebet, it's better to have three instead of one. They'll be fighting each other instead of us."

Wéshkebet looked from the fire to Siggenauk, who was still holding the piece of obsidian to the firelight. "If three of our tribes descended on Boston to fight, White people wouldn't see anything advantageous about the situation."

"They would if one tribe had its foot firmly on their throats, and the two others might remove it."

"Ending up with three feet on your throat is another possible scenario." Wéshkebet ran his fingers along a ragged scar on his wrist and looked at a group of children who were throwing a stick for a dog. "Well, they're gone for now." He smiled at Siggenauk. "Thank you for killing me. You saved my life."

Siggenauk put his large, paw-like hand on Wéshkebet's shoulder and smiled, exposing the large gap between his front teeth. "Use it wisely."

The drums began at noon. Marguerite's cousins, step-children, and the elderly wgema who had made her his wife when she arrived three months pregnant with Schlosser's child—all gathered around her small body. Even her estranged brother Gnêw arrived, his spine bent,

45

his face deeply furrowed. A young woman helped him to sit on his mat, and he chanted the funeral prayers for his sister.

Men, women, and children approached the fire with sacred tobacco pinched in their fingers, offering up a prayer for Marguerite's soul, as they cast the tobacco into the flames.

Wéshkebet stared at his mother's body. This river-drift of skin and bone could not be her. He closed his eyes and tried to picture her as she had been, but the horrible reality would give him no peace.

His mother's younger sister put a pinch of tobacco into the fire and began to sing:

What sound do I hear?
It's the wailing of women.
Why do they grieve?
Because she is gone
Far beyond the river's bend
Far beyond our lands
To a place that's neither day nor night.
She is gone
To the bottom of the river
To the sand
To the rock
To the pearls.
Who can help us in this darkness?
Mishipeshu, goddess of dreams.
When will She come?
At the end,
When the rivers swell.
When the stars fall.
When the tail bites the head of the snake.
She is gone
To the bottom of the river
To the sand
To the rock
To the pearls.

Marguerite spent three days among the living and then a cold front blew her through the pine trees, past the Wintermaker's stars, and into the Spirit World.

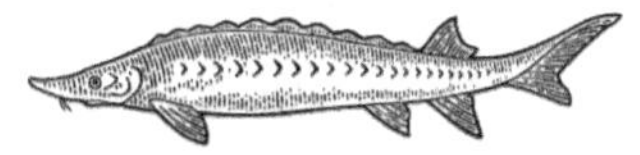

MORNING

Mishipeshu sat upon the flat rock in the river. Thoughts buzzed around her head like angry hornets. She had found a hatchet on the river bottom, which she gripped with white knuckle force. Namé was at her side, his enormous, spiked body undulating in the river current.

"Two-leggeds and their infernal bartering!" said Mishipeshu. She pressed her hands together in prayer and mimicked the sanctimonious tone of her petitioners, 'Oh, sweet Goddess, rip out my still beating heart, but please don't let them take my lover from me.' 'Take my great, fat cow, only grant me a week of rain.' 'Here, goddess, six silver coins, please carve out the intestines of that son-of-a-bitch who stole my wife.' As if their cows, hearts, and coins meant anything to me.

"And, Namé, you know that old woman who came to barter with me just now?" Namé swished his tail in assent. "She was a Medéwewen, a clever one. What does she do? Sacrifices herself for the sake of two mortals, who are no better than stinking effluent. I never asked for her life in exchange for theirs. She practically threw herself into the Sanctuary of the Dead."

Namé lifted his snow-white whiskers and said, "Her life was the most precious thing she had to offer, Mistress."

"Precious to her." She looked up at the river's rippling surface, as if seeking assistance there. "Gods want power, knowledge, healing. Why do mortals not understand that?"

"The thoughts of men and gods seldom converge," he observed, the drooping sides of his mouth giving his words a sadness he did not feel. In fact, the water's icy freshness made him so giddy he would have rocketed through the river's roof and into the overwater. But he saw the dark look in his mistress's eye, so he rubbed his belly on the gravel.

She sighed. "And this old woman, *she* knew the art of *nabagûck*. Understood its power. She had a magic book, filled with drawings of my plants and potions." The goddess shook her mane of dark hair. "Oh,

I would give much to have that book, to keep it from malicious two-leggeds. Yet now she's in the spirit world, a place I dare not travel.

"How is one to talk to them, Namé? How can I get them to tell me where my sister is? I wonder how my mother does it…"

"She talks to them when they dream, Mistress," said Namé.

"Dream?"

"Two-leggeds spend much of their time in dreams. They lay unmoving, unseeing, unhearing, yet they live." He swung his great body around to face the current, letting the water rush into his gills. "In sleep, their minds are moved by forces beyond their control."

"Spirits shape their thoughts?"

The great fish shook his white whiskers, "I could not say."

"I've looked at these men, many look," she shuddered, "ripe with decay. Yet others sparkle with a lightness and warmth that pleases me. Manitou warned me not to give my love to men. I suppose, my sister must."

Mishipeshu rose from her seat, put her hatchet in her belt and fitted the pearl encrusted harness around the great sturgeon's snout. "In vain, I seek respite from our search, Namé," she said, putting her new hatchet in her belt and fastening his harness. "Let us go."

She felt the current pass through her fingers. In the patterns of the eddies, she could feel cold dread. A dark night was approaching on a blackened earth.

CHAPTER 4

ISAAC MCCOY, EDUCATING THE SAVAGES

~ 1828 ~

Wabaunsee had never seen a battlefield, but he'd seen men die, not the heroic deaths they might have imagined for themselves when they were applying their war paint and sharpening their hatchets, but pathetic, gasping, shuddering, moaning, glamor-less, miserable deaths that sometimes dragged on for weeks. The mortal injuries—the deep gash in the belly, the missing hand, the crushed spine—did not convince their demented hearts to stop beating. It was clear to Wabaunsee that reason did not rule the heart. Nothing reasonable would have kept those broken bodies breathing.

Wabaunsee's uncle had been such a warrior with such a heart. Death had found him one night as he tip-toed through the village on his way back from the wigwam of another man's wife. He was stabbed forty-one times, and he lingered for a week, his heart refusing to give up until it had pumped every last drop of blood from his desiccated body.

But for most of his life, his uncle had been more hunter than prey. He fought in the Osage Wars, and the scalps of the men he'd killed nearly filled a large earthenware pot he kept by the side of his bed. He had a casual familiarity with his victims' hair, which he braided when he had nothing better to do. He felt no remorse—these were the scalps of men who had been destined to die—just as he was destined to live. Yet, as Wabaunsee had observed, destiny favored the warrior with the more reliable gun.

His uncle arrived on the battlefield with his "Mackinaw Musket," wrapped in painted deer skin and decorated with eagle feathers, and with a deafening, sky-splitting crack dispatched his victims to the spirit world. The teachers at the Mission had told Wabaunsee that the sound of the trumpet announced the Kingdom of God, but he felt certain that there could be nothing more solemn or final than the thunder of his uncle's gun.

This morning, the battlefield Wabaunsee contemplated was not the kind his uncle had seen. On this cold morning in the Month of the Long Night, he had stopped on the way back from the outhouse to decode the agitated surface of the snow, and, as he examined the tiny tracks, a battle unfolded before his eyes. A large snowy owl had spied a shrew scurrying to the woodpile. The owl had spread his silent, powerful wings—all knives and softness. What was it to him, the life of so small a thing? The shrew had no doubt felt the gust from the owl's great wings. Did he feel a sudden chill of ice crystals swirling against his sightless eyes? Had he sensed what might come next?

Wabaunsee looked up into the cluster of pines behind the wood pile. Maybe the great white owl was there still, somewhere hidden on a high branch. Maybe, as the sun rose, and the owl closed its weary eyes against the piercing light, the shrews' bones churned in its gut. And when the bones were properly covered with his victim's own fur, the owl would spit them out as an offering to whatever god owls pray to.

Wabaunsee knocked the snow off his moccasins and went into the small log house that served as a boys' dormitory at night and a classroom during the day at the Carey Mission, a Baptist school in the Michigan Territory. Little clouds of vapor hung above those boys awake enough to talk. Spider webs of frost covered the small glass panes that let in winter's blue-gray light. Wabaunsee knelt before the wood stove, poked a red-eyed ember and added a few more pieces of wood. A puff of wood smoke escaped into the room, irritating the lungs of the boys with the flu and sending them into coughing fits. Wabaunsee quickly closed the stove door and took his place on the bench with the other boys waiting for their lessons to begin.

The Mission's poverty wasn't something widely known, so it wasn't surprising that his aunt, after both his mother and father had died, decided that Wabaunsee would have his best chance at survival here away from his village where drinking had become the most predictable activity. Reverend McCoy had promised his aunt that her nephew would be fed, clothed, and taught to read. And, to drive home the point, Mrs. McCoy had immediately brought him a pair of thin wool pants and a jacket. Those meager clothes would prove typical of the Mission's threadbare charity. Luckily, he had a deerskin tunic he'd brought from home. Without it, he wasn't sure he could have survived the winter.

He'd lost weight at the Mission. For the past three months, his diet, like everyone else's, had been cornmeal gruel and weak tea. The missionaries weren't able hunters, and he was not allowed to hunt, even if he shared his kill with others. Rev. McCoy was concerned hunting would encourage Indians to forsake the more godly pursuit of agriculture. When Wabaunsee closed his eyes, he could smell venison cooking and hear the fat snapping as it dripped into the fire.

Reverend McCoy's wife arrived, carrying an armful of primers, which the older boys distributed to the younger ones already seated on long benches. The sleepy girls arrived wrapped in shawls made from the same bolt of brown wool Mrs. Wright, the blacksmith's wife, had bought at half price from the trading post in Fort Wayne.

The girls were White, Myaamia, Bodwéwadmi, and mixed. Yet there was something that united them on a more profound level: they all possessed a level of political astuteness that was remarkable for their tender ages. Completely deprived of power or resources, they had to strategize in order to avoid the worst chores, commandeer the choicest scraps of cloth, and merit the most coveted tasks. Baking, for example, gave them access to sugar. Collecting berries in the meadow freed them from mind-numbing kitchen work as well as the mission's surveillance. A trip to the trading post might involve a pony ride and a gift of a ribbon or a piece of candy from the shopkeeper's wife.

Complex alliances and long-standing feuds connected and divided the girls in ways invisible to a casual observer. With their thin bodies swaddled in wool and their noses streaming freely onto their sleeves, they stoically accepted the primers the boys handed to them and seated themselves at their places.

Mrs. McCoy lowered her arthritic body onto a straight-backed wooden chair near the woodstove. Her stiff, black, wool skirt radiated out around her small form. In all things, she resembled one of the primer's crude woodcuts: everything about her that wasn't covered in black was paper white.

"A" was for Adam: "In Adam's fall/ We sinned all." "B" was for Bible: "Thy life to mend/ This book attend." And "C": "The cat doth play and after slay." Mrs. McCoy closed her eyes tightly, as if summoning her last bit of strength to speak to them. God was always testing Mrs. McCoy. He watched her day and night, just waiting for her to sin, so he could strike.

They were just about to begin the Bible lesson for the day when the older children's teacher, Mr. Lumpkin, appeared at the door carrying a wrapped parcel. Lumpkin's round, wire-rimmed glasses steamed up immediately. His beard was whitened with the recent flurries, and his brow, as always, was deeply furrowed, as if he were hard at work on some vexing problem. He spoke with Mrs. McCoy in a hushed voice then left. A wave of cold air from the opened door circulated through the classroom, punctuating his departure.

"Kewanee. Please come here." Mrs. McCoy looked up from the package on her lap to the benches where the girls sat. All of Mrs. McCoy's emotions—anger, suspicion, contentment—flitted across the white expanse of her round, blank face like shadows of passing clouds. Wabaunsee suspected she was unable to feel much of anything after burying six of her own ten children. Too much scar tissue around her heart.

Kewanee was a quiet, watchful girl just a few years younger than Wabaunsee. Her arms were as thin and as strong as willow branches, and she could climb trees more quickly than anyone he had ever known. Her fingernails were always amber with pine sap. She knew by heart all the Christian hymns, and her voice warbled in a way that sent shivers down his spine. Reverend McCoy said that she sang like one of God's angels.

Everyone turned to look at her as she walked slowly towards Mrs. McCoy, dragging the fingers of one hand through her tangled black hair.

"Kewanee, two generous, Christian ladies from Boston have decided to become your sponsors." She consulted the piece of unfolded stationary that lay in her lap atop a square parcel. "They ask that you be named Harriet Emma Ober, the name of their society's secretary." She looked up at Kewanee. "This is an honor, Kewanee, and very encouraging that Christian ladies should show such kindness to one less fortunate than themselves. They've sent you a dress and a Bible."

Kewanee looked at Mrs. McCoy then away. A fragment of a smile flitted across Mrs. McCoy's face. The children shifted uneasily in their seats; they could see the ribbon of poison wrapped round the gift. "Take the package...Harriet," she said, pushing it toward her.

Kewanee took the package and looked to the bench where the other girls sat. "From now on, boys and girls, Kewanee will be called Harriet." The girl stood rooted to the spot where she'd been summoned; her gentle features hardened into a mask of fury. She stared into Mrs. McCoy's eyes, burning a hole through the dimly-lit chaos of the older woman's thoughts. There was a flash of something that could have been fear, anger, or maybe just discomfort in Mrs. McCoy's face. "You may take your seat," she said. Kewanee looked at the floor and walked back slowly to the bench.

"Josephus, will you begin the reading for us?"

Josephus was Mr. and Mrs. McCoy's son. "Ezekiel chapter 34, number 16, 'I will seek that which was lost, and bring again that which was driven away, and will bind up that which was broken, and will strengthen that which was sick: but I will destroy the fat and the strong: I will feed them with judgment.'"

"Josephus, can you tell us? Why would God destroy the fat and the strong?"

Josephus looked up from his folded hands and cleared his throat. At the moment, all he could do was envy "the fat and the strong." He had just passed the worst of his bout with influenza but still had occasional coughing fits. All eyes turned toward Josephus's waxen face "Because they are prideful."

"And why would God, if he is truly good, 'destroy'?" asked Mrs. McCoy, arching her eyebrows slightly but remaining otherwise expressionless.

"A good God still needs to enact divine justice and that sometimes causes him to destroy things."

To the other children, Josephus seemed not entirely human. He retained countless hymns and Bible verses and retrieved them effortlessly without substituting a similar word or pausing for reflection. Everyone would look to Josephus when they got to the third or fourth stanza of a hymn, and he would lead unerringly to the end. Random conversations, the instructions for making soap, the names of all the trees and birds—everything became part of the vast storage house in his head.

The snow was falling fast when Mr. Lumpkin announced with two blasts on his bugle the end of morning classes. As the children left the school room to start their chores, three girls followed Kewanee who was looking straight ahead, her small nose turned slightly upward. Lydia, a girl with dark ringlets that framed her heart-shaped face, pushed her lower lip out and asked: "Can we see your new dress...Harriet?" Kewanee ignored her and walked toward the kitchen where the other girls had already begun grinding dried corn into cornmeal. Once, she had drawn a picture of Lydia that faithfully depicted the girl's angelic doll face but added a demon's tail that peeked out beneath her skirts. Lydia had sought vengeance ever since.

Outside the schoolhouse, the long-suffering Mr. Lumpkin shoveled the snow that wasn't content to simply fall from the sky but drifted horizontally into his freshly shoveled paths.

Wabaunsee had heard that Lumpkin had left Ohio to join the Mission after the woman he'd married died of typhus. Maybe it was his grief that drove him to embrace drudgery. He'd never seen anyone so drawn to repetitive, mindless labor. When land was being cleared for tilling, and a tree was felled, Lumpkin would, ax in hand, fall on the matted roots with all the ecstasy of a lover. Snow presented him with endless opportunities for the kind of back-breaking, fruitless labor he relished. Despite Reverend McCoy's praise of Lumpkin's diligence, none of the children wished to be like him.

Lumpkin stuck his shovel in the snow before him and leaned his weight upon it, breathing heavily. "Go break the ice on the water troughs, lads, and get some firewood for the classroom and kitchen." Wabaunsee and Josephus set off toward the barn along one of Lumpkin's newly shoveled paths.

"You'll both be coming with me and Reverend McCoy to get supplies from the river men," Lumpkin called after them.

After delivering the firewood to the kitchen, Josephus and Wabaunsee hitched a stone boat with runners to the old, swayback mare Jezabelle and set off behind Reverend McCoy and Lumpkin for the river.

The Reverend's frame was small and wiry; his shoulders, narrow. Despite the fact that he was well into his fifties, from the back, he looked like an adolescent boy. As always, he wore his parson's hat, which provided no warmth.

Reverend McCoy stopped and closed his eyes, pinching the bridge of his nose with his fingertips. Mr. Lumpkin looked closely at him, "Another headache, Reverend?"

"Yes, like a nail being driven into my skull. Anyway, it passes. If I could just sleep…God gives me this pain because he knows I'm strong enough to endure it, so I rejoice."

Wabaunsee, who had been at the Mission for a year and a half, could speak, read, and write in English. Words that were new to him found their way to his tongue, as if he needed to taste each one. "Rejoice," he whispered, "rejoice."

Josephus looked furtively at Wabaunsee and said in a voice too soft to be heard by his father or Mr. Lumpkin, "I had a dream last night." Reverend McCoy had forbidden the children to speak of their dreams. Reason would lead them to God. Only primitive people, he had said, believed in the significance of dreams.

"What was it?"

"I dreamt that I was walking in the woods. It was summer, and all the trees were leafed out." He looked above at the bare branches as if seeing his dream again. "I looked down at the ground beneath my feet, and I saw something wriggle. And I saw something wriggle in the bark of the tree and then in a cloud. I realized that everything was wriggling because everything was made out of snakes. What do you suppose that means?"

"I don't know. Some dreams don't mean anything. Some mean a lot."

Josephus stopped and looked at his friend. "How're you supposed to tell the difference?"

"The ones that show you something new," Wabaunsee said, shrugging his shoulders. "The ones that teach you to think different about things—they're the good ones."

"But I'm not sure what the snakes mean," muttered Josephus, who was clearly uncomfortable with the ambiguity.

"Maybe they don't mean anything."

When they reached the river, Wabaunsee saw that it was frozen with the exception of an expanse ten-canoe-lengths wide of open water. He remembered what the same river had looked like at the height of summer when he had filled a large, leather pouch with freshwater clams. His grandfather had praised him, saying he must be part heron, and each morning afterward Wabaunsee awoke hoping to find that blue-gray feathers had pushed their way out of his naked flesh. He wanted his useless, soft lips to harden into a dagger-like bill.

He closed his eyes trying to will those days back, and, for a moment, he was surrounded by fresh wild ginger, the musky scent of beaver, and the drone of bumblebees. But the sound of the men shouting to one another across the frozen river broke the spell. He looked up at the gray sky that had forgotten that there had ever been a thing called summer.

Two men stood on the opposite side of the river unloading burlap bags from a sledge onto the ice. The taller of the two men, who wore a fur hat, began chopping a line in the ice with his hatchet. His last decisive chop un-tethered the frozen mass from the river bank, and the man nearly lost his balance as his makeshift ice-raft broke loose. The fur-hatted man's traveling companion was attempting to do the same but looked less practiced.

The man with the fur hat used a long pole to guide himself to the opposite side of the river where he grabbed hold of a heavy tree limb.

Wabaunsee, Josephus, Mr. Lumpkin, and Rev. McCoy ran to the ice-raft and began to unload the supplies.

Suddenly, they heard splashing. The inexperienced trader had fallen into the river after his pole got snagged. The young man's face was red; his eyes, wide with terror. The older trader grabbed a rope out of his pack, ran along the bank, and threw an end in the direction his friend was headed. The young man's head suddenly went below the water's surface.

"James!" the trader bellowed.

Painful seconds passed without a ripple, then suddenly a head appeared by a cluster of dead wood. Quickly tying his end of the rope to a tree, he waded into the water, and threw the rope directly in front of the drowning man. "Take it, James! Take the rope!"

With a gesture that seemed almost casual, James reached out and took the rope. "Good! James, hold on! Hold on tight!" He pulled the man towards him, grabbed him by his soaked jacket, and dragged him to the frozen bank where the men stripped off his wet clothes and wrapped him in a saddle blanket. They covered him with whatever clothes of their own they could spare.

"How far is your mission?" asked the man in the fur hat.

"A little over a mile," Lumpkin answered, taking off his scarf and wrapping it around the young man's head.

The trader produced a piece of flint from a leather bag, and they all began wrenching whatever dead branches they could find from the snow.

Isaac's voice could be heard from afar, calling for assistance. He had followed the younger man's abandoned ice raft as the current pulled it north. Josephus looked at Lumpkin with uncertainty. "Go help your father, lad."

The trader stripped pieces of bark off the trees, and they laid the shivering young man on the bark before the fire. Wabaunsee gave an extra saddle blanket to the now inadequately dressed older trader.

Reverend McCoy and Josephus returned, burdened with sacks of flour and dried beans they'd rescued from the run-away ice-raft. Josephus approached the fire where a silent vigil was being kept around the stricken man. They all knew how fast even healthy young men could die in water that cold.

"I thought we had lost everything, but I managed to recover every bit of it. God be praised. I think this man here lost his hatchet." He then looked around at the tense expressions of the assembled group and noticed that the young trader was still shaking violently. Reverend McCoy solemnly removed his hat and, standing over him, said: "Holy Father, give us strength as we confront the moment of our death, comfort us in our suffering, give us peace from our fears, surround us with Your loving presence in our loneliness."

The trader shook even more violently, and the Reverend, raising his thick dark eyebrows in troubled surprise, stepped away.

Gradually, the young trader's shaking subsided. When his hands and feet began to warm, they transferred him to the horse, and, with the stone boat lightly loaded so as not to overtax the horse, they shouldered the remaining supplies and trudged through the snow to the mission.

Darkness had fallen by the time they reached their destination. Mrs. Wright wrapped Mr. Johnson, the young trader who had fallen into the water, in a blanket and had him sit near the woodstove. She gave him a cup of sassafras tea and bowl of hominy grits—exactly the fare they themselves had had for the past two months. His hands still shook too much to bring any of it successfully to his lips. Mrs. Wright, who had once been an attractive woman, watched him, thinking only of his head full of dark, glossy ringlets that were, she thought, so wasted on a man.

It was two hours past dinner time. The residents of the Carey Mission had been waiting for the party's return, trying unsuccessfully to ignore their empty stomachs, but now, at last, the adults were seated at the crude wooden dining table. As there were so many mouths to feed at the table and so little space, meals were accomplished in shifts. The eldest of the children ate late with the adults, since they could endure hunger longer.

Wabaunsee would eat with the adults tonight. He'd returned too late to eat with the children. He took a place on the bench next to Josephus. Reverend McCoy sat at the head of the table with Billy Killbuck, the older trader in the fur hat, on his right. Wabaunsee looked around the table at the pale, thin, and pinched faces staring vacantly at steaming pots of hominy and tea. Mrs. Wright appeared to be suffering from an eye infection. The thin face of one of the older boys would flush vivid red when he coughed then gradually return to its customary sallowness.

McCoy would have to say grace before they could eat. Wabaunsee could hear Josephus' stomach growling as they waited for the Reverend to find a verse from the Bible. The pages crackled like dry leaves beneath his calloused fingertips. Wabaunsee studied McCoy's face—his hooded eyes, delicate nose, full, sensuous mouth, and thick, black hair, now heavily streaked with gray. Despite his life of penance and self-denial, he radiated physical intensity. It was as if a fire continually burned in his gut, a fire that grew hotter the more he tried to smother it.

Reverend McCoy cleared his throat, pursed his lips, and, pressing long fingers that resembled tapered candles to his breastbone, read from the Bible. The table followed the reading with a collective: "Thanks be to God." Mrs. McCoy took hold of the ladle to begin the much-anticipated distribution. Her task was more demanding than it appeared. All would be sensitive to any accidental surpluses or deficiencies on anyone else's plate.

After several minutes of silent, appreciative eating, interrupted now and then by a pause to remove a cornhusk from a tooth or spoon, Reverend McCoy turned to the older trader. "And where are you from, Mr. Killbuck?"

Billy wiped his lips on the piece of cotton he'd been given. "I'm from Michigan Territory—a village on the Barbue River."

Eager to show his knowledge of Indian tribes, McCoy said, "So, you're Myaamia."

"I'm what you might call mixed, sir. A little of this and a little of that."

Short and long tufts of Killbuck's hair stuck out from under his fur hat, looking, at least to Wabaunsee, as though rodents had chewed it. He was stocky, though slightly doughy—a man who would quickly turn to fat if his life were less arduous. He favored one corner of his wide mouth when he spoke, which gave everything he said a conspiratorial air.

"Will you be leaving soon, Reverend?" Mr. Lumpkin asked.

"End of the week. I have to talk to Burnett about another loan, and then there's that business with the baptism."

"Baptism?" Lumpkin squinted his tired eyes behind his glasses.

"Yes." McCoy smiled indulgently. "It seems the man they call 'The Bishop' would like for me to baptize his dead mother."

Lumpkin also smiled good naturedly. "Oh dear. Bit late for that." He stood up as he buttoned his coat and addressed the group. "I bid you good night, gentlemen. And, ladies." Mrs. McCoy and Mrs. Wright were conversing in the back of the room and did not hear him. "Thanks to you, Mr. Killbuck and your partner Mr. Johnson," Lumpkin nodded to the young man who was hanging his felt boots by the fire, "my Jezabelle will get a little corn tonight."

"Happy to hear it. Better keep Jezabelle inside. Folks further south said a huge bear tore through their village a couple of nights ago. Apparently, got one of their sheep. Must be somethin' wrong with him. Bears don't like to leave their dens when it's cold like this. They say the scratch marks he's been leavin' is well above a tall man's head. Good night, Mr. Lumpkin."

"Thanks for the warning, Mr. Killbuck. Good night."

"Did Kewanee get her package?" McCoy asked.

"Yes, she did."

"Did she seem pleased?"

Lumpkin paused for a moment. "I don't know. I left the package with Mrs. McCoy. I had shoveling to do," then added with forced joviality, "Well, good night!"

Mr. Lumpkin closed the door and the cold air felt good on Wabaunsee's face. He was hoping that the adults wouldn't notice that it was past his bedtime. His stomach was full, and he was overheated. He couldn't remember a time in recent history when he'd experienced both states at the same time. Even the smoke, Mr. Johnson's perspiration-soaked boots, and the sour, marshy smell that came from Reverend McCoy's mouth did not make him wish to leave his place at the table.

Wabaunsee didn't understand what was amusing about 'The Bishop' wishing to baptize his dead mother. It seemed a natural thing, even a good thing, to try to protect one's loved-ones in the afterlife.

Killbuck yawned into his hand then sat up straight as if willing himself awake and asked, "So, you'll be traveling again soon, Reverend?"

"Another trip to Washington—my last, I hope. If I succeed in getting the permissions I need, I'll return to the mission and then we'll all, God willing, be traveling west."

"West?"

"Yes, we're relocating our school and all our aborigines west. We're waiting for government approval to relocate them to Kansas."

"Seems as though you've got space here. Why you gotta move?"

"Settlers. That's why we have to move. More and more of them move here every year and with them comes more and more whiskey. Our red brothers are helpless against it. Believe me, we would not encourage them to leave their homes if it were not absolutely necessary."

"Have you been to Kansas, Reverend?"

"No, I have not."

"It is a hot and sickly place filled with horse flies. Water is scarce. It's Pawnee, Choctaw, Cherokee homeland. Bodwéwadmi and Myaamia will find no welcome there."

McCoy exhaled heavily. "We, at the Mission, have consecrated our lives to the improvement of the aborigines, and they are not improving here. They are becoming worse."

"If you can't stop settlers from giving Indians whiskey here, how do you expect you'll do it in Kansas?"

"Moving them there will give us time to teach them the habits of civilized life."

"Like drinking whisky." Killbuck smiled his crooked smile.

"Mr. Killbuck, perhaps I seem naïve to you. Perhaps there is no way the evil of ardent spirits may be checked. But God has given me hope, and I do believe I have the best interests of the aborigines at heart. Kansas is a fertile land, and I have been advised that the corn that was planted in that land by the missionaries throve well. If corn can grow, men can feed themselves and their pigs. I believe it will be a new beginning."

"Indians hunt, Reverend."

"That was in the past. 'He that tilleth his land shall be satisfied with bread.' Civilized men till the land, and the aborigines must be civilized. We cannot let them give in to their savage propensities for war and the chase." McCoy pinched the bridge of his nose.

"Something the matter, sir?" Killbuck asked.

"Sleeplessness, Mr. Killbuck. If I could only sleep…Everyone has his cross to bear."

"I have medicine for pain. It also puts you to sleep. It's in my bag." Billy motioned to where his bag lay on the floor next to the now sleeping James. "Would you like some?"

McCoy remained silent for a moment. His eyes widened. He wished for something, anything that would call off the hounds of his own thoughts that chased him remorselessly till dawn. Glory would certainly follow all his sufferings, and, though he would never fault God's wisdom for having cursed him in this way, he couldn't help but think of all the good he could accomplish in His name, if he could only sleep. Depraved men, shallow men, men without character or purpose in life lay their heads down at night confident that sleep's sweet oblivion would find them. Yet he, a righteous man, found no such peace.

"I doubt it will work for me. Is it an Indian potion?"

"Indians use it, but your people take it too. Some take it for visions."

McCoy closed his eyes and folded his hands in his lap primly. "Mr. Killbuck, God speaks to us through the Bible and our reason. Reason is the light that leads us toward God. I know your people put great stock in dreams, but here at the Mission we consider them nonsense. We do not discuss them."

Killbuck dug through his pack and returned to the table with a small, calico bag. He poured water from a ceramic jug on the table into the wooden mug in front of McCoy and then sprinkled a little of the powder from his fabric bag into the water. "You won't need much of this."

"I'll need twice the normal dose, I'm sure. I've tried various tinctures and herbal teas—all without effect."

For a moment, Killbuck looked steadily at McCoy, yet he added no more powder to his drink. McCoy emptied the cup, grimacing slightly at the medicine's bitter flavor.

Wabaunsee knew from Killbuck's description that he must have given McCoy the potent nabagûck. As a member of the Medewin, Wabaunsee was shocked at the casual way in which Killbuck had given away this sacred and deadly medicine.

McCoy, as yet unaffected by the drug, wrapped himself in his thin, woolen coat, placed on his head his black, felt, parson's hat, and rose from the table.

"Good night to you, Mr. Killbuck. I thank you for your tonic." McCoy closed the door behind him with far more force than was necessary.

"Mr. Killbuck, won't that kill the Reverend?" Wabaunsee asked.

"I gave him so little, son," Killbuck said with his twisted smile, rising from the table to put more firewood in the stove.

Snores from the shadowy heap of sleeping men at the far end of the room and the occasional snap of the fire in the stove gave the cabin a fragile domesticity that pushed back against the suffocating silence of the winter night. Killbuck, Josephus, and Wabaunsee remained silent and unmoving at the candlelit table.

"I know your face, son. Well, not *your* face, but your grandfather's, Wéshkebet-mbo's. It's Wéshkebet I see lookin' out at me, when I look at you." He leaned back in his seat. "I don't suppose he'd be happy to see you here. Did you know about McCoy's plans to move the Bodwéwadmi west?"

"No. First I heard of it was tonight." Wabaunsee looked up into Killbuck's dark, watchful eyes and wondered if his grandfather had liked this man.

Killbuck interlaced his fingers and placed them carefully on the table. "Tomorrow, we're headed north. There's a group of Bodwéwadmi at their winter camp with pelts to trade. They're hunters not "tillers of the soil," but they ain't drunkards neither. They'll be headed north into Canada when spring comes." Killbuck rubbed his eyes and stood up. "I've got to get me some sleep. If you want to come with us, git your things and come back here. We'll leave at dawn."

Wabaunsee nodded. Both boys wrapped themselves in their jackets and walked outside. They stood for a moment in the cabin's blue shadow and looked above to the distant moon. Josephus walked ahead, and Wabaunsee remained behind. Two years ago, he had stood in this very spot with his Aunt. The five log cabins that constituted the entirety of the Carey Mission had been floating in a field of buttercups and Queen Anne's lace. His Aunt had held his hand tightly in hers, but he could feel that she had already hardened her heart to him—not because she was cruel or indifferent. She was the type of woman who cried for rabbits caught in snares. And not because she did not love him—she would rise early every morning to make his breakfast of wild rice and cranberries. But she'd lived long enough to see what whiskey could do. She'd seen her sister stabbed to death and old people of the village abandoned. There was no reason to think it would ever end. She was doing what she felt she had to do. However strange the people at the Mission might seem, they did not drink, and that was all the recommendation she needed.

He could hear wolves howling in the distance. Jezabelle snorted and stomped the ground in her paddock. Wabaunsee quietly stepped into the dark cabin where the boys slept. The acrid, musty odor of adolescent boy that was thick and pungent in summer had become a delicate bouquet in the winter's cold.

Josephus was already in the dark corner of the room where the bedrolls were kept. If he was going with the traders, Wabaunsee needed to collect his things, though he had only a few possessions. He felt dizzy, as if he stood at the edge of a precipice. Nothing tethered him to his past, and now his future was entirely undetermined.

"Are you going with them?" Josephus whispered.

"Yes. I think I am."

"I want to go too," he said in a slightly higher pitch.

Wabaunsee considered this for a moment. "They'll look for you."

Josephus exhaled softly in the darkness. "I...I know. What will you do with your book?"

"I'll bring it with me." Wabaunsee looked up into the rafters to the place where the manuscript was hidden. He stood silent for a few moments and then shook his head. "No, I can't. It's too big. I'll ruin it."

"I can keep it for you…until you come back."

"What if I don't come back?" Josephus was silent. Wabaunsee realized that he had already considered this outcome. "If I don't come back, give it to my older sister Angelique Navarre. My grandfather didn't want it to go to her on account of her marrying that White trader, but she's the next in line. It was my grandmother Marguerite's book. She would have wanted it to go to a Medewin like me. Angelique is not Medewin, but the book must have a keeper, and she is family."

Wabaunsee gathered his bedroll, his collection of colored pebbles, a wool hat, and a beaded belt his Aunt had given him.

"I'm sorry," Josephus said as he lay on his back staring at the ceiling.

"For what?"

Several seconds of silence followed. "Sorry about my father. Sorry about you having to leave."

"It's not your fault."

"I hope…I hope everything works out for you. I hope we meet again."

"You've been a good friend to me. I'll miss you."

"I'll miss you too."

Wabaunsee was overcome by a wave of panic. He couldn't say that he'd had a good life at the mission, but it had been a stable one. He just didn't feel like the sort of person who could spend his life raising corn and reading the Bible. "Good-bye," he said quickly, as he lifted the ice-cold door latch, and exited before he had time to reconsider.

After saying their prayers with folded hands on either side of the bed as both had been taught to do as little children, they stretched themselves out upon their straw mattresses. They were skeletal as a result of years subsisting on a sparse, flavorless diet, interrupted by frequent bouts of illness. Mrs. McCoy dropped like a stone into a deep slumber, and, as usual, Reverend McCoy could only watch her enviously.

Sleeplessness was just one of many crosses he bore: the ceaseless worry that the Baptist Missionary Society would discontinue its financial support (which was barely sufficient as it was); the overtaxed, long-suffering missionaries whose help they could never rely on for more than two months; the endless variety of illnesses and injuries that befell them; crop failures; disease among the livestock.

He stretched out on the bed, feeling the jagged topography of his spine against the unyielding surface of the straw mattress. He waited, vigilant to any alteration in his consciousness. Nothing. The tonic should have been stronger.

In the darkness, somewhere above his head, he heard a light, occasional scratch. *Hoo hoo hoooo. Hoo hoo hoooo.* He stared at the dark ceiling. The owl must have flown away. He closed his eyes.

Familiar and grotesque faces mixed freely in his imagination. Bright pools of orange, blue, and purple met and merged with darker pools of gray and black. This was exactly the sort of wakeful dream his brain devised to torment him each night. He wondered how many hours he still had to wait before dawn.

Finally, he got out of bed and went to his cabin's one tiny window; its thick glass made from bottle ends distorted more than it clarified. One section of the glass provided a fairly accurate view of the outside. He could see the naked torsos of the oaks and sycamores that marked the borderline between the mission and the forest.

Out of the corner of his eye, McCoy saw movement—a dark shape. His heart beat faster. He stared at the moonlit expanse of snow and waited. Nothing. Again, he saw a dark shape moving in the trees. Then, it was gone. He turned back to look at his sleeping wife. He could see her nose sticking out of the blankets. Maybe he should wake her. What could she do about the dark shape in the woods? He thought of the large bear Killbuck had mentioned. He thought of Jezabelle in her stall. He thought of the children.

He sat on the edge of the bed and carefully reinserted the piece of newspaper that covered a hole in his worn, deerskin boots. Then, he wrapped his wool jacket around his body. He had no gun. Men of God had no need for firearms.

He stepped outside and closed the door behind him. The bright points of the stars sparkled. The moon was directly overhead, and the cold's grip on the land was absolute. Time itself had frozen solid. He inhaled the frigid air, and it caught in his lungs and made him want to cough. But he needed to be silent. Something was out there with him.

Just as he started walking away from his cabin, he saw it. The black, shaggy carpet of its enormous body swayed back and forth, and its head moved slowly from side to side as if seeking something buried in the snow. It was the largest bear McCoy had ever seen. Mr. Killbuck had a rifle. Maybe Mr. Killbuck was still awake. The bear raised its head and smelled the air. McCoy was close enough to his cabin to make it back inside if the bear charged, though sometimes the latch stuck, particularly in the cold.

The bear headed for the children's cabin. Thank God they were behind a closed door, and there was nothing inside the cabin to entice a bear. He did wonder if children were more appetizing to bears than grown men. Children's skin smelled sweet like berries. Their soft flesh would certainly be easier for bears to sink their teeth into.

The bear stood on its hind legs; its claws reached past the cabin's little window next to the door. McCoy saw that it was easily twice his size. He remained perfectly still. The bear dropped back down and lumbered away.

But the door of the children's cabin opened. A girl's slight form appeared. McCoy thought it looked like Kewanee's small, willow-tree shape. She pushed the door closed, and it banged loudly against the door jam. The girl went down the steps and walked along the shoveled path in the direction of the outhouse, keeping her eyes on the path before her. There was nothing fearful or tentative about her. There never was. The bear raised its head and sniffed the air.

The bear charged, closing the distance between itself and the child instantly. Horror and panic overwhelmed McCoy. He wanted to cry out for help, but he did not want to draw the bear's attention to himself. The child disappeared beneath the bear's bulky body. He could hear snapping and cracking, as the bear whipped its head back and forth. Blood and saliva sprayed across the snow. The bear turned around to where McCoy stood; the girl's head was in its mouth. The bear pawed at the now motionless body. It pulled off an arm, took several bites, and after pushing the mangled pieces of the child's body with its nose, sauntered off. The stars still sparkled brilliantly in the sky.

Reverend McCoy could see the dark pieces of what was left of the child's body scattered across the snow. He stood rooted to the same spot: both alive and dead. The bear would have killed him, but it had killed her instead. He'd go back inside his cabin, take off his boots and jacket, and tomorrow morning he would pretend to be just as shocked and horrified as the others. Maybe, in time, he'd forget. Maybe he'd convince himself it had never happened. He'd contact the Christian women's society in Boston to see if he could transfer her dress and Bible to some other child. No, no need to do that. They didn't know that there had ever been a girl named Kewanee. As far as they were concerned, another child could have been the recipient of their kindness. It wouldn't matter to anyone.

He went inside. No need to kick the snow off his boots, since he hadn't ventured more than five feet away from the steps. His wife was still asleep. It was strange to think that her husband of thirty years could have committed such an unspeakable act of cowardice just outside her window, yet there she slept so very much at peace. He lowered himself into the bed as if it were his grave.

"Isaac! What ails you?"

He opened his eyes. Morning light filled the cabin. He saw his wife's pale-blue eyes before him. He remembered what had happened the night before. Why was she looking at him like that?

"What is it?" he asked.

Mrs. McCoy was studying him with a look of cold assessment. "You've been asleep a long time. The children are already at their lessons."

Had they not found the body yet? Was she testing him?

"Mr. Killbuck gave me some sleeping powder. Is he still here?"

"No. He and the young man, Mr…Mr. Johnson left early."

"I'll be up shortly. Is everything fine then?"

"Yes, Wabaunsee is not feeling well. Josephus said he was still sleeping." She looked at him as if she could see his coward's heart beating in his chest. He looked away. She left.

Broad shafts of daylight shown through the window. Had it not happened then? He dressed hurriedly and went outside: no child's body, no blood, no bear tracks. God in heaven be praised.

He hurried to the schoolroom. Mrs. McCoy looked up in surprise from her primer. He scanned the room. Kewanee looked up. Her eyes were dark and inscrutable, and a reverence came to him that was like love. He cleared his throat. "No need for Kewanee to change her name. No need. Sorry." The children looked at him blankly. He hurriedly closed the door and went back outside.

Yesterday's clouds had departed, and a bright, limpid light defined the wooden shingles of the main cabin and the tree tops beyond. Delicate wisps of smoke floated from the chimney like the breath of an angel.

CHAPTER 5

MEN SEEKING FORTUNES IN THE PROMISED LAND

~ 1836 ~

"I have found them to be designing, intriguing men determined to get as much as they can for as little as possible by whatever means necessary," said Alexis Coquillard as he dipped the tip of his quill into the blue glass inkwell on his desk. This was his assessment of his competitors in the local fur trade, the Ewing brothers, W.G. and G.W. His assistant, Raymond Steel, had heard this assessment many times before and knew that his own commentary on the brothers' characters was neither expected nor desired.

Tuesdays they oversaw the ferry that brought passengers from one side of the St. Joseph to the other. Wednesdays they assisted Coquillard's brother Michael with his accounting at the tavern. Mondays were devoted to meetings with bankers, government officials, or surveyors. All other days, like today, they were at the crude log building in a forest clearing that served as a major depot for the local fur trade. As an agent of John Astor's American Fur Company, Coquillard could add a two and a half percent commission to the price of each of the pelts he purchased from the Natives.

Alexis Coquillard was laboriously transferring into the ledger the figures from the receipts, orders, and promissory notes that Mr. Steel had just given him. Coquillard, the third of ten children born to a French-speaking family in the backwoods around Detroit, had taught himself to read and write as a young adult and was slow at both. Mr. Steel was accustomed to taking over whenever his employer threw down his pen in frustration and stormed off.

Coquillard's business ventures had made him a very rich man

at forty-two, and he was about to become even richer. An old Indian portage, about two miles long, connected the St. Joseph River to the Kankakee, a river which eventually emptied into the Mississippi. Coquillard was making that portage obsolete by digging a canal connecting the two rivers. Recognizing the canal's commercial potential as well as its convenience, he was already building a saw mill and two flour mills. He had hired a New York company with experience planning and digging the Erie Canal to guide the work, and there had been no shortage of offers locally to assist with the digging. He knew people called it "Coquillard's Folly," but he felt sure it would be a gold mine.

"Chief Peepenawah is out on the trading grounds, Mr. Coquillard. He says he wants to speak with you," said Mr. Steel, a man in his early thirties with straight, precisely combed, reddish-brown hair, and an intense, accusatory gaze.

Alexis sighed deeply, "How much does he owe us still, Mr. Steel?"

"Ten thousand. We plowed their land three times. They bought seeds, pans, blankets, and ammunition—all on credit."

Alexis' pen stopped mid-air as he listened. "Is he here to pay his debts?"

"He seems to be asking to borrow more money. His men are with him. They've got a few more pelts."

Alexis leaned back in his chair; his silver eyes became little frozen pools. He shook the ink out of his pen and set it on the blotter. Tiny drops of ink transformed into dark, menacing shapes. He took out his gold pocket watch, checked the time and caressed it lightly with his forefinger. "Sic transit Gloria mundi" was engraved on its back: "Thus passes the glory of the world." For Alexis, the glory of the world was just unfolding.

The watch was a gentleman's possession, and he was now a gentleman. Silks for his wife; engraved silver spoons and glass goblets for his household; and, for himself, a gold watch. It had been the first in a series of many elegant and beautiful things he had purchased for himself and his family. Given the way his various enterprises were prospering, there would be many more.

With determination, Alexis lifted his six-foot, four-inch frame out of his chair and walked out of the counting house and into the trading yard. Trappers yelled their greetings to him in French and English, and workmen with mud-covered trousers wearily trudged toward the counting house to receive their pay.

Carts filled with muskrat, wolf, and raccoon pelts groaned under the great weight they carried. Countless over-burdened wagons had cut deep furrows in the ground from years of nearly constant traffic. Hundreds of pelts leaving from this point in the wilderness today would meet hundreds of pelts coming from Detroit, Chicago, Montreal, all converging on the warehouses of New York where they would become thousand-pelt high stacks before being shipped off to London, Shanghai, and Le Havre.

Alexis walked through all this activity purposefully, noting with pride that men recognized and acknowledged him as one above the rest. He wasn't one of those men in top hats from the East who used a Latin word here and there just to remind you whom you were dealing with. He was called a "man of action": a title he embraced. He rounded the barn where oxen and horses were being watered, fed, and harnessed and saw the group of Miami sitting beneath a cluster of oak trees.

Chief Peepenawah rested a foot on a large rock while he attempted to remove something from his teeth. Locals called Alexis "Potawatomi Chief" because of his knowledge of Native languages. Alexis had discovered that the memorization of approximately one hundred and fifty phrases in Potawatomi and Miami was sufficient to do business with the native population. It had certainly impressed General Tipton, the Indian agent in Fort Wayne, who had eagerly issued Alexis a license to do business with the Potawatomi for three thousand dollars. The Indians were less impressed with his facility in their languages. To them, he sounded both impaired and aggressive.

Striding directly toward Chief Peepenawah, Alexis said in broken Miami, "You here to pay debt. You owe ten thousand dollars." Chief Peepenawah pretended not to hear Alexis and continued to clean his teeth.

Chief Peepenawah had broad shoulders, a tapered narrow waist, and eyes so dark they absorbed all light. He wore hawk feathers in his thick black hair, a wampum and leather band around his arm that drew attention to his well-developed muscles. He wore a necklace with silver ornaments, all in the shape of quarter moons. Resigned to the necessity of dealing with Coquillard, Peepenawah slowly turned towards him. "You buy our furs cheaply and sell them at a profit. You owe *us* money."

Coquillard's brain spun through its list of memorized phrases, but nothing he could think of was an apt reply. Without warning, Alexis reached out a hand and snatched from Peepenawah's neck the silver necklace with the delicate half-moons. He stuffed it rapidly into his pants pocket and strode back toward the counting house. Peepenawah and his men stood for a moment in stunned amazement. The warriors shouted "thief" and "white dog" at the retreating Coquillard, and two workmen tending their horses at the barn went for their guns.

In the counting house, Alexis Coquillard calmly returned to his ledger after throwing the silver necklace on the desk. "How much is this bit of tinsel worth, Mr. Steel," he asked.

Mr. Steel, who was more concerned than his employer about the increasing volume and frequency of shouts and war-whoops outside, examined the necklace. "Thirty dollars? It's a fine piece of work."

Coquillard took it back from his assistant and brought it to the safe. "Subtract thirty dollars from the good chief's account. He's still $9,970 in arrears."

There was a loud knock at the door.

"Let them in," said Coquillard who was squatting at the safe with his back to the door.

Steel went to the door reluctantly. He wasn't eager to take either a bullet or an arrow for his employer. Coquillard hadn't always been so casual in his treatment of the Indians and traders. But, at some point, his rapidly accumulating wealth began to seem less like the result of good fortune and more like his due.

When Steel opened the door, a burly man of sixty with a very red nose, triangular white beard, and a large wart on his ruddy forehead stepped inside and looked around for Coquillard. "Chief Peepenawah would like to speak with you. We can shoot him, sir. Do you want us to shoot him? I mean, we can just shoot him."

"Dead Indians can't pay their debts, William. Send him in."

There was a loud rap at the door. Coquillard grabbed a small club from under his desk and walked quietly to the hinge side of the door. He opened the door while keeping himself concealed behind it. Chief Peepenawah walked in cautiously. Coquillard leapt out and hit the Chief over the head with the club. Peepenawah's dark eyes registered surprise as he collapsed to the floor.

Coquillard stepped over the motionless body of the Miami chief and went outside. "William! Come help the good Chief out of the counting house."

The same burly man with the white beard came into the room. He stood staring wide-eyed at Peepenawah. "Is he dead?"

"What did I just say, William? Dead Indians can't pay debts. Give him back to his people and remind them we still require the $9970."

Peepenawah's men had been outmaneuvered outside the counting house by a group of trappers with rifles. William shouted to a friend for assistance, and the two of them carried the limp, handsome body of the Chief outside, depositing him in the mud by a wagon of pelts at the feet of his enraged but powerless men.

NOON

There were no shadows here—just the rock, the Old Oak, and the river. Muskrat had been sent to find Mishipeshu, and now they both awaited the arrival of Manitou.

Mishipeshu splashed water on the rock because it was too hot for her to sit on. Muskrat used both hands to pull up pondweed and push it into his mouth. Mishipeshu looked at him with disgust. "Do you never stop eating, Muskrat?"

Muskrat stopped chewing and stared at her for a moment with his black, beady eyes. He pushed more pondweed into his mouth.

Mishipeshu sighed, shook her head, and arranged her hair while looking at her reflection in the water. Lazily, she detached the snails from the rock where she sat, pulled off their shells, and threw their wriggling worm bodies into Namé's large, open mouth.

Bear, Quail, Wolf, Beaver and Buffalo had joined Muskrat on the riverbank without Mishipeshu noticing. They turned East and walked several paces then turned West to return to the same spot.

"Manitou, first god of the heavens, why have you abandoned us?" they said in unison, looking up into the sky. "What have we done that you have brought this plague of men upon us?"

They looked up into the sky and waited in silence. An acorn fell. The animals once more walked East and then West.

"Manitou, we cannot see what is to come. We do not have the gift of prophecy. Yet we hear the dark wings of fate above our heads. The men who have come into this country have killed so many. Our home, once filled with flowers and honey, has been felled by axes. Guns have silenced the birds' songs. Hear our prayers, oh Manitou. We beseech you. Make them go."

A strong wind blew in from the west and then died. One-by-one, the animals departed from the riverbank.

Mishipeshu looked at the place on the riverbank where the animals had recently stood. "Manitou has called for us, yet not appeared. Very troubling, my friend. Very troubling." She stroked the sturgeon's head, and the great fish rubbed his head affectionately on her hand. "Your barbels are frayed, my darling."

"Oh Namé," said Mishipeshu. "Time travel makes me sick. Day and night flash by so quickly. My head aches and still we find no trace of Meskwaki."

Namé raised his head above the water to feel the sun's heat. Droplets fell from the four sharp barbels beneath his chin and radiated outward in ever widening circles. Mishipeshu nestled her long body between the ridges of Namé's spine and took up the silver, pearl-encrusted reins. They dove beneath the surface of the water and a cloud of bubbles followed after.

CHAPTER 6

"COQUILLARD'S DITCH" AND THE MYSTERY OF THE MISSING WATER

~ 1837 ~

Sixteen-year-old Josiah Lamb sat on a stump gnawing the stale white bread he'd bought the day before from Bartlett's Bakery on Washington Street. He had just thrown down in disgust the shovel he'd been using since daybreak to dig 'Coquillard's Ditch' and was now taking what he thought was a well-deserved break.

Josiah squinted into the late morning sun and continued his narrative to Ian Carr, the twenty-two-year-old Scot who'd been appointed his supervisor for three months of work. "So, like I was telling ya, time passes and some of the men starts wonderin', 'What's keepin' em?' and all, so they turn their horses round to find out. Well, wouldn't ya know. They was all dead and scalped. Their horses gone, and their wagons on fire."

Ian Carr was only six years older than his employee, Josiah, but he felt the distance between them was decades-long and continents-wide. All of Josiah's stories ended with someone being scalped or shot. Life was just meaningless filler between acts of violence. Ian reminded himself that he would soon be saying good-bye to Josiah. Tomorrow, the canal would be complete.

For three months, Ian had shoveled, pushed, and dumped muck. His first days on the job had made him more tired and sore than anything he had ever done in his life, and his life had not been lacking in punishing physical labor. Daydreaming about what he would do with the money he earned had made it easier for him to accustom his body to the hard work. He felt strong, and he knew he had this work to thank for that. Still, when they dug the final shovelfuls tomorrow, and the water of the Kankakee took its new course, he would be happy to collect his pay and move on to whatever came next.

Ian received sixteen dollars a week for his labor, like the other thirty men digging the canal. Assistants, like Josiah, were paid eight. Two miles of land was the only thing obstructing a three-thousand-mile waterway, stretching from the St. Lawrence Seaway's cold, gray waters to the warm, blue-green Gulf of Mexico.

Natives and then White settlers had dragged heavy boats and supplies over this two-mile piece of land without ever thinking there might be an alternative. Not Alexis Coquillard. He had invested one hundred thousand in the construction of the canal and was building a flour and saw mill and lathe works to profit from the water flow. When the canal opened, he'd be ready for every opportunity to make money. Property values of land adjacent to the canal had already increased ten-fold, and a new network of roads crisscrossed land that had been wilderness just a few years before.

Of course, what they were doing to the Indians didn't seem right. Soon, they said, the Indians would all be driven west, and their land would be up for sale.

Ian's own family had been run off their land in Scotland for not making the landlord enough money. They were evicted for being "backward" and "unprofitable." Ian and his two younger brothers had been off in the hills before dawn to mind the sheep. They smelled smoke, and, looking down into the valley, saw flames shooting out of their family's cottage. They ran home as fast as they could, but they were helpless against the blaze. Ian's uncle told them that he had seen the landlord's assistant gallop off with a lit torch in his hand. Ian's mother had refused to believe it.

A rifle shot rang out close by, which brought Ian out of his reverie. They could hear men shouting in the distance.

"Quail hunters?" said Ian, looking at Josiah. This would be the fifth group of hunters they'd encountered in the past three days.

South of the pin oak grove, close to where Ian and Josiah were digging, was a thicket of sumac. A quail flew out of the thicket and then a cocker spaniel emerged followed by two hunters. The hunters shouldered their rifles and blasted three holes in the late morning's canopy of rhythmic chirps, calls, and songs. A bird's body froze mid-flight, then started its heavy arc toward the earth. Two more birds were flushed out and suffered a similar fate. The hunters walked deeper into the woods and swamp.

Their momentary distraction gone, Josiah lifted up the wheelbarrow's handles, pushed hard to counteract the load's inertia, then fought to keep it upright along the rutted path. Ian returned to his shoveling.

It had started with a gentle wind from the northwest. As Ian and Josiah washed the day's muck from their feet, clothing, and tools, Isaac noticed that the leaves of the aspens had taken on a silvery look—a look that had, in the past, preceded the arrival of violent downpours. A stillness settled over the land. Somewhere close by, a morning dove cooed, then that too stopped. Everything was listening, waiting.

"Let's put the cover over the wagon and tighten it. I think it's going to storm," Ian said. Joshiah took his hat off, scratched his head, and examined the stretch of sky above their heads. "I don't feel nothin'."

"Listen. You hear it?"

A moist wind blew through the clearing and far off they heard a rumble like cannon fire from a distant battle. They stretched the canvas tarp over the wagon; beneath it, they stowed shovels, saws, and picks.

Ian watched the darkening northwest sky. A breeze sprang out of nowhere, whipping through a cluster of trees and freeing basket-loads of leaves yellowed by the recent drought and shortening days. Some of the leaves were lifted high into the sky where they were indiscernible from the small birds racing off to escape the coming storm.

Cool drops fell irregularly, bringing relief wherever they fell on Ian's body. Josiah looked up, felt the rain, and disappeared into the wagon. But Ian stayed outside enjoying the freedom from Josiah's company and feeling the cool, fresh air wafting in from the icy north, perhaps the same air he breathed in now had once drifted through an immense stand of pine trees or a snow-covered, rocky mountain range.

Blue-black clouds darkened the sky, and the rain, tentative at first, was now steady. Still, Ian remained outside. The raindrops ran through his hair and down his face. A sudden flash illuminated the entire grove. Then, a tremendous, shattering clap of thunder followed; it reverberated through his chest and head. During that brilliant flash of lightning, he had seen workers running off in different directions to escape the downpour. Reluctantly, Ian got into the back of the wagon where Josiah already lay with a blanket over his head.

Ian listened to the rain waxing and waning long into the night, drifting between sleep and wakefulness. In a dream, he saw images: a canal filled with dead quail; a treeless landscape beneath a blood-red sky.

The wagon's white canvas ceiling was glowing with morning

sunlight when Ian awoke. A crow perched on the wagon called in its loudest, raspiest voice. Josiah raised his head slightly, groaned, and pulled a blanket over his head.

When Ian emerged from the wagon, he found the entire glade newly polished and pristine. Sparks of red cardinal flowers and white stars of Kankakee mallow edged a thick grove of oaks. He closed his eyes and smelled warm mint and heard a whippoorwill singing somewhere above their heads.

He walked toward the canal, buttoning his shirt, assessing the damage done to their work by the previous night's rain. Some of the mud Josiah had taken out of the canal had washed back in, but the ditch that should have been filled with rainwater was empty. Ian looked down the length of the canal and saw that the other men who had just emerged from their wagons were noticing the same thing.

"Stand back!" the men shouted, as they removed the last shovel-fuls of muck dividing the Kankakee from the St. Joseph.

They watched and waited.

"Where's the water?"

By the time Alexis Coquillard arrived at the canal, it was already twelve o'clock, and the sun beat down on the empty canal with an intensity more typical of July than mid-September. He got off his horse quickly and strode purposefully toward the canal, stopping, putting both hands on his hips, and staring at the empty ditch. One of the consultants he had hired from a New York firm arrived shortly afterward, looking a bit tentative and incredulous as he too surveyed the ditch.

"Mr. Coquillard, sir, perhaps the canal needs to be deeper," suggested the consultant. "Maybe another foot down would give you a firmer base."

Alexis pushed back his sweaty hair from his forehead and called to his foreman, "Tell the men to dig another foot down." Alexis grabbed a shovel and jumped into the ditch, sticking the end of the shovel into the soil at different points. After about ten minutes, he climbed back out, and, handing his shovel to the foreman, told him, "Another foot down!"

Mr. Greene, Coquillard's foreman for the canal work, was a small, wiry man of fifty with large, expressive, blue-green eyes and a gray, bristly beard. "Sir, the men were expecting to receive their pay today. They worked for three months, and they done what you asked them."

"You can see yourself, Mr. Greene, that the job isn't done yet.

There's no water in the canal. A canal is not a canal if it does not have water flowing through it. Isn't that right, Mr. Greene?" said Alexis, looking down with ferocious intensity at his foreman who was a good foot shorter.

But Mr. Greene raised his gentle eyes to Mr. Coquillard and said, "There's no water in the ditch, that's true, Mr. Coquillard, but the contract with the men says that they were to dig a ditch thirty feet wide and four feet deep, which is what they done. Nothin' was said about there needing to be water in it, sir. You can't expect em' to do more work till they're paid for what they done, sir."

The men, guessing at the subject and tenor of the two men's conversation, were silent. Alexis stared aggressively at Mr. Green but then looked round him furtively. Thirty-five men held pickaxes and shovels staring intently at Alexis Coquillard.

"All right then, if they don't fancy getting the job done, tell them they can go home," Alexis said.

With both hands on the end of the shovel he had planted into the ground before him, Mr. Greene pensively studied the patch of ground before him, "The men will go home, sir, after you pay them."

"I will send Mr. Steel with the cash box," said Alexis, who got back on his horse and left the men standing by the empty ditch in the afternoon sun.

"Mortgaging your farmland and city lots to the State Bank should bring you," said Mr. Steel scribbling numbers on the papers before him on Mr. Coquillard's desk, "$45,639." Alexis paced with his hands behind his back. He had summoned his assistant to his home on a Sunday and then was uninterested, even hostile, when he answered his questions.

"That still leaves $54,361 to be paid," said Steel.

"I know how much that still leaves," said Alexis quietly, tapping his forehead lightly with the fingertips of both hands. He walked into and out of the pale patch of November sunlight on the floor. He stopped and rested his hands on the back of a leather upholstered chair that he had had sent from Philadelphia the previous year at great personal expense. "And how much did we take in from ferry tolls?"

Mr. Steel flipped pages in the ledger and quickly added the numbers in his head. "$910. We'll probably take in another $50, provided the ice on the river doesn't come early and stay late, as it did last year."

Alexis looked out the window at the river that had followed its own blind will since time immemorial. But those days were ending. The river would henceforth serve men.

"I could deed the canal to the State. The new canal will be worth at least $30,000 once it's dug to the proper depth."

"The canal might be worth thousands of dollars in time, sir, but that is not its current value."

There was an uncomfortable silence. "Quite right. Let's get back to our enumeration of assets and liabilities, Mr. Steel. I am owed ten thousand by the Miami, am I not?"

"Yes, nearly that for plowing their lands for the past two years. But they're unlikely to be able to pay. Demand for furs has fallen, as you know, and they don't have any other resources, except annuity payments from the government for their land, and those are barely sufficient to cover their needs."

Mr. Steel looked thoughtfully at the glass paperweight on the desk without really seeing it. "We *could* ask Mr. Tipton—he's still the Indian agent in these parts—to take the ten thousand out of the government annuities before it gets to the Miami."

"Tipton will be moving them out soon, won't he?" asked Coquillard.

"Yes, that should have happened already," said Steel, dipping his pen in the crystal well. "Another reason to get the money now. You'll never see it once they're on the other side of the Mississippi."

"How much did Tipton get from the Government to move the Indians out?"

"Thirty-five, forty thousand."

Coquillard looked out the window at the leafless trees. "If I could get *one* such contract, my debts would be nearly paid. Perhaps, I could get a percentage of Tipton's contract." He straightened his back and put his hands on his hips.

"Mr. Steel, write to Mr. Tipton and offer him our assistance, particularly in the capacity of translator. I think it would be an advantage to him to have someone managing the effort who is already familiar with this territory and the natives."

Mr. Steel took out a piece of paper to begin writing the letter.

Soon, all his enterprises would be back in their proper order. Not only would his debts be paid, he'd be turning a healthy profit.

"I'll be back this afternoon to sign it," said Alexis, checking his pocket watch. "I'm off to inspect the new flour mill."

"Mr. Coquillard, what about the payment to the canal workers, sir? It's been two months since they finished the project."

"The answer to *that* is very simple. There's no money to pay them. That's the short and long of it. They'll have to wait until my finances are settled with the State Bank." Alexis moved his watch into the exterior pocket of his thick fur coat, which he cinched around his large frame with a leather belt. He left without saying good-bye.

Alexis followed a path through a wooded area close to the river. His horse's hooves landed hard against the frozen earth newly covered with a dusting of snow. Above his head, a flock of Canadian geese in V formation headed south.

Christmas this year would not be as full of cheer as the last, yet he still had prospects. He still had connections, and, in no time at all, he'd be back to where he should be financially. If he could secure some of the government contract money for the Indian removal, he'd have his debts paid off by this time next year.

Alexis thought he heard a horse's whinny. His own horse was slightly agitated, so he tightened the reins, clucked his tongue, and urged her on with his heels. At this point, he should have heard something: lumber being sawn, nails hammered, men shouting to each other. But he heard nothing—just the wind in the dry leaves. They'd never finish before the first serious snowfall if they didn't work Sundays. The men would have plenty of time to rest in winter. He stopped to listen. He smelled smoke.

The path that traversed a grove of quaking aspens opened into a clearing where the blackened skeleton of his flour mill stood. The long, charcoal rafters reached toward each other like fingers on opposite hands—fingers that no longer touched. The large, wooden doors, newly whitewashed, were peppered with soot. In a trance, he dismounted, tethered his horse to a post and walked around the charred remains. Steam rose from the still hot timbers as snowflakes fell softly from the sky.

"Hallo?" he called. "Hallo?" he repeated with a strained insistence in his voice. No response—just more wind in the trees. He pushed a door open. The smoke and wet ash smell were even more intense, though fresh air and light circulated freely in the now roof-less mill. The ladder leading up to the second floor was still intact. A few of the joists looked solid. Perhaps there was something yet salvageable.

He stared in disbelief. He needed the income from this mill to pay his debts. How could this be happening to him, Alexis Coquillard, his father's shrewdest, most industrious, and favorite son? Had some vagrant or Indian done this? Tipton would surely give him the contract once the word got out about what the Indians had done—well, had probably done.

Adversity was something men like himself, men of stature, dealt with heroically. No doubt there was some way to work this to his advantage. There was always something that one could do, if one had the proper temperament and will, and Alexis had proven again and again that he had both. And, he resolved, clenching his back teeth, he would prove it once more. No matter how great the challenge, he would rise to it, and others would respect him even more.

Alexis went up the first few steps of the ladder to see what was left of the second floor. Some of the joists connecting the east and west walls looked solid, and the wall on the opposite side was still intact. He inched cautiously across the first couple of feet of one of the beams and then walked more confidently when it held fast. But something broke free, and he felt himself fly through the air, the ground seeming to pull him toward it. Quite suddenly, his forehead slammed against something unyielding. Everything went dark.

After a few minutes of absolute quiet in the ruins of the mill, Peepenawah stepped from behind the wall and walked toward Alexis' body. The Miami chief had watched from a distance as some of the unpaid canal workers had set the mill ablaze earlier that day. And now, quite unexpectedly, Alexis had fallen to his death without any assistance from Peepenawah. He knelt by Alexis' body and turned him over. His eyebrows were raised as if in mild surprise.

He reached inside Alexis' pocket, finding his handkerchief, papers, and then the gold watch. Peepenawah felt the cool weight of the pocket watch in his hand. He pulled gently on the stem; the front opened, revealing a pure white face with a black tracery of numbers and golden hands. He held it to his ear, and the ticking found its way down into the deepest recesses of his heart. A smile brightened his careworn face. He stuffed the watch in his leather pouch.

He freed Alexis' horse from the post where he'd been tied, and the mare ambled off in the direction of the town. Peepenawah used the dead man's fur coat as a blanket for his own horse and headed south towards home. The flurries thickening into the season's first snow.

At midnight, on the second day after he had left the blackened shell of Coquillard's mill, Peepenawah reached his village on the Yellow River. The air was cold and still. He tied up his horse and entered the longhouse. His eyes adjusted to the darkness slowly, and he moved forward cautiously. The sounds of snoring, coughing, and the shifting of bodies on mats came from all corners. He placed his new fur coat by the door and moved carefully past the sleepers to find his mat.

"Peepenawah," a man's voice whispered. "Chief Menominee wants to see you."

"It's late. He's sleeping," Peepenawah said.

"No. He's been fasting for three days, waiting for a vision," said the voice.

Peepenawah was so tired he had several times almost fallen from his horse, but he grabbed a blanket and reluctantly left the long house to search for Menominee. In the moon-less night, he saw a dark figure by the fire pit. Peepenawah approached, not entirely sure of the figure's identity.

"Why aren't you sleeping, brother?" Peepenawah asked.

"I'm thinking." Menominee looked up at Peepenawah through the tangled, matted hair that framed his deeply-lined face.

"Alexis Coquillard is dead," said Peepenawah matter-of-factly, sitting down by the fire next to Menominee and wrapping his blanket about his shoulders.

"Did you kill him?" Menominee asked, turning slightly to watch Peepenawah in profile.

"No, he fell from a beam of his new mill. I took his fur coat." He thought about the gold watch but said nothing. "I'm avenged."

Menominee sighed. "You're *avenged* are you, my friend?" He snorted unpleasantly. "I don't suppose he returned any of our land before he expired, did he, my friend?"

Peepenawah ladled out some venison stew from a pot above the fire and raised the ladle questioningly to Menominee who brusquely shook his head. After Peepenawah had swallowed some mouthfuls of the stew, he raised his spoon as if lecturing the fire and said, "I prayed to Mishipeshu for Coquillard's death, and I prayed to her for our land.

She chose to answer one prayer but not the other. The desires of men and gods seldom converge."

Peepenawah gazed thoughtfully at the fire. "Coquillard never did understand why his canal didn't fill with water." He had a few more spoonfuls of stew and then addressed Menominee's profile. "Everyone knew he was digging that canal along a crest. On one side, water went toward the Mchëzibe; on the other, it went into the Mishigami. You could see that on any rainy day. Anyone could have told him that."

"Anyone *you* know could have told him that," said Menominee.

Peepenawah rubbed his eyes. "Why did you want to talk with me?"

Menominee was silent for a while, staring expressionless into the fire. "Why has Manitou forsaken us?"

Peepenawah continued to spoon the hot stew into his mouth. In general, he was not interested in theological questions, and Menominee knew he was not. Etiquette, however, required him to stay with Menominee and listen.

Menominee watched him intently. "I've fasted three days and nothing has come to me but more questions. We used to have potent medicine. Our Medewin knew how to bring us power. But our Medewin have dispersed and taken what magic they had with them. I have heard rumors that our sacred book has fallen into the White man's hands." He smelled the soup. "Give me some too, my friend."

Peepenawah found a clean bowl outside the long house, filled it, and handed it to Menominee. "Friend, it's late. You're tired. Why don't you eat and go to bed? There's a time for many thoughts, and there's a time for sleep. This is a time for sleep."

Menominee burned his mouth with the soup and, vexed, set the bowl down roughly. "And tomorrow I will wake up and still have no answers." He stared up into the heavens as if it were the stars he was addressing. "White men are closing in on us from the east, north, and south. The only direction for us to go is west. Even if somehow our enemies were to welcome us there, I don't know: Will we be the same men under a foreign sky?" He stretched his stiff legs towards the fire. "I grow impatient with our gods, and I do not believe in theirs. Nabagûck could once bring us visions, but we've forgotten how to make it."

He turned towards Peepenewah who was facing the fire and continued, "When the White men first came, do you know what they offered us? They offered every Indian a rifle, a blanket, and a brass kettle if they would just move out and go west. We laughed. We didn't know that that would be their best offer."

They fell silent, but each was still alert and listening to the fire snap and crackle. A small cluster of clouds parted, revealing a slim crescent moon.

"When I sat at this fire with my father on nights like this, we heard the wolves talking to one another. One wolf would say something, and another one far off would answer. Wolves have hundreds of words for the moon. But, this year, when the leaves began to fall, we heard no wolves."

"The White men are chopping down all the forests, and the wolves have nowhere to hide."

"There's nothing more for us here," said Peepenawah. He wiped his mouth, put his bowl to one side, and warmed his hands by the fire. With his back against a stump near the firepit, he pulled his blanket over his head so only his nose and mouth were still visible. Gradually, he drifted off to sleep.

Menominee continued to stare into the embers until the horizon warmed to a soft rose beyond the fragile weaving of leafless branches.

Chapter 7

The Vision Quest of Pierre Navarre

~ 1864 ~

Pierre Navarre was a man who had outlived his time. Nothing he knew was worth knowing anymore. He could hurl a tomahawk, track a bear, buck a tree, and find his way through the Kankakee swamp in a blizzard, but none of that mattered anymore. Men these days didn't know how to do any of that, and they didn't care that they didn't know. They wore tall black hats and silk cravats and doused their heads in hair oil. Merchants these days knew nothing about the fur trade, and they wouldn't pay you a nickel for a good hide. The town was filling up with useless folk—grog sellers, confidence men, curiosity seekers.

Maybe his manner was plain and coarse. Maybe city folk could tell he was backwoods raised, but he was a decent man, and that was more than he could say for the trash moving into town or the cold-hearted bastards who had taken his wife.

Pierre's gray, wiry eyebrows framed eyes so deeply set, they seem to have been shaded with charcoal. He gazed out of these dark holes with glowing enmity, discouraging even the best-intentioned visitors.

His rocking chair was old and warped, squeaking and twisting sideways on each backward rock, but Pierre scarcely noticed it.

His yard was a thicket of untamed vegetation surrounded by neat rows of new wooden houses built with uniform, sawmill-processed lumber. The little trading post in the wilderness called Southhold had transformed overnight into the city of South Bend. Now there were even factories. The Studebaker brothers manufactured wagons to carry sol-diers, wagons to carry guns, and wagons to carry soldiers shot by guns. The town had churches, grocery stores, brothels, a new railroad, and, encircling those, an ever-expanding sea of farmland, acre after acre of corn and wheat. The forests that had so recently dominated the landscape were vanquished.

A compact, dark-skinned man of medium height wearing a white hat approached Pierre's cabin. The intense, mid-day sun reflected off his white hat, making it appear to be the man's most significant feature. On these muggy August days, the metallic rattle of the cicadas would ceaselessly crescendo and subside until the coolness of the evening air silenced them.

The man in the white hat was Peter, Pierre's second and most conventionally successful son. Peter got on well with his carpentry business and had recently moved his wife and three children into a fine, white, two-story house with a bit of gingerbread at the eaves and an ornamental wrought iron fence in the front yard.

He mounted the porch stairs with a heavy tread, lowered himself into the rocking chair next to his father, the same chair that his mother had sat in years ago, and, taking his hat from his head, wiped the perspiration from his brow with his neatly folded linen handkerchief.

"Mornin', Pa," said Peter.

"Mornin'," answered Pierre, looking slightly irritated that his solitude had been disturbed. They sat in silence for a bit, rocking and surveying the tangle of trees and bushes and the river beyond.

"You want me to fix that squeaky chair of yours?" asked Peter, wincing when his father began to rock and squeak.

"Why?" Pierre stared at his son as if he'd been insulted. "Nothin' wrong with this chair."

Peter looked down at his hat pensively and nodded his head in agreement. "Listen, Pa, I've been thinkin'. It's no good you livin' alone like this. You need to be around family."

"I need my own place, and this one suits me fine. Besides, your youngsters wouldn't like having an old man around all the time, and I'd be another mouth to feed for your wife."

"That's not true, Pa," he said, knowing that that was precisely how his family would feel if his father were to move in with them.

The cicadas' drone intensified. Peter smoothed the wrinkles from his pants and rocked in his chair, turning his gaze to the river. "Remember the swimming contests we used to have? When I told my boys about it, they didn't believe we used to swim clear across the river at Baugo Creek."

Pierre's eyes wrinkled a bit at the corners and his toothless mouth pulled up into something that resembled a smile.

They both fell to reminiscing. His father told him about finding his sister Judith twelve feet up a sycamore tree in pursuit of a baby raccoon in the dead of night. How eight-year-old Anthony had made his own raft and paddled it all the way to Niles, Michigan, before they discovered he was missing. How Peter had given him the scare of his life the night they both got caught in a blizzard on the road from the Coldwater trading grounds. Peter had been shaking like a leaf, and the only thing that kept him from freezing to death were the beaver pelts one of his customers had, just by chance, failed to pick up. They were all stories Peter knew well, and, with repetition, they had acquired their own predictable turns of phrase.

His father had fallen in love with the children they were, and, as they had grown, they had slipped into a world of shadows for him. Six magical, exquisitely beautiful creatures had shared his cabin, but they had all, one by one, disappeared into the gray, undifferentiated mass of humanity. Peter the child, even if he was just a memory, was clearly dearer to his father than Peter the grown man sitting beside him. In fact, when listening to his father's stories, Peter himself preferred Peter the child to Peter the man.

"Anthony'll be arriving from Kansas on Friday, Pa."

"Your brother?" Pierre knitted his bushy eyebrows, stopped rocking in his chair and looked at Peter.

"Yes, Pa, Anthony." Peter walked his fingers around the perimeter of his hat.

"The one who joined the Mormons?"

"He says he's done with all that. He wants to work for the tribe now. He's got plans for gettin' some land back."

The furrow between Pierre's eyebrows deepened. "Not sure how he's goin' to do that, even with Joseph Smith and all the angels at his side. The time for making things right has passed."

He turned towards his son, and his eyes were wide in their dark sockets. "The men who drove your mother's people off their land have gotten rich, fat, and powerful. Who's gonna touch 'em now? Who's gonna tell them that they got to give it all back? Not them whose houses are also settin' on Indian land, and that's pretty much everybody."

"They're working with the law and the politicians now, Pa. That's a lot more likely to get results than asking the Great Spirit to change the White man's gunpowder to sand." Peter smiled good naturedly.

His father turned his body towards his son, his eyes were even wider. "Weren't many who thought that would help, and that weren't the reason they lost everything. Things was stacked against them from the start."

They sat in silence, and his father's chair continued to squeak.

"I'll bring Anthony by on Saturday night then?" Peter remembered that his father frequently forgot what day of the week it was, so he added, "That's *five* days from now. Will you be amenable to that, Pa?"

A shadow of fear passed across his father's face. "I expect he won't be staying here, with me?"

"He can stay with us, Pa," said Peter, noticing that his father looked slightly relieved. "Well, I gotta get back to work."

"Hey." His father narrowed his eyes and looked toward the river. "Who's that lady who's been walking along the river at night? She walked straight into the water the other night."

His son turned his head slightly to one side. "Straight into the water, Pa?"

"Well, that's the very thing. It's not clear what she's doin'. She's down there at night sometimes—not every night, but, you know, often."

"Old woman? Young woman?"

"Young, I think. She's got lots of," he gestured around his head, "hair. See if anybody else knows who she is. Strange for a woman to walk around by herself at night like that."

They both looked towards the water as if expecting to see her.

"I'll ask around. See you, Pa."

Pierre lifted one hand in response and settled back into his rocking chair.

"But how much do you suppose your father's property's worth? The cabin's of no account, of course, but what about the la-and?" Peter's wife, who came from Massachusetts, gave a special nasal quality to the "ah" sound in "land." "What with it being on the river, you'd think there'd be some value in that. Maybe some new textile mill might want it."

Peter's wife, Olive, carried a pot full of water from the sink to the stovetop. Peter had already asked himself this, but he thought it unseemly for her to do so.

Peter was sitting at the kitchen table, tracing the perimeter of his hat with his fingers. "Steam power's the thing these days," he said. "The river's not so important anymore. Besides, we're not going to have to think about selling Pa's place any time soon, I hope. He's not ready to drop into the grave just yet."

"I didn't mean that. I was just…"

He hesitated a moment and said: "Your quiltin' still set up in the parlor?"

"Yes. Why?"

"Anthony's comin' from Kansas on Friday. I was thinking he could sleep in the parlor."

His wife turned her red, meaty, perspiring face towards him with a look of unmitigated hostility. "There's no room for him here. Why didn't you tell him that?"

"I didn't get his letter until yesterday. He'll sleep wherever. He doesn't care."

Her pale blue eyes that he had initially found so attractive now made her look as cold as a January sky. "If he starts in again with his preachin', there'll be nowhere to escape him."

"He could stay in the boys' room."

"No! I don't want him filling their brains with all kinds of crazy talk about healing the sick and raising the dead. If he could really raise the dead, folks would be falling all over themselves for the chance to put him up." She pursed her thin lips and cut the ends off the green beans she was preparing to boil. "Why can't he learn a trade the way other men do? He went to school, didn't he? All this gallivantin' around without ever settlin'." She lifted her head tartly, pushing with the back of her hand the strands of dark hair from her sweat dampened temples.

"No doubt it's the Indian in him," Peter said, looking down at his hat and tracing the perimeter once more with his fingers. "Restless and unaccustomed to work."

"Stop playing with your hat. It's irritatin'."

She wiped her hands on her apron and dumped a pan full of green beans into the boiling water. "Well, he's just going to have to be satisfied with a cot in the garden shed, cause that's all I've got the time to get ready for him."

Peter was too tired to argue about his brother's accommodations. He hoped that she'd relent by Friday evening. If his brother had dropped the Mormon preaching, as he said he had in his letter, the family might be more welcoming. He stood up, examined a spindle on the chair, and went out the back door. He still had work at the shop to tend to. Thank God, he always had work at the shop.

The sun had set, and a cool, moist breeze was blowing in from the Kankakee marsh. Peter waited for his brother by the hitching post at the stagecoach stop. Soon there'd be a train connecting South Bend with points west, but, for now, travelers had to endure the dusty road.

There was not much traffic on South Street tonight, just an occasional horse-drawn cart. A tall, thin woman with a careworn face partially hidden beneath a large, floppy bonnet was hurrying home. A stooped old man in dusty overalls was using a long pole to light a gas street lamp on the corner.

Peter heard the jingle of the harness from the stagecoach and turned to see the driver nearly dislodged from his seat after his carriage wheels hit a large tree root in the unfinished road. "Woah!" called the young driver.

A lad with a sunburnt neck darted off the porch where he had been sitting and grabbed the horses' reins from the driver. The driver jumped to the ground and then sprang immediately onto the back of the carriage, unloading trunks, soldier kits, and wrapped parcels at a furious rate in the hopes of getting tips. The coach doors opened. Legs, arms, petticoats, rough leather boots suddenly erupted from the sides of the overloaded vehicle.

Peter saw Anthony's familiar mop of curly, black hair now streaked with gray. He was wearing a fashionable, light-weight, tan jacket and bowler hat; his mustache was impeccably trimmed. Where was the shabby vagabond with the fire of God in his eyes? This was a changed man. Yet, he wore the same look of bewildered innocence that Peter had seen many times before. The innocence had become less hopeful, more under siege.

Anthony raised his hand and waved when he saw his brother and made his way swiftly through the dispersing passengers. He dropped his luggage when he met Peter and shook his hand with genuine warmth.

"God, what a long trip," said Anthony. "Didn't get a genteel wink from St. Louis to Logansport, but, no mishaps. Calvary man I was sitting next to told me a coach got robbed on the same route bout' two weeks ago."

Peter bent down to pick up one of his brother's bags, noticing its ornate stitching. Anthony brushed the dust off his jacket.

"Traveling is a dangerous prospect these days," Peter said. "Let's go to Union Tavern. Olive's putting up green beans. We'd have nothing but a cold supper tonight."

Anthony wondered if there was something more to this, since his brother had said it quickly, as if getting something unpleasant out of the way. A wave of regret passed over him as he remembered the self-righteous preaching he had indulged in during his last visit.

"This place sure has changed," Anthony observed as they walked north on Michigan Street. "Must be twenty new store fronts we've passed in two blocks."

"Everything's gotten more crowded and louder. Whatever's on its way to Chicago—steam engine, circus act, disease—stops here first. We've got organ grinders coming in this weekend from Elkhart," said Peter, as they walked along Michigan Street.

"Organ grinders? What have the good people of South Bend done to be so sorely afflicted?" said Anthony.

Piano music and the sound of loud, drunken voices spilled out the open windows of Union Tavern. Peter promised the coat-check boy a few extra coins to watch Anthony's bags. The tavern's uneven wooden floor was sticky with spilled beer. They sat at a table in the corner, farthest from the piano where a group of soldiers and keelboat men were belting out *Billy Barlow*.

"'What shall I hunt?' says Dan'l to Joe
"'Hunt for a rat,' said Billy Burlow

They ordered pork chops, fried potatoes and two whiskeys. They looked at each other's faces, noting changes. Peter tried to avoid looking in mirrors these days. The bags under his eyes were more pronounced, and the deepening creases on either side of his mouth made him think of the phrase from the Bible: "a man of sorrow and acquainted with grief."

"Place has gotten livelier since the last time I was here," observed Anthony, surveying the dining room and the bar's collection of sunburnt and weather-beaten faces. There were small and wiry keelboat pilots and broad-shouldered and brawny construction men. Mixed in with the mostly male clientele were solidly built women wearing incongruously delicate, white lace collars. A couple of pimply, Union soldiers still in their teens leaned heavily against the bar. A pantheon of stuffed moose, buck, and bear heads surveyed the crowd from above.

"A little too lively. I've replaced more legs from these chairs..."

Peter said, shaking his head. "The keelboat boys come in on Friday and Saturday nights. After a couple of drinks, they yank the legs off and beat each other senseless. Not complaining. Keeps us carpenters in business." He smiled into his whiskey. "You still teaching?"

"Oh, no. Ancient history. I've been working with the tribe—negotiatin' with government agents to make sure the tribe gets their annuities. I've also got some money-making projects on the side." Anthony looked sheepish. "I know, I know, all my treasures used to be in heaven. But those spiritual riches are not, I've found, legal tender." He smiled a smile that looked practiced, as if he had said just those words with just that expression on his face many times. "No, I just got tired of trying to live on moonbeams. At some point, a man has got to start looking at the way things are instead of dreaming about the way they should be."

Peter shrugged his shoulders. "How's the tribe?"

"Not good. Not good at all. They always end up being in somebody's way—no matter how far they are from White settlements. And White folks are forever suspecting them of something. If a group of Indians from the north visits a group of Indians in the south, suddenly everyone's calling it a war council. But it's not just the White folks that are the problem." Anthony shook his head. "Let's face facts, Indians don't know how to work things to their advantage. There are so many ways a man can make a fortune out West. Does the Indian take advantage of the opportunities? No." He drained the entirety of his whiskey glass.

Peter had never seen his brother drink like that before. He had also never heard his brother refer to '*the* Indian.' "Speculating and making deals wasn't ever what Indians did," Peter said.

"But if they want to survive, they've got to learn." Anthony stroked his mustache with his thumb and forefinger, suddenly thoughtful. "You know, I don't feel entirely at home with White people or Indians. Seems like I'm forever saying things that upsets one side or the other even though I'm forever trying not to offend." A dark cloud passed over his features. He leaned back in his chair. "Look at you, though. You're White by marriage. Have you managed to wash off all the red?" He laughed a forced laugh and raised a finger to the waiter and pointed to his empty glass.

Peter was insulted by this, but the thought of trading angry words with his brother pained him more than overlooking the comment. "I work with wood, not people. It's easier for me not to fret about how people see me."

He ran his tongue over his teeth then looked directly at his brother. "Look, I don't try to be White. I just try to fit in." He lowered his eyes, took a drink of whiskey. "I don't know. Maybe that does mean trying to be White." He paused and looked around the room. "All I know is that these people aren't going back to where they came from. *Three hundred new families have settled here just this past year.* They're so awfully sorry about the Indians being driven off their land. But they also think having their own farms with lots of land is a very good thing. You've got to make your peace with it."

Neither said anything for a few moments. The apple pie arrived. Anthony thought he should ask about Olive. He guessed that his brother's marriage was more difficult than most, that it caused him pain, and that he did not want to discuss it. Peter had never been one to belabor problems that had no clear resolution. "How's Pa?"

"He's doing about as well as you might expect. Ornery. Sometimes downright rude. Says crazy things sometimes. Keeps askin' about a woman he sees walking along the river at night. Said he's seen her walk into the river."

"You sure there *isn't* a woman walking around there at night? Pa was always pretty observant."

"I can believe some woman is taking late night walks, but a path leading *into* the river?"

"Maybe he shouldn't be living on his own. I guess we can talk about that after we see him. How're the boys?" Anthony asked. Peter immediately relaxed and began a long description of the boys' pet raccoon and tricks played on a disagreeable neighbor.

They talked about family for another hour after dinner, then collected Anthony's luggage from the coat check boy. Anthony gave the boy a generous tip to bring his bags to Peter's house. Peter noted the wad of bills in his brother's wallet. Perhaps seeing his brother's expensive luggage would change Olive's views on hosting him.

They walked out onto the broad, dirt street where the smell of sweat, perfume, and whiskey gradually dissipated into the night's cool air. Soon the sound of voices and music was replaced by the lowing of cows, barking of dogs and the pulsing rasp of the katydids. The trees closed in around them, as they followed the narrow roadway that led to their father's cabin.

So, this was how a man lost his mind, Pierre reflected. It didn't bother him much, but, sometimes, depending on how it manifested itself, it could be unsettling.

At his age, there was nothing particularly salutary about being in your right mind. You could feel the broken pieces of tooth in your gums, the stench of your own breath, the pain in your joints. The real world, the world he'd spent his whole life living in, was turning its back on him. He couldn't hear the birds' songs anymore. His grandchildren seemed to speak in garbled whispers. Landscapes and people blurred at a distance. Memories intruded on the present in unexpected ways. His toddler son crouching to examine a beetle was also a grown man with a white hat in a rocking chair.

She had brought him another tear-shaped vial. He couldn't see her well, but he imagined that she was young and beautiful. She told him to take the potion, so he could be with her, not as he was in this life, but as he had been—strong, commanding, virile. He didn't know what she wanted from him. Her body was always close enough to touch, but she passed through his hands like water.

He removed the stopper and drank the liquid. The liquid burned his throat. In a few moments, he would be able to smell the apples ripening in the orchard and see the glow of distant fire flies.

A sudden whirlwind launched some leaves and branches into the air, and, as he watched, they coalesced into a figure—a woman. Her dark hair was long, thick, and lustrous and wrapped itself around her face and torso. A sudden gust blew the hair from her face. Her eyes were red and burned into him like coals.

His heart beat faster as she approached. Just as his hand touched her face, her body burst into a hundred white doves that flew off to every corner of the sky.

He stood alone in an empty field. He looked down. Angelique's old medicine book was open at his feet. A single red, water lily blossom fell from the sky and landed on the page.

Anthony and Peter heard moaning from their father's cabin. They ran up the steps, pushed open the front door, which was always kept unlocked, and stepped into almost total darkness. Peter went into the kitchen, recognizing by feel the pump, sink, and the shelf where he knew his father kept matches and candles. He found both, lit the candle, and held it aloft.

A chaotic jumble of broken furniture, blankets, books, and burlap bags was illuminated by the amber light. Pierre had been sleeping on a platform that Peter had built for him in a corner of the room. The candle light revealed his father's long, thin body beneath a woolen blanket. He drew closer and saw that his father's mouth was open wide enough to howl, yet just a weak "ahhhh" sound was coming out. On a table next to the bed was a small tear-shaped vial.

"Maybe he took some of this," Peter said. He held the bottle up.

"Maybe too much of it. Probably ought to get him to throw it up. Don't you think?" said Anthony, deferring, by habit, to his older brother. Anthony pulled out a pocket watch and, pushing back his father's sleeves, began to count his pulse.

"I was just here a few days ago. He was distracted and clearly wanted to be left alone, but he's been like that for a while."

"Pulse is slow, but regular."

Anthony, who hadn't seen his father for several years, was taken aback. The change in him was stark. The contours of his skull were emerging from beneath his waxy, translucent skin, and his thin, bloodless lips were taut against his toothless gums. Large tufts of wiry, white hair emerged from his temples and continued towards his jaw to form wildly overgrown mutton chop sideburns.

Peter found an oil lamp, which he succeeded in lighting. A scruffy, black and gray, striped cat ran out of its hiding place, its ribcage shuttling back and forth beneath its fur. In the oil lamp's bright halo, they took stock of the sixteen-by-eighteen foot room in which they had slept, played, fought, and eaten—such a small stage for so many actors and so much drama.

A sudden motion caught his eye. Peter lifted the light higher. A round figure with sloping shoulders sat in his mother's rocking chair.

"Theresa! Why didn't you say anything?"

A middle-aged woman with a slightly bulbous nose, stretched her arms above her head and rose slowly from the rocking chair. "I was asleep," she said, yawning and pulling the red jacket she was wearing snuggly across her round belly.

"Is Pa sick?" Peter asked.

"No, he's fine. He just took some nabagûck. It's a good tonic. Puts him right to sleep." She looked up. "Anthony! Well, my goodness, haven't seen you for what? Two years? Why, don't you look fancy." She put her hands to her face in mock amazement. "Who'd a thought you could make so much money preachin' nonsense."

Anthony had come forward to embrace her, but she made no effort to come to him. "You sure there's nothing wrong with Pa?" he said.

She rubbed her eyes. "Well, he's *old*." She put a hand under her loose shirt and scratched herself. "You boys been out on the town. You smell like whiskey."

"We went to the Union for a drink."

She smelled the air reverently. "I could do with a drink." She still wore her hair in braids as she had done as a girl, but now they were mostly silver. While Peter and Anthony had inherited their mother's more delicate features, Theresa was big-boned and had her father's prominent brow.

"So, Pa's been taking this navaguk…" Peter said.

"Nabagûck," Theresa corrected him.

"He take it often?"

"Twice a week—sometimes, three. I make sure he gets a very small dose. It's potent stuff. There's a young woman who sells it down by the river. She doesn't charge much for hers. Not as much as she should. It's getting hard to find. I used to make it myself, but my legs got bad. I can't go wading into water like I used to."

"You don't think it's too strong for him? He sounded distressed," Peter said.

"He's more distressed without it," she said sharply. "You think Pa'd be at Union Tavern dancing if it weren't for the nabagûck?"

"I'm just questioning the wisdom of giving him strong drugs," Anthony said.

She didn't try to defend herself but walked stiffly to where the old man lay and looked at him thoughtfully. "Times have moved ahead and left him behind. He was a man of the wilderness, but the only wilderness he's got left is the one in his head."

Pierre lifted an arm and then let his fingers drop to his forehead.

"What did you see, Pa? What did you see?" Theresa spoke to Pierre in Potawatomi, a language her brothers had mostly forgotten. Despite Anthony's years with the tribe in Kansas, all of his business dealings were in English. The brothers were reminded of the world they had left behind—a world their sister still fully inhabited.

Pierre looked up at his daughter's face. "White doves. She turned into white doves," he said. His voice was raspy, as if he'd spent several hours screaming at demons. Pierre's opalescent, cataract-covered eyes turned toward Anthony. "Who's here?"

Theresa switched to English. "It's your boys. Peter's here and Anthony too."

Pierre had more surprise than pleasure on his face. "You come here to see me?"

Anthony moved closer to Pierre's bedside. "How you feelin', Pa?"

"I'm feelin' like somebody stole *my* body and gave me some old man's."

Peter and Anthony relaxed and smiled. The old man still had some life in him. Theresa retreated to the kitchen while Anthony sat at the end of his father's makeshift bed, narrating his recent business dealings. Peter examined the squeaking rocking chair.

Anthony continued in a self-congratulatory tone, "Then, of course, it was clear he wasn't going to make the payments for the second parcel. I knew that from the beginning, so I..."

"Theresa, what do white doves mean?" Pierre asked, not appearing to notice that he had interrupted his son. "I mean when you dream about them."

"They mean love, Pa. Love." Theresa passed around mugs of hot tea. "Or that somebody's going to lose a tooth." She smiled, revealing a bottom row of corn-kernel, yellow teeth.

"What's a man supposed to make of that?" Pierre asked, then shook his head. "I'm already forgetting the dream. It had something to do with that book. I've got to get rid of that book."

Pierre pushed himself up from his bed, and, after many awkward, unnecessary moves to the left and right, he brought his feet to the floor. He stood up, looking as if he would immediately sit back down. Yet he straightened his back, picked up the oil lamp, and set off toward the back room before his surprised sons fully realized the potential dangers of letting a drugged, old man take possession of a burning lamp.

With one hand against the wall for support, he moved slowly but steadily towards what had been a bedroom but was now serving as a storage room at the back of the house. Bags of onions and potatoes littered the top of the wooden bed where Pierre had slept until the sagging ropes supporting the mattress created a depression so deep that he could no longer pull himself from the center without assistance.

Pierre grabbed a broom from the corner of the room. He squatted down stiffly by the bedside and placed the lamp on the floor. He shoved the broomstick's end beneath the bed, sweeping it back and forth until the end met a resistant object. After much pushing and prodding, the corner of a rectangular object wrapped in pieces of stiff, old leather emerged from under the bed. Pierre, breathing heavily from the exertion, sat back on his heels and surveyed the parcel gravely.

"What is it?" said Anthony, squatting down and examining the package. "Should I unwrap it?"

Peter raised the lamp higher. Pierre nodded his head wordlessly and wiped the corners of his mouth with the back of his hand. "Be careful. It's old," he said.

Anthony and Peter unwound the uncooperative packaging, revealing a large, leather-bound manuscript. It smelled of pine needles and moist earth. The leather cover was embossed with a sinuous pattern in gold. Anthony opened it.

Delicate, exquisitely rendered drawings of plants and flowers filled each page: pale green Jack-in-the-pulpits; bright yellow black-eyed Susans; lavender trumpets of hairy beardtongue; pine bark; oaks; and willow—all rendered in precise detail and rich color accompanied by foreign script.

"How did you get this book, Pa?" Peter asked.

Pierre squinted up at him into the lamplight. "Belonged to your mother. Some boy from the Carey Mission—one of the McCoy boys brought it to her. Told her that she was next in line to own it. Your mother was the granddaughter of the half-breed woman it belonged to. Marguerite, your great-grandmother."

Theresa, who had sat down on the bed, took the massive book and put it on her lap, gently turning each page after studying the pictures. "Pa, I've heard about this book. This is the missing Medéwewen book. Why didn't you say something about this? This should go to the tribe."

"What's the tribe goin' to do with it?" Anthony asked, narrowing his eyes and looking at her as if she'd suggested something outlandish.

"This is Bodwéwadmi, Ojibway, Myaamia, Nadwék—Native wisdom. All the things they learned from the land. All the things they believed in."

"Well, it's not goin' to help them now," Anthony said. "If we give it to the tribe, they'll trade it for whiskey, or it'll end up as wallpaper in some sod house in Kansas."

"You don't know that." Theresa stared at Anthony as if it were the first time she was really seeing him.

"We can't risk it," Anthony said, wrinkling his nose. "Maybe we should sell it to a collector."

Theresa's mouth dropped open. "What?"

Peter, looking for a way to diffuse the conflict, asked his father, "What do you want us to do with the book?"

Under her breath, Theresa said, "Stick it under our beds for a few decades, like he did."

Pierre furrowed his brow, as if not comprehending how his

intentions should be unclear. "Keep it from *her*—the lady in the river with all that black hair. Hide it somewhere."

The siblings said nothing but stole furtively glances at each other.

"Clearly, Peter should take it," said Anthony. "He's got the big house. He can store and protect it."

"But he knows nothing about medicine or healing," said Theresa.

Anthony turned to his father. "Would you feel better, Pa, if Peter took the book with him?"

Looking a bit vacant, Pierre bit his lower lip. "Yes, I suppose I would."

"What?" Theresa stared at her father and shook her head in disbelief. "The manuscript should go to me—it should go to the tribe. Peter doesn't want it." She turned to Peter. "Do you?"

Peter looked at her with his puffy eyes. He didn't want it, but he also didn't want to be dragged into this conflict, particularly on his sister's side. He cleared his throat.

Theresa rose and handed the manuscript to Peter. "You think I've grown greedy in my old age. My youth gone—and we all know I never was a beauty—and now I want money. Is that what you're thinking?" She looked toward Peter and Anthony but did not meet their eyes.

"But what we have here, gentlemen," she gestured toward the book in Peter's arms, "is a book of magic. Not one filled with tricks and charms—it's full of wisdom. I'm telling you: we all will pay the price if it's lost."

"The drama is totally out of place here, Theresa," said Anthony, shrugging his shoulders. "It's a book with pretty pictures."

"Gentlemen, it's late. Good night." Breathing heavily, she shuffled down the dark hallway, towards the cabin door.

Peter could hear her labored gait as she descended the cabin's wooden stairs. He should have put a handrail on those stairs a few months ago but hadn't gotten around to it.

"How 'bout you come home with me, Pa," Peter suggested. "Anthony is staying with me too."

"No, no…" the old man shook his head, "I'm staying here. I'm not going anywhere in the middle of the night."

Anthony said that he would stay with him and turned his attention to removing the onions and potatoes from the rope bed.

When Peter held the manuscript upright, intending to rewrap it in the piece of leather, a letter dropped out on the floor. It was yellow from age and sealed with wax. He showed it to his father. "Ever seen this before?"

"No. Have an address on it?" Pierre asked, squinting at the letter over his son's shoulder.

Peter flipped it back and forth in his hands. "Looks like it's in French. You can read French, right?"

Pierre shook his head. "Not anymore. Never use it. And the script's too small."

Anthony agreed to bring it the next day to the courthouse. He had a friend there who could read French.

Peter rewrapped the manuscript and carried it with him, wishing Anthony and his father a good night as he headed down the front steps. Nothing like an heirloom—even if it's just a book—to sow hate and discontent in a family, he reflected, as the crickets and a gentle breeze welcomed him into the quiet of the night.

As he walked under the broad-leaved sycamores that grew along the river's edge, Peter felt he could breathe easier now. People could be so taxing, even your relatives—especially your relatives.

He took the night air deep into his lungs. The wind tousled his hair and whispered down his neck. His senses were suddenly alive to all the night's softness.

A shadow detached itself from a tree by the river, supple, graceful, feminine. He stopped. The figure disappeared behind a cluster of trees. He waited, but it, or she, did not reemerge on the other side. Was it the woman his father had seen?

He heard a cry. He drew closer to the river. The surface was agitated, the wind had picked up. Was someone swimming out there? He heard the cry again. It was plaintive but also…sensual. He put the manuscript down on the grass, so he could push back the willows. His socks were getting wet.

"Peter?" A man's amiable voice called him. He saw a lantern in the bushes.

"Yes?"

"It's the constable. I'm not wearing my constable hat because I've misplaced it. Your wife sent me to look for you. She said you'd be coming this way." He held his lamp aloft. The light penetrated a few feet into the turbid water but no further. Moths flew about the lamp.

Peter realized that he was standing in the river up to his knees.

"Did you lose something?"

"No, I thought…I thought I heard a cry."

"Your wife wants you home. I can investigate the cry." Peter walked out of the water, and the constable handed him the manuscript. "This is yours, right?"

Peter thanked him and headed home. He did not know what had possessed him to wade so far into the river. If the constable hadn't called to him, how much further would he have gone?

When he opened the door to his house, he heard anxious voices, hurried footsteps, and a child crying. A lamp was burning in the parlor. Anthony's luggage was set up neatly by a cot covered with fresh, white linen. Peter put the manuscript down on a table, took his jacket off, and went up the stairs. A shrill, angry cry came from his son's room, and Sarah, their new baby girl, was crying as well.

"Oh my God, where have you been?" said his wife who met him outside the boys' room. "Michael's sick. He's got diarrhea, and he's vomitin' water."

There was a knock on the door, and Peter descended to admit Dr. Josephus McCoy into their small parlor. He took Dr. McCoy's coat and hat. The doctor pointed upstairs questioningly even though he already had a foot on the steps. Josephus, now in his fifties, had been practicing medicine for twenty years since leaving Carey Mission for good. He had seen more cases of cholera this year than ever before. Peter's children were not, he discovered, dangerously ill. The fate of the little boy next door was less certain.

The children had taken their tonics and had drifted off to sleep. The parents thanked Josephus profusely, and he had reassured them that he could let himself out.

As he walked toward the front door, he noticed a parcel tied up with saddle straps lying on a table. There was something about its size and shape that gave him pause.

Peter followed Dr. McCoy to the front door. "I wanted to let you know that people have been helping themselves to the lumber from your father's old school," Peter said.

"I'm not surprised," said McCoy, latching his apothecary case. "Frankly, I'm pleased that people are finding new purposes for whatever's left of the place. Every time I pass by it, I see something new has collapsed or been covered by poison ivy,"

"Do you want me to ask a friend of mine, who lives out that way to keep an eye on the place for you?" Peter suggested.

McCoy smiled wearily. "Thanks, but no. It's not worth preserving. I would be surprised if anyone had happy memories associated with that place. Let nature lay its claim." He straightened his cravat, his eyes resting once again on the parcel, and left.

Peter hired more carpenters to keep up with demand. His household now had luxuries his father's generation could never have imagined. A box of Nova Scotia dried cod appeared regularly at their doorstep, a piano forte graced their parlor, and Olive had just replaced her tired looking cotton upholstery with an opulent, teal-colored wool.

During one of the hottest summer days on record, Pierre saw dark clouds on the horizon and warned anyone who'd listen of an impending blizzard. He wrote a letter to his dead wife, saying he'd soon be joining her in Kansas, and the next day they found his body along the road that ran south-west to Logansport.

Years passed before Olive discovered on a basement shelf a dust-covered parcel wrapped with saddle straps. She remembered that it had come from her father-in-law's filthy cabin. As far as she was concerned, he'd never owned anything worth having. She marched it outside and dropped it with the other bits of refuse on the burn pile.

CHAPTER 8

HENRY PORTER'S MYSTERIOUS DISAPPEARANCE

~ 1887 ~

"Shallow, bourgeois entertainment. That's what you thought of it, right?"

Henry's face assumed a slightly sardonic expression as he struggled to open his umbrella. Sarah tied the black, satin ribbon of her bonnet under her chin. He took her arm, and they both walked briskly out from under the bright red awning of the Oliver Opera House and into a fine, blowing rain.

"You sure you don't want to get a cab?" he asked.

"No, no, not unless you do. Do you?" She looked up at him questioningly. Her large dark eyes were framed by long lashes. She was so lovely and so very clever, but far too accommodating. He didn't answer. As a rule, he didn't answer unnecessary questions.

She thought about asking him another question about the magic lantern performance, but she didn't think it was fair that she should be forever fetching fuel for conversations. She didn't want to feel resentful, but she did. She looked down at the wet brick pavement beneath her feet, dark and mottled, the color of dried blood.

"I'm not sure I understood the premise," Henry said, resuming their previous conversation. They stopped in the middle of Michigan Street to let a cart carrying lumber pass.

"I think it was simple. They were asking us to appreciate the beauty of the natural world, as it's perceived by two people incapable of speech."

"Why would the fact that they're both deaf mutes make them especially good at conveying the beauty of the natural world? I think I would have enjoyed the subject more if presented by people who were capable of speech."

"But it would have been a different sort of presentation."

"Decidedly better."

"Henry, that wasn't the point. It's true they could have given far more information had they both been able to speak, but they gave us a window into their world. Didn't you notice that their paintings were more sensual? It was as if they had simultaneously felt and seen the flowers. Weren't you impressed by that?"

"No."

"Well, I'm sorry you didn't like it."

The rain had stopped, and they paused while Henry shook the water from the umbrella and put it away.

"I didn't say I thought it was without merit. Truly, these people have no other way to earn a wage than contriving a carnival show to wring pity and money out of people like us."

"So, it was a political parable for you—like everything else." She smiled at him, and he pulled her arm closer.

"To a man with a hammer, everything looks like a nail."

"Nice to hear *you* say that." She nestled into his arm and felt the warmth of his body radiate to hers.

They left behind the city's brick buildings and smokestacks, passed Navarre Street where the cabin of one of the city's founding fathers still stood, and walked north amid the modest, two-story homes on quarter-acre lots. Some had leaded glass doorways and lamp posts; others still had outhouses; one had a skinny goat with a bell.

A blustery late October had stripped most of the golden leaves from the tall oaks that lined the road, leaving only the most tenacious to endure the winter. Before them lay a field of brush, willows, and sweet gum with stinking pools of effluent from the city's paper and textile mills. A calf with two heads had been born on Kunstmann's farm near the river last year, and the locals said it was the poisons in the river that caused it. Old Kunstmann thought it was the devil's work.

A young man approached them from the opposite side of the wooden bridge that crossed the St. Joseph River. His blond hair was tousled by the wind, and he had a thick red scarf around his neck. As they drew nearer to one another, Sarah gripped Henry's arm and said, "Oh, it's Fritz!" The young man recognized her at the same moment. His handsome face instantly brightened. "Sarah!" he yelled at the top of his voice and took off running to meet her. The two embraced on the bridge, and Fritz, a full head taller, picked her up and twirled her around. The two of them were so filled with childlike joy, Henry felt more envy than jealousy.

Seeing that Henry was standing awkwardly to one side fingering his umbrella, Fritz went to him with his hand extended. His expression and manner were so artless, so full of good will, he was immediately predisposed in his favor. "So, you must be Henry. I hope you'll forgive me. Sarah and I grew up together."

"Henry, you remember me telling you about my dear friend who'd been spirited away by the Brothers of the Holy Cross?"

"Sarah, you make it sound like an abduction. They gave me a scholarship to study botany. I'm so sorry I missed the wedding. I was working out East and, unfortunately, couldn't get away." Then, turning towards Sarah said, "But I'm back now with a vengeance and in search of work."

"Where are you staying?"

"With my uncle on Taylor Street by the lumber mill. He puts up with my plant collection, and I put up with his snoring."

They were silent for a moment and a flock of sandhill cranes passed over their heads.

"Those look like snow clouds on the horizon. Are you headed to your uncle's now?"

"Yes, I just dropped by your house and left a note."

"Fritz, you've got such a long way to go and no hat!"

"Look, I'm wrapping my scarf around my head in a great snow turban. Are you happy now?"

"Yes, you look ridiculous but warm."

"We'll be in on Friday. Come by then."

Fritz clicked his heels and saluted, "Aye-aye, captain." Still keeping a soldierly demeanor he turned towards Henry and saluted once more. "Till Friday."

He skipped off in the direction of the town, turning once to wave. Sarah and Henry waved back.

Sarah took Henry's arm as they continued to walk across the bridge and spoke to him in a confidential tone. "I know, you probably think he's very eccentric, and that we're both half-mad. But believe me, once you know him, you're going to love him."

Hidden in a cluster of trees, Henry, Sarah, and Fritz sat on a sandy ledge with cool river water up to their necks. Church bells rang, and a train whistle blew in the distance, but, in their sun-dappled, green world of mid-August, these sounds were alien and inconsequential. Light and shadow modeled their young features as if they were vaudeville players illuminated by lurid stage lights. The ferns that grew around them had been set in gentle motion by some unfelt breeze. Damselflies met and mated like amorous acrobats.

Fritz had immersed the lower part of his face, so he could be eye-level with the water bugs. Sarah looked up at the light shining through the canopy of leaves. Henry, having found a mossy rock against which to lean his back, closed his eyes and dug his feet into the sand.

"Let's sell our house and live in the woods," Sarah said.

Henry opened his eyes and looked at Sarah who was still studying the interplay of leaves and light above her head.

"Can you think of any home that matches this for beauty?" she said.

Henry had his arm and shoulder fully underwater to extract a rock poking his leg. "I'm sure Clem Studebaker's mansion will."

"Have you seen the interior yet?"

"No, but I've heard it will rival the grand estates of Europe."

"I'm surprised Clem would want to live in anything without a smokestack," Sarah said.

Fritz pulled himself out of the water and sat on a rock. A lock of his blond, wet hair dripped into the water as he hung his head down. He wrung the water from the lock and then coiled it into a comical knot on the top of his head and made a face at Sarah, who laughed.

"Do you remember that old book I rescued from your mother's burn pile when we were kids?" Fritz asked.

For a moment, Sarah looked at him without comprehending and then said, "Yes, yes, of course. I remember you felt so guilty about that. You brought me over to your house and showed it to me. It was, unfortunately, so like my mother to think it was rubbish."

"That book was really the beginning of my interest in botany. Did you ever find out where the book came from?"

"I'm not sure, but I thought it might have belonged to my grandpa Navarre. When he died, there were a lot of strange things that showed up at our house: sacks of dried beans, pelts, gun parts. My mother threw them all away."

Henry, who had been working on creating a more comfortable

underwater seat for himself, suddenly asked: "How much are they paying you at the switching yard?"

Sarah looked sharply at Henry. "Henry, that's rude to ask that."

Fritz laughed. "No, Sarah. No need to worry. Henry and I have had lots of conversations about wages. He may work in management, but he's a union man at heart. Seventy cents, Henry."

"For Christ's sake. Seventy cents for a ten-hour day in the switching yard. That's insane."

"Can't you find a position for Fritz in the office where you work, Henry?"

Fritz smiled indulgently at Sarah. "Henry's suggested that several times, but I don't want a long-term commitment. I want to earn enough money to go back to school. I also don't want to sit behind a desk. At the switching yard, I work outside all day. I use my arms and legs. I like the physicality of it. I'll have plenty of time behind a desk once I'm back to school. Besides, it's educational in its own way."

Henry thought of his own tame, safe existence. He was twenty-six and already suffered from piles. He looked down at his pale, soft flesh beneath the water.

"But, Fritz, I think it's a shame. Your skills are wasted at a switching yard," Sarah said.

"Are they? What about your skills, Sarah? Or Henry's? We're all wasting our talents in one way or another. Now this…" he said, settling himself back into the water and turning his face toward the sun shining through the trees, "is not a waste of time."

"Clem Studebaker would say it was," said Henry.

"Then he's not entirely human, is he?" Fritz said, letting his arms float in the water. With his eyes now closed, he added, "I want to give that old botanical manuscript back to you, Sarah."

"Why? You rescued it. It's yours," she said.

"But it was in your family and would still be yours if your mother hadn't failed to appreciate it."

"I'm happy with you owning it. I would be less happy if *I* did."

Fritz stood up, and Henry admired his friend's well-developed arms and shoulders. Fritz returned his gaze with an unnerving frankness. Henry put his hand through his thick, dark hair which also grew in great tufts on his chest and back. He inched himself slowly into the water until he was entirely immersed. He stayed under long enough to make Sarah anxious then burst to the surface.

"Henry! Don't do that."

"What? Make you worry? Let's swim. Shall we go into the river?"

"Oh, you city boys," said Sarah. Henry had grown up in Pittsburgh and moved to South Bend when his father had opened his first medical practice there. "This," she said, "is not a good place to swim. The current is too strong here. Besides, *She* might get you," said Sarah, opening her eyes wide and clawing the air.

"She?" Henry also clawed the air.

"Mishipeshu. She's the Potawatomi river goddess. She especially loves beautiful young men. She caresses them while they swim and then pulls them into the depths."

"Might not be half bad. Sort of like Hades dragging Persephone into the underworld," said Henry.

"Or Mr. Mole making off with Thumbelina," said Fritz.

"But Mishipeshu never lets her men return to the surface."

"I wouldn't think her victims are much fun after the first five or ten minutes."

"No, I suppose not."

Fritz went underwater and came to the surface holding a white stone. He held it up so Henry could see it and threw it back into the water. Henry dove to retrieve it. Henry could see the chalky white stone make its final zig zag to the river bottom. He was just about to grab it when Fritz's long, thin body knocked him out of the way.

Beneath the water, Fritz seemed to have a golden halo around his body. Henry came to the surface to breathe, but Fritz grabbed his leg and pulled him under. Fritz looked directly into Henry's eyes, and Henry looked into his. Henry felt that there was something unfastening, a curious unraveling going on inside his skull.

Henry pulled away first and burst into the air with a wide-mouthed gasp. Fritz surfaced slowly with quiet dignity.

"I thought I was going to have to go down after you two! You alright?"

"Oh, fine, for Christ's sake," Henry said. He was back to being the old Henry—at odds with himself, at odds with everything. He cast a furtive look at Fritz. Whose smile had a faint trace of amusement about it.

Sarah had gotten out of the water and was wrapping her hair in a towel. "I thought Mishipeshu had gotten both of you."

Fritz collected his clothes from the rock where he had spread them out, and without turning towards her, said: "She did."

Henry had just gotten another promotion. He was clever with numbers and had an instinctual ability to divine the wants of those in power. He solved problems both large and small without fanfare and little self-promotion. He was poised to become a very successful man. Yet he was not entirely at peace. He followed the Chicago Haymarket affair in the papers every day and saw that any worker who said he wanted more than survival wages for himself and his family risked being fired. And, if that worker organized with his co-workers, he'd be silenced with a truncheon. On Henry's ascent up the company ladder, he could not help casting his eyes below at the undifferentiated legions of men who arrived just after dawn with hollow eyes and shapeless, wrinkled jackets to take their places on the assembly line.

Fritz had become an essential part of their domestic life. He never foisted his company upon them, but if Henry didn't invite him for dinner on Saturday night, Sarah did. There were others they included in their outings, but it was a thing understood that they were the principal three.

Henry lost his temper with Sarah with increasing frequency. She was forever missing his point mostly because she didn't read enough. He didn't know how she could invest so much of herself in her drawings. The act of mechanically reproducing what one saw could hardly be helpful in developing one's mental faculties. If she would just read the papers as he did, perhaps they'd find more common ground. Fritz always understood him. Talking with Fritz wasn't hard work at all; they were entirely compatible.

To Henry's surprise, Fritz had not lost his closeness with Sarah. In fact, their ties had grown stronger. They talked for hours about their shared interest in plants and art. Sarah clearly felt that Fritz was primarily *her* friend, and, as she subtly and sometimes not so subtly pointed out to Henry: if anyone was an interloper in their relationship, it was Henry.

A chasm was opening between them that, despite their considerable affection for one another, they were powerless to bridge.

It had been a busy day. Henry had just checked in with one of the warehouse accountants on an inconsistency he had found when examining the books that morning. He needed to finish writing an article advertising the company's new "Extension Top Carriage," and, to do that, he'd need to speak with the carriage designers and machinists in Design House Six, about a quarter mile away but still within the Studebaker compound.

He didn't know what time it was because his pocket watch had fallen into a puddle a month ago, but his rumbling stomach told him that it must be about noon. The whistle confirmed this. He put the ham sandwich Sarah had packed for him into his pocket with the intention of meeting Fritz for lunch at the Lake Shore Depot, which was on his way to the Design House.

The depot was a hub of activity: coal trains arrived full during the day and rattled off empty in the night. Twenty boilers devoured the coal and sixteen dynamos gave the men the power to create enough buggies, sleighs, wagons, and carriages to fill the Studebaker showrooms around the world.

Henry put on his top hat and stepped out. The October air was ice cold and saturated with the yeasty smell of the neighboring brewery. Men filled the courtyard. Some men, like Henry, wore top hats, long woolen coats, and black polished shoes. Other men wore baggy trousers, woolen caps and had grease on their faces. Henry felt in his pocket to make sure he had remembered to bring an article he had clipped out of a Chicago workers' newspaper for Fritz.

At the depot, Henry saw a group of men on a bench opening their lunch pails. Henry often came to the depot at lunch to see Fritz. They recognized him, and a few nodded in his direction. He thought he saw one smirk and say something to his neighbor that made them both laugh. Henry felt self-conscious for a moment and then saw Fritz jumping off the back of a railcar he had just finished unloading. Henry had seen Fritz prance across the top of the railroad cars like a ballet dancer. Fritz yelled something to another friend on the loading dock. When he saw Henry, the smile that had been on his face vanished. A strange look, part accusation, part forgiveness, took its place.

"You free for lunch?" Henry said, walking toward a bench close to the depot. Assuming that Fritz would be, he was already removing from his pocket the article he wanted him to read. "There's an interesting piece I read about the railroad workers' strike. I didn't realize that their pay is forty-three percent less than it was ten years ago!"

Henry sat down on the bench; Fritz remained standing. He looked up at Fritz, anticipating he'd have some response to what he'd said, but Fritz was studying him.

Henry said nothing, but his heart went suddenly cold, as if a crime committed long ago had finally caught up with him.

Fritz's gaze was unflinching. "Henry, you come to the switching yard most lunch times. I see you every Saturday, and...," he turned to look in the direction of the other men, "we both look forward to it." He paused for a moment and looked into the distance behind Henry's head then directly into his eyes.

Henry felt joyful and terrified, aroused, and panicked. He was overwhelmed, as if he'd been walking down a garden path and suddenly found himself floundering in the ocean. But fear drowned out all else.

Henry stared at his shoes. He had never felt so weak. He knew he couldn't meet Fritz's gaze. Fritz had seen into a place in his heart that was carefully and thoroughly roped off. "I'm hungry," he said weakly, looking down at the cobblestones then back to Fritz's face.

Fritz gave him a sad smile. "I'm skipping lunch today." He backed away slowly from Henry.

"I'll... we'll see you on Saturday?"

Fritz squinted his eyes and shook his head. He turned and walked back to the depot.

Henry stood staring at the place where he had stood.

A train was approaching on the Lake Shore line, and the whistle sounded like a chorus of the damned; black smoke rolled from the train's metal chimney.

Henry carefully refolded the article he had taken out, adjusted his top hat, and headed back for his office. He decided he didn't feel up to visiting Design House Six.

No single idea clearly formed in Henry's mind. He stood before the drafting table in his office, shuffling through the papers he had already read that day. The words on the pages seemed meaningless; zigzags and curly-cues that had nothing to do with him. Minutes passed during which he simply stared at the page. Finally, he decided to read the words out loud, but the sounds turned immediately into nonsense.

Henry gave up trying to focus on his work. He stared through the dirty window to the brick courtyard below. He decided to go home early. He wasn't feeling himself.

Fritz returned to the depot. His lunch was unappetizing—just a rind of cheese and sausage he had grabbed off the counter.

The broad-shouldered Polish boys had gathered and were taunting each other as they unwrapped and began to eat their meat-filled pierogi. One or two looked his way, noting perhaps that his meeting with Henry had been brief. He was sure their relationship was a subject of amusement for the young men. Their own comforting bonds of masculinity brought them together yet kept them safely apart. The collective had decided the few whose lives would be mangled by this arrangement were no real loss.

Fritz climbed into the train car where they had just loaded a shiny, black landau bound for Washington, D.C. The well-polished lantern and brass carriage door handle reflected the weak light from the open door. He checked the ropes that tethered this glittering jewel in place. In the darkness of the railroad car, he was free to let his usual cheerful expression evaporate from his face. Henry was brave enough to proclaim the virtues of anarchism to the titans of industry, but too afraid to listen to his own heart.

"Fritz? You in there?"

It was the foreman. He was a neatly built man with a bushy mustache. "We've got to move a train off track seven. Can you help?"

Fritz quickly clambered down from the car with the landau and followed the foreman across the tracks between the new brick administration building and the depot. A stocky man with an oil can in his hand and dirt on his face was working on the switch engine. Another train approached, rhythmically panting steam into the cold air.

The foreman stopped to talk with a tall man with white hair wearing a Lake Shore railroad cap. The tall man told him to send Fritz up top to put the brakes on. Fritz enjoyed the sensation of walking on the top of the train while it was moving. As the train moved forward, he could walk backwards. No one else could do that. No one else even wanted to try.

Another train arrived and its whistle howled, silencing the voice of the elderly man who yelled: "Hold tight!" The yard crew had switched the arriving train onto the wrong track. Fritz's black jacket disappeared in a cloud of steam.

Between lunch that day and his walk home, Henry had resolved to speak frankly with Fritz. Somehow, he thought, they would come to some happy resolution. He wasn't sure what that resolution would look like, but he committed himself to the hope that such a resolution was possible.

Sarah was growing poinsettias in the basement as a surprise Christmas gift for Fritz, and Henry was helping her re-pot them when a man from the depot came to deliver the news. Sarah followed Henry out of the house, where he fell to his knees in the garden.

After the funeral, Fritz's uncle gave Sarah the manuscript. He said he was sure Fritz would have wanted her to have it. He also brought over all of Fritz's plants.

As the winter's darkness made the outdoors less welcoming, Sarah copied sketches from the manuscript while Henry pretended to read. She was particularly attentive to him, and her pity revealed how much she had guessed about what was in his heart, and this pained him even more.

"Would you leave South Bend?" Henry asked her one evening, as they sat by the fire.

"Yes. I would," she said. "I think that would be a very good idea, Henry."

Snow blew across the intersection of Washington and Taylor Streets, down the steeply pitched roofs of the stately Victorian homes, and into the open collar of the driver, who urged his horses and the heaving, creaking carriage up the lane towards the Studebaker mansion.

Tonight, the light cast by its long, elegant windows was the color of brandied peaches, and the driver, his thoughts disordered by the cold, quickly tethered his horses and propelled his numbed limbs toward the door. No one responded to his clumsy whacks with the brass door knocker, so he pulled the great door open. Dazzling kaleidoscopic colors greeted him on the other side of the door along with drunken laughter and the smell of baked fruit pies and roast duck.

Sarah, wearing a dress made from cranberry-colored silk trimmed with black lace, stood at the bottom of a broad, carved wooden staircase, her dark hair coiled atop her well-shaped head. She recognized the driver and crossed the floor rapidly to speak with him.

"Another hour or so at least, Walter. We got a late start this evening. Why don't you go into the kitchen and get something warm to eat." She noted his red face and slightly desperate air. "Is it really that cold out? Your eyebrows are covered in frost."

She caught the arm of a passing servant. "Geraldine, would you kindly take Father Christmas here to the kitchen for a little dinner? Henry and I aren't ready to leave yet."

Geraldine took the arm of the coachman and led him towards the kitchen, telling him, as if speaking to a co-conspirator: "The mercury was at nine degrees below zero this afternoon."

"Cold enough to freeze the tail off a brass monkey, ma'am," the coachman said, rubbing together the tattered leather of his gloves.

She laughed. "What a strange thing to say!"

This evening's banquet was foremost an opportunity to drink punch and eat duck at company expense, but it was also Henry's going away party.

A waiter balancing on his shoulder an enormous tray piled high with dirty plates and glasses caught his foot on the rug and drove the whole tinkling, clattering collection into the carpet with a stupendous crash. Reverberating silence followed. Then an enormous chorus of whistles, jeers, and applause broke out in the ballroom, and the piano music began once more.

Henry, seated at a table, caught Sarah's eye across the room and raised his eyebrows in a silent question: *"Can we go home yet?"* She responded by cocking her head to one side, her eyes widening in a gentle plea: *"Please, I haven't been out in so long. Can't we stay a little longer?"* He shrugged his shoulders in resigned assent and looked away.

One of Sarah's friends grabbed her arm and led her toward the ballroom, waving comically to Henry who smiled and waved back. He fingered the antique gold pocket watch he had found at a local shop: "Sic transit Gloria mundi" was engraved on its back. He liked the cold smoothness in his palm and its precise craftsmanship—a harkening back to a time before assembly lines.

Henry would be leaving Studebaker to take up a position in Philadelphia. At least, that's what they all believed, including Sarah who had spent the previous week with her friend Martha packing dishes.

Actually, there was no position for Henry in Philadelphia, or anywhere else for that matter. There had been a position in Philadelphia, but it had fallen through, and, strangely enough, he hadn't cared. He should have talked it over with Sarah. He should have had an alternative plan by now.

Suddenly, he was at the massive wooden doors with Sarah, saying his thank-yous and good-byes. He laughed, and he thought it sounded like a good imitation of himself.

Out in the moonlight, their bodies cast towering, blue shadows on the snow. Sarah got into the carriage quickly and huddled beneath a pile of blankets. Henry let the cold air find its way around his scarf and into his jacket. His face felt wonderfully numb.

"Henry! Get under the covers! You'll catch your death of cold."

To please her, he pulled the blankets over his legs. He looked down at her dark, sparkling eyes and loathed himself for not wanting to be with her. He squeezed her arm with affection but looked away.

On the way home, they crossed the Michigan St. Bridge. It was the same bridge on which he'd first met Fritz. The horses walked slowly across the frozen, wooden boards, giving Henry a chance to look at the river. It was frozen and snow-covered where it was shallow; there was a dark, open artery where it ran deep.

As soon as they clambered down from the sleigh, Sarah muttered something about hot tea and darted into the house. Henry paid the driver. The horses blew steam into the cold, still night. The driver cracked the whip, and Henry watched the sleigh until it merged with the darkness of the night and all he could hear was the distant jangle of bells.

He buttoned up the great woolen coat Sarah had given him that Christmas. He took his gold watch from his pocket and opened it: 1:00 a.m. He wrapped it in his handkerchief, stuck it in the letterbox next to the door. He followed the track made by the sleigh.

The land north of the river had been recently cleared to make room for the brick manufacturing plant, yet where the land sloped down to the river, thickets of tangled willow branches and brush remained. He could just make out the dark edge of the Michigan St. Bridge—the point where "civilization" began.

The river was the only thing moving, the only thing with a clear direction and purpose that would not be stopped by the cold. Henry wondered how cold it would have to be for how long before the center froze?

A path of sorts extended from the wheel track to the river's edge, probably the tracks made by a dog chasing a river otter. Henry imagined the dog's wild excitement as he followed his bounding, zigzag path with his own measured steps.

At the river's edge, as he breathed in the frigid air, he could feel the full dimension of his anguish; it spanned the length of his arms and filled his gut and chest. He had brought his great, tormenting love down to this river tonight hoping that the night air would extinguish it, but the cold air only numbed his flesh, and left a leaden core of concentrated pain.

What troubled him as he walked across the ice weren't thoughts of Sarah. She was still young and attractive, and, though he suspected her of nothing, felt confident suitors would soon be queuing up. No, the idea that nagged at him as he approached the black, open water was the possibility that this oppressive, unreasonable, fanatical love might just be the best part of him.

Henry's body was found that March by a group of spear fishermen when their torchlight revealed a white object on the surface of the water. They planted their spears into the river bottom around the body to keep it from being drawn again into the current's power and then summoned the police.

When the coroner, Israel Underhill, examined the body the next day, he was surprised by the absence of clothes. Henry had last been seen alive fully dressed and wearing a long overcoat.

Henry's body was taken from the river, completely naked except for a stocking on the right foot and, wrapped around the left, a bit of his red flannel underclothes. Though his face was disfigured by its five weeks in the water, his dark hair was beautifully ornamented with the sweepings of the river, which Sarah lovingly pressed between the pages of the ancient manuscript.

AFTERNOON

Mishipeshu's cave faced the entrance to the Sanctuary of the Dead—a black hole ringed with jagged rocks and tractor tires. Bison-spirits, wolf-spirits, the spirits of bobcats and two-leggeds—all the souls of the local dead floated through her garden on their way to the Underworld.

She was accustomed to seeing spirits pass by her window: one in the morning, another in the afternoon.

But then, one afternoon, the taste of bitter wormwood was in her mouth, and she knew that something was very wrong. She looked out the window into the garden, where the pondweed gently swayed in the current. A pigeon spirit floated towards the black entrance. Then two pigeons, then five, followed quickly by ten and twenty. Soon, a raging torrent of white and brown feathers thundered past.

No sooner had the pigeons passed, than quail and beavers—two, five, ten, and then hundreds, thousands joined them. Bears, wolverines, bison followed—so thick and fast they could no longer be counted. A multitude of fur and feathers hurled itself towards the dark entrance—a colossal migration to the land of the dead.

Days, weeks, months passed, and the torrent continued, flattening Mishipeshu's garden and blasting the loose stone and dirt around the Sanctuary's entrance.

At last, the flow tapered off.

"So many dead…" Mishipeshu said, shaking her head.

A school of bluegills approached. One fish said, "A two-legged has gone astray in the pondweed."

"His heart is still beating," another said.

"Must have died for love," they said in unison and swam on.

Mishipeshu had ferried more two-leggeds to the Sanctuary of the Dead than she cared to remember. Fish were not permitted to do so. Most of the time, it wasn't difficult to put things right—free their coat from a branch; pull them from a churning eddy. Usually, it was a mechanical problem. Sometimes, she did turn people around, away from the Land of the Dead, but only at the request of a Medéwewen, and they rarely made such requests.

Shafts of pale green light fell about the two-legged caught in the weeds. As she untangled him, she saw his face. He seemed to be dreaming—or communing with the stars. "He died for love," she whispered, repeating the blue gills' words.

She put her ear to his heart. She heard a gentle beat, like the sound the rain makes underwater—soft, hollow plunks. She put her finger on his lower lip—marble-cold.

He still wore clothes, which, she felt, made him less attractive. She took off his long woolen coat. Beneath that, he had another woolen jacket, a cotton shirt, an undershirt, and pants. She removed them all, except for a red flannel sock—she thought the color suited him.

From now on, he would belong to her. She took a red water lily blossom from behind her own ear and tucked it gently behind his. She put swamp thistle blossoms and black-eyed Susans in his dark hair. She stepped back, so she could appreciate the full effect. He was beautiful. She leaned over his face. His eyes, framed by dark brows, were closed. She brushed his lips with her own.

"Mishipeshu!"

It was Manitou's voice.

Mishipeshu lifted her head and saw the white light of the sun above her. What harm could one kiss do?

"Their love is like poison," Manitou answered, hearing her thoughts.

Reluctantly, Mishipeshu finished untangling him and pushed him into the current. He floated away. She followed behind, watching as he passed though the black tunnel and into the Sanctuary of the Dead.

Manitou was gone. Mishipeshu was angry—angry with Manitou for making two-leggeds, and angry with herself for trying to kiss one. Two-leggeds were killers. Had she not seen all the bodies of her dead brothers and sisters—all the animals who had passed by on their way to the underworld? Her dark eyes flashed red, as she made her way back to her cave. The small fish darted away.

Chapter 9

Father Nieuwland's Tincture of Love and Death

~ 1914 ~

Father Julius Nieuwland took the Colt semi-automatic pistol out of his pocket, aimed at a branch of an elm twenty feet above his head and fired. This was his standard method for collecting botany specimens from trees. There were just tiny nubs on the branches at this time of the year, so it hadn't been worth the noise, but it delighted the older boys in his class and, of course, Nieuwland himself.

Carrying an unlit lantern and some burlap sacks, Nieuwland followed the muddy forest path with surprising deftness for a man of his size. Seven young men and boys followed after him, making brief, off-trail forays to climb on boulders or tightrope walk across fallen limbs.

Prof. Greene trailed behind Father Nieuwland's group with his own band of smaller children. They had been frightened by the loud report of his colleague's gun, and many still had their hands over their ears.

Greene stopped, took off his wire-rimmed glasses, and polished them with his handkerchief, trying to banish the flood of images the gunshot had conjured: the flash of artillery and smoke on the horizon, the wagons laboring through mud, the blindfolded deserters waiting to be shot. Greene had been an infantry soldier in the Union Army, and even now, at the age of seventy-two, not a day passed without some reminder of his three years in the war.

"No cause for alarm, my little scholars! Just Prof. Nieuwland bringing order to the natural world," said Prof. Greene smiling in a slightly pained way. The children looked into their teacher's kindly, doughy face, framed with flyaway white hair and found reassurance there. They forgot their fears and advanced down the trail.

Nieuwland had been one of Greene's students at Catholic University, and the two, who shared many interests and convictions, had become fast friends. Now that Edward was at the end of his career, he also felt a fatherly tenderness for his brilliant student whose ambition and interests had, unfortunately, at least, as far as he was concerned, led him to chemistry and away from botany.

Greene's group emerged at a clearing by the river where Nieuwland's older boys had already arrived and were variously engaged in skipping stones, sticking their shovels into the wet earth, and peeling bark from the trees.

Father Nieuwland stood on a stump near the river and addressed the group: "Boys! Listen up! We'll be looking about two to three feet out into the water for lily pads growing along a quarter mile strip. Starting here." He held his hands aloft and brought them down on either side of where he stood. "If you spot anything, please give me, Jeremy, or one of the older boys a holler. Remember, use your shovels gently."

Jeremy Thorton, Father Nieuwland's lanky, curly-haired teaching assistant, added, "DON'T yank the foliage on top. It'll break off, and we won't have the root. Understand?"

Father Nieuwland headed north along the river, stepping over hedges of blackened, water-logged branches with his large, muddy boots while scanning the water for the lilies. The sun was edging toward the horizon.

Greene stopped with his group beneath a large sycamore twenty feet from the river. "Children! Gather round!" Greene said.

David Meyer, who had just turned eight, tugged at whatever plant material he could get his hands on and then shredded it, and some of the other children, impressed by David's display of strength, did the same. Greene noticed that David was starting to tug on a green shoot of trillium that had just poked its head out of the soil in search of sunlight.

"David Meyer, *what* are you doing?"

The boy turned his freckled face to Prof. Greene and looked at him blankly from under a fringe of red hair.

Prof. Greene addressed the group. "Children, which of the rocks is alive?"

The children looked at each other blankly. "None of them," said Andrew.

Green smiled, "Isn't it possible that stones have their own language?"

"They don't have any mouths," said the very angular Cecil who stood near the back of the group.

"How do we know that a thing needs a mouth to communicate? What if the rocks, the trees, the plants, the river, the sky—everything around us is connected and communicating all the time?"

One boy of ten with dark eyebrows, wearing a frayed, wool coat he had clearly outgrown said, "Why aren't they speaking to us, Prof. Greene?"

"Perhaps you aren't listening?"

Prof. Greene signaled the group to follow him closer to the river where he pointed out and described the plants and the animals that made the river their home. Nieuwland's enormous forehead, waxen features, and mouth that resembled a line segment suddenly appeared at the edge of Greene's group of boys. Nieuwland's intensity made him impossible to ignore.

"Yes, Prof. Nieuwland?" Greene asked.

"Sorry for the interruption, but one of the boys has just found what might be the water lily you described. Would you mind taking a look?" Nieuwland asked.

"Excuse me, boys. Please use this time to find a plant and sketch it. Nathan?" he turned toward a slightly older, dark-haired boy of ten or eleven. "Could you make sure that everyone has what he needs and stays together?"

"Yes, Prof. Greene," Nathan said, eagerly. Cecil rolled his eyes.

Greene carefully picked his way through the branches and whole trees deposited by the river during last year's flood. Nieuwland charged ahead, practically vaulting over the stumps and logs. Just beyond a particularly large pile of branches, two boys were squatting, observing a single lily pad a few feet into the river. Greene and Nieuwland joined the group.

Greene thought he saw a spot of red on one of the buds. As they watched, the red spot grew larger. The light was fading, so it was difficult to say if the bud would open fully. They waited a little longer in silence. A cold wind blew through the branches. The descending temperature made many of the boys wish they had brought their jackets, but they remained and watched as the blossom began to spill out its red petals.

"That's it! You've found it!" said Greene, surprised by his own exuberant excitement.

Father Nieuwland stood up and shouted to a few of the boys, "Bring a shovel and a sack."

"Wait, Julius," Greene said. This was a spectacle Edward had longed to see for decades. He looked at Julius' expressionless face. There was no awe, no wonder. For him, this lily was a thing to be acquired and then taken apart. Years of education and a brilliant mind had not given him what was necessary to appreciate the beauty of a flower.

As a younger man, Greene might have chastised Julius, but a hopelessness and resignation had crept over him these past few years. "Oh, never mind. Go ahead." He went back to supervise the children, but tears welled up in his eyes. He took a handkerchief out of his coat pocket and blew his nose to demonstrate that the tears in his eyes had nothing to do with any pain in his heart. He finished the children's lesson and waited while they gathered their pencils and papers.

Julius, looking quite pleased with himself, waited for Edward at the beginning of the trail that led back to the school. The lily had been packed up, and the lab equipment accounted for. It was almost dark, and the older boys counted and corralled the younger ones into small groups so that none could stray on the return trip. Carrying aloft kerosene lamps, the groups set off down the trail, baying like wolves and hooting like owls.

"You were right. It was exactly where you said it would be," Julius said smiling down at Greene, who was quite a bit shorter. Julius' enthusiasm was tempered by his friend's initial unwillingness to collect the sample. Edward could be a bit deep and moody at times, and Julius could seldom read his thoughts and motives.

Julius walked ahead purposely to address the group. "Boys! If you're carrying a lantern, watch your footing! It's getting dark. Knute, stop throwing the football!" At this, his barrel-chested lab assistant stopped mid throw, screwing his kindly face into an apologetic smile.

Julius rejoined Edward, observing, "I'm losing my chemists to football."

"It's a nasty, brutal sport. I wish they'd find some other way to occupy their time."

"I don't know. The game toughens them up, if it doesn't kill them," Julius said. There was a silence between them as they walked down the wooded path. "I received a letter from my cousin in Hansbeke yesterday. She said a German zeppelin flew over their town on its way to the French border. What do you make of that?"

"The Germans seem to be quite head-and-shoulders above the rest of us in engineering and chemistry," Edward said lamely. He didn't follow political developments in Europe very closely.

"The Germans are advancing in all areas but frequently by stealing ideas from their trusting neighbors. My parents' friends say that the universities are rife with German spies."

Edward looked around at the darkening tree tops buffeted by a wind that had come up just as the sun had set. The cherry trees would no doubt have leaves next week, and the hardwoods would leaf out shortly afterward. He was going to point out a red-tailed hawk that had landed in the branches above their heads, but his friend's attention was on the troubling situation in Europe.

"How are the experiments going, Julius?" Edward asked, in part, because he was curious and, in part, because he wanted to drag his attention back to something less vexing.

"A bit slowly, at the moment," he said. "My students are excellent, but it takes so long to train them before they're useful. It's dangerous work as well, and I have to make sure I don't send them back to mother and father minus a nose or a couple of digits."

Edward smiled and shook his head. "Julius, why don't you stick with botany? Botany keeps one rooted in Mother Earth. Chemistry… chemistry is Mephistophelean."

"Oh, come now, Edward. You can't believe that. God gave us an entire pharmacy of plants for all possible ills. Nature is the best chemist in the world. It's our job to unlock its mysteries."

"But, Julius, you're not just unlocking mysteries, you're creating monsters. Things that never before existed."

"Steam engines, cameras, telegraph machines, incandescent light—all these things didn't exist, yet they're not evil. All the ingredients for them were just waiting for someone to find and put together. I feel that way about my synthetic rubber experiments too. It will be useful in ways I can't imagine."

Edward looked at his friend's proud face, "It might also be damaging in ways you can't imagine. Don't you remember that unfortunate cocktail you mixed up in the lab—the one that created the plume of green gas and sent you to the hospital for several days? Some sort of acetate solution you were playing with, wasn't it?"

Julius' thin lips curled into a smile, "If you hadn't dragged me to the hospital, that would have been my last experiment." He paused, and the smile gradually disappeared from his face. "You know, Edward, as far as the government is concerned, that greenish-yellow cloud I invented *was* a great success."

Edward looked at him quizzically, "What do you mean?"

Julius lowered his voice somewhat, and Edward, who was slightly deaf in the ear closest to Julius from gun and cannon fire, had to work hard to make out Julius' words.

"About a month ago, a mysterious visitor from Washington, D.C. stopped by my office. He said he was interested in my dissertation research. But then it became clear that he was mostly interested in how I had created the fumes that sent me to the hospital." Julius stopped, looked at Edward directly and said, "I'm quite sure he was considering my experiment for military purposes."

"Poison gas?"

Julius pressed the back of his hand to his mouth and held it there for a moment before letting it fall back again at his side. "If it should turn out that...that I had inadvertently invented a weapon of war, I would not, I could not, feel entirely...remorseful. If it were something that would, say, sicken the Germans."

"'*Sicken*'? Julius, don't be naïve. War has never been about 'sickening' the enemy. It's always been about killing him."

They emerged from the woods and onto a dirt road. A big, black, shaggy dog ran at Edward and Julius, barking and baring its teeth. Julius recoiled. Edward extended his hand tentatively to the dog. The dog continued to bark then wagged its tail. Finally, he sniffed Edward's outstretched hand and stopped barking altogether.

The students now looked like an irregular shadow on the road far ahead. Julius could see Edward's profile—his friend was tired. He remembered how energetic and vital he had been, how he had paced in front of the classroom, his black robe covered in chalk dust. Greene's lectures had made him feel transported into a lofty, higher realm. Now, the once scintillating Prof. Greene was a tired, old man. One day, he reflected, one of his students would look at him and think the same.

"The first three boxes of your herbarium arrived," said Julius.

"Oh, splendid."

"The administration was thrilled when they found out they'd not only be adding you to the faculty, they'd be the new owners of your entire herbarium—the same collection the Smithsonian was vying for. But, of course, that didn't keep them from being careless in its retrieval. It was lucky that Brother Crowley was waiting at the train station to collect the first boxes. If a parcel isn't immediately claimed, the freight men abandon it on the platform and continue on their merry way to Chicago," said Julius.

Edward shook his head, "Well, it's been risky every time I've moved the collection. I certainly never expected to move it once, let alone three times. No matter. I feel as though it finally has a good home, Julius, under your watchful eye."

Ahead, they could see the golden dome atop the main classroom building and the spire of the church. The children ran up the steps eager to take their places at the dining tables. Edward was seized with a fit of coughing on the stairs. He was red in the face and his eyes were bulging by the time the fit had passed.

"Go ahead, Julius," Edward said, taking out a handkerchief and mopping his brow, which was covered with sweat. "I'll be right in."

"No, no, I'll wait with you. I'm enjoying the night air. I was incarcerated for so long this winter with pneumonia. It feels good to finally be liberated."

Edward folded his handkerchief and placed it neatly in the interior pocket of his jacket. "Julius, I meant to tell you that there's something special in Box 46 of the herbarium." Edward stopped speaking, still trying to catch his breath after his coughing fit. "Box 46 has a manuscript in it. It's a botanical manuscript of great historical and personal value. I don't think I've told you this before, but I was married once. The manuscript belonged to my wife, who died thirty—oh God, is it really thirty years ago? Yes, it is." He shook his head. "Anyway, the manuscript seems to be from the eighteenth century, though I was never able to establish its true provenance."

"That sounds intriguing," Julius said, scrutinizing his elderly teacher as if he were seeing him for the first time. The idea was jarring that this quiet, methodical, grandfatherly man could once have shared his bed with a woman.

"The book itself, the binding and paper, that is, is probably French or German, but the plants are from this area," Edward said, finally continuing up the stairs. "I knew about the lily you found today because of this book. It's an ethnobotanical book with instructions for making medications—it even has some seeds from that time period. The lily seeds are psychoactive. If you prepare them according to the instructions, and ingest them in small amounts, it's a hallucinogenic. Native Americans used it for vision quests."

Julius smiled. "Edward, you chastise me for creating Mephistophelian poisons in my lab, and yet you've apparently been making hallucinogens. The lily's poison is no less poisonous for being natural."

"The book might have its share of hocus pocus, but it's a work of great artistic and scientific merit. It also means a lot to me personally, for whatever that's worth, and I'd like for you to take good care of it."

"Yes, of course, Edward. You know I will," said Julius, clasping the other by the arm. "Let's get you something to drink."

They both climbed up the stairs and found themselves in a great hall where young women in dark blue dresses and white aprons were delivering plates of steaming mashed potato and roasted chicken to the eager boys seated at long tables.

Father Nieuwland stared out the train window. The copy of the *New York Times* he had picked up at the train station lay abandoned in the empty seat next to his. April rain cascaded down the glass, and, in the woods beyond the glass, he could see that even the coarsest knots of tangled bushes were now trimmed with pale green. It had been a very long winter. Julius sat on the train trying in vain to find the space to stretch out his long legs. He was on the way to Edward's funeral.

Edward had returned to Washington almost a year before to supervise the packing up and shipping of the rest of his herbarium and to fulfill his responsibilities to the Smithsonian. They had found his body in his spare, single room at Catholic University when he failed to come to breakfast. He had been withdrawn of late and had complained of not getting enough sleep. A sleeping tonic of some sort in a tear-drop shaped vial was found on the nightstand next to his bed.

Julius had been looking forward to having Edward close by, and now the great tree that had towered above all else in his education had unexpectedly fallen. If he was honest, he had to admit that he hadn't given much thought to Edward in the past few months. He'd been so involved with the effort to raise money for the now German-occupied Belgium. When the boxed materials from the herbarium arrived, he hadn't had time to supervise their unloading and cataloging and had left the work to his student assistants.

Julius grabbed the folded *New York Times* and opened it. Bloomingdales was having a white sale. A letter to the editor complained that Times Square dance halls were too crowded. Americans tangoed and polished their new automobiles while war took its toll on the other side of the Atlantic. What were the Old Country's turf disputes to them? More than three thousand miles of ocean separated comfortable Americans from European battlefields; the war might as well be on a distant star.

Photographs, Julius mused, were the only thing that occasionally perturbed the general indifference: images of German officers in comical pointed helmets, miserable looking men in rain-filled trenches, soldiers marching down boulevards lined with shocked locals.

The train picked up speed as they pulled out of Toledo. There was still such a long way to go. The rain came down harder.

How many years ago was it now? Did it matter? Each memory was still perfectly intact in his head. During his few moments of quiet, when his other responsibilities were temporarily silenced, he would select a memory as if it were a delicate glass object on a shelf. Here's the memory of them sitting at the beach at night. Here's the one in which they are hiding from her brother at her family's farm in Hansbeke. None of it mattered now. He was a priest, and she was a married woman living in Ypres thousands of miles away.

Would he even recognize Hansbeke now? It had been such a safe, little backwater in his youth. August changed all that. A barrage of German artillery knocked down the church steeple; stones that hadn't moved in centuries fell like meteors into the town square. The steeple that had always told travelers from afar that ahead lay the sleepy village of Hansbeke crumbled and fell. Executions of civilians, arrests for singing the national anthem, and late-night disappearances of Belgian men who ran off to join the Allies at the Front—all that had followed.

In her last letter, Rachel had told him that her family had moved in with relatives in Ypres so they could all be together, and that the tulips, indifferent to artillery, were blooming under the Flanders spring sky.

Julius wished that he could provide some sort of assistance to Rachel and her family, but how could he? He had to resign himself to helping her indirectly by raising money for Belgium. So, here he sat thousands of miles away from her on the safe side of the ocean. As the landscape darkened outside his window, he saw more distinctly his own luminously pale, plain face reflected in the glass.

The laity could indulge in "what-if" scenarios, but God determined the lives of priests. Wasn't that the way it worked? How could his life be other than what it was?

As Father Nieuwland's eyes closed and his relaxed body rocked back and forth with the rhythm of the train, far away in Ypres, dawn was breaking over the rooftops, meadows, and grazing cattle.

Rachel went outside to get some fresh air after a sleepless night. A strange, greenish-yellow cloud appeared on the horizon. It rode a gentle, morning breeze over Flemish fields. It passed silently over the city's earthen ramparts, kissing the parted lips of those still lost in dreams.

CHAPTER 10

ROOSEVELT'S WINCHESTER

~ 1918 ~

President Theodore Roosevelt—*former* President Roosevelt—pushed open the screen door of Colliers Hunting Lodge. Hands on hips, he surveyed the vibrantly blue mid-morning sky with an air of critical evaluation. A lilac bush full of blossoms draped itself wantonly over the railing, making the air sweet and heavy with its scent.

Roosevelt's guide for the day, Jeremy Thorton, was a slim, young man full of enthusiasm for things few young men cared about—plants, birds, reptiles. Fifteen years before, when the President had come out to the Kankakee Swamp for a similar hunting trip, it had been Jeremy's uncle who had served as the President's guide.

"Here's your Winchester 76—cleaned, polished and ready to 'go out and win the West', Mr. President," said Jeremy, coming briskly up the porch steps to hand it over to Roosevelt for inspection.

The president lit up at the sight of the gun; the wrinkles around his eyes radiating outward from his wire-rimmed glasses. He ran his hand down the length of the polished barrel. He stepped to the edge of the porch and checked the sights, aiming it at a branch near the top of a stately sycamore.

"Don't shoot!" called a tall, trim man in a tweed jacket. He had a well-manicured, gray mustache and wore the kind of black-banded Panama hat popular among much younger men. He held his hands above his head as he walked toward Roosevelt in a half-hearted way, looking uncommitted to his own joke.

Freddie Vanderbilt was Teddy Roosevelt's age, sixty, yet still crisp and fresh as new linen. "I was worried you'd mistake me for a Hun, Teddy." He studied the President's portly physique. "You're looking bully. Heard you had surgery. Thought that might have knocked some of the wind out of your sails, but I see I needn't have worried."

Roosevelt smiled warily at Freddie as he shook his hand. Freddie nodded to Jeremy with a trace of social condescension.

Roosevelt handed Jeremy the gun. "Could you take the rifle down to the boat? I like a 45-calibre bullet backed by about 150 grains of powder. I'll join you after I've had my breakfast."

"Right, Mr. President. I'll go to the kennel first for Sparky. Meet you at the dock then," said Jeremy, giving a formal nod in Freddie's direction.

"I read about the men you sent to France to rebuild the rail lines. Fine thing to do, Freddie," said Roosevelt, squinting at him behind his gold-rimmed spectacles. Freddie was not sure what to make of the Colonel's apparent sincerity, a quality considered bad form by his own social set.

"Yes, well, we all must do our part for the war effort... to drive out the Hun," and then, as if entirely losing the will to parrot popular rhetoric, he added flatly, "... as it were." He took off his hat and wiped his brow. "How's the family? You've got sons who've gone off to fight, haven't you?" Freddie asked.

"Yes, both. Some men think their own necks are never worth risking. I'm glad to say that my sons are not in that category." Roosevelt delivered his next words with an orator's vibrato, "Great victory requires great sacrifice."

Freddie looked beyond the President to the bough, dense with lilac blossoms, "Sacrifice might not seem quite so lofty in the trenches."

Roosevelt was preparing to counter with examples from his own experience in the Spanish-American War but was interrupted when the front door of the lodge opened and a rotund, middle-aged woman came out, dusting the flour from her apron. She wore a smile that looked more like a dogged commitment to cheerfulness than genuine pleasure, "Mr. President, your breakfast is ready."

"Mrs. Collier, that is music to my ears. Thank you, my dear lady. I will be there presently."

"There's plenty of coffee, Mr. President. Just the way you like it." Mrs. Collier acknowledged Freddie with a degree of trepidation. "Will you be joining us for breakfast as well, Mr. Vanderbilt?"

Freddie thanked her but demurred, which seemed to bring Mrs. Collier a measure of relief. "Tonight, we have something quite special prepared—an evening of music and poetry. Mrs. Cybil Manchester is down from Chicago with her husband for some picnicking. Cybil has a beautiful voice. A real nightingale."

Clasping his hands in front of him, Roosevelt shook his head regretfully and said, "Mrs. Collier, unfortunately, I will no doubt miss Mrs. Manchester, as I'll be spending my day with Jeremy and Sparky hunting and searching for the elusive prothonotary warbler—a small, yellow song bird that makes its home in swamps."

"Well, that little bird better pack his bags," Mrs. Collier said merrily. "The Kankakee River Improvement Association goin' to make sure there's no more swamp around here."

The sound of something substantial hitting the floor in the dining room absorbed all of her attention. She cast her eyes to the heavens, and her arms went limp at her sides. "Excuse me...," she said before throwing the door open and storming back into the house. "Maude! Git!"

Roosevelt smiled. "Maude is Mrs. Collier's dog," he said, kicking a small branch off the porch in an affectionate, proprietorial way. "Are you sure you can't join me for breakfast, Freddie?"

"Thank you for the invitation, Colonel. You're most kind, but I'm planning to catch the 9:10 back East, and I'm already running late."

"You don't think they'd hold the train for the Director of the Erie Railroad himself?" Roosevelt asked, inviting Freddie to bask a bit in his exalted title.

"Not if they want to keep their jobs," he said. He ran ahead to open the front door for Roosevelt who strode purposefully forward.

"You and Mrs. Roosevelt must pay us a visit at Pine Tree Point this summer. We have a copy of your book on birds. I'm sorry. I'm forgetting the title..."

"*The Summer Birds of the Adirondacks.*"

"Yes, that's right. Anyway, you must come and stay with us."

"Yes, we'd both like that very much."

"Good luck with the hunting. Not much wildlife to shoot at anymore, what with the new canal. That's progress for you," Freddie observed as he lingered on his way up the stairs, trying not to appear eager to terminate the conversation.

"Safe travels!" Roosevelt called after him. A friend had told him that Freddie had built his Adirondack "camp" in the Japanese style and required his servants to dress in that country's native costumes. It would be a cold day in hell before he'd visit Freddie's ridiculous Japanese playhouse, yet he had just told him that he would very much like to visit. Polite society made lying so hard to avoid.

Soon he'd be out on the marsh with his hunting dog and Winchester, and the world would once again be delightfully straightforward. When he had finished his hearty breakfast of eggs, bacon, biscuits, and was on his third cup of coffee, Jeremy came in.

"Did you get your breakfast, Jeremy?" asked Roosevelt with sincere paternal concern.

"Yes, Mr. President, thank you. Ready to go whenever you are," said Jeremy, looking a bit fondly at the buttered toast.

"Fine then. I'll get my hat and meet you at the boat in ten minutes." Roosevelt stood up, crushed his napkin in his fist, and tossed it on the table.

Jeremy had been paddling for an hour already as the sun climbed higher in the sky. Roosevelt checked his watch; it was half past eleven. He looked back over his shoulder and asked, "How much further?"

Jeremy examined the landscape around them, "Another fifteen to twenty minutes."

Roosevelt looked at the borders of the river that were now "improved" by steam dredgers and felt an ineffable loss. He remembered how he had set off from the same point some fifteen years ago into a dense morning mist along the then winding Kankakee. The river lost itself amid mysterious islands of sycamore and sedge grass. Then, the hunter entered a foreign land, where water turned into dry land and back into water again with little warning. In those days, the swamps were a profoundly disorienting experience. Things that looked familiar at first glance felt alien upon a second.

"It's up ahead, to the right," said Jeremy indicating a short dock, which was actually just a couple of pieces of driftwood lashed together. They pulled the canoe into the sedges and followed a narrow, sandy footpath through the woods. Their cocker spaniel, Sparky, had been so excited at the prospect of being on dry land, he made a wild jump for the beach and landed in the shallows. Unfazed, he swam to shore, shook the water off his coat, and raced down the path. Roosevelt, cheered by the dog's display of enthusiasm, followed down the path after him, enjoying the motion forward. He felt youthful and energized.

Unbidden thoughts of an unpleasant recent exchange of letters between himself and the Secretary of War came back to him. He had offered to lead a battalion to the front, but it was clear they thought him too old for the task. Perhaps he was. His hearing was practically gone in one ear, his vision compromised, and his digestion permanently disordered by his nearly-fatal trip to the Amazon. But, damn it, he was still a vigorous man and would be willing to test his mettle against a thousand younger men on the battlefield.

The day was passing pleasantly. Though it was impossible not to compare today's sparse wildlife with the dense flocks that crowded the sky on his last visit, he was satisfied with the wood duck and mallard he had shot. Mrs. Collier had packed a picnic lunch of cold chicken and potatoes, which they were enjoying on an open sandy ridge.

A slender column of smoke rose from what Jeremy called "Indian Island," a half-mile to the west. The grandson of a Potawatomi man, who had hidden in the swamp rather than be "removed" to Kansas by Tipton's men, lived there, hiring himself out as a guide, breeding coon dogs to sell to the local hunters, and trading in local plants and herbal remedies. They decided to pay a visit to the island after lunch.

The second time they docked the canoe, Sparky took off up the sandy slope with even greater determination. Several minutes passed, and then another dog began barking furiously somewhere ahead of them.

"Hullo?" called Jeremy when they reached a small log cabin.

A brindle-colored dog barked and strained at the rope that tethered him. The smoke that they had seen from a distance was coming not from the cabin's chimney but from a fire pit in the yard. Just beyond the fire pit was a small domed structure covered in animal hides; it was ten feet in diameter and only four feet high. Just outside the entrance was a deer skull on a post. Roosevelt stopped and surveyed the odd hut. Jeremy was trying to grab Sparky's collar without success. The dogs sniffed each other energetically.

The door of the cabin opened part way, and a slight man peered out. His long, steel-gray hair was braided with a piece of bright red wool. Jeremy could smell the familiar earthy sweetness of dried plants emanating from the man's cabin.

"Hullo!" Roosevelt called to the man, removing his hat and walking toward him with a relaxed, confident stride. The man studied the large hand outstretched to grasp his own, offering his own with a bit of reluctance. Deep lines ran from his nose to the corners of his mouth. His eyes were golden brown.

Jeremy, who had just succeeded in grabbing Sparky's collar, smiled and squinted at the man in incredulity. "Don't you recognize this man, Mshkiki?"

A pause followed. "Sure. Think I might have seen his face in the papers," he said impassively, refusing to be impressed by his guest's eminence.

A silence followed during which they all looked at the dog.

Roosevelt pointed to the small, domed hut. "What's that little house for? Curing meat?"

"That there?" the man asked, pointing a bent, arthritic finger towards the hut. "That's a sweat lodge."

"Oh, yes, I've heard of those," Roosevelt said walking towards the hut. "What exactly happens in a sweat lodge?"

"We heat stones in the fire pit. And then we bring them in there." He moved aside the piece of animal hide to show the hut's interior. "There's a pit of sand, see?" The man got down on his knees, and Roosevelt did too to look into the dark interior. "We use that hollowed out old gourd to pour water from that bucket over there onto the stones. The steam rises, and we sweat. The sweat lodge heals your body and cleans your soul."

Roosevelt leaned back on his heels. "We could all do with cleaner souls."

Mshkiki gave him an appraising look and nodded, then said, "Come back tonight. You can try it out."

"Colonel," Jeremy interrupted, feeling as though he had let this conversation go on long enough, "I think you said that you needed to send a cablegram this evening."

Roosevelt cast Jeremy a brief, stern look. "We'll come back tonight, Mr. . . .Mr. ..."

"Mshkiki. Call me Mshkiki. Tonight's a full moon—good time for the sweat lodge, Colonel."

"Thank you, Mshkiki." Roosevelt smiled and nodded his head. "I will take you up on your invitation—as long as I can bring supper."

"Sure. Why not?" Mshkiki smiled.

As they were preparing to leave, Mshkiki went into his cabin and returned with a small bundle of wet, bright-green plants. Jeremy counted out coins into Mshkiki's palm.

"Just about impossible to find 'em now, kid." Reluctantly, Jeremy opened his leather purse and placed a few more coins in his still open hand.

While they were setting a time for their return, Sparky, who had been staring up at Mshkiki's roof, now shrank toward the ground and flattened his ears.

A large, black, furry shape appeared at the roof's edge. "Good God, man! That's a bear!" said Roosevelt.

Mshkiki smiled like a proud father. "Jimmy's a real handful."

"He's a pet?" asked the Colonel, greatly amused.

"Jimmy's a damn good bear when he's not eating my food or shitting in the house. I expect somebody shot his mother when he was still a cub."

"Mshkiki, aren't you worried he's going to hurt you?" asked the President.

"He hasn't hurt me yet. I don't suppose he'd have much reason to."

"Bears aren't known for their capacity to reason." Roosevelt shook his head, wishing he had the time to tell Mshkiki and Jeremy about an encounter he'd had with a grizzly out West.

Jeremy made one last attempt to dissuade the President from coming back, as he paddled the canoe to the lodge. "What would Mrs. Collier do," he pondered aloud, "without a President to show off to her other guests?"

In response, the President, who was facing the prow, turned his cumbersome body around and glowered at Jeremy, saying nothing.

"I'm sorry, Colonel. I've heard of people having bad experiences in sweat lodges."

"It will be fine. *I* will be fine, and if not, *that* will be fine."

With little clearance, they passed beneath Dunn's Bridge made from salvaged pieces of the great Ferris wheel from the Chicago World's Fair. Although it had seemed a good idea at the time of construction, the semi-circular pieces were so heavy they were pushing the modest structure deeper into the swamp every year. Boaters, fearful it might collapse on their heads, passed beneath it as quickly as they could.

They stopped at the few remaining patches of hardwoods and listened for the yellow warbler, but they heard only red-winged blackbirds and cowbirds. A chugging, percussive rattling drowned out all other sounds as they progressed up the river. A dredger belched black smoke and took huge bites from the river bottom with its steel jaws.

"They dig up a lot of dead Indians with that thing. They found one last week wearing a silver earring. Seen enough?" The President indicated that he had, and they headed back to the lodge along the tamed and straightened river.

Roosevelt went to his room with every intention of writing a cablegram to the Secretary of War, but instead, when he took his boots off and reclined on the brass bed, he immediately fell asleep. Jeremy went to the President's room to confirm a departure time, but, as he raised his hand to knock on the door, he heard the President snoring. Jeremy quietly retreated to the porch to tie flies for the next day's fishing adventure. Maybe the Colonel would sleep so late, he'd consider the sweat lodge adventure no longer feasible.

But Jeremy succeeded in tying only two flies before the porch door flew open. Roosevelt adjusted his collar. "Ready?"

Darkness fell as they paddled past the steam dredger and under the crowning glory of the Chicago World's Fair, now slowly sinking into Kankakee mud. Mist arose from the warmed earth and into the cool, night air.

Jeremy recounted for the president how his family had lived on the river in a small cabin on stilts but then had moved to higher, drier land after his successive bouts with pneumonia as a child. He told him about his studies with Professor Nieuwland and finding among the boxes of dried plants a curious manuscript with information about local plants and their medicinal properties. He was trying to use one of these 'recipes' to make a painkilling elixir from water lilies, but he was having a hard time translating the instructions. Roosevelt praised his industry and expressed his hope that Jeremy's drug might be used in field hospitals to further the war effort.

The river's twists were hard to negotiate in the darkness, though at least the current was on their side. Evening brought a resurgence of bird songs and chatter as they found the last seeds, bugs, and worms for the day and settled into their chosen roosting spots. When the birds quieted down, the bullfrogs warmed up.

Roosevelt watched the swallows as they performed their aerial acrobatics, flying top speed within inches of the water's surface, then soaring to the treetops. He thought of his son, Quentin, a fighter pilot at twenty-one. He pictured Quentin at the controls of his open cockpit biplane, strafing the enemy with precisely aimed aerial fire, then swerving and dodging the hopelessly outclassed Huns who followed in pursuit. Roosevelt's leg muscles tensed and his heart beat faster as he imagined himself racing through the clouds at Quentin's side with the emerald patchwork of the French countryside below.

"You smell wood smoke, Colonel?" Jeremy asked,

Roosevelt lifted his face into the night air. Jeremy caught a glint of reflected light from his wire rim glasses, as the latter sniffed the air. "No, nothing," he said.

After five or ten minutes, they heard a dog bark. "That's Mshkiki's hound," said Roosevelt authoritatively. Sparky had been left behind at the lodge to avoid another boisterous encounter.

The moon was illuminating the sky now, and they discerned without too much trouble the cluster of trees that marked Mshkiki's dock. They pulled the boat up onto a sandy knoll and retraced the path they had walked just hours before, now with far less energy.

The smell of wood smoke was thick and pungent with aromatic herbs and grasses. Mshkiki was tending the fire.

After eating their supper, Mshkiki gave the President a flask of water, which he urged him to drink. Roosevelt stripped down to his silk shorts. His abundant pink flesh looked as soft and vulnerable as a baby's. He tipped the flask and drank greedily then choked and spluttered.

"What is this?" Roosevelt's face was contorted in the firelight.

"Special medicine. It will help you see things in the spirit world."

"What did you put in there?" Jeremy asked, shaking his head in disbelief and digging in his knapsack for his own water to give to the Colonel.

"Nabagûck. Only a very, very little. A man his size. He will barely feel it."

"Why? It's dangerous." Jeremy had spent many hours creating the elixir in his lab, but he had never tried it.

"All journeys into the spirit world are dangerous," said Mshkiki with a look of incomprehension on his face.

The Colonel mopped his watering eyes with a handkerchief and waved off Jeremy's flask. "When a man is no longer capable of meeting new challenges, Jeremy, mental or physical, he is no longer a man. I have faced down grizzly bears, charging rhinos, and gunfire. I think that I can handle a little liquor and a bit of heat, even at my advanced age. Cowardice is *the* unpardonable sin."

Jeremy had endured his own privations and tests of courage and did not risk his safety or the safety of others lightly. If the Colonel was staking his manliness on participating in the sweat lodge ritual, there was no point in trying to dissuade him. Jeremy sat down with his back against a stately oak, removed a tobacco pouch and pipe from an inner pocket, and, then, looking around, asked, "Where's that pet bear of yours?"

"He's out for a walk," said Mshkiki in an off-hand way. "He likes to go for a walk after he's had his dinner."

Jeremy looked around apprehensively. He filled his pipe and settled in for a long night's watch.

The President ducked his smoothly shaven neck beneath the leather flap that served as a door and went into the sweat lodge.

Not more than five minutes had passed, but already Roosevelt felt as though he'd been in that hell hole for an eternity. Mshkiki dipped the gourd ladle into the water then broadcast droplets across the heated rocks. Steam filled the President's nose and lungs. He closed his eyes, fearing his eyeballs might sear. His heart raced. No time limit had been set on this torment. Panic set in. He shifted nervously on the dirt floor, straightening his back and exhaled a heavy, ragged breath. In the darkness, Mshkiki reached out and put his hand on the Colonel's. This act of familiarity overwhelmed him with indignation, yet he felt an even greater countervailing reassurance that he was not alone in this bizarre, unpleasant experience.

With a sing-song rhythm, Mshkiki chanted in Potawatomi then in English, "Grandmother, oh Sacred One. Guide our feet on the path that leads to wisdom and give us the strength to see what we must see in the darkness."

Mshkiki continued his chanting. Roosevelt had heard this type of rhythmic, atonal song when he'd been out in the Dakotas and had been unimpressed. Its lack of vocal range and the monotony of the sounds and rhythms made him dismiss it as "uncivilized." Yet now, he heard it in his bloodstream, and it spoke to him of love and loss.

Suddenly, he remembered Alice, his first wife, and her lifeless face against the pillow—her lips and eyes both sensual and angelic. Months before giving birth to their first and, as it turned out, only child, she had looked at him with her meadow-green eyes and wondered aloud if the dying felt as she did—their bodies advancing inexorably toward the great unknown, compelled by a force they could neither see nor understand.

His throat contracted as if Alice had died that morning instead of thirty-four years ago. He had felt it was a disloyalty to his second wife to mourn the death of his first. But here in the darkness, the tears flowed down his cheeks. He didn't care what Mshkiki thought.

Images flashed through his head: the frozen buffalo he had found in a snowdrift one winter in the Badlands; the broad, wraparound, wooden porch at Sagamore, his Oyster Bay home, crowded with some of the nation's most important men. Then, he was back playing hide-and-seek with his son Quentin and his friends in the attic of the White

House. He saw vividly the house's sturdy rafters in half-darkness and heard the delighted shouts of little boys.

These memories so engaged him, he was surprised when Mshkiki told him that it was time to "purify" in the river water. Roosevelt obediently left the sweat lodge, went down to the river, and stood thigh-deep in the muddy Kankakee. He was silent; his mind still full of images of the past.

During the second session in the sweat lodge, he felt that his senses had become keener.

Now, he could hear all the subtle cadences of Mshkiki's chant he'd been deaf to before. He saw shades in the blackness that surrounded them. The smells of all the sweet herbs and grasses spiraled away from him, altering their characteristics before they could be identified.

After the second session in the lodge, they stood once again in the Kankakee; a blood red moon filled the sky.

"You've seen enough, Colonel," said Mshkiki, as he stood in the water studying Roosevelt. "Rest now and then go home."

Roosevelt rubbed his fleshy arms and chest with the water in a way that made it look as though he were anointing someone else's body. A light mist had settled over the land and water. Mosquitos landed on his back; he did not swat them away. "I think one more session, Mshkiki. You said the Potawatomi have three sessions. I want to do that too."

Yet, as soon as Roosevelt took up his place again on the sweat lodge floor, he felt that it had been a mistake. The novelty had worn off entirely. He was after all, only sitting on the dirt in a small, overheated hut—there was nothing remotely heroic about it. He sighed and settled in to patiently endure the passage of time.

Mshkiki added charcoal from the outdoor fire pit, and Roosevelt's eyes were drawn to the glowing embers, which, without his glasses, lost their defined edges, pulsating and shifting their shapes. He watched in a disinterested way as one fiery figure's head inflated and burst. Two dwarfish demons copulated and incinerated. One demon, bent with age, snatched another and began to devour it. He hadn't realized before that all one had to do was watch the embers and a drama unfolded; the actors grew, metamorphosed, and died, usually violent deaths.

Gradually, blackness swallowed up all the red figures. Only that which appeared to be a small, red box remained. The box folded and refolded, getting progressively smaller until it folded itself up entirely and disappeared. Roosevelt was left staring at what was now just an undistinguished point of darkness, yet, gradually, that point receded into a deeper plane, sucking in the less dark spaces after it.

Suddenly, it was light around him, but his eyes were covered. He had somehow returned to the White House attic, where he was once again playing hide-and-seek with the children. He could hear their suppressed laughter, taunting him with light taps on his arms and legs, scurrying away before he could catch them. He scissored his arms before him in a mechanical way to make himself seem more frightening, and the children shrieked delightedly and ran away.

Off to his right, he heard the lid of the cedar chest being carefully lifted by small hands. This was Quentin's favorite hiding place, and the Colonel moved toward it confidently, despite the blindfold. He found the chest's edge with his foot, bent down, and lifted the polished lid.

He tore off his blindfold. It was Quentin, not the small boy he had heard laughing, but Quentin the athletic, handsome twenty-one-year-old whom he had last seen in his pilot's uniform, his cap perched rakishly to one side. He had saluted his father joyfully as he headed out the front door with his army-issued duffle bag.

But this Quentin would never smile again. The Quentin that he saw before him in the cedar chest was lifeless—a gaping, jagged wound across his eye and forehead. Quentin's childhood hiding place was now his coffin.

He understood, with dazzling clarity, that he had sent his son, his greatest treasure, without which his own life was meaningless, to his death, and that *it need not have happened*. No patriotic slogan, impassioned speech or brilliant passage of rhetoric would ever justify the loss of a life so precious. He had spent a lifetime glorifying the "ultimate sacrifice" without ever fully understanding what it meant.

He came to himself howling and rocking violently back and forth. Jeremy and Mshkiki were dragging him from the sweat lodge, and he was breathing the staccato breath of a child who had just cried his heart out. They laid him out on the grass under a woolen blanket. He stared up at the stars, their clear, white light was a welcome antidote to the riotous and obscene red embers.

"What the hell happened?" Jeremy asked Mshkiki in an accusatory voice, as they stood at a slight distance to observe the President.

"I told him not to go in a third time. The third time is for vision seekers." Mshkiki sat down next to the President whose chest was still heaving.

Roosevelt fell into a deep sleep and did not wake even when Mshkiki's pet bear sniffed and licked his hair.

He woke to the sound of the distant whistle of the 6:05 Erie-Pennsylvania train as it arrived in Kouts Station. He dressed in the cold morning air and walked with Jeremy back to the boat. As they rowed against the gentle current, a great sandhill crane lifted its blood-red head from the brush and spread its great wings in flight. The Colonel instinctively raised his Winchester, aimed, then lowered the rifle.

TWILIGHT

Bullfrog began to sing. He blew out his bagpipe throat in a strong, bass C. The birds settled into their roosts to listen. A cool breeze wound its way through the trees to caress Mishipeshu's bare, wet shoulders. She shivered. The sun slipped below the horizon.

She stood and raised her arms to the sky, letting herself be moved by the low, percussive beat of the frog: jug-a-rummm, jug-a-rummm, jug-a-rummm.

She raised one foot from the rock and then the other. Each time her foot fell, a tremor found its way to the Earth's core.

She twirled her hands above her head, snatching fistfuls of the sky at sunset: wild rose, firefly-orange, shimmering amethyst. Her hips moved like water, making circles as voluptuous as the full moon. Red-Tailed Hawk pierced the sky with his shrill cry.

Mishipeshu extended her claws. She threw her head back, and her black hair nearly touched the ground. She snapped her head forward, and her hair raced through the air like a wave about to crash. She crouched low, coiling her whole body tighter and tighter, then sprang high into the air—a red-hot tongue of flame leaping upward. She spun once toward the rising moon and once toward the setting sun, twirling faster and faster until Earth melted into sky and water.

Then, all was quiet, except for Bullfrog who said jug-a-rummm, jug-a-rummm, jug-a-rummm.

The first stars appeared. Mishipeshu rested on her rock in the river. Hundreds of fish had gathered in her shadow to worship. She shooed them away with a flick of her wrist.

Manitou had watched Mishipeshu dance. She stepped from the shadows, star-light dancing on her golden antlers. "Now, I see what you have become. I sought to protect you, but I must now share with you the vision which robs me of all peace."

Mishipeshu stood before her mother as the sun slipped below the horizon, and a great silence spread like water across the land.

"I see fire, smoke, floods." Manitou raised her hand and ran it slowly across the horizon. "All my creatures consumed, and two-leggeds reigning as gods. And, you, my daughter, perish with the river."

"But I am immortal, Mother—born when you created the rivers from the great sea." Her thick, dark eyebrows knitting above her flashing eyes. "I have always lived in the river, and there I will stay."

"Your life is one with the river. When the river dies, so do you." Manitou moved to embrace her daughter, but Mishipeshu broke away and strode to the river's edge. She crossed her arms over her chest and looked pensively at the turbulent water.

"But this means my sister will also die along with everything that calls the river home." She looked at her mother tentatively, hoping for contradiction, but Manitou mournfully nodded her head.

"Alas, you were too mild." She looked directly at her mother. "Mortals were never like your other creatures." She shook her head. "They will destroy everything, and they will do it before the world can be renewed."

"Time can follow many paths," said Manitou. "Perhaps I see just one path."

"You see the most likely path, Manitou," Mishipeshu said, her voice bristling of anger. She returned her gaze to the river. "With Namé, I have traveled many paths. In each, two-leggeds' power grows. I cannot keep them from their terrible weapons, but I might still keep Nabagûck beyond their reach. It must be ours alone."

Manitou reached into the folds of her sky-blue robes. "Take these red and black agate bracelets, forged from the North's cold lava and iron. They will help you find your way into the world of men. The red agate is for you; the black is for your sister. Once, there was one of yellow that belonged to Thunderbird, but that was lost long ago.

"Stay close to the river. And, Mishipeshu, do not give your love to men."

Her daughter's eyes flashed red in the moonlight. She dove into the river.

CHAPTER 11

KATY McQUILLAN'S TRIP TO SHANGRI-LA

~ 1938 ~

Katy opened the door into the kitchen and caught a glimpse of Charlie's short, black, well-oiled hair. He was reading the newspaper as he did every morning before leaving on his coal delivery route. Keeping her head down, she walked quickly through the kitchen to the drafty entryway where she picked up the mail from the floor: Zell's Funeral Parlor, Hudson Lake Casino, City Wide Liquor. She brought in two bottles of frozen milk from the recent March snow.

Katy bent down to light the stove; the black hinges shrieked. She could feel Charlie's eyes on the back of her brown, woolen skirt, and fear made her heart beat faster. Each whispery rustle of his newspaper registered on her inner ear.

"The *Shadow's* on tonight, nine o'clock," he said, clenching and unclenching his jaws.

Katy's tongue lay heavy and motionless in her mouth. Silence had become both her prison and defense.

She heard herself asking, not because she cared but because it was a line from the script she had inherited from her sister, "You git coffee?"

"I had the cold stuff in the pan," he answered. Still staring at the newspaper, he added, scratching the back of his scalp, "I put a bucket under the place where the roof's leakin' upstairs. Check it today and make sure it don't overflow."

He put on his coat, picked up from the table the gray, metal lunchbox Katy had packed for him, and left. When the front door closed, the familiar silence rushed in to fill every corner of the house.

Katy now slept where her sister Bridget had, next to Charlie with his .22 rifle between them. Fear, according to Charlie's father, taught women respect.

Katy stayed awake nights remembering the crack her uncle's rifle had made after he cornered a raccoon in his barn. She could feel the cold, polished surface of the gun barrel against her arm. She didn't dare relax or close her eyes. She imagined the pain and the warm trickle of her own blood. She heard phantom gunshots in half-dreams, thunderous explosions, again and again.

Plain, dutiful, sixteen-year-old Katy had been sent by her parents in July to take care of her sister who had fallen ill after giving birth to a baby girl. Bridget recognized Katy at first, but then her mind unraveled like a ball of dropped knitting yarn. She thrashed and tugged on her sweat-soaked nightgown. Finally, she settled down, lifting the rim of countless imaginary teacups to her lips. After two days of encouraging improvements, Bridget died.

Bridget never called for her husband Charlie, even on her deathbed. When her sister breathed her last exhausted, rattling breath, her husband was fast asleep in a lounge chair at Hudson Lake Casino.

Katy agreed to Charlie's request that she stay on for a while to help take care of the baby, at least until other arrangements could be made, though neither could imagine what those other arrangements might be. Katy was devastated when her sister died but was so occupied with caring for the baby, she didn't have time for grief.

She had found in her sister's medicine cabinet a blue glass bottle. She held it up to the light.

> ***Soothing Lily***
> *Contains valuable tonic and nerve stimulant*
> *properties of the water lily. A drug known and used*
> *by Indians to induce restorative sleep and relieve pain*
> *the natural way.*
> *Jeremy Thorton, Chemist, Sole Proprietor.*

She poured the fluid into a teaspoon and drank it. She felt its warmth radiate through her chest. She didn't feel so anxious, and the day passed like a dream.

Taking care of the baby confined her to the house until a neighbor brought over their old pram for her to use. It was hard work for small girl like Katy to maneuver the heavy, steel-wheeled conveyance up and down stairs, but it was worth the trouble to get outside. Katy had been born with a slightly twisted left foot, which had left her with a limp. The pram provided her with pleasant support.

One July afternoon, she was pushing the pram along the river. The baby was fast asleep after a long crying fit. Katy saw a bench, parked the pram, and sat down to watch the river and rest her foot. A tall woman with dark hair and a broad-brimmed hat sat down next to her.

"I certainly hope that's not *your* baby," the woman said.

Katy smiled shyly. "No, it's my sister's."

"So, you're giving your sister a break from the little one?" Katy saw that the woman had lovely, smooth, dark skin and eyes so dark they were almost black. Her dress was sky blue and made from a type of shimmery silk Katy had never seen before.

"My sister's dead, ma'am."

"I'm very sorry. I know what it means to be without a sister," she said gravely, staring out at the river.

Katy felt tears well up in her eyes. Compassion was something rare and unexpected for Katy, like the appearance of an exotic butterfly.

The woman leaned closer and asked, "So, you are Medéwewen?"

Katy stared at her blankly, "No, ma'am, my name is Katy."

The woman eyed her critically. "Then you've taken nabagûck—a medicine? You wouldn't be able to see me, otherwise."

"I've taken nothin'," she stopped short. "No, that isn't right. I took my sister's medicine."

"Is she Medéwewen?" The woman was sitting close to her now. Her gaze was intense, and her eyes had an inexplicable red glow.

Katy felt nervous and looked around her. "No, ma'am. Her name was Bridget."

The woman looked up into the clouds, as if seeking answers there. "Katy, will you bring me this medicine you took? You see, you, or your sister, have found a sacred elixir—a drug that could be very dangerous, if it found its way into the wrong hands. There are evil men in the world. We, sisters, must do everything in our power to stop them."

"Ma'am, I'm sure my sister bought that medicine, she didn't take it from nobody."

The woman put her large hand on Katy's, and Katy felt an electric current run through her hand to her heart. "I'm sure that it was hers," the woman said reassuringly.

The baby began to cry. Katy promised to bring the elixir and said a hurried good-bye.

As Katy limped along the LaSalle Bridge, she turned to look at the park bench; the woman was gone.

In December, Charlie bought tickets to the new movie "Lost Horizon" to have, as he put it, "a little Christmas." In the theater, Katy was transported to *Shangri-La*, a warm, Tibetan paradise where everyone was beautiful, and no one ever died. But when the lights turned back on in the theater, she saw again the shredded lining of her tweed coat and the pool of melted snow beneath her scuffed and dirty boots.

She remembered too how Charlie had approached her later that night, smelling like salami and whiskey. She remembered his clumsy embrace that had momentarily made her close her eyes and believe that she was a movie star, but then everything quickly turned into a nightmare of warm, sticky breath, cold belt buckle against her stomach, and pain. Stifled rage and revulsion for him quickly overcame her. Hatred wrapped its roots around her heart.

The woman on the park bench had been right. There are evil men in the world; sisters must stick together.

Only the changing geometry of the shadows on the walls and floors told Katy that time was passing: she emptied the pan filled with water from the leaking roof; she laundered the bed linens; she swept the kitchen floor; she fed the baby. She poured herself a teaspoon of the Soothing Lily and drank it. She felt its warmth radiate through her chest.

That evening, when Charlie had finished plowing through a steaming plate of pot roast and potatoes, he raised his head and looked into Katy's arctic blue eyes: their tiny pupils focused on some bleak, interior landscape. He wiped the gravy off his mouth. "Full. Can't eat another bite." He stood for a moment, gripping the back of his chair and sucking bits of pork out of his teeth. Katy cupped her left elbow in her right hand and pressed her fingers gently against her lips, like a child who has forgotten her lines in a school play.

"Well," he said, stretching his arms above his head. "I'm goin' to Jimmy's tonight. You just, you just relax here and listen to the radio." He leaned over and gave her an awkward, folksy pat on the shoulder. He left, and, for a while, she continued to stare at the door. She stood up and cleared the dishes from the table. She took just a spoonful of her sister's medicine to calm her nerves.

Later that night, she listened to the radio and comforted the crying baby. Katy walked back and forth across the braided rug, patting the baby rhythmically on the behind. She'd wait till eleven to give her a bottle; she'd sleep better that way. She squirted some of the milk on her wrist to check the temperature. Finally, she sat down in the rocking chair, and the baby, frantic with excitement, latched onto the nipple.

On the radio, an organ progressed through a series of disquieting minor chords with increasing volume.

"Paul Gordon, listen!"
"I can't see anyone. Who's that?"
"I am the Shadow!"
[The sound of Gordon whimpering]
"Stop! We haven't much time. We must hurry, Gordon, you're in the Death House charged with murder."
"Yes, I'm innocent! I'm innocent, but nobody knows it!"
"Take courage, Gordon. The Shadow knows."

She rocked the baby back and forth, back and forth. At last, the baby fell asleep, but Katy still felt anxious, restless. She gently placed the sleeping baby on the sofa and took a little more of her sister's medicine.

She returned to the rocking chair, pulled an afghan over her, and fell asleep. When the wall clock struck three, she awoke. The house was dark and quiet. Charlie must have come home, turned the lights off, and collapsed upstairs on the bed.

The beautiful woman in the blue dress was calling to her again.

Katy got up and walked up the stairs. Charlie's long, ripping snores increased in volume.

In the dark, her fingers searched for and found a small, glass, faceted doorknob. She turned it and let her fingers palpate the fabrics in the closet, feeling for the long, silvery-blue, silk scarf that an elderly neighbor had given Bridget. She had said that it would look pretty with her long dark hair. Katy had always thought the fabric was the work of angels. Her rough fingers caught on the feathery silk, which she disentangled from the coarser garments in her sister's wardrobe. She wrapped the scarf around her neck.

The tired metal bed springs suddenly compressed and released. Charlie's snores stopped. She stood paralyzed, rocking with the tempo of her own furiously beating heart. Her eyes strained to see movement. A drop of water fell from the ceiling to the waiting bucket. Charlie muttered something unintelligible, puffed out a syllable of air, and began once again to snore.

When Katy's uncle had shot the raccoon, he had steadied the rifle against his shoulder then pulled the trigger. She tiptoed closer to the bedroom. The sheer that covered the window glowed white with the streetlight. She walked toward the rifle's dark silhouette, reaching out with both hands. She closed her right hand around the metal barrel and the left, round the wooden stock. She handled it awkwardly, maneuvering it gradually until the butt was against her shoulder. She inched forward noiselessly in her freshly laundered cotton socks until the barrel was two inches from Charlie's forehead, right between his eyes. Her finger explored the delicate curve of the trigger.

The pull and the gun's loud crack were one event. She stepped backwards, her ears ringing. A delicate wisp of smoke hung in the air like the blue incense that sometimes lingers after Sunday mass. Katy laid the gun down at the side of the bed. Charlie had a small hole between his eyes, and he wasn't snoring anymore.

She retraced her steps down the corridor and descended the creaking wooden stairs. She walked through the kitchen, stopping briefly to hang up Charlie's coat that he had flung carelessly on the table, then went into the living room where the baby still slept on the sofa. She put on her coat, wrapped the baby more snuggly in her blanket, and nestled her against her shoulder. She opened the front door.

A frozen fog was suspended in the March air, and each streetlight on Francis St. illuminated no more than the circle of mist that surrounded it. She descended the wooden stairs and turned right. Her boots crunched through the ice-lacquered snow as she headed towards Navarre Street. A light came on behind a curtain in the neighbor's house. Had they heard the gunshot? A few seconds passed; the light went off again. She followed Michigan St. until it intersected with LaSalle then turned left toward the bridge.

With the heavy snows in mid-February and the thaw that followed, the river had crept up and over its banks. It caressed the underside of the bridge and submerged the park benches to their armrests.

Katy tried to focus her nearsighted eyes in the darkness. Streetlights in the shape of grand candelabras glowed softly along the bridge. Soon, she'd be with Bridget; they'd have their own house—somewhere beautiful where birds sang and flowers bloomed all year round—just like *Shangri-La*.

The baby was preoccupied with the fresh wind on her face and the curious, unfamiliar objects passing before her eyes: the smokestack sentinels on the river's far side; the black, tangled branches now visible as the sky began to brighten.

Katy smoothed the child's silky hair and laid her down gently on the bridge's walkway. She tied one end of the scarf to her neck and the other end to the baby's. She pictured Charlie lying in the dark with a hole in his head. He would never see *Shangri-La*. Such places were not meant for men like Charlie.

In the fragile light of dawn, she could just see the shape of a woman, who sat on a park bench mostly submerged by the raging river.

"Katy!" the woman called.

The woman's eyes glowed red, and Katy was frightened. She had not thought to bring her the medicine.

She held the baby tightly against her chest, placed her foot on the bridge's lower railing, and launched herself into the river.

She heard the woman yell, "No!"

An implacable cold enveloped her; the water pulled the baby from her arms and tangled Katy's long, straight hair. A chaotic montage followed of bubbles, gray sky, and brownish-green water. Everything swirled and churned until it fit on the head of a pin.

Katy's body was seen as it fell over the French Paper Factory Dam thirteen miles downstream. The baby was found in a tangle of leaves, branches and newspaper above the dam. Her little legs were drawn up as if she'd been on a pony ride.

Inspector Jason W. Hull found a nearly empty bottle of "Soothing Lily" in the medicine cabinet in Charlie's house—a medicine that had been taken off the market after several lawsuits. No motive was found for the crime.

Chapter 12

Flight and Transfiguration

~ 1957 ~

Angela looked outside into the brilliant morning light and recoiled. She hadn't slept at all the previous night on the bus. It had been Irina's turn to sit by the window. In her aisle seat, she'd been unable to rest her head on anything except her friend's small, bony shoulder. She desperately wanted to rub her eyes, but she was still wearing makeup. She never appeared in public without makeup.

Irina was ahead of her in line, wearing her big, movie-star sunglasses inside the dark lobby of South Bend's LaSalle Hotel. She was tiny, and her glasses made her look bug-like. She was nearing the front of the queue of dancers waiting for room keys. She looked for Angela and waved for her to come to the front of the line. They were rooming together, as they always did.

Irina craned her neck to look out the window. Angela knew she was looking for the musicians' bus, which was usually late, since the driver, at his passengers' request, took frequent cigarette breaks. Irina's latest admirer, Salvador, was an oboe player. Irina looked up hopefully when the shadow of a bus passed across the mosaic floor of the hotel lobby. It was the truck with the props and scenery. Irina turned her attention back to the reception desk.

The corridor that led to their room was long and ended in a floor-to-ceiling window covered by a pink sheer drenched in spring sunshine. Trays with half-eaten sandwiches and empty bottles of champagne cluttered the corridor. They could hear laugh tracks from TVs and the voice of a small child. The smell of Lysol and coffee intermingled in the stagnant air. Angela tightly gripped the room key with an enormous wooden bauble at the end, as if she feared someone might take it from her. Room 747, at last.

Irina threw herself on the bed. "Smells funny in here." She wrinkled her tiny nose.

"The exterminator's been here."

"Cockroaches better than that smell." She put a pillow over her face.

"I don't think you mean that," Angela said in a business-like voice, as she arranged her purse and the room key on a dresser.

Irina removed the pillow, stretched her arms above her head, and closed her eyes.

"You're not going down to breakfast?" Angela asked.

"No, I can't," she said, shaking her head.

"That means no food unless we sneak out between the rehearsal and the show."

"I don't care," Irina said, her voice already becoming faint.

Angela placed her cosmetic case on the night table and her suitcase on the floor. She would skip breakfast too. But before she could sleep, she'd have to remove her makeup—all the layers of "flesh-colored" foundation to "correct" her skin color.

"You look almost Italian!" one of the dancers had said once as Angela was putting the finishing touches on her hair and make-up in the dressing room.

She pulled aside one of the drapes to look out their seventh-floor window and pressed her forehead to the cool glass. She could see the bridge and a black triangle that must be the river beneath it.

Be yourself, people said. But she knew there could be unpleasant consequences for being herself. Anyway, why would she want to be *just* herself? When the music started, she could be a snowflake, a princess, a cat. Being a swan was what came most naturally to her. The ballet master told her that he had never seen a dancer become a swan so effortlessly. Everything that was young woman in Angela melted away, and everything that was swan rushed in to take its place.

The sun was just peeking above the abandoned, brick, industrial buildings across the river. A red-tailed hawk landed on the ledge outside her window. Angela's heart leapt, as if it were a long lost friend. She looked into his dark eyes, and, for a moment, imagined that she could see what he saw. There were four gray pigeons perched on the telephone wire below, oblivious to any threat from above. The pigeons were warming their feathers in the morning sun—dreaming of hawthorn berries or little green beetles. Angela tapped on the glass; the pigeons flew away.

She dug her travel alarm clock out of her luggage, stretched herself out on the bed, and closed her eyes.

Sophie Verzul, a stately matron who wore her steel-gray hair in a bowl cut, sat at the piano, never altering her demeanor, no matter what scenes of hysteria, rage, or exultation took place on the stage before her.

She bowed her head slightly, acknowledging the ballet master's request for the allegro moderato from *Dances of the Swans*. Sophie had to play loud enough to be heard over the sound of toe shoes slapping the wooden floor. Miguel Terechensky, the ballet master, counted as the four ballerinas, one of whom was Irina, linked arms, and moved diagonally across the stage.

Angela had slept a few hours and downed two cups of syrupy, black coffee from an urn in the lobby before hurrying to rehearsal with Irina. By two, they were both beginning to feel light-headed from hunger. Irina finished rehearsing her part, and they both changed into their street clothes to find something to eat. The pavement was radiating heat, and a warm breeze carried the smell of car exhaust and lilacs.

They found a bakery, The Moderne, with a glittering, old-world, green and black stained-glass storefront. They went inside, found a booth, and ordered two eclairs a piece, which they washed down with mugs of hot chocolate. They sat stunned and glassy eyed.

When Irina left for the restroom, Angela took out her compact to check her make-up and noticed the letter she had pushed to the bottom of her purse. It was from the ballet company's director, Alexsey Morozov. She wasn't sure that she wanted to look at it again. Morosov had written that he was looking for ways to feature her in next season's ballets. Would she be free to talk after the show—perhaps over a drink?

She hadn't mentioned the letter to Irina, even though they kept few secrets from each other.

Irina returned to her seat. She held the edge of the table, turning to crack her spine, then her neck. Angela quickly scanned the room to see if anyone had noticed. Such a petite, feminine creature doing something so uncouth in public was comic but also slightly embarrassing.

"Did you notice that Nina wasn't riding with Morozov. She was on our bus. I wonder if something happened," Angela said.

"She's gettin' too thin." Irina winced.

"You suppose she's sick of him?"

Irina lifted her eyebrows in faux shock. "That's not the way it works, darlink. Men like Morozov always want something new." A police car passed by with the siren on, and Irina looked out the window. With her winged eyeliner and dark hair, she reminded Angela of some Egyptian queen.

"You suppose she'll just go back to being in the corps? I mean, if it's over between the two of them?" Angela asked.

Irina shrugged. "Maybe she'll go somewhere else. She's had big roles. Maybe she could be principal—someplace not so big."

Angela thought of Morozov: his deep, bass voice, his Mercury coupe, his voluminous, black, belted overcoat, the way he would emerge from a veil of cigarette smoke to deliver some command to the stage crew or dancer. After shows, he'd sit backstage with the ballet master and drink whiskey. Had he been watching her during rehearsals? The thought triggered a wave of warmth, which she could feel rising into her cheeks.

"You going to eat that donut?" Irina asked, pointing to the partially eaten eclair Angela had left on her plate.

"No, no. Take it, please."

Irina wrapped up the eclair in a napkin and stuffed it in her purse. Angela sometimes forgot what kind of life Irina had left behind in Soviet Russia.

Angela looked at her watch. "Oh, God! We've got to go." They plucked coins from their change purses to pay the bill, then went back out onto the street. They squinted in the bright light; Irina dropped her movie star sunglasses from the top of her head to her eyes.

"You meeting Salvy after the show tonight?" Angela asked.

Irina smiled coquettishly. "*May*-be. Why you don't meet with his brother Francisco? Francisco is out his mind for you."

"Oh, maybe, sometime. He just seems like, like… such a boy."

"What's wrong with boys! Boys are nice. Boys are sweet."

"I don't want sweet. I want something else," Angela said, putting her hands in her pockets and gazing up into the rooftops.

"What?"

"I don't know." She stopped, then smiled and continued on. "I do know—power."

Irina turned her plastic, bug-eyes toward Angela and shook her head. "No, my darlink, you don't want that."

"Why?"

Irina shrugged. "Well…well, you can't have it, so no point."

Sunlight reflected from a hundred different points of steel and glass on the city street and coalesced in Angela's head like a scream. On their way back to the Morris Theatre, the young women turned north on Michigan Street, where a herd of cars with steel-toothed radiators were waiting to race south and into the endless cornfields.

The ache at the base of Angela's skull migrated to her eye where it began to pulse. She needed her medicine.

"I've got to pick something up at the pharmacy. See you back-stage," Angela said over her shoulder as she quickened her step.

Irina watched her friend, with her ponytail of black curls, maneuver around a group of parcel-laden women with small children who were standing at a bus shelter. Even when Angela wasn't wearing toe shoes, she moved as if some force were pulling her skyward—as if she would spring into the clouds if there weren't so many people watching.

Backstage, Angela cast her eyes down the row of dancers seated before the lit make-up mirror—everyone was busily correcting major and minor imperfections with wax, powder, and paint.

She looked in the mirror and saw that Irina was smiling slyly and doing a mazurka step as she approached with a letter pinched in her fingertips. She put the letter on the table in front of Angela with a dramatic flourish and mazurka-ed away. The handwriting was Morozov's. She'd wait until after the show to read it.

The swans adjusted each other's costumes on their way to the stage and nervously whispered words of encouragement. Angela saw Morozov as he went out on stage to deliver the introduction to the ballet. His dress shoes slapped the floor as he approached the microphone. She imagined how he appeared to the audience—his well-tailored black suit, deep voice, exotic Russian accent. Was there something in his voice tonight for her? Was he thinking of her and wondering if she was backstage listening to him?

The curtain went up on the evil sorcerer Rothbart's kingdom, bathed in blue moonlight. Rothbart transformed all the women into swans, and then hunters with bows appeared, frightening the swans. Odette, the beautiful swan queen, and Siegfried, the handsome prince, fell in love—just as they'd fallen in love every Saturday night at around 7:45 p.m. in every small city between Tallahassee and Toledo. And every time they fell in love, Rothbart, dressed in a glittering black cape, sent his scheming, beautiful daughter, who looked exactly like Odette, to lure Siegfried away. Every time, he fell for it and realized too late that he'd missed his one chance to free his true love from her enchantment.

Applause thundered throughout the theater, the curtain came down, and the house lights slowly came back up.

As soon as she was in the dressing room, Angela tore open the letter. Morozov wanted to meet her in the bar in the theater's basement. She took off her swan costume and handed it to Sophie Verzul, who was collecting them. Angela's gaze rested a moment on Sophie's implacable face and matronly bosom. She'd commit suicide rather than change places with Sophie, she thought. But what had this woman done to provoke such horror?

As she walked along the dark, backstage hallway to the exit, she saw that one of the heavy metal doors had been propped open to let in fresh air. Irina and Salvador were out on the fire escape. He had his arm around her neck and they were laughing as they shared a drink from a paper cup. Irina wouldn't be looking for her any time soon.

In the hotel room, she rifled through her suitcase, looking for her orange satin dress with the plunging neckline. Nicky the violinist had said she looked "delicious" in that. She held the dress up to her face and looked in the mirror. Yes, she actually did look Italian. She tossed her head back. This was how she'd smile when she saw him—free and easy, just like they were old friends. And this is what she looked like when she laughed. She tilted her head back and opened her mouth in a wide smile. God, what the hell was she doing?

She pursed her lips. She needed lipstick. Sophia Verzul's dry, bloodless lips suddenly presented themselves to her imagination. She shuddered. How old was Sophia? When would her own plump, kissable lips look like that?

It was 10:15 p.m., according to the clock by her bed. He had set their meeting time for 10:30 p.m. How did he know that she'd be free then? Had it actually been a request?

She changed into her orange dress, put on her tan high heels and threw a light-weight sweater over her shoulders. Should she wear the yellow agate bracelet her mother had given her? It was a family heirloom passed down from some unhappy ancestor whose story she couldn't remember. The bracelet was too big for her tiny wrist, so she slid it up her forearm. She looked at herself in the mirror: her black hair hung loose about her shoulders; her brown eyes, direct, magnetic. She caressed her face and called herself "Raven," just as her mother had done. A faint shudder passed through her.

She could feel the familiar ache at the base of her skull. She might as well take a dose now before her migraine got any worse. She extracted a tear-drop shaped bottle from her make-up bag, removed the cork, and drank some of the bitter liquid. She had bought it from a woman selling botanical medications outside the pharmacy. Couldn't hurt, she thought. Just plants. She sat for a few moments on the edge of the bed to collect herself. She should probably be measuring this stuff. The important thing was that it worked.

She locked the door and left the key at the front desk for Irina. She didn't want to run into any of the other dancers on her way to the bar to meet Morozov, but she knew that was more than she could hope for. More than once Francisco had asked her to meet him for a drink, but she had always come up with an excuse. What if he saw her with Mr. Morozov? Listen to her: "Mr." Morozov, as if this weren't the man who had asked her out for a drink. Should she call him "Aleksey"? Or "Alyosha"—that's what his Russian friends called him. She made herself take a deep breath. There was nothing to worry about: it was just a drink.

The interurban rattled out of sight as she left the hotel. An elderly couple were walking arm and arm as they left the theater. The old woman looked at Angela and then whispered something to her husband, who also threw her a furtive look. Angela rolled over on her ankle awkwardly as she stepped off the curb. God, she needed to be more careful. Who'd promote a lame ballerina to principal?

Tiny leaves were just beginning to unfold on the trees outside the theater. Moths fluttered against the marquee lights—*Ballet Russe de Monte Carlo, Tonight, Sold Out*.

She was surprised by the sparkling gilt and white columns in the theater's foyer; the back entrance used by the dancers and musicians had been far less prepossessing. She followed the arrow directing customers to the basement bar. As she descended the curved staircase, she let her hand glide along the cool, reassuring marble handrail. Big band music played in the bar—the kind of music old people listened to. A young man bounded up the stairs with a cigarette precariously perched on his lower lip; he smiled at her knowingly. She put her head down.

She opened the door of the restaurant. In a spotlight, a woman dressed in an emerald green gown pressed her lips against the microphone with her eyes closed. Angela scanned the crowd. All the tables were two-tops in a faux French bistro style. A woman in her forties with dyed hair leaned forward, displaying her cleavage as she smoked a cigarette. A fat, balding man with tired eyes struggled to extract bills from his wallet at the bar. She could feel covert glances directed her way from around the room. She tightened her grip on the handle of her purse.

A man's large hands suddenly grabbed her waist from behind.

Angela stood stock still, shocked by the forcefulness of his grasp. His hand then traveled to her forearm as he pulled her toward one of the tables. She was flustered and took a bit too long before meeting his gaze.

"You thought I wasn't coming, didn't you?" Morozov said.

"I didn't know what to think," she said gravely. Then, deciding that was not the persona she wished for tonight added, "Well, I wasn't kept in suspense for long." She smiled.

The waiter came to the table. He was Black and looked at Angela a little longer than she felt was necessary.

"What will you have? Anything you like," Morozov said.

"I'll have a whiskey and soda."

"Girl after my own heart. Make that two."

The waiter left. The woman in the emerald dress sang: "*Is that all there is, is that all there is? If that's all there is, my friends, then let's keep dancing. Let's break out the booze and have a ball…*"

They both looked at the stage. The music was loud enough to make conversation difficult. She noticed that he was looking at her profile. The music was over. Everyone applauded.

"You look beautiful. Absolutely stunning." He leaned back and surveyed her as if he was admiring a painting he'd just purchased. She thought she heard a little click from his mouth, as if he had too much saliva.

She gave a flicker of a smile in polite acknowledgement of his compliment. "Why did you invite me out?"

He raised his eyebrows and then gave a controlled chortle. He bit his lower lip and looked down, suddenly slightly demure. "I thought *that* would be clear." She noticed that his cheeks were smooth like a baby's. Had he shaved himself or gone to a barber shop that morning to get someone else to do it for him in anticipation of this evening? He leaned back in his seat with both hands cupped round his on-the-rocks glass, silent as if he were struggling with the dark, mysterious world of his emotional life. Finally, he brought out: "I admire you." He locked her in his gaze for a moment.

She was conscious of the way the orange dress clung to her chest as she breathed. She felt the wet cold of the glass against her lip. "That's very kind of you." She thought that sounded like something her fourth-grade teacher would have said, but she let it stand. She wasn't sure where she was going with this.

"So, the two of us haven't had a chance to talk." He leaned across the table and patted her hand, taking charge of the conversation. She noticed he was wearing a large ring that glittered. Not a wedding ring; it was a red stone. Garnet? Ruby? She could smell his aftershave lotion. It was a dark, musky scent that evoked a previous era—like the smell of an old lady's fur coat.

"So, tell me: what you think of my company?"

"It's a wonderful company. Miquel does such a great job. He's demanding, but he's forgiving. I guess you could say the choreography, well, it's a little trite—I mean, that is what some of the newspapers say—but audiences want the classics."

He looked puzzled by what she had said, as if he hadn't fully understood but didn't care enough to ask for clarification. "And what do you think of Alicia, eh?"

He was referring to Alicia Alonso, the world-renowned Cuban prima ballerina, who was traveling with the troupe as a guest star.

"Flawless. You can tell the Cubans…"

Morozov motioned to someone he recognized at the bar. He got up from the table with some difficulty. "You'll excuse me for a few moments, Angela." He put his hands on her shoulders in a heavy caress. "I see an old friend." Angela watched him saunter over to the bar where a small man was smiling intensely through his black mustache. Morozov clapped him on the back then kissed him on both cheeks. He put his arm around his friend's neck as if he was letting him in on an important secret. The other man smiled and looked in Angela's direction. Angela sipped her drink and looked around the room. She saw Salvador's back. He was giving a few bills to the bartender. Had he seen her? Irina must be back in the hotel room changing. They'd find some bar where there was cheap beer and rockabilly music—someplace where everyone was young, and the dance floor was crowded.

Morozov returned to the table. He put his hand on her arm. "You were saying how much you liked Cuban ballet."

She didn't bother to correct him. They talked about the guest artists. Igor Youskevitch, the male lead, and Alicia's partner.

"Igor said to me, he said: I'll never work for you. And look, you see, how the mighty fall?" Morozov laughed. One of his teeth in the back of his mouth was gold. The music started again, and they both looked at the singer. Angela wasn't really listening. When the set ended, he leaned over, letting his arm touch hers.

"You want to go for a walk?" he asked, as if his words might be code for something else.

"Okay," she said.

Morozov tipped the waiter extravagantly, perhaps for her sake. He put his hand up to silence the waiter's protests.

A warm breeze tousled the ruffled hem of her dress as soon as she went outside. A pigeon fluttered to the ground to pick at a dropped pretzel, and Angela looked up to see if there was a hawk watching. The "Hertz Rent-a-Car" sign pulsed a violent, blood-red.

"We could walk to the river?" Angela said. Ahead, she saw a white barricade with red diagonal stripes; "Bridge Closed" the sign read. A strong wind came out of the East, tossing the branches with their newly formed buds this way and that.

He belted his coat and pulled her close. "Why not? Anything you say." Soon, she thought, he would say something cornball like "you are the princess of my heart." But not yet. It was a bit soon for that. She could smell his sweat. Why did he always wear that big coat? What was he hiding?

Angela wondered if she should have had a drink after the medicine she took. She usually didn't go for any homeopathic stuff, but she thought it must be healthier than the low-strength butalbital she'd been taking. And she really liked the glass vial it came in.

"I've been thinking about adding a new kind of dance to our performances, and you have been my inspiration."

They walked around the wooden barricade on the bridge. What was that strange sound she heard? It wasn't normal speech—just s's and th's. Like the sound of snakes whispering.

"I'm thinking of adding something entirely new—an African dance. Maybe a piece that features Zulu warriors."

Her heart was beating so fast. She felt as though she needed to operate this creature called Angela even though she no longer fully inhabited her body. She needed to make this Angela-doll say something appropriate.

"Will I wear toe shoes or dance barefoot?"

Morozov chuckled. "Toe shoes on Zulu? Very funny."

The whispering was getting louder. And she could hear the water—a rushing that filled her ears. She could even see underwater— the black leaves rotting; the silvery sway of fish. She knew that Morozov was still walking next to her, and that she would have to make Angela say something to him.

"I'm feeling a little lightheaded."

Beneath them, a branch that had been blocking the water suddenly broke free, and a wave of silt and mud was released into the water. A hawk pushed off from a sycamore branch above their heads. The beating of its wings was deafening, but she could see that he heard nothing.

Cascading water and the turbulent air of the approaching storm filled Angela's consciousness, but, as if through a small window, she could still see Morozov—the chubbiness of his smiling cheeks. He reached out and put his index finger to her nose, "You, my darling, are not used to drink. Whiskey's a man's drink."

Angela's pupils had become dark caves. They were standing on the bridge above the bend in the river. The lights of an old brick power plant came on. Morozov was watching her intently, like a predator watches its prey. In the chaos that had now flooded her every thought and sensation, she was struggling to remain aware that he was there at all.

"Penny for your thoughts," Morozov said, putting his hands around her waist and drawing her closer to him. Angela stared straight ahead. He moved in closer. His lips brushed her ear: "Would you like to dance?"

Angela smelled whiskey, Eau de Cologne, and decay. Her heart turned into a wild animal caged in her chest, but it had nothing to do with Morozov. The words were perfectly articulated in her head: *She* is here. Over Morozov's shoulder, Angela could see a figure on the opposite side of the bridge.

Morozov nuzzled her neck, and his hands moved up to her breasts. Angela caressed his hand, tenderly stroked his fingers, and brought his hand to her lips. He howled in pain, backed away and held his bleeding hand to his chest. She had sunk her teeth into his palm.

"Go," Angela said. Her voice was deep and stern and impossible to challenge.

Morozov stared at her and shook his head. "Crazy woman. You… you never dance with my company again." His smooth, chubby cheeks trembled like an injured child about to cry.

Angela felt no regret. She was happy that he no longer obstructed her view of the beautiful woman with the long black hair across the bridge. The woman looked at the retreating figure of Morozov with her eyes glowing red and claws extended.

"No," said Angela.

"Do men behave…thus?" The woman's voice echoed in her head.

"Power ruins some," said Angela, who knelt and bowed her head as the woman approached.

Clouds raced across the face of the full moon.

"Rise, Thunderbird!"

Angela's blood seemed to boil, and a pins-and-needles sensation enveloped her skin. Hard bristles emerged from her pores, becoming long, black feathers, iridescent in the streetlight and rustling like silk. Her arms turned into wings. She flapped them gently, admiring their strength and beauty. A strong gust of wind blew in from the East. She jumped onto the bridge's railing and looked into the dark, turbulent waters, swollen from the spring rains and snowmelt. She lifted her wings and the air carried her up into the sky. She hung there suspended, then, fell rapidly twenty feet towards the river, flapping her wings helplessly. She pitched her body forward and flapped as hard as she could. Her wing tips dipped into the cold water, but she beat them furiously and began to rise.

She used her shoulders and her back, flapping her wings until she had reached a great height above the city where gusts of air carrying vaporous clouds flew past her. Below, she saw tiny streetlights and headlights that merged into rivers of light, as she flew higher. She lifted her head and gave a loud, guttural cry of joy.

Rolling out beneath her was the illuminated grid of the city streets and beyond that the occasional barn light like a beacon in the blackness. She could smell the newly-tilled earth and sense the other birds—the quick tempo of their hearts as their brains whirled with trajectories of flight.

She looked up. She had forgotten about the sky. All her life, she had never looked up. Everything below was untethered and subject to change, but the dark sky was eternal.

As she descended, the great cacophony in her head fell silent. The sound of the river was now nothing but a distant murmur, and the pigeons offered up their throaty coos to the rising sun.

Angela heard a light switch snap on.

"Well, some people know how to have good time," Irina said, looking both amused and relieved.

Angela detached the hair glued to the side of her mouth with saliva. She looked around the sunlit hotel room.

"You took too much of this," Irina said, holding up tear-shaped glass bottle. "I told Morozov when he came to the door last night that you were asleep. He laughed. The bus is waiting. You have to hurry."

All the images from the previous night came back to her. She was still wearing her orange dress and agate bracelet. For the first time, she noticed that the pattern on the stones resembled a map—veins of blue crystal looked like rivers; white ridges, like mountains. Could it be pointing her in some new direction?

"You can do your makeup now. I'm out of bathroom," Irina said.

Angela propped herself up on her elbows and saw that a pigeon was sunbathing on the ledge outside their window.

"No, I'm not doing the makeup anymore."

CHAPTER 13

THE POWER PLANT

~ 1970 ~

Storms in Chicago delayed Alan's return flight. He didn't get back to South Bend until after 10 p.m., but he wasn't going to let that stop him from doing the job site inspection. He didn't want to be the cause of another hold-up in construction.

Besides, this inspection wasn't for another burger joint or strip mall. This was a big-budget, civic building project, unlike anything the city had seen in years. They'd scrapped plans for an interior courtyard filled with peacocks and toucans, and the one-hundred-foot catwalk was rejected out of safety concerns. But a gleaming edifice of concrete, steel, and glass would arise from the crumbling mills and factories that lined the St. Joseph River.

Alan parked his blue Dodge Charger next to a beat-up, silver Mustang with a flat tire in an otherwise empty parking lot. He walked past the unoccupied guard house. He unlocked the gate and turned on the flood lights. One padlock to protect an eleven-acre construction site? What were they thinking?

The construction aggregate was too coarse and the rebar insufficient, but things otherwise looked ready for the footers. Next, he'd take a look at the old hydroelectric power plant. The New York City architects wanted to know how much, if any, of the seventy-year old building could be saved.

The power plant was a squat brick building astride a canal made from diverted river water. He went to the side entrance they'd left unlocked. Hundreds of moths congregated like supplicants around the light in the graffiti painted doorway. Alan put on the miner's headlamp his wife had given him as a birthday gift, kicked away some empty beer cans, and tugged open the huge metal door. Cold, damp air reached out of the dark, chilling his bare arms. He walked along a concrete platform to a spiral metal staircase—the building was part submarine, part mausoleum. Hard to believe that when his grandfather had worked in this plant, seventy years ago, it had been state of the art in hydroelectric facilities. The turbines had lit up the six-story Oliver Hotel and Opera House.

At the bottom of the spiral stairs, there was another large metal door with blistering paint. He couldn't get it open more than about eighteen inches, so he turned his body sideways and shimmied in. His headlamp wasn't enough to illuminate the large turbine room, so he took out his aluminum flashlight. Several of the railings intended to keep workers away from the transformer were missing. There were significant gaps in the grated, metal flooring above the turbines. A large rat scampered off under the duct work.

Seventy years ago, it must have been deafening here. His flashlight illuminated the ballooning dark spots on the ceiling where there were leaks in the roof. The concrete floor had puddles; a grayish-green mold was creeping up the stone walls. If they wanted to turn this building into high-end apartments, they had a lot of work to do.

Alan walked between the turbines and had just found the intake pipe when his flashlight died. "Damn it," he whispered. He was going to have to swap out the batteries from his headlamp to use in the flashlight.

Luckily, a little light was coming in from the row of windows above his head. An odd feeling crept over him. He looked up. Someone was standing at the window, pressed against the glass, looking in. Despite the darkness, he felt sure it was examining him, as if he were prey. The eyes reflected a red light. A fine comb ran over his back and down his arms.

He didn't want to turn on his flashlight. He didn't want to do anything to reveal where he was, but he also didn't want to fall twenty feet onto concrete. He felt for the railing closest to the turbine and followed that to its end. Then, he found the staircase, and when he reached the top, he knew where the metal door should be. His shin ran directly into a metal pipe. He suppressed a howl of pain, while his eyes teared up. Why was he letting this unnerve him, he thought, as he made his way in a panic up the stairs. He opened the door, where the muffled flutter of a hundred moth wings greeted him.

Whatever it was had been outside. Now, he was out there with it. He walked swiftly across the construction site and fumbled briefly with the combination lock, looking back quickly over his shoulder at the power plant. His blue Dodge Charger was bathed in the glow of the blue, mercury vapor light. He could hear the whistle of a freight train in the distance. He got into his car and locked the doors.

Alan hadn't slept well the night before, and the local historian's lecture was not helping him stay awake.

"The Potawatomies were a dignified and friendly tribe accustomed to dealing with White traders. South Bend was principally a trading and portage area for them rather than a home base." The historian paused and with one finger pushed his heavy black glasses back up the bridge of his nose. He looked pointedly at Alan, as if aware of his lack of engagement. He took a sip of water and continued. "Coquillard wished to supervise this forced emigration to ensure that the Indians would not suffer undue hardship. While the friendship between the Indians and White settlers was deep and real, the Indian influence was truncated in South Bend by the 1840 resettlement."

The District Attorney, late to the 9:00 a.m. tax commissioners' meeting, spotted Alan and quietly made his way to his side of the board table, sinking into the chair next to him with the air of having just outrun a rabid dog.

"The early traders were great friends with the local Indian tribes and spoke their languages well," the historian continued.

"Hey, Alan," the District Attorney whispered, laying a hand on his shoulder. Alan picked his head up. He'd had his chin in his hand and had been doodling a picture of a large eyeball on his otherwise blank legal pad.

"Hey, Jerry."

Jerry still had his high-school era surfer-boy cool, despite his slightly receding hairline and the reading glasses he self-consciously slipped out of his pocket whenever handed a document he needed to sign. He wore his sideburns long like men twenty years younger.

They both feigned interest in the speaker for a few moments, then Jerry leaned over to Alan and said, "Did you get a chance to visit the site last night?"

Alan immediately saw before him the red eyes he had seen in the power plant. "Yeah." He studied his legal pad for a moment.

"Well?"

Alan took off his wire rim glasses and began to clean them with a small, white cloth. "There are railings missing around the transformer, wide-open twenty-foot drops onto concrete floors, rats. Egress windows and doors are inadequate, meaning that there are none. Most of the interior space is located within the river's flood zone. Overall, I'd say, it's structurally unsound and dangerous to human life."

Jerry smiled and ran both hands through his tousled hair. "So ready for occupation."

"If you like lawsuits," Alan said, putting his glasses back on.

"And you know I do. Our New York City architects may want the power plant preserved, but the locals want it gone. What I really need is a report laying out the pros and cons. They can argue about it, resolve it, and my office can move on."

Alan shrugged. "It really depends on how much of the original building they want to keep. Are they thinking about preserving the old millwork and beams?"

Jerry smiled at the presenter then put his head down and whispered: "Look, I don't know anything about the architectural or construction stuff. I just agreed to act as legal counsel. Rodger's our building supervisor, so I'll connect you with him."

"OK. You got some format for this report?" Alan asked, as he clicked his pen.

"Yup, Rodger's got that too. It's pretty straightforward."

"I'll shoot for getting that to you by Friday."

"Great," said Jerry, pushing his chair back decisively.

"Oh, wait. I didn't get a chance to check out the transformer. Somebody's got to get that out of there, but I'm not sure how difficult that's going to be."

"You can add an addendum about the transformer later. You free on Friday night? I was thinking we could go out for a beer."

"Sure. Wife's out of town. I've got nothing on my calendar."

"Great. You okay with Kubiak's? Not too low-rent for you?"

"It'll be fine," Alan answered with a deadpan expression. "I'll bring my own brass rails, ferns, and mahogany."

Jerry gave him one of his election-winning smiles and took his official seat at the head of the table.

Alan went back to drawing eyes on his legal pad.

A thick layer of smoke made Alan's eyes water as they opened the door to Kubiak's. It was already crowded, and it took them a while to work their way to the last two unoccupied stools at the end of the bar.

The bartender wiped down the counter in front of them with one hand and picked up an empty beer glass with the other.

"Gentlemen?"

"Give me a Pabst," Jerry said.

Alan cast his eyes along the rows of jewel-colored bottles, then focused on the tap handles. "Got any Drewry's?"

Jerry looked at him with feigned disgust. "That's an old man's beer."

"I *am* an old man, my friend."

Alan reached into his back pocket to get out his wallet.

"No, it's on me tonight." Jerry turned to the bartender. "Open a tab." Jerry gestured to two women with sky-blue eyeshadow and long blond hair who were standing by the small stage having a heated conversation with the owner. "Exotic dancers tonight."

"I wouldn't call them 'exotic.' Look local and corn-fed to me," Alan said, sipping his beer as he leaned against the bar. "You heard anything about kids or vagrants hanging out at the power plant?"

"Sure. Plenty," said Jerry, as he lowered himself onto a barstool. "But the DA's office has the right to reject cases when the offense occurred at a nonresidential property. We hear about people trespassing, but nothing gets prosecuted. Why? Did you see something?"

"Yeah, I saw somebody when I was doing the inspection Tuesday night." He shrugged his shoulders and looked vaguely at the stage where the performers were still setting up. "The light wasn't good. Just curious."

"Jerry!" A broad-shouldered, tall guy with a wind-burnt complexion and a bristly gray flattop was vigorously shaking Jerry's hand.

Jerry leaned over to Alan, "You know Jack?" Alan shook Jack's big, leathery hand.

Jack gave him a good-natured smile and turned his attention back to Jerry. "Did you buy that Arctic Cat we saw up in Kalkaska?" They launched into a conversation about snowmobiling, and Alan drifted back to his own thoughts. He hadn't expected to enjoy himself at Kubiak's. He knew that he needed some way to punctuate the end of a work week and get his mind off that weird thing he'd seen in the power plant. So, it wasn't unusual for vagrants to go looking for a little heat and shelter at the power plant. The red eyes must have been a reflection.

Jerry and Jack had to shout at each other to be heard above the music. As the noise level in the bar inched up a few more decibels, Alan felt himself detach. The multi-colored liquor bottles behind the bar, the couples dancing near the stage, the two men playing pool in the corner all became part of a show he was watching.

Jerry finished one beer and then ordered another. A friend brought him a whiskey, and he ordered himself a second. It was now clear why Jerry had suggested that Alan drive. A diminutive brunette with tight curls led Jerry out onto the dance floor. When they returned to the bar, he was leaning on her for support, and she was wincing, eager to get away.

A man with a red baseball cap and thick tortoise shell glasses stood up at the bar and said with a smirk, "Hey, everybody, a toast to the District Attorney!"

Jerry's eyes were now watery, pink, and unfocused. He raised his glass and addressed the crowd at the bar. "To Truth and Justice!"

"To Truth and Justice," they answered with faux solemnity. Jerry polished off his fourth whiskey.

Alan turned away from the spectacle that Jerry had become. A striking young woman with long, glossy, black hair was walking unsteadily past the pool table in the direction of the ladies' room. Some local farm boy with sunburnt cheeks and a green Pioneer Seed Corn hat paused the shot he was lining up to watch her walk past. Alan's heart started to beat faster as if he was planning to leap to her defense, but the kid went back to his pool game.

Alan looked at his watch. Ten minutes had passed since the woman went into the bathroom. He waited another five. Maybe she'd OD'ed on something. He was a forty-two-year-old without kids. He didn't know anything about drugs, and he wasn't interested in learning. Someone should check on her.

Alan left his stool at the bar and went to find the owner's wife, Julie Ann, who usually worked in the kitchen. He'd been a few years behind her in high school. A wave of heat hit him as he opened the door to the kitchen. The back door was propped open, and the guys who had been making the burgers all night were outside playing toss with the empties. He could hear glass breaking and cheers. Julie Ann, a faded beauty wearing a bandana and blue jeans, was cleaning the grease out of the exhaust fan.

"Whacha need, sweetheart?"

"A young woman went into the ladies', and she's been in there for fifteen minutes."

Julie Ann twisted herself around to look at him. "Sometimes ladies take a while, hon."

"She looked like she was very drunk or high. I was thinking someone should check on her."

"Oh. Okay."

Julie Ann went to the sink to clean the grease off her hands. She couldn't find the soap, so she used Comet. Her hands were bright pink, the color of fresh hamburger, when she was finished. She grabbed a large set of keys from a hook hanging in a cupboard and went out into the crowded bar. Alan followed. She knocked on the bathroom door, waited, unlocked the door, and went inside. Almost immediately, she stuck her head out the door, glanced around for him, and motioned him in. The young woman had passed out and fallen to the floor.

"Poor dear," said Julie Ann. "Help me get her into the kitchen. There's a daybed in there we can put her on."

Alan picked her up. She was tall, willowy, but solid. She didn't have that superfluous softness most women had. Julie Ann moved a crate of plastic ketchup dispensers off the "daybed," which was actually a canvas cot. Alan gently put her down.

Julie Ann said that one of the bar's regulars was a doctor; she went in search of him. Alan was left alone to gaze at her. Even the harsh florescent light could not diminish the soft, warm glow of her skin, the rose-petal tenderness of her lips, the iridescence of her hair.

The doctor put his head around the edge of the door. He had short, curly, reddish blond hair and a cigarette stuck to his lower lip. "Whaddya got in here?"

Alan moved so the doctor could wedge his round beer belly through the partially open door and into the cramped kitchen. He was red in the face and sweating. He checked her pulse, looked at her fingernails, and felt her forehead. He was about to check her eyes but then seemed to decide against it.

"Pulse is slow but regular. Skin's cool and dry like she's dehydrated. Man, she's got well-developed pectoral and latissimus dorsi muscles. Must be a swimmer. She yours?"

"No, I just saw her go into the bathroom," Alan said, as if responding to an accusation. "She didn't look good."

"Finders keepers, I say." The doctor gave him a friendly nudge with his elbow. "Give her lots of water when she wakes up. Otherwise, she's fine." The doctor returned his gaze to the woman, as if compelled to do so. "Very fine."

"Thanks, Doc!" Julie Ann called out as she nudged a plastic bussing tray piled high with dirty plates and beer cans onto the already crowded countertop. She took a tablecloth out of a cupboard and draped it over her like a blanket. "She can stay in here and sleep it off." She went back to cleaning the exhaust fan.

When Alan returned to the bar, Jerry was whistling at the women who had come back on stage for an encore. Another whiskey arrived for Jerry. Alan's head was beginning to pound, and he wanted to leave. It was impressive how far Jerry had gotten in life with so little self-control.

The dancers quit the stage and moved to a small table where they unzipped their boots and rubbed their calves. Julie Ann's husband, who was carrying the cash drawer, sat down with them. The crowd slowly cleared except for a few guys who were still playing pool. Jerry was engaged in a heart-to-heart conversation with a sixtyish guy in a light-blue leisure suit.

Alan put his hand on Jerry's shoulder. "Hey Jerry, I want to go home."

Jerry looked at him as if he'd just materialized out of thin air. "Are you in a hurry or something?"

The bartender slung a dish towel over his shoulder. "Closing time, boys and girls!"

A harsh overhead light came on, which scattered most of the remaining customers.

Jerry said good-bye to his new friend and started weaving his way to the exit.

"That girl's still out. Can you take her home, hon?" Julie Ann had her hand on Alan's arm and was looking at him earnestly.

Alan had stopped by the door, so Jerry could sit down again. It was the third time he'd needed to sit down since leaving his barstool. "I've already got my hands full."

"I'd take her, hon, but we've got Phil's mom living with us, and she's sleeping on the sofa."

Alan rubbed his forehead. "Let me get Jerry out to the car. I'll be right back."

Jerry walked out to the parking lot as if he were walking into a strong wind. He leaned against Alan's Dodge Charger and threw up.

Julie Ann held the kitchen door open for Alan. Her pink tank top was wet with sweat, and a bra strap had fallen over one shoulder. Alan stood over the unconscious woman unsure where to put his hands. He'd have to get one under her thighs and the other under her back.

Electricity raced through his body when he picked her up: pure, radiant energy. He had never felt so alive.

Julie Ann walked ahead of him to open doors. One of the guys playing pool picked his head up and stared. His face looked as if it had been crudely chipped from an irregular piece of granite. Alan's attention was focused on steering a path between tables and chairs.

Outside, moonlight had enchanted the gravel parking lot, his Dodge Charger—even Jerry's slumped figure in the passenger seat. Alan placed the woman reverently in the back seat.

"Good night, hun." Julie Ann turned off the "open" sign. Alan could hear her talking softly but authoritatively to the guys still playing pool.

He thought about trying to secure Jerry's safety belt, but that was more than what he was willing to do for him at the moment. Alan sat behind the steering wheel. Unlike Jerry, it would never have occurred to him to go to a bar, get shit-faced and expect other people to take care of him.

He looked in the rearview mirror when he stopped at an intersection, but he couldn't see her. He turned around. She was facing the upholstery of the back seat. He could just see the soft slope of her hips. He felt an electrical current whip through his groin. He rolled down his window and let in the cool night air and the smell of new-mown hay.

Jerry lived in a sprawling suburban ranch with self-important pillars on opposite sides of the driveway. He hosted cocktail parties next to his inground pool that were meant to look like the advertisements in glossy magazines. The sprinklers were on when Alan pulled into the driveway. A plump, orange tabby cat looked out the picture window. Jerry's wife, Susan, quickly appeared and gave a cheery wave to Alan, as if he'd stopped by to play cards.

"Hi, Alan! Thanks a million for getting him home," she said, flashing him a super-white smile. There were smudges of mascara on her cheeks.

It took both of them to get Jerry into the house. Susan didn't appear to have noticed the woman in the backseat.

Alan got back behind the wheel. He lived northeast of town in a new subdivision, where the lots were smaller than in Jerry's neighborhood. He looked at the black macadam of the road before him, but his inner attention was focused solely on *her*. He imagined how her body was responding to every turn of the steering wheel, every bump on the road.

Who knows what would have happened if he had left her at Kubiak's. She'd be grateful to him when she woke up. She'd understand how vulnerable she'd been. A car was suddenly coming straight towards him and blasted its horn. He'd strayed into on-coming traffic. God, he needed to get a hold of himself. She was just some bimbo. Yet every cell in his body resisted that idea. He took some deep breaths.

He pulled into his driveway. It was a split-level gray house with yellow shutters. His wife had wanted an attached garage, so she wouldn't have to walk through the snow with groceries. She hadn't been thinking that it would also enable her husband to carry unconscious, beautiful women into the house without the neighbors noticing. He smiled, but then imagined what that smile must look like on his face under these circumstances. He shuddered.

He propped the house door open, picked up the girl, and kicked the car door closed. He carried her across the living room's deep pile carpet and laid her on the sofa like a holy offering. The faux gold mantle clock chimed: one, two, three.

Alan placed a large glass of water on the table next to the sofa. The doctor had said she was dehydrated. Impulsively, he took an English muffin out of the refrigerator and put it on a plate. What if she got sick? It wouldn't do for her to be on her back. She should really be on her side. He gently took her shoulders and rolled her onto her side, then put a pillow behind her back to keep her on her side. She sighed and her long, dark, lustrous hair fell across her face. The floor gave way beneath his feet.

The refrigerator switched on, and Alan heard the coolant trickling through the aluminum pipes. He turned on a light in the bathroom and slowly backed into his bedroom. What else could he do but leave her there?

He didn't feel like brushing his teeth. He lay in bed staring at the ceiling. His wife Wendy seemed so distant from him now. Had he ever really loved her? She was a kind person, a good person. He thought of her stiff, white, flannel nightgowns. And he was a faithful spouse—whatever that was worth. Now, Jerry, on the other hand, was a goddamn embarrassment—ogling women half his age.

Alan stared at the ceiling. These same ugly, square, acoustic tiles had kept him from seeing the night sky for what, a couple of decades now?

He was tired. Images of peoples' faces paraded through his head. Random construction sites. Bits of conversation partially heard. A balloon man twisted his thoughts into surprising, colorful shapes.

But there was a sound that did not belong to the jumble of thoughts and emotions inside his head. It sounded like steam escaping from somewhere. It was rhythmic. It had a texture to it and a bit of irregularity. There was a question-answer quality to it. He listened. It was breathing: inhale, exhale, inhale, exhale. He felt his entire body relaxing into the soothing pattern. The breath stopped. He opened his eyes.

The dark-haired woman lay in the bed next to him. She was watching him. Her eyes were huge and dark.

A car passed by the window, a block of reflected light raced across the wall of the bedroom.

"Do you want me to take you home…or something?" he asked. "You know, I'm sure I would remember if we had met."

"Do you time travel?" He heard her musical voice in his head.

He shook his head.

She gave him a confiding look and said, "Different paths lead to different times, you know. It all depends on your trajectory."

"Are you an astrophysicist, or something?"

She laughed. "I have found many doors into your world. I was off-course tonight. The time travel made me ill." She caressed his face with her hand. "I don't usually let mortals see me, unless I want them to."

Her words were crazy, but Alan had no doubt that they were true.

She held out a small teardrop shaped bottle in the palm of her hand. It was such a beautifully shaped piece of glass. He took the bottle from her hand. "Take some, if you want to travel with me."

"I don't take drugs," he said, handing it back to her. "And you shouldn't either. You could have easily ended up in a very bad situation tonight, if…."

"If you hadn't been there to rescue me?" she said, laughing. "Well, don't take it, if you don't want to." She looked into his eyes and continued. "If you *don't* want to be with me."

He grabbed the bottle, removed the cork, and drank.

Fred had been weeding the soybean field with a hoe since six-thirty in the morning and had only taken a break once to check on the Tigers-Yankees game. He'd really let the weeds get ahead of him this year. It was nearly three-thirty in the afternoon, and rivulets of sweat streamed down his back and face; his eyes stung from the salt. He had taken his t-shirt off to swat gnats in the morning, but, now, even the gnats were holed up someplace to escape the heat. Countless times that day, he had scanned the distance between the red barn and the field where he was working, hoping to see *her*.

In the shade of the house, he primed the old water pump, yanking the handle up and down until the water began to flow. He ducked his head and neck beneath the stream. He grabbed a towel from a nail-peg and dried his hair as he walked to the back door.

Women didn't get under his skin like they did for most guys. His brother went to pieces after losing the "love of his life." All the romantic stuff was bullshit.

"Anybody here?" he yelled, standing in the middle of his kitchen, the big, steel fan blowing his wet hair against the sides of his head. Barney, his shaggy black and white mutt, came into the kitchen to greet him, his tail wagging fiercely. Fred bent down and scratched the dog's head.

The telephone rang. Fred turned the fan off and answered it.

"Hello?"

"Hey, Fred, it's me, Mark."

"Hey, Mark."

"You were telling me about that woman you met. The one with long, dark hair who was walking along the river?"

Fred hadn't remembered telling Mark this, but he'd had a lot to drink the night they went out. "Ah, yup."

"Well, I think I seen her."

Fred swallowed hard. "Where?"

"I was playing pool at Kubiak's, and this beautiful chick walks in. Lots of black hair, like you said. She looked stoned, man. She kept her head down and went to the restroom."

"So? What did she do when she came out?"

"I don't know. I left with Joanne while she was still in the ladies room. But then I was talking to a friend of mine today, and he said that a guy carried her out of Kubiak's and put her in the back of his car."

Several seconds of silence. "You know who it was?"

"Yeah, it was one of the guys sitting with the District Attorney."

"You know what kind of car he was driving?"

"Come on, Fred. You're not going to go after him or anything, are you?"

"Some asshole drags *my* girlfriend home with him, and I'm not supposed to do anything? What would you do?"

"My friend said he was older. He could have been taking her home, Fred."

"Come on. I just want to know."

There was a pause. "It was a blue Dodge Charger."

Fred sat at his kitchen table with the red and white checkered gingham tablecloth his mother had made. He held the telephone receiver with one hand and scratched the dog's head with the other.

"Good afternoon, District Attorney's Office." A woman's voice chirped on the other end of the phone.

"Hi, this is Kubiak's Bar and Grill. One of the District Attorney's friends left a set of keys at our place a couple of days ago, and we'd like to return them. Could you ask him if he knows the address of the guy he came in with last Friday? I think he was driving a blue Dodge Charger."

"Okay, I'll see if he's still here. He might have gone home for the day." The woman put the phone down. "You mind if I put you on hold for a minute."

"No, no. That's fine." Fred listened to music as he sketched an eye on the corner of the newspaper.

"Hello, sir? Sorry about the wait. Do you have a pen?"

"Yes, yes, I do."

"Alan Greer. 17803 Tally Ho Drive, South Bend, Indiana."

"Thank you."

"You're welcome. Have a nice…"

Fred hung up the phone. He already had the map of the city spread out on the kitchen table. He found the street. It was curved without having any reason to be curved. It was the kind of place where guys with desk jobs lived. He circled it three times.

Barney swung his thick tail back and forth and barked.

"Yes, Barnaby, it's dinner time. We're going to get you fed, and then Daddy's going to go get Mommy."

Fred mixed some canned and dry dog food in a bowl and gave it to Barney. He took his wallet off the table and shoved it in his back pocket. He put on his John Deer baseball hat, stuffed the keys for his pickup truck in his pocket, and grabbed from the kitchen closet the shotgun he kept in a brown canvas case.

To the west, where the St. Joseph river ran, the sun smoldered above the sycamores. Fred walked across the gravel drive to his pick-up truck. He wasn't sure what he was going to do. Fragmentary images of her long, black hair and lips went through his mind. Then, he saw a stranger's hands on her hips. Intense desire and humiliation mixed until he felt helpless before the firestorm of his own rage. Who was this office prick? Some pretty boy friend of the District Attorney. She hadn't *chosen* to leave with him. That's why he had to carry her out—like a prize at the county fair.

He rolled down the window, and the sweet smell of corn drifted in. The small, teardrop-shaped vial that she had given him hung from his rearview mirror.

Fred slowed down in front of Alan's house. What if they'd given him the wrong address? There was no car parked out front. He drove past the house. There was a dead end with an empty lot where he could park and keep watch without being conspicuous.

Two girls rode bicycles with pink and yellow streamers on their handlebars. The light faded. A train whistle blew downtown. The moon rose above the rows of tidy homes, sprinklers, and chain-linked fences. The garage door opened, and a blue Dodge Charger pulled out. Fred started the engine and followed.

Alan heard a mourning dove. He sat up and looked around. He was alone. The numbers on his alarm clock, hummed, vibrated and flipped: 9:15. He never slept that late. His eyes throbbed. Memories from the previous night flooded back. On the nightstand, he saw a small, tear-shaped glass vial.

Was she still in the house? He checked each room with a mixture of fear and longing. She was gone. He sat on the bed. He could see his wife's clothes hanging neatly in the closet. Ever since they'd been married, she'd dedicated her Sundays to washing and ironing their clothes in preparation for the work week. He had no doubt she'd continue that routine until she dropped dead. He looked at a wedding picture on the bookshelf. He studied his own young, goofy face, and now he could see it clearly—the panic, the regret.

He gathered up the bed sheets and put them close to his face like a bouquet. None of her scent remained. Nothing. He looked at the pillows. There, on the white cotton pillowcase, was a long, black hair. His heart fluttered. Carefully, he picked the hair between his fingers. He pressed it to his lips. He spent the next hour winding the black hair around his pinky and then attaching it to a piece of yarn, which he tied about his neck. She had singled him out for a reason. The scorpion tail of desire whipped through him with a ferocity that left him weak. He picked up the teardrop shaped vial and kissed it.

He couldn't lose control of himself like this. He needed his normal routines. He needed to remember who he was. He'd go to the power plant and finish inspecting the transformer. If he went at night, he wouldn't have to worry about getting in the way of the construction crew. Sure, it was a Saturday night, and that would seem pathetic if anyone found out, but the job needed to get done. His dedication would be appreciated by someone…maybe?

He made himself a cup of coffee. He was already feeling better. Everything would go back to normal once his wife came home.

The metal door to the turbine room was still partially open, just as he had left it when he'd been in there last. He hadn't been able to find his headlamp, so he had brought his aluminum flashlight.

Despite the late hour, it felt good to be back at work. He'd get over this. He imagined himself narrating the events of the past few days to Wendy. She'd laugh and say she hadn't realized what an active imagination he had. Then he'd say that he hadn't realized it either. But he knew he wouldn't laugh about it, and he also knew he wouldn't tell her.

The floor was settling unevenly in the turbine room. Of course, none of the wiring would be up to code. The iron piping would have to be replaced by PVC.

Alan heard a thump. It seemed to come from the other side of the metal door. Maybe a cop had seen his car and had come to investigate. He waited, listening. Nothing. He pointed his flashlight into the old turbine and shimmied into an irregularly shaped alcove to check the wiring.

A piece of metal flexed someplace in the direction of the doorway. Alan lifted his head and listened. He looked at his watch: 11:00 p.m. It would take him at least another half hour, or forty-five minutes before he finished with the transformer.

A large sack fell somewhere above his head. He froze. His heart thundered in his chest.

"Damn it." The voice echoed. "Hey, anybody down there?" It was a man's voice.

Alan pointed his flashlight up at the man. "Sorry about that. Yeah, building inspector. I'm down here looking at the transformer. I didn't get a chance to look at it when I was here last."

"You came back at eleven at night on a Saturday. That's dedication."

The man had a shaggy beard and was wearing a John Deer baseball cap. He was carrying a canvas bag.

"I don't have that much more to do. Just wanted to get it done, so I don't have to think about it next week." Alan trained his flashlight on the transformer again.

"Is that your blue Dodge Charger in the parking lot?"

"Yup. That's mine." Alan got down on his knees and shined the flashlight along one side of the turbine.

"You know if this place has another exit?"

"No, this place was built at the turn of the century. No rules about having a secondary means of egress." Alan grabbed his clipboard and wrote down some figures.

The man leaned heavily against the railing that ran around one of the turbines.

"I wouldn't trust that railing, if I were you. Some of those haven't been replaced for seventy years."

The man backed away from the railing and came closer to where Alan was squatting next to the transformer. He sat down on a metal stair and pointed his flashlight at the ceiling.

"What kind of flashlight you got? That looks like an old one." Alan observed.

"This here? This here's a Big Beam."

"Like it?" Alan asked in a distracted voice as he jotted more numbers down on his clipboard.

"Yup. Keep it in my truck. It's good for coon hunting." The man's voice was tense and loud enough to echo in the concrete chamber.

Alan was silent, then said, "I imagine you need a bright light for that."

"I like it cuz you can put it down, and it'll light up a whole area. You can use both hands in the dark."

Alan thought he heard a zipper. This guy was a little weird, but harmless. "Mine's a piece of garbage. The metal support's flimsy. Falls over all the time."

The man kept a steady beam of light pointed at the ceiling. "You ever go to Kubiak's"

Alan stopped writing and looked through a network of dark pipes at the man who seemed to be studying the ceiling. "Yeah...I was there this past Friday. Why?"

"I'm just askin'." The man's voice had suddenly become more strained and slightly higher pitched. "I'm askin' cause a friend of mine saw this guy carry an unconscious girl outta that bar, and that guy was driving a blue Dodge Charger." Alan heard a gun being cocked. "You wouldn't be the asshole who did that, would you?"

"What? No!"

"Yeah? Well, who was it then?"

Fred was standing a little above him with the light of the Big Beam flashlight illuminating his baggy trousers. The upper half of his body was shrouded in darkness, but Alan felt sure he was pointing a shotgun at him.

"Look, she came in and passed out in the ladies' room. There was…there was nobody to look out for her. I took her home because there was no one else to watch out for her. It was the *decent* thing to do."

"And what you did to her afterwards? Was that the '*decent* thing to do'?"

"She was all over me. I left her alone. She came after me."

"You lie!" A huge metal hammer seemed to strike Alan's head from all directions simultaneously. He scrambled away like a terrified beast. His flashlight rolled off the metal grate floor and landed next to one of the turbines, giving a soft glow to the chamber beneath them. He was curled up into a ball. All this guy had to do was lift his flashlight, and he'd see him.

"Look. I'm telling you the truth."

Fred took his big flashlight and his shotgun over to where Alan was cowering. "Do you love her?"

Of course he couldn't love her. He didn't know her. Yet it defied everything in his soul to say that he did not. His life had been so full of ambivalent emotions, "unconditional" commitments that were, at the end of the day, conditional, and he realized with a feeling that was not unlike joy that what he felt for her was love. He loved her as certainly as he breathed.

"I…I do."

Another blast reverberated through the old power plant. Fred sat down and put his gun away. There couldn't be two of them loving her like that. It had to be one or the other, and now it was just him.

He heard a light tapping on the window above his head. A woman was standing there. Well, hallelujah, it was *her*. His heart knocked hard in his chest. It took his breath away. *She* had come back to him. He was the one she loved. She'd understand that he had done this for her. A ladder on the wall led to the window where she stood.

"Wait there, sweetheart! We're going to South America."

Fred grabbed his flashlight and started climbing the metal ladder. He wasn't sure how she'd managed to get herself on that platform. He guessed she'd been trying to get away from that bastard and was frightened. Fred was breathing heavily by the time he reached the top. The window was open, and he crawled out onto the concrete ledge, facing the river. He'd looked at the moon so many times with indifference, but tonight it whispered to him of all that was mysterious, sacred, and just beyond his grasp.

She stood with her back to him; the long, black tendrils of her hair blowing gently in the breeze from the falling water.

"He…he won't hurt you anymore, angel," Fred said awkwardly and reached out for her.

Her hand clamped hard around his wrist.

Murder stigmatizes real estate. The building commissioner had discovered this the hard way several years ago, and he wasn't going to make the same mistake with the power plant. By September, bulldozers had transformed the old power plant into neat piles of brick and pipe.

Jerry stood with Wendy on the Colfax Bridge overlooking the river and the construction site. Wendy zipped up her caramel-colored ski jacket to keep out the cold wind that had unexpectedly kicked up. Jerry wondered if she skied, and was about to ask, when he realized it wasn't the kind of question you asked a woman whose husband had just been murdered. Wendy had a pleasant, round face framed by bangs cut in the popular feathered look. Her button nose was red in the cold.

"I don't know what I'll do with the house. So many memories."

Jerry remembered the new apartment complex going up on Darden Road and thought about recommending that, but that too didn't seem appropriate. "Yeah, I can imagine."

Wendy dug both of her hands deep in her pockets and looked up at Jerry and then away. "The worst part is feeling that I didn't really know him. I thought we were so close. I thought we shared everything."

"I'm *sure* that was true, Wendy," Jerry said, trying unsuccessfully to sound sincere. "Alan was just being Alan—decent, kind, responsible," he said, realizing there was no top button to close the neck of his new cowhide jacket. "He got me home safely from Kubiak's, and he brought that woman home because there was no one else to take her. She just happened to be the girlfriend of a jealous, homicidal maniac."

He looked away from her and out at the river. "If I hadn't gotten myself so stewed at Kubiak's, he wouldn't have had to deal with that situation alone."

Wendy reached into her coat pocket and extracted a strand of red wool with a little bundle of hair tied to the end. She held it up. "They found this around Alan's neck. They didn't think it was significant, so they gave it back to me along with his other personal effects."

Jerry shook his head. "That was a bad idea."

"The yarn is mine. He got it out of my craft drawer. It's where I keep supplies for my second-grade kids. But the hair…the hair isn't mine. It's long, and it's black." Wendy looked into Jerry's eyes, silently challenging him to come up with an explanation. She stuffed it back in her pocket.

Jerry stared at his feet. "The residue in that glass vial they found in his pocket had a lot in common with LSD and other hallucinogens. That probably explains some of his strange behavior."

"It's not like Alan to take drugs," Wendy said with authority, then shrugged.

"When we find the woman, we'll get some answers," Jerry said with a conviction he didn't feel. "I can't believe she's just vanished."

Wendy leaned against the handrail and looked out gravely across the river. "I can't help thinking that she might be right here, and we don't know it."

Jerry was going to say that the descriptions provided by Julie Ann, the doctor, and the guy playing pool at Kubiak's had left little doubt that the woman was extraordinarily attractive. But pointing out the attractiveness of the woman her husband had died for would, of course, provide little comfort.

"If she is close by, we'll certainly find her, and then we'll know a lot more than we do now," Jerry said in a serious, take-charge voice. Inwardly, he recoiled at the stupidity of his own words. He doubted that they would ever really "know" what had happened with Alan. *Knowing* someone, even a spouse, was always provisional. He took Wendy's arm, and they headed back across the Colfax Bridge. In the shadow of the bridge, a dark figure slipped beneath the water.

NIGHT

Mishipeshu waited by the entrance to the Sanctuary of the Dead. The moon's golden orb threw shafts of light all around her.

She was in love with the man who wielded the silver torch—the one who had carried her in his arms. She stood at the entrance of the Sanctuary of the Dead ready to bar his way. She would keep him with her in the river. Muskrat said that she must feed her lover pondweed every day, and he promised to bring her as much as she needed. She thought the man would not like this food, but she hoped he'd find pleasure enough in his new life with her to make up for that.

Mishipeshu had dragged the one who had killed her darling from the power plant rooftop to the Sanctuary entrance, then shoved him down the dark passageway. Manitou had said that there were consequences for taking men's lives. If there were no consequences for the millions of bison, pigeon, bear, and bobcat lives that men had taken, why should there be for him?

In the distance, she saw a dark shape floating towards her. He was still wearing the ugly work boots he'd had on in the power plant. She swam to him and grabbed his pant leg to keep him from drifting toward the Sanctuary entrance. His head had been quite badly damaged by the loud firestick. She pressed the pondweed to his broken skull, and the wound swiftly disappeared. She repaired his broken glasses.

She put her face close to his and studied the thick eyebrows that framed his closed eyes. He looked calm. He had made his peace with his gods. She felt his arms; he was strong, though no longer young. Silver hairs had made their appearance among the black. There was a great gentleness in his face. She brushed her lips to his nose, his eyes, his forehead. His eyes slowly opened, and a look of terror filled them. He recoiled from her, kicking and flailing his arms. He saw the dark entrance to the Sanctuary and struggled towards it. She swam after him and caught him. She grabbed his clenched hand, unwrapped his fingers, and gave him the present she'd hoped to give him later: his aluminum flashlight.

Alan knew that he was dead. He knew that a beautiful woman's crazy boyfriend had followed him into the power plant and had shot him at point-blank range. He concluded that this must be what his nervous system had generated before signing off for good. And looking around at the fish, the moon above, and the woman, he was impressed—he had not believed himself capable of conjuring all this, even as a grand finale.

She lifted the pondweed to her lips and took a nibble, nodded, then held it out to him. He took some, opened his mouth, and water rushed in. It flooded his lungs, his head, his throat. He saw her pointing frantically to the pondweed, which he crammed into his mouth, chewing with a kind of frenzy. He was able to get down a mouthful along with about a quart of water. Calm took root in his abdomen, unfurling sleepy tendrils into every corner of his body. She held his hand in hers and looked into his face with love and bewilderment.

With a clarity that he had lacked in life, Alan saw vividly what lay ahead. He saw the goddess on a bed of water lily blossoms, freshwater pearls in her hair and passion on her lips. He saw their chubby child playing in the tall underwater grass. Then, he saw a concrete wall, weathered black and covered in moss and snails. The wall was so high he could not see the top, and he knew with certainty that the wall was both impenetrable and unending.

He pulled her hands to his lips and kissed them, and then, before she'd had a chance to respond, he threw himself headlong into the black maw of the Underworld.

The goddess watched him disappear into the darkness—the fire of her love smoldering into hatred.

CHAPTER 14

THE RARE BOOK ROOM

~ 2017 ~

"Assume every book could be Shakespeare's First Folio. We're looking for historic significance, mint condition, illustrations—you've got the checklist."

Ingrid Streeter, the bibliographer for the Rare Book Room, was in the library's basement instructing her assistant, Carol Bouchard, on how to handle the stacks of boxed books delivered the previous week from Nieuwland Hall—long the dumping ground for homeless books. But now, with new physics laboratories being added to the building, the vast motley collection had been sent to the Rare Book Room for review.

Ingrid looked down at the paperback she held in her small hands as if it were a dead rat. "This sort of schlock"—she held up a copy of *The Unwanted Wife*—"goes directly into the toss pile." She let the book drop into a large box marked "Book Sale."

The buzzer sounded, which meant there was a patron with a question the undergraduate manning the front desk couldn't answer.

Using a nearby chair for assistance, Ingrid rose heavily to her feet, wincing when she put pressure on the knee she had fallen on last winter.

"We'll go through as many books as we can each day and make decisions about where they need to go. I always knew we'd end up getting some God-awful mess when they decided to clear out Nieuwland." She put her hands on her square hips then adjusted some imperceptible imbalance in the line of her well-tailored, wool skirt. She shook her head as she surveyed the stacks of boxes. "I had no idea it would be on this scale."

Like a ship's captain who had just addressed the engine crew,

Ingrid turned away and walked with a bit of limp down the narrow passage between the stacks to the elevator. Carol wanted to ask what percentage of her time she would be expected to devote to this project, but she knew that Ingrid had already turned her orderly, well-regulated mind to other projects.

Carol pulled up a chair, sat down, and placed her laptop on the floor. She cast her eye over the towering piles of boxes. It looked to be the size of a quarter-acre lot. She'd process the first twenty boxes, then she'd know the average number of books in each box.

After four years of graduate work, here she was, working as a librarian's assistant—a job any conscientious high-school student could do. So much for "following your bliss." She should have been more realistic. Poor kids studied business or engineering, not history.

Carol had completed all the course work necessary for a doctorate, but then her stipend ended, her bank balance plunged, and bills piled up. She had taken this job at Notre Dame's Rare Book Room at the prompting of one of her professors. He thought they might have useful resources for her dissertation. Sadly, she'd made no progress on that front.

She'd seen other graduate students enter this academic limbo where she was now. It was called "All-But-Dissertation" (ABD). It sounded like a legitimate stage on a normally progressing career path, but for grad students in her financial situation, it was the end of the line.

She opened a box and looked in: *The History of the Boston Massacre*, volume five from the American Heritage collection on the Civil War, and a complete set of Star Trek novels, signed by the author. She wrote descriptions of the condition of each book's binding and pages, title, publication date, physical dimensions, signatures, marginalia.

It was tedium on an epic scale, but she swept her emotions to one side and focused on the work.

She looked at her watch: 4:15, and she had just finished her fourth box. If she continued at this rate, it would take her about eight months. Ingrid had said *we* would be processing the books, but it was clear she'd be doing this on her own.

She pulled the next box towards her. This one was made from wood and looked very old. She could just make out the number "46" that had been painted on it. The top, which had been nailed shut, was loose on one end, and it made a loud squeak when she pried it open. Even before she removed the old newspapers, issues of the *Notre Dame Scholastic* from 1926, she smelled old leather and decaying vegetation.

She carefully pushed aside the remaining papers, expecting to find a nest of dead mice. A brown leather cover filled the entirety of the crate; its delicate gold filigree reflected the basement's fluorescent light. She wedged her fingers down along its sides, lifted it up, and carried it to a metal table at the end of one of the stacks.

Gold scrollwork ornamented the perimeter of the leather cover. She ran her fingertips across it lightly. She examined the binding; it was hand stitched and delicately tooled. This was definitely pre-nineteenth-century. She opened it gently.

A microscopically rendered mass of roots, which started at the very bottom of the page, exploded into a hundred different stems with pale green, lacy fronds. Globes of soft pink blossoms peeked out from behind large, tongue-like leaves. Clusters of evergreen needles—some long and thin, others short and stubby—were paired with their corresponding cones. Linear Latin, and French and German with their respective circumflexes and umlauts filled the margins along with transliterated written Algonquin, which she recognized from her work with Jesuit documents from New France.

How did something of such obvious historical significance wind up among boxes of sci-fi paperbacks and Michelin guides?

She knew what she needed to do next, yet everything inside her rebelled against doing it. She should let Ingrid know immediately about this incredible find. Ingrid would bring in all her identification resources to establish the date, value, and author. Then, she would offer it up as a prize to the appropriate on-campus faculty expert.

Just this past summer, a collection of early twentieth-century Irish music had been donated to the library, and Ingrid had immediately handed it over to a senior, tenured professor in the history department. There had been a junior faculty member in ethnomusicology who would have benefited far more, but Ingrid had chosen to bestow it on the one with the established reputation, who thanked her profusely with flowers, concert tickets and invitations to dinner parties.

If Carol revealed what she had found, Ingrid would hand over this amazing treasure to someone who had a name, and she, Carol, would go back to describing dog-eared paperbacks in the basement. Was it unethical for her to keep this, at least for a little while, to herself? Since all the boxes had been put in the basement at random, this box that she found her first day might just as easily have been found on the last.

Carol was certain Ingrid would not be sympathetic to her desire to study the manuscript first. Her credentials as a historian would not make up for her youth and lowly status. Giving first viewing privileges to her assistant would earn Ingrid no points with the people whose opinions she cared about most.

She looked at her phone: 4:40 p.m. The library closed at five. She would have to go back to the first floor now, or Ingrid would come down to look for her. She picked up the manuscript and carefully placed it back in its box. She covered it with a more recent wrinkled newspaper and put the original packing material in an empty box. In a dark, distant corner of the basement, she found a high shelf with room enough for her two boxes.

A text from Ingrid appeared on her phone. She could hear the recorded chime and message, notifying patrons that the library would be closing soon. She dusted off her skirt and sweater, pulled out and opened another box in the improbable event that Ingrid would notice that some of Carol's time was unaccounted for. Carol doubted that this would happen. Though suspicious by nature, Ingrid was not terribly observant, at least when it came to Carol. Even after being her supervisor for several months, she'd had difficulties describing Carol's appearance to a colleague who was supposed to meet her in the parking lot. Ingrid, who was on the phone with the woman, had stood up from her desk and walked over to look at Carol who was shelving books and said, not caring if Carol overheard: "Tall with dark hair." For Ingrid, Carol was a replaceable subordinate, best kept in the outer reaches of her social circle.

Carol switched off the lights and stepped into the elevator. When the doors opened, she saw the familiar expanse of harvest gold carpet, floor-to-ceiling bookshelves behind glass, and heard the quiet, comforting purr of the ventilation system. Ingrid, predictably, was not at her desk. Like clockwork, she locked the door at exactly 4:58.

"What took you so long?" Ingrid called from the other room. "I thought you'd fallen asleep down there."

"I'm working out a system. It's kind of overwhelming," Carol said, taking her jacket from the hanger in the closet and grabbing her umbrella.

"Nothing to be done about that. I don't want anyone who hasn't received proper training doing that work," Ingrid said, then added with a knowing smile, "just because it's too tedious for our more educated employees." Ingrid made sure to expose to ridicule any feelings of wounded pride Carol might harbor.

"Ingrid, would it be okay if I put in some extra hours processing those books. Say, a couple of hours every evening?" Carol worked hard to keep her face and voice indifferent.

"I can't pay you overtime." Ingrid looked in a hand-held mirror, repositioning a few misplaced hairs on her well-coiffed, gray head.

"No, I didn't think so. I was just hoping we could jump-start the process a bit," Carol said, freeing her hair from the back of her coat and regarding Ingrid with a steady gaze. It occurred to her that Ingrid might want to impress higher-ups with her speed in cataloging this massive influx of books.

"Well, you could stay in the evenings if you want," she said, as if granting a special favor. "I had forgotten that you're only getting minimum wage." She locked her desk drawer and tied the belt of her rain jacket. "I could pay you an extra fifty dollars a week."

"That's fine," Carol said, thrusting her hands into the pockets of the trench coat. She'd bought it on clearance just two months ago, and her fingertips were already poking through the poorly stitched seams. "See you tomorrow," she said brightly.

Everything was still wet and quietly dripping from the recent rain. She could hear the cars on the roads splashing through the deep puddles. In November, the gray clouds would move over the city where they'd remain parked until mid-March. But in September, there were still clear, sunny days to look forward to.

Her request to work evenings had been totally spontaneous. She had surprised herself when she heard the suggestion come to her lips so seemingly devoid of ulterior motive. She smiled when she thought how she'd kept the discovery of the manuscript to herself. If she—sweet, gentle, truthful Carol—could deceive Ingrid in this way, entirely new ways of being in the world were possible.

Without paying much attention to her surroundings, she completed the thirty-minute walk to her apartment on the second floor of a house that faced the river. She fed her cat Godfrey and made herself a bowl of instant oatmeal. She read the news on her laptop until her email pinged. She switched to her inbox and saw that her 23andMe report was in. She hadn't really been able to afford the hundred bucks the test had cost. Her adoptive parents were loving and attentive, but they knew nothing about her birth parents.

She took a deep breath and opened the geographic ancestry page. She scanned it to the bottom: "0%" Wait, how could she be zero percent? She went on to the chromosome ancestry: "100% unassigned." She typed an angry email to the company, reread it, and deleted it. Why would they care that she was an orphan? She wrote a more measured response and sent it. A hundred bucks down the drain. Godfrey jumped onto her lap.

While she petted the cat, she looked at the pictures she had taken with her phone of the manuscript. She compared them with photos of similar manuscripts on the Web and decided that it was closest in appearance to those from the late 1700's. The craftsmanship looked more Old World than New—maybe France, Germany? Carol didn't know much about plants, but they obviously weren't tropical.

As Carol was getting her clothes ready for the next day, she felt excited for the first time about going to work. She'd need to start packing dinners as well as lunches: she put four envelopes of instant oatmeal in her computer bag.

She lay in bed making plans. She would streamline the cataloging system so that she could process the same number of books twice, maybe three times as fast as she had today. That would allow her to devote all work after-hours to the manuscript. To what end? She wasn't sure, but this could be the dissertation topic she'd been looking for.

Carol couldn't believe it when she looked at her phone the next day and saw it was already 4:40. She had processed all the books in five boxes. She went upstairs to report to Ingrid, who was talking with a library patron. Judging by the expression on her face, it was some "average Joe"—her term for anyone showing a non academic, non-professional curiosity about something in their collection. Once, Ingrid had been curt with an "average Joe" who turned out to be a wealthy donor. She was sufficiently chastened by the event to maintain a chilly pleasantness at all times to everyone.

"Anything noteworthy down there?" Ingrid asked casually, instantly dropping the forced smile from her face as soon as the "Joe" stepped away.

Carol's heart skipped a beat. "Depends on what you call noteworthy. . . I unboxed and cataloged the thirty-five-volume collected lectures of John L. Goddard, sixteen French Michelin guides from the 1960s splattered with red wine stains, and a book from a pessimistic alum called, *Is Germany Incurable?*"

"Well, that sounds like you're keeping yourself entertained, not at the expense of speed or efficiency, I hope."

"Actually, I already processed three boxes," said Carol casually.

Ingrid unlocked her desk and extracted her purse and car keys. "I spoke with Security. I told them that there would be a staff person working late."

Carol wondered how late was "late," but she knew the question would sound odd, a bit too eager. She was making this up as she went along. Ingrid shut the door, and Carol watched her stride purposefully towards her undoubtedly clean car and well-ordered home.

As Carol descended into the library's basement, a slight smile played about her lips. She was Howard Carter lifting her lamp above the treasures of Tutankhamun.

She found the box with the manuscript, reopened it, and carefully extracted her treasure. She cleared a metal table beneath one of the brighter, fluorescent lights and sat on a folding chair she had found in a closet. Again, the scent of pine needles and autumn greeted her, as she opened the manuscript. She took a legal pad, along with the Latin and Algonquin dictionaries, from her computer bag. The Algonquin dictionary was from the 19th-century, so its usefulness was dubious. She'd have to order a better one through interlibrary loan. She put on a pair of thin rubber gloves. If she was going to keep this manuscript to herself for a little while, she didn't want to be responsible for diminishing its value.

The pen-and-inks with watercolors had been executed on vellum and were backed by heavy paper. Every illustration was luminous and precise with touches here and there of uncontrolled imagination. She returned to the first page where the title was written: *Plantarum Americae Septentrionalis et usu medicatis.* Carol wrote both the Latin title and the English translation, *Plants of North America and their Medicinal Use.* Interspersed with the drawings were steps in the preparation of medicines. The manuscript was not only beautiful, it was useful. If a plant could be eaten or used as a purgative, purify the blood, counteract the venom of a snakebite, it was noted.

Carol's phone timer went off. It was 3:00 a.m. She had decided that this was the latest she could stay and still keep her wits about her the next day. She'd sleep on the weekends.

She flipped through her ten pages of notes; it had been a productive night.

Three months passed. The leaves had fallen from the trees, and the sky was the color of concrete. Glittering veils of snow and an occasional iris-colored sky usually brightened the seasonal drabness, but this year, more rain came instead. It thundered down on rooftops and pooled in the coarse bristle of harvested cornfields. The St. Joseph and Kankakee Rivers crested their banks and did not retreat. And still the rains came, surpassing all records. New forms of molds and mildews appeared that no one had ever seen before. The rain made it easier for Carol to turn her back on the world and descend into her cave.

Friday came, and Carol was in her usual end-of-the-week exhaustion. In the process of taking off her coat, the sleeves of her blouse, sweater, and wool coat had become so knotted, she could not extract her arm. She pulled frantically at her sleeve while wishing she could give up, collapse on the floor, and sleep.

"Carol, we've got a bunch of workmen in the basement this morning. With all the rain we've been having, they're checking the steam tunnels for flooding and the basement for cracks. I thought I smelled mold last time I was down there."

Carol was shaking her afflicted arm in an effort to free herself from her sleeve. "I haven't smelled mold. I haven't seen any leaks."

Ingrid was silent.

"I mean, I've been thinking about that possibility myself and was surprised that there was absolutely no moldy smell." She finally succeeded in shaking herself free. She stepped out of the closet where she was visible from Ingrid's desk. Ingrid took off her cat's eye reading glasses, narrowed her eyes and examined her. Carol continued, "Should I go down there and help them?"

"No, Carol, I don't see any point in that unless you've got experience in plumbing. I've got plenty for you to help me with up here. You can start pulling the books on this list." Ingrid got up from her desk and handed Carol a legal pad. "When you find them, put them on my desk. I'm looking for interesting covers. I want to put together an exhibit displaying our collection on baseball.

"Before you start on that, there's a patron in the reading room who's looking for information on Father Nieuwland. I told him that all that information is in Archives, but he still wants to check through our collection. Can you deal with him first?"

Carol looked at the clock. It was 9 a.m. The titles on the legal pad were blurring together. Her brain refused to engage in anything. She went to the ladies' room and splashed cold water on her face.

When she came back, she found a man in his late forties with salt and pepper hair, sitting at the reading table and making notes in a small, leather-bound notebook.

"The bibliographer said that you were looking for information on Father Nieuwland?" Carol said, a bit tentatively. The man turned towards her, revealing a handlebar mustache—a disarming contrast to his humorless face.

"No," he said, snapping his notebook closed and fastening the clasp. "I'm looking for a manuscript formerly owned by Edward Greene, the botanist and Nieuwland's mentor," he said, sounding as if it were the third time he was explaining his objective to her rather than the first.

"We have his two-volume history of botany. Would you like to take a look at that?"

"Yes," he said, as if choosing from a menu which offered nothing to his liking.

She started to leave, relieved to have an excuse to get away from him, but then stopped. "You'll need to fill out a request form first."

He narrowed his eyes and stared at her. "Why can't you do that for me?"

"Because, because it's a form that patrons need to fill out."

He shook his head with disbelief. "Right."

She gave him the form, which he filled out in a microscopic script. After a fifteen-minute trip to the basement, she returned, placing the book he'd requested before him as carefully as if it had been spun from the finest glass.

"This isn't the book I wanted," he said flatly.

"I'm sorry. That's the book you asked for."

"Could I speak with your supervisor?"

Carol was dumbfounded. "Sure. Absolutely. I'll get her." She told Ingrid what had happened.

"Do you have the form?" Carol handed it to her. "Well, that's what you gave him," Ingrid said, returning to her scrutiny of old photos of baseball players. "Send him to the Herbarium. He said he worked for a pharmaceutical company. Tell him they have people with scientific expertise over there."

"I can't see him being happy with that suggestion."

Ingrid shrugged her shoulders.

The man was staring intently at his phone when Carol returned.

"The bibliographer suggested you try the Herbarium over in Jordan Hall. You'll find Nieuwland's collection of specimens there as well."

"I'm not looking for a dried plant," he said with dismissive condescension. "I'm looking for a botanical manuscript, and this," he said, holding up the book she had brought him, "is not one."

He stared fixedly at Carol, as if seeing the ghost of the manuscript on her retinas. Carol summoned all her self-control to put on a what-has-that-got-to-do-with-me face, but she could feel that panic was getting the upper hand. What if Ingrid had mentioned the massive collection of books from Nieuwland Hall beneath his feet at this very moment?

"Do you have a reference number for this manuscript?" she asked.

"No. If I did, I would have written it on the form."

"Everything we have here has a reference number."

"You don't have anything that hasn't yet been cataloged?"

"We don't assign catalog numbers to new acquisitions. That's the job of the main library. You might want to check there."

He exhaled and closed his eyes briefly. "Are there any other institutions that might have Nieuwland or Greene's works?"

"Maybe Catholic University? Greene was there for a while. Or the Smithsonian."

"Maybe I'll find more help there." He put away his notebook and shut his laptop.

"Sorry."

"Me too," he said without moving a single facial muscle. He put his pen and notebook in their designated compartments, latched his briefcase, rose to his feet, and left.

Carol was sure that her manuscript was the one he was looking for. She had wondered if Greene had sent Nieuwland the manuscript along with the herbarium plants. But why would this guy's pharmaceutical company be interested in a manuscript that was based more on folk wisdom than chemistry?

For Nieuwland and Greene, discovering and classifying a new species of plant was an effort to figure out where they fit into God's divine order. But Nieuwland's students could have been motivated by financial gain. It wouldn't be surprising at all if at least one of them who was familiar with the manuscript had pursued a career in the drug industry.

Carol couldn't summon the necessary mental energy to think clearly about what this meant. By repeating the cold-water treatment every two hours, she was able to get through the entire work day.

"Are you sure you want to stay late again tonight?" Ingrid asked, unlocking her desk drawer and retrieving her car keys. "You don't seem yourself. You could be getting sick. I don't want you coming in if you're sick. *I* just *can't* get sick. My colds become bronchitis, and bronchitis turns into pneumonia."

Carol cleared her throat. "I'm fine. Just a little short on sleep."

Ingrid eyed her as if she had morphed into a giant virus. "Suit yourself."

When, at the day's end, Carol locked the door behind Ingrid, she heaved a great sigh of relief and descended into the basement to set up her work station. She reached up to the top shelf to retrieve the box with the manuscript. It wasn't there. She frantically moved boxes around, thinking she'd misplaced it the night before. The workmen must have moved it, but why? It wasn't close to anything that could leak. She sat down and took some deep breaths; she needed to take stock of the situation. It was difficult not to conclude that someone had taken it. She sat on the metal folding chair staring at the empty pool of fluorescent light before her. She packed her bag and headed out into the cold drizzle.

She slept until three in the afternoon on Saturday and two on Sunday, in part from exhaustion, in part to escape the painful awareness of what she'd lost—the months of late nights translating, analyzing, decoding the manuscript. She was still only halfway through the book. No one wrote a dissertation on half of a book.

She arrived at work on Monday morning entirely coherent and utterly dispirited. As she removed her boots, she could hear Ingrid on the phone, talking about how to display some baseball ephemera. She walked into the reading room. Box 46 was on a long mahogany table in the center of the room. She went over to it and peered inside. There were the recent newspapers she'd used to cover the manuscript. She picked it up; the manuscript was still inside.

"No, that's going to make it too late. I need to have this all put together by April..."

Carol eyed the elevator. She'd have to carry the box past Ingrid's office. Did she know what was inside? Her heart was racing.

"That will be fine then. I'll expect them on Tuesday. Good-bye."

Her opportunity to do something, anything, with the box had passed.

"Carol?" Ingrid called from her office in a slightly peremptory tone.

Carol closed her eyes. "Yes?"

"Can you come in here please?"

As Carol walked into Ingrid's office, Ingrid examined her above her reading glasses, which had descended to the tip of her nose.

"Carol, I know what you've been doing in the basement...and I appreciate it, but I found out last week that there are going to be budget cuts. I'm afraid I'm not going to be able to pay you for your extra hours."

"I'm making a lot of progress. I think I could be done in three months," she said, trying to keep her voice more plucky than pleading.

"Well, you've certainly been single-minded about it." Ingrid leaned her elbows on her desk and rested her chin on the palm of her hand for a moment. "I can give you two," she said.

"Okay. I'll see what I can do." Carol turned to leave Ingrid's office.

"Oh, Carol, one of the workmen found a box that was left open on a desk in the basement. They needed to get the desk out of the way, and he didn't know what to do with it. He left it on the table in the reading room. I've been so busy here this morning, I haven't had a chance to do anything with it yet."

"That's fine. I'll take it back to the basement."

Carol couldn't believe that she had forgotten to hide the manuscript. Sleep deprivation, as it turned out, wasn't something she could just power through. She grabbed the box and walked slowly past Ingrid's office to the elevator.

She was still getting used to having legs, but her lungs were struggling to process oxygen. Mishipeshu tried to avoid the broken glass and twisted metal as she dragged herself across the icy rocks along the river. A sickly, orange vapor blocked her view of the full moon she knew was there. All coordinates pointed to this place at this time, though it certainly wasn't a time she would have chosen.

She wore a human dress the raccoons had found for her. It was made from a cotton print covered with wild strawberries and smelling strongly of garbage. She had freshened it up by swimming in it for several days.

Namé was waiting for her close by in a deep hole in the river bottom. He couldn't swim very far without being blocked by a dam.

Houses trimmed in Christmas lights lined the snow-covered riverbanks. Though it was the dead of night, a TV screen in someone's living room flashed with images of race cars and palm trees.

Mishipeshu rubbed her legs to get the blood flowing into them and then crept up to a house with a screened-in patio. The windows were dark. She wrenched the patio door off its hinges, went inside, and propped the door back in place. The smell of moisture led her to the kitchen, where she turned on the faucet. She took huge gulps of water then blew it violently out of her mouth and nose. Chlorine.

The scent of humans was faint, and Mishipeshu concluded that the house, at least this part of it, was abandoned. She found a blanket, put it in the tub, then filled the tub with water. She got in, nestling into the blanket's wet folds and covering her nose with a cotton t-shirt to lessen the chlorine smell.

She heard someone run up an outside staircase. A door opened overhead and then closed. Water ran through a pipe above her head.

She rose from the tub. The time had come.

Since September, Carol had identified about eighty percent of the plants in the manuscript; the remaining twenty percent she guessed were no longer in existence. All were native to Northern Indiana. The plant names were written in Miami and Potawatomi. Their medicinal properties, therapeutic applications, and associated religious rituals, were in French. Latin terms were sometimes used for clarification. Abundant references to the cosmology of the Medéwewen, a secret Native American society of healers, had found their way into the manuscript: the world began on a tortoise shell and would end with a giant flood.

It was Wednesday night around 2 a.m. one week before Christmas. Flipping through the manuscript's last pages, she found a long lock of black hair encircled at one end with one row of dyed porcupine quills. She let her fingers travel down the length of the glossy shafts of hair, which was black with a bluish iridescent gleam. She braided the lock into her own hair and looked at it in her phone's camera. It suited her.

At a quarter to three, she left the library. A train whistle blew someplace south of town. There weren't very many passenger trains anymore, so it had to be a freight train. She could hear the drone of the big rigs, hurtling west along the Indiana Toll Road towards Chicago. Before their journeys ended, the trucks would pass through the charred landscape of steel mills, past glittering refineries, and beneath the towering flames of gas flares.

The rain had stopped. Carol picked a path around dark pools of water and hard lumps of ice-covered snow. The campus was empty; it was winter break. She walked past the faux gothic brick buildings and into a brightly-lit, empty, parking lot. She rubbed away the drip that was forming on her nose. She could smell the manuscript on her fingers. Pine needles and a rich, musky scent. If you pressed your whole face into the fur of a bobcat, you might smell something like that. She looked around her: asphalt illuminated by high pressure sodium lamps. An orange veil of ambient light ensured that it was never fully night.

If only she could see what this place had looked like before the streets, the houses, the cars, the lights—before every square inch of land had been measured out, sold, and "developed." She passed the graveyard at the edge of campus. It was a little haven of darkness with a trace of something elemental—big trees wrapping their roots around the bones of the dead.

A caution light pulsed at the intersection where she turned south. From this point, the sidewalk descended towards the river. A car's headlights appeared behind her; it was a pickup truck with a rattling exhaust pipe. The truck came to a stop next to her, and a window on the passenger side rolled down. A man with a red beard wearing a wool cap leaned out. "Hey bay-bee! Wanna go for a ride?"

Before she had time to reflect on what she was doing, she picked up a large rock and hurled it directly at the strip of metal roof above the man's head.

"Jesus! What the hell?" The driver hit the gas. They sped through the red light at the bottom of the hill and crossed the Michigan Street bridge into the city.

Carol ran to her house a block away. She was less afraid of the men than her own monumental rage—she felt she could have ripped them limb from limb. She ran up the staircase to her second-floor apartment and locked the door behind her. She usually had a cup of tea before bed, but tonight she poured herself a shot of vodka. She stood at the sink in a daze, filling and emptying the shot glass.

Adrenaline could certainly make people capable of all kinds of things. But it was amazing how she had landed that rock right where she wanted it. She squeezed her shoulder and arm and felt a tentative wonder at herself. How had she had the strength to do that? She should have played softball with an arm like that. She opened and closed books for a living. It didn't make any sense that she'd been able to hurl a rock like that.

She wandered into her tiny bedroom and switched on the light beside her bed. She held the purring Godfrey tightly to her chest and breathed deeply. She brushed her teeth and got her clothes ready for the next day. She pulled the curtain across the sliding glass door that led out onto a sorry little balcony facing the river. She got into bed and switched off the light.

The deadline Ingrid had given her was a good thing. The manuscript was taking a toll on her health; she needed to be done with it, but her endgame was still uncertain. On the day before the deadline, would she say, "Wow, Ingrid! Look what I *just* found?"

And who was the manuscript's rightful owner? Someone who legally owned it had given it to the university, presumably. But in terms of culture, religion, history…well, that was far more complicated. She stared at the ceiling tiles and drifted off to sleep.

She was awakened by the sound of Godfrey growling. He stood by the sliding glass door, switching his tail, which had fluffed out like a bottlebrush. The door was locked, wasn't it? She distinctly remembered locking it sometime in late fall—one of the last nice days before the weather closed in. But it was also possible that she had left it open.

She got out of bed and drew back a half inch of the curtain covering the door. She saw the balcony railing, illuminated by one of the lights on the Michigan street bridge. She moved closer to the cold glass and pulled the curtain back a bit more. She saw a powerline, a green plastic planter. A bit more of the curtain. Now, she could see most of the balcony—it was empty. She sighed. Godfrey, you stupid cat.

When she turned away from the window, she saw her, standing in her bedroom doorway. She was about her height with long, black hair. For a moment, Carol wondered if she could be looking into a mirror. But the eyes were alien.

"Meskwaki." She heard the woman's voice inside her head.

Images flashed through her mind: a woman's hand holding a piece of glowing pyrite, the moon reflected on the water, a dark cave, a muskrat swimming with green leaves clutched in his mouth, water lilies. But she didn't know what it meant.

The woman with the dark flowing hair shook her head, as if she could bear no more sorrow. She wiped her tears with the back of her hand and left.

A feeble light illuminated the bedroom curtains. The cat was curled up by her feet, fast asleep. She rolled over and grabbed her phone. Something pulled at her hair, and she disentangled the black hair amulet she had found in the manuscript. She couldn't believe how careless she'd been. It was a museum piece, for God's sake. She put it carefully on the nightstand, pulled the blankets up to her chin, and drifted back to sleep.

Friday was her last night with the manuscript. Ingrid had been unyielding with the deadline. But Carol had almost finished taking pictures and had enough material to send to her adviser in Montreal. She was hoping he still remembered who she was.

It was early February and Carol's last week with the manuscript. She was in the basement emptying book boxes when her phone buzzed. Ingrid said she was needed upstairs.

A trim man of medium height in his mid-to-late twenties was in Ingrid's office. They were both examining something on her desk. The man was listening to Ingrid attentively but with a hint of detachment, as if he were reserving judgement on what she was saying. The alert concentration of his face contrasted with his rumpled chinos and untucked shirt, which, judging by the folds, had only recently been taken out of its packaging. He had thick, dark brown hair in need of trimming. His wire-rim glasses were so out-of-date they looked as though they could be an ironic statement. Carol felt sure that they were not.

"Carol, can you help us with this? You've got some experience translating old French, right?"

The man focused his dark eyes on her, and Carol felt as though he could see all the way to the back of her skull. He quickly recognized, no doubt from experience, that that sort of intensity was off-putting and extended his hand to her with a smile. "Hi, I'm… Derrick—Derrick Fischer."

"Nice to meet you." Carol could feel the trace of a smile play about her lips. It felt like a smirk, so she tried to correct it.

Derrick turned back to Ingrid. "Actually, a friend told me about Ms. Bouchard's expertise, and I was hoping she might be willing to help."

Ingrid continued the introduction, "Mr. Fischer is a graduate student in the biology department. He also works part-time at the Herbarium. He's writing his dissertation on evolutionary botany. Did I get that right?"

"Yes, I work mostly with plant physiology and the relationships among plants over time. But right now, I'm working on a very interesting, well, interesting to me, historical issue." He took in a breath, as if preparing to launch into a lengthy description of his research, raised his eyebrows, but then said nothing.

"What's the historical issue?" Carol asked.

"So, I've been trying to find early accounts of the kinds of plants that grew in the Kankakee Swamp before it was dredged. I've come across a letter from a botanist who was working in this area in the eighteenth century, but it's written in French, eighteenth-century French. I'm not having much luck with translating it myself."

"Do you know the name of this botanist?"

"Yes, his name is Francis Schlosser. I have his letters to a botanist in Leipzig, Christian Gottlieb Ludwig." He turned to the overfull backpack that he had put in a chair and began rummaging through the disorderly contents. "The letters are about the plants he's found and what medicinal properties the Native Americans attributed to them." He extracted a manila envelope, which, after a moment's pause, he handed to Carol. "Schlosser might have been stationed at Fort St. Joseph or Michilimackinac. He must have had a very close contact, or contacts, among the Native Americans. It's unlikely he learned as much as he knew about the plants on his own."

"There are a few dictionaries in the reading room. Let's go in there." She grabbed a pencil and notebook from Ingrid's desk and then walked off toward the reading room. "This way," she said and gestured toward the room with the long mahogany table surrounded by bookshelves of ancient-looking tomes. She took from the shelves a couple of dictionaries and sat down at the table."

"Sorry, I'm not going to be very speedy with this. I hope you're patient."

"Trust me. It took me weeks to mistranslate a few sentences. He couldn't have been writing about a trip to visit relatives and a search for fence posts."

"Oh dear, a four-page letter about fence posts. I wouldn't have been so willing to help if I had known." She arranged her paper and dictionaries and began to read the letter.

Derrick started to clean his glasses with the end of his shirt. "Oh, sorry to interrupt, but does the library have any old maps of this area?"

"How old?" she asked, looking up from the letter.

He stared at her a moment as if not entirely comprehending what she said, "Oh, the map! I guess the oldest ones you have. Sorry, I thought you were wondering how old I was."

Carol thought he seemed a little agitated and smiled at him reassuringly. "We have an impressive collection of maps of the Great Lakes, but you have to make an appointment to look at the originals. Here, I'll get you our index." She went to the shelves and pried out an unremarkable three-ring binder from between two far more impressive volumes with stamped leather bindings. "These are just pictures of the maps, obviously, but it will give you a good idea of the breadth of the collection, so you can decide which originals you want to look at more closely."

"Oh, thanks!" He looked at her with a kind of puppy-dog glow, but then, mildly embarrassed, reined in the warmth of his smile.

Carol returned to her seat and looked at the letter. She recognized the handwriting instantly as the same that was in the manuscript. The letter even had a date: 1763. Her temples were throbbing. Did he know what she had in the basement? She looked at him quickly. He was turning the pages of the notebook as she had suggested. No, he didn't have a clue.

It took her more than an hour to translate the letter. She read through what she had written, moving her lips as she did so. She erased bits and scribbled in new material.

Derrick had spent the time looking through the map index, lifting his head occasionally to steal covert looks at her.

"Okay," she said decisively, rubbing the end of her nose with her forefinger. Derrick's reverie was interrupted, and he looked at Carol with an unfocused gaze. "His French is pretty good for a non-native. This guy doesn't seem like your typical soldier in a wilderness outpost. Turns out...," she raised her eyebrows and tucked a lock of dark hair behind her ear. "It's a love letter. I'll read it:

Fort Pontchartrain, August 25, 1763
My dearest Marguerite,
My father's position in the army convinced me that I too should be a soldier, but, unfortunately, did not ensure I'd be a good one. Now, I must live with the fact that I set my pastime above the lives of fifteen good men and endangered your life as well.

I don't remember much of the trip to the fort. I was in a lot of pain. I remember the forests we passed through seemed endless. Eventually, the trail we were on ended in an open plain. There were square white houses surrounded by split rail fences and orchards, but the houses were empty. I heard gunfire from the fort. The Oddawa and Huron had surrounded it.

Your brother's men traded me for four Potawatomi and Myaamia warriors. Gnêw did not look me in the face during the entire journey. I felt he would still rather have killed me, even though I turned out to be valuable in getting his people back.

Carol looked up from her translation and said, "Here, it looks as though time has passed because the ink and handwriting look slightly different."

"I've been walled up in this stinking hole for three months. I'm much stronger now, and I'm hoping to join a group of soldiers headed west. For now, my plan is to find work and make some money.

I'm entrusting this letter to a Potawatomi woman who's traveling along the Sauk trail to the lands beyond the Theakiki to return to her family. She said that she knows your mother, and I am hopeful this letter will somehow find its way to you.

I will do all I can to get another letter to you. I hope you've been able to protect the manuscript, though I understand how difficult that must be. During all these dark days, my heart lifts when I think of you.

All my love,

Francis

When she read the reference to the manuscript, her heart stopped. Yet, looking up from her notebook to Derrick, she managed to say in a casual tone, "So, you're familiar with this manuscript he mentions?"

"No…I mean, yes. Schlosser mentions a manuscript in his letter to Gottlieb, but, no, no one has ever confirmed its existence. Now, we know it *did* exist, and that in the 1760s it passed into the hands of the Potawatomi. Actually, it's doubtful it still exists if it hasn't turned up by now. I've looked in all the major collections for it."

"Where'd you find the letter?"

"A friend of mine was researching Roger's Rangers and found a reference to Schlosser's death in the British *Annual Register*. The *Register* article said that Schlosser was eventually reassigned to Fort Stanwix in Syracuse, New York." He took the envelope he had given her and extracted a few pages, which he placed before her. "Here, it says he was shot dead by an 'Indian slave.' That was in 1768. His remains and personal effects, which included this letter, were sent to Montreal, which was then controlled by the British."

"Why was there a letter he wrote to someone else in his possession?" Carol asked.

"The letter has a stamp on it in the corner." Derrick leaned across the table and pointed to the edge of the photocopy. "You can just barely see it, but it's a stamp from the South Bend courthouse, 1864. Maybe it was included with his personal effects."

"So, both the letter and maybe the manuscript were still here in 1864. And the way he died…" She frowned, letting her gaze travel to the books above his head. "You don't suppose it was Marguerite's brother who finally did him in?"

He looked a bit surprised and smiled. "Yeah, I didn't think of that. Guess we'll never know."

Ingrid opened the glass door to the reading room where they sat. "It's closing time, Carol." The library's recorded chimes and message to patrons confirmed this.

Carol looked at her watch. Ingrid noticed Carol's new bracelet, "Where did you get that? I've never seen you wear it before."

Carol looked at the bracelet, as if noticing it for the first time. "This one? Found it outside my door."

"Looks like black onyx. You should get it appraised."

Carol shrugged her shoulders. "Appraisals cost money—money I don't have."

Ingrid looked slightly embarrassed. "Make sure everything is locked up and remember we have to finish the baseball project tomorrow."

"Okay. See you tomorrow," Carol said, indulging herself by giving Ingrid a bit of a hard stare.

Ingrid left.

"I'll make you a copy," Carol said, turning to Derrick and holding out her hand for the translation. "If you were able to locate this manuscript, how would it help you?"

"Well… it would save me an enormous amount of work." He put his hands into his thick dark hair at the back of his head. "Right now, I'm dependent on seeds and pollen from sediment samples to reconstruct a plant ecology people have spent the last two and a half centuries altering or destroying. The habitats left that even remotely resemble the original ones are the size of postage stamps."

She looked out the glass door Ingrid had just exited, lowered her voice, and moved closer to him. "And what next, after you figure out what used to grow there?"

He inhaled and briefly closed his dark eyes. "Well, it might be naïve, but I hope someone, someday might be interested in restoring it."

"And you would like to help with that?" she asked, looking at him intently.

He looked slightly uncomfortable, then resolved. "Yes. Yes, I would."

"Do you know anything about chemistry?" she asked.

He gave her a puzzled look. "I've survived several classes of it."

Carol opened the glass door and looked out. "Okay. She's definitely gone." She crossed her arms over her chest and said in a voice so hushed it was barely audible, "I want to show you something. It's in the basement."

Derrick gathered his jacket and backpack and followed her to the elevator, which they rode to the basement.

Carol went directly to the box with the manuscript, extracted it, and put it on the metal table she'd been using every night.

"Oh my God, is this it?" He dropped his backpack and coat on the floor. "Is this the manuscript?"

Carol nodded and beamed. After all these months of secrecy, she was finally showing it to someone who appreciated its beauty and value. Derrick spent the next hour pouring through it, commenting on things he recognized, expressing wonder at what was unfamiliar.

"*This* is what I found three weeks ago." Carol took a glass bottle out of her backpack. "I found it wrapped up in newspapers under the manuscript." She handed it to him. It was a square, blue glass bottle.

He held it up to the light and read,

> *Soothing Lily*
> *Contains valuable tonic and nerve stimulant*
> *properties of the water lily. A drug known and used*
> *by Indians to induce restorative sleep and relieve pain*
> *the natural way.*
> *Jeremy Thorton, Chemist, Sole Proprietor.*

"Take a look at the last page of the manuscript," Carol said.

Derrick carefully turned the pages. "A water lily with bright red blossoms. That's unusual for this part of the world."

"According to the manuscript, it opens only at night."

"That's got to be wrong," Derrick said, a sudden intensity replacing his former easy-going demeanor. "That type of lily exists only in Southeast Asia."

Carol was silent for a moment, furrowed her brow, then said, "Well, that feature does seem pretty unusual." She pointed to the text at the right of the drawing. "But the description is lengthy and detailed. Doesn't seem like something they'd make up," Carol said, rubbing her nose. "According to the manuscript, the lily's Algonquin name is nabagûck. It was used in vision quest rituals."

Derrick interlaced his fingers and rested them in his lap. He stared at the ceiling and leaned the folding chair back at what looked to Carol like a dangerous angle. "I guess it's possible that night-blooming water lilies *used* to grow here." He rocked forward; the chair legs dropped with a thud. "I mean, there are plants that grow here now that could be very different from their ancestors in all sorts of ways—the chemical composition of their seeds, the color of the blossoms…"

Derrick picked up the blue, glass bottle Carol had placed on the table before him and held it up to the light. "It's still full."

"Do you know of anyone who could test this?" Carol asked.

"I can ask a chemist friend of mine if she can do it."

Carol was standing just outside a pool of fluorescent light, which left half her face in darkness. "I found Jeremy Thorton's name on a class roster for Fr. Nieuwland. He's listed as an undergraduate and then a graduate. I think he must have been using the information in the manuscript to make drugs."

Carol continued, "About a month ago, a guy showed up from a pharmaceutical company, asking about the manuscript. I'm guessing he found a record of the Soothing Lily drug in their corporate archives. Maybe their documents even mention the manuscript."

"Does the guy have a handlebar mustache?"

"Yeah!"

Derrick smiled and shook his head. "That guy showed up at the Herbarium too. Super uptight and aggressive?"

Carol nodded vigorously.

"He wouldn't let this friend of mine alone. Said he was a research chemist and demanded access to our collection. He kept asking about a plant—she didn't say which it was. She got so sick of him, she told him that she had seen it growing abundantly by the river downtown."

As Carol and Derrick took the elevator back upstairs, she told him the story of how she'd discovered the manuscript six months ago and turned it into her dissertation topic.

He put on his coat and gathered his things and noticed that she wasn't doing the same. "You're staying here?"

"Have to. I've only got until the end of the week to get this done," she said, rubbing her temples with her fingertips. She opened the door for him, and he went out into the corridor.

"I'll try to get you the lab results by Friday," he said, laboring to put his heavy pack back on his back. "Meet you here at the end of the workday?"

"Three a.m.?"

He closed his eyes and shook his head. "Wait, that's how late you've been working every night?"

She shrugged and looked at him from behind the still open door with a guilty smile.

He backed down the corridor, holding the straps of his backpack. "Okay. Well, I'll see you, if I don't fall asleep."

She waved and watched him walk, a bit asymmetrically, down the corridor to the exit.

She returned to the basement, feeling lighter and happier than she'd felt in a long time. The manuscript, and the necessity of keeping it a secret, had become an increasingly heavy burden since she'd made her discovery in September.

Of course, she hadn't told him everything. She hadn't told him about the weird underwater dreams she'd been having, but then who talked with total strangers about their dreams?

Late Friday afternoon, Carol came up from the basement and found Ingrid in conversation with the executive from the pharmaceutical company. Dread washed over her.

"Catholic University doesn't have it; the Smithsonian doesn't either. It *has* to be here."

"We don't have any record of this manuscript, Mr…"

"Blackmole."

"Carol, is that you?" Ingrid said with a sharp edge to her voice.

"Yes," she answered, as if she wasn't entirely sure of her own identity. She stepped into Ingrid's office.

"Mr. Blackmole is here from Parke-Davis, and he's trying to locate a manuscript," said Ingrid.

Carol raised her eyebrows and crossed her arms across her chest.

"Mr. Blackmole, without having any reference numbers, we're really unable to help you. Before any of our new resources come to us, they get numbers. We simply don't have anything that's uncatalogued…except, of course, the books we just received from Nieuwland Hall. Carol, you haven't found anything that fits Mr. Blackmole's description?" Ingrid looked at Blackmole. "You're looking for a botanical manuscript from which time period?"

"Nineteenth century, perhaps even earlier," he added.

They were both looking at her. She could feel her temperature rise. She willed all expression from her face. "I'll get my laptop. We can look at my inventory spreadsheet."

She sat down at one of the large mahogany tables and opened her laptop. She scanned the list for an entry she knew wasn't there.

"The closest thing I have on my list is a couple of lab notebooks from a botany class Nieuwland taught in 1912. Would you like to look at those?"

Blackmole turned away from Carol and looked intently at Ingrid. "Could I see this uncatalogued collection?"

Ingrid looked slightly offended. "Mr. Blackmole, I'm afraid we don't allow patrons in the stacks."

"My company is prepared to pay a lot of money to…find the manuscript."

Ingrid's eyes lit up at the mention of money but clearly didn't want some outsider on her turf. "How many boxes of uncatalogued books are left, Carol?"

"Twenty-four"

"Well, then you'll have your answer shortly." Ingrid smiled and stood up from her desk.

Blackmole very slowly turned his expressionless face towards Carol. "I'd be happy to help your assistant with the remainder of the boxes."

Carol held her breath, contemplating the prospect of spending time with Blackmole in the basement.

But then, as he turned towards Ingrid, his face suddenly transformed. He radiated warmth, even charm, "I'm an executive at a large corporation now, but I started my career as a chemical engineer at a research university. I know how tight university budgets can be. People don't understand that good science demands significant resources."

Here he stopped—his rhetoric demanded a comparison with the needs of non-scientific university libraries, yet he clearly didn't feel they had the same claim on resources. "So, I understand the frustration of trying to work within tight university budgets. Believe me, Park Davis is prepared to make a significant donation."

Ingrid's manicured eyebrows slowly elevated. Her chilly smile disappeared, and her lips parted. A sultry warmth spread across her wrinkled face. "There's certainly no denying that buying and caring for rare books is an expensive proposition, and we are always looking for ways to expand our collection."

The closing chime sounded.

"We're closing for the day, Mr. Blackmole," Ingrid said apologetically, reluctant to let this big fish off the line. "Why don't you come back tomorrow morning, and we can start a thorough search of the basement. Maybe I can get some undergraduates to assist?" They continued discussing their plans for the next day as Ingrid showed Blackmole to the door.

Ingrid had picked up the scent of cash. Blackmole, who had previously appeared to her as an interloper, had identified himself as very valuable asset. Carol, having thwarted the cash-laden Blackmole's objectives, was now the enemy.

Ingrid instructed Carol to put together in one pile all the remaining unopened boxes for Blackmole to look through in the morning.

"Make sure he has a chair!" Ingrid called to her as she headed for the elevator.

As the elevator doors closed, Carol rolled her eyes and sighed. It didn't make sense to her that someone like Blackmole would be so interested in the manuscript. His company had already developed, tested, and marketed "The Soothing Lily" in the 1920s or 30s. Unless they had lost all the information in a fire or through an act of industrial sabotage, they must know the water lily's chemical properties and could surely make a synthetic copy.

She didn't have the time to think about his motives. She needed to focus on the manuscript. She needed to take more photos, double check spellings, and verify that her figure references were correct. To these tasks, she devoted an hour, but then her mind returned to the question of Blackmole and his pharmaceutical company.

Of all the manuscript's medicines, those made from the water lily seemed the most potent—visions, states of ecstasy, communion with gods, prophetic dreams, painful death. Yet the "Soothing Lily" label advertised the drug's ability to combat insomnia and relieve pain—modest claims considering the powers ascribed to it by Native tribes. She had assumed the claims made on a twentieth-century medicine bottle were more reliable than those in an eighteenth-century manuscript. Perhaps that was wrong.

She also wondered if there wasn't something more to be learned from the Father Nieuwland collection in the Archives. He had taught at the University for thirty-two years and was a prolific correspondent. Most of his research was in chemistry, but he had been trained as a botanist and taught the subject. His association with Greene, who donated the Herbarium, made Nieuwland the manuscript's most likely owner. The newspapers used as padding inside the manuscript box dated from the early twentieth century—Nieuwland's era, and the manuscript was found in the building where he had spent most of his career.

Carol looked at her watch: 11 p.m. If she was going to revisit Father Neiuwland's papers in the Archives, she needed to do it now. Ingrid kept a set of keys for library offices in her desk drawer. Was it breaking and entering, if she had a key? She was library staff and, even though she didn't have authorization at this moment, she had been granted access to Archive resources. She was doing legitimate research.

Carol took the elevator to the first floor and went to Ingrid's office. She retrieved the conveniently labeled Archive keys from Ingrid's desk drawer, locked the Rare Book Room door, and walked down the granite corridor to the Main Library. To her right, the soaring window wall stared out into the dark, wet night.

A girl with a head full of auburn curls was at the circulation desk, her face dangerously close to the pages of a fat textbook. Students in sweatpants and baseball hats sprawled across lounge chairs and ottomans with their laptops and take-out coffee cups. Carol got into the elevator and pushed six.

The elevator door opened into an empty hallway illuminated with sterile, white-blue light. Her boots slapped against the tile floor. Ingrid's key didn't fit the lock on the Archives' metal fire door. She kept trying. Clearly, forcing it would not help. Christ, what if she got the key stuck in the lock? She took a few deep breaths, adjusted the key's angle by a nanometer—the door opened.

After stumbling around for a few minutes, she found herself in the dark but familiar reading room. A red light blinked in the corner. Security camera? From the room's large windows, she could see the lights of the golden dome on the Main Administration Building and the outline of Nieuwland Hall's rooftop. She opened a glass paneled door and entered the stacks. A motion detector turned on the lights automatically, startling her.

She found the N's in the floor-to-ceiling metal bookshelves that filled the room.

"N," "N-i," "N-i-e," Nieuwland. She grabbed three large cardboard boxes off the shelf and brought them back to the reading room.

She flipped through the index, looking for the correspondences between Father Nieuwland and Father Greene. Time-yellowed paper was interspersed with hand-typed documents. The handwriting was elegant but inscrutable. Luckily, some conscientious library scribe had deciphered the early twentieth-century penmanship and typed the text on heavy weight paper.

Her tired eyes scanned through the documents looking for some mention of the manuscript or lily. Many of the letters had to do with arcane but hotly felt disputes concerning botanical taxonomy. One letter dated 1918 had an attached tracking sheet with the words: "Student letter to N?" She read the following paragraph:

I had been assured that it was a very small dose for a man of Roosevelt's size and vigor, yet I'm telling you that in the course of not more than three hours, he was reduced to the condition of a mewling baby. On the return trip to the lodge, the Colonel told me that he had had a vision of great clarity and horrific content. When I pressed him, in so far as politeness and his position in the world allowed, as to the subject, he reluctantly told me that it had involved his son, Quentin. As you know, just two months after the Colonel's "vision," Quentin was shot down by a German aircraft.

Not only will this water lily elixir eliminate pain and insomnia, it appears to endow one with prophetic powers. Imagine how this could have aided us in the war? And, of course, there's an enormous amount of money to be made.

Carol sat back in her chair and let the words echo in her head: "there's an enormous amount of money to be made." For thousands of years, the lily's power had been sacred knowledge—a way to commune with the gods. But, today, for a company like Park-Davis, it was a potential blockbuster drug, a profit engine.

She took a picture of the letter and returned the materials to the shelf. She felt dizzy as she carefully returned everything to its place. She had never done anything remotely this criminal before, but she had learned an important part of the puzzle.

"You definitely work late," Derrick said, stepping into the Rare Books Room and pulling back the rain-soaked hood of his oversized sweatshirt. He immediately ran his foot into a table leg. "Jesus! How do you function in total darkness?"

"I'm used to it. I keep the lights off, so I don't get any visits from security," Carol said, moving confidently around the shadowy masses of furniture and turning on a reading light. They sat down opposite each other. The manuscript in its original box was on the table between them.

She told him about Blackmole's visit and Ingrid's sudden

willingness to give him access to the uncatalogued material, after he suggested a possible donation. She also told him what she had just found in the Archives about the drug's prophetic powers.

He fixed her with an inquisitional look. "You're not skeptical about 'prophetic powers'?" he asked.

She rocked her head back and forth. "I've had so many weird things happen since I've been working on this manuscript, I just don't know anymore."

"You've been short on sleep too, right?"

She looked at him as if she were going to say more on the subject, but then asked, "What did you find out about the 'Soothing Lily'?"

Derrick reached into his coat pocket, took out the bottle and put it on the table. "Psychoactive alkaloid aporphine. It's a hallucinogen, anxiety reliever, sleep aid. It's been in that bottle for about a hundred years. Probably not very effective anymore."

Carol took the bottle from his hand and examined it. "Science drains all the magic from things, doesn't it?"

"I bet your brain chemistry feels pretty magical on that stuff," he said, smiling and awkwardly trying to shove his phone back into his pants pocket.

She folded her hands in her lap and sighed. "It's a shame someone like Blackmole will end up with the manuscript." She looked at Derrick and then at some distant point behind his head. "Can't you picture Marguerite and Francis? I can see them in the candlelight—their heads bent over the manuscript. I can see them by the river looking for wild ginger, or with Medéwewen elders, asking them which elixirs could be made from the leaves of stinging nettles."

Derrick was studying her intently. "You've got the opposite of prophesy. You see the past."

"Retrocognition," she said.

"Impressive."

"Honestly, I just looked that up the other day." Suddenly dispirited, she looked contemplatively at the manuscript box and pulled a tiny splinter off of it.

Her melancholy put him ill at ease. "Maybe it's not so bad that Blackmole and his pharmaceutical gang get the manuscript," he said, shrugging. "It could potentially benefit people with all sorts of afflictions. And what's so wrong with profit being the engine of that process?"

"Because all that leads to the manuscript ending up in a climate-controlled glass box accessible only to experts or people who have purchased tickets to see it. Blackmole and his company will have it thoroughly commodified. They have no interest in keeping the manuscript…sacred. He wants to exploit it."

They sat in silence for a minute. Then Carol suddenly gripped the edge of the desk and leaned forward. "Were any of the books from Nieuwland Hall brought to the Herbarium?"

Derrick rubbed his face with his hands. "Let me think. Yes, three or four boxes. Why?"

"Did they open them yet?"

"No, as far as I know, they're still under a desk in the reception room."

Derrick looked at his watch, "Christ, it's almost six."

"We could bring the manuscript to the Herbarium," said Carol with sudden eagerness. "The manuscript box could just as easily have wound up there."

"Moving it there isn't going to protect it for very long. Plus, if it's not documented and given a home somewhere, you can't write a dissertation on it. A work of fiction maybe, but not a dissertation."

Carol rested her hand on the manuscript box and scrunched up her face. "Should I hand this over to a pharmaceutical company, so I can publish a few articles for an audience of what— twelve?"

"That *is* what academics do. Besides, it's light already. People are up and about. They'll see us carrying the manuscript box."

"Not if we take the tunnels."

He stared at her blankly. "Wait, those tunnels aren't for pedestrians. They're for heating and cooling."

"A friend of mine got a tour of the tunnels once. She said they're narrow but clean and well lit. When we had all that flooding, I saw workmen get into the steam tunnels from the basement." She leaned forward and touched his arm. "I don't expect you to go. You've been great."

A slightly ironic smile played on his lips. "Oh no. If it gives me the chance of being scalded alive, I'm all in."

They took the elevator to the basement, and Carol headed directly for a closet door. "*Yes*, unlocked," she whispered excitedly. She fumbled along the wall for the light switch. Derrick found it and flicked it on.

It was a small closet with a mop, a bucket, a broom, folding chairs and a fuse box. They moved some of the chairs out of the way and saw the outline of a trapdoor with a recessed metal handle. She pulled it, but it didn't budge.

"Do you need a key?" Derrick asked.

"I don't know. I don't see a keyhole anywhere."

Derrick pressed the latch down then up; it opened. A metal ladder descended into the darkness. Derrick held up his phone's flashlight. They could see a concrete floor six feet down. "It doesn't look clean or well-lit down there," he said.

Carol gave him an apologetic smile and handed him the box with the manuscript as she positioned herself to climb down the ladder.

The tunnel was six-feet high and four-feet wide. Enormous metal pipes ran the length of the concrete walls. The air was hot and heavy with moisture.

Derrick had put the manuscript box in a garbage bag he found in the closet and was now gingerly descending the ladder. "Which way?" he asked. "Jordan Hall must be mostly east of here and a little north." He repositioned the box so he could see his phone. "My phone compass says left."

Carol could see the glow of an emergency light up ahead. She had been hoping for the kind of tunnels that ran beneath Disney World—painted with bright, cheerful colors, the floor gleaming with new polish. This tunnel was oppressively dark and smelled of mice and mildew. The pipes hissed constantly and occasionally clanged. Derrick closed the hatch; the only light remaining was from their phones.

"Okay. I just dropped a pin," he called, his voice echoing.

The heat and humidity worsened as they advanced down the tunnel. Carol could feel the sweat dripping down her shirt. The hissing made it sound as if the walls were made of snakes.

"There's a map here!" Derrick called out.

Carol walked back to where he was standing to see a small schematic diagram high on the tunnel wall; there were black shapes representing buildings. He pointed to the largest black rectangle. "That sort of looks like Jordan Hall. Maybe just keep on walking until we see an opportunity to turn left? Remind me to drop another pin when we do that."

As she moved along in this hissing darkness, it suddenly felt uncannily familiar. She had been here before. She could almost grasp the butterfly wing of some distant memory, a long-forgotten dream. All at once, she seemed to be falling into a very deep well.

She was swimming against a current under a hazy gold full moon. She saw the water as she had never seen it before—endlessly cascading, sparkling, alive. Heard its sweet, ringing voice. Green trout, sturgeon, muskrat surrounded her, welcomed her. A woman with long, flowing hair swam before her—showing her the way, and Carol wanted nothing more than to follow.

She heard Derrick's voice as if it were coming to her from a great distance. "Are you okay? You're weaving all over the place. We need to turn north, not south. South goes to the river."

She could smell the river and taste it in the tunnel air; she instinctively turned towards it. "No," she whispered, "not yet." She shook her head and forced herself to go left.

"I'm okay. Just…sleepy."

Up ahead, she could see another red emergency light and then the contours of a ladder mounted to the tunnel wall. Derrick climbed up it and pushed at the door above his head. It was stuck. As Carol held the flashlight, he pulled and pushed violently on the handle for several minutes, cursing at it and enlarging the sweat stains under his arms. Finally, it broke free; gray light filtered into the tunnel. Carol handed him the manuscript box, his coat, and the backpack that he had shed. They emerged into a storage room—green plastic tarps, bags of soil, fans, and earthenware pots filled the shelves.

"Bingo. Basement of Jordon Hall. Under the greenhouse," Derrick said, wiping off the dirt and dust from his jeans.

After cautiously opening the storage room door and making sure no one was around, they climbed a flight of stairs into the blinding sunlight streaming through the greenhouse roof. The air was thick with the smell of wet, lush vegetation. From the greenhouse, they stepped into a long hallway with a vaulted ceiling and crossed its shiny marble floor inlaid with self-important, academic medallions—biology, chemistry, physics.

Derrick took out his keys and opened the Herbarium. Carol closed her eyes for a moment; her closed eyelids felt like the sweetest balm. She was standing behind Derrick and thought she could smell his sweat. It smelled a little like the pastrami sandwiches her mother used to pack for her school lunches. "You don't have any food, do you?"

He smiled. His eyes were puffy. "Half an egg salad sandwich I got out of the vending machine. Interested? Sorry I don't have anything better. I've stopped caring much what I eat—works out pretty well when you're on a tight budget."

Carol put her hand up in protest. "Thanks, I'll wait."

A phone was ringing somewhere in the suite of offices connected to the Herbarium. Derrick put the manuscript box down on the long, wooden table in the reception area and went to answer it.

The Herbarium was also a museum of biodiversity with displays of skewered butterflies, fan-shaped fossils, and taxidermied trout. As she studied the trout's brown dots, the upward curve of its lower jaw, Carol slipped into the phantasmagorical world she had encountered in the tunnel. She was once more swimming against the current...

"That was my supervisor," Derrick said and put his hands to his temples. "Shit. Maybe I shouldn't have picked up. This isn't my morning to work. She said she just got a call from the Rare Books Room. They're searching for a missing manuscript, it seems." He sat down at the table. They both gazed fixedly at Box 46 with furrowed brows.

"I've often wondered if the Pokagon Band of Potawatomi would take it," Carol said, turning her gaze to Derrick. "I'm certainly not in any position to offer it to them. It's the University's property."

"But you said it's not an ordinary artifact, right?" said Derrick. "It's a sacred text." He leaned forward. "If it's a Native American sacred text, some representative should be invited to look at it. There might even be grounds for repatriation."

Carol suddenly stood up. "Can I use your phone? Mine is dying." Carrying Derrick's phone, she walked decisively towards a cubicle in a far corner of the room.

They heard someone fumbling with keys at the door. Derrick grabbed the manuscript box and stuck it in a closet, flinging a pair of rubber boots and wool scarf on top of it and closing the door.

A short, full-figured, middle-aged woman with a grey bob entered the room. A sky-blue barrette swept her bangs to one side. She carried a lunch bag, purse, and backpack, which she had accessorized with tiny plush toys, key rings and iron-on patches from National Parks.

"Derrick, I'm *so* glad you're here," she said slightly out of breath. She noticed Carol talking on the phone and looked questioningly at Derrick.

"That's Carol. She works in the Rare Book Room," said Derrick. Carol leaned back in her chair and waved to Margaret, who gave her a cheery smile.

Margaret moved closer to Derrick and lowered her voice, "She wasn't *sent* over here, was she?"

Derrick shook his head and scowled, as if offended by the suggestion.

Margaret shimmied herself out of her book-laden backpack. As soon as she was free from her burden, he put her hands on her hips, stretched, and arched her back. "Do you know anything about this manuscript they're looking for?"

Derrick, who was unused to duplicity, hesitated. There was a knock at the door. Margaret hung her colorful, quilted jacket on a hook by her desk, ran her fingers through her hair, and went to the door.

"It was a *tremendous* task." It was Ingrid's voice. "They dumped hundreds of books on us. No organization whatsoever. But six months of hard work and late nights paid off," she said in a self-congratulatory tone, not immediately seeing Carol, who was sitting at a cubicle at the far end of the room. Carol, who was cradling the phone between her neck and shoulder, waved with exaggerated perkiness to Ingrid, who loosened her silk scarf as if it had suddenly become too tight.

Blackmole, looking disheveled, entered the room behind Ingrid. His shoes were muddy and one of his pant legs even had dirt on it. As Carol watched him, she wondered how he justified his arrogance—a rational man of science forced to navigate alone the stormy seas of human behavior.

Ingrid introduced Blackmole, putting particular emphasis on his title—*Vice President* of Research. She said he had reason to believe that an old botanical manuscript of great interest to the pharmaceutical company he worked for was somewhere on campus. She explained that they had already searched the remaining twenty-four boxes of uncatalogued materials in the Rare Book Room; the Herbarium was the next logical place to search.

"We do have four boxes from that collection," said Margaret and dragged the boxes out from under her desk. They opened them and found they contained an Idaho fly-fishing guide, physics textbooks, and a series on homesteading.

"That's certainly an eclectic mix. I doubt the main library will want any of these," Margaret said as she stood up from the floor where she was unpacking them with Ingrid's assistance. "I guess that settles it. I'm sorry we couldn't have found the manuscript you were looking for, Mr. …Blackmole, it sounds like quite a treasure."

Blackmole stared at Ingrid, looking incredulous that she would allow him to be thwarted in this way.

Ingrid responded to his displeasure. "Well, we can cross these boxes off our list, but the Herbarium's collection could also be searched."

Margaret narrowed her eyes, as if she hadn't heard Ingrid. "Everything we have has a catalogue number. It's not on our shelves unless it has a number."

"I think…Mr. Blackmole, correct me if I'm not understanding you right. Mr. Blackmole believes that the manuscript could have been… misshelved."

Margaret shook her head as if trying to disperse a thick mental fog. "It couldn't have been misshelved if it doesn't have a number. We know what *is* and what *is not* part of our collection because we have barcodes, circulation software, the Library of Congress system. What's the good of a library that can't keep track of its own collection?"

She continued, her face growing redder. "Is it possible for a few books in our collection to be misshelved or even lost? Sure. Do I wonder if I'm going to discover a first edition of Darwin's *Origin of Species* on the Herbarium's shelves? No."

There were several knocks at the door. Margaret furrowed her brow. "We're so popular this morning." She returned with three under-graduates—all looking as if they had just woken up.

"I hired these students to help us with our search," said Blackmole, addressing himself in an indirect way to Margaret. "You two," he pointed to a student in the black baseball cap, who put his hand to his chest with an uncertain look, and another whose thick shaggy bangs hid his eyes entirely. Blackmole nodded curtly. "Yes, you two. Go through the collection in the backroom and check for anything out of place. And you," he pointed to a round-faced girl with blue glasses. "Check the closets and storage areas." She looked as if she were going to object but then walked uncertainly after the others.

"Mr. Blackmole," said a visibly distraught Margaret. "I have my own *trained* staff."

Ingrid stepped forward. "Margaret, I know this might seem like overstepping your authority."

"Seem?"

Margaret walked decisively to her desk and picked up the receiver of her university-issued, black, plastic phone.

The usually unflappable Ingrid leaned against a table and studied her glossy leather pumps.

Carol, who had finished her call, pulled up a chair and sat down at the table. Her eyes met Derrick's briefly; they both looked away.

Blackmole joined the students to oversee their search of the collection. As their search dragged on, Ingrid fished paperwork out of her briefcase, while Carol and Derrick pretended to immerse themselves in books they had grabbed at random off the shelves.

After more than an hour, the round-faced girl returned to the reception area, and, on her way to retrieve her backpack, noticed the closet next to Ingrid's desk. Derrick and Carol watched the girl open the door and go in. They looked at each other. The metallic shriek of heavy coats being slid back and forth reassured Carol that the student's search was cursory.

There was a long pause and then the door opened. The girl backed out of the closet carrying the box with the manuscript. She placed it on the table and studied it critically before extracting the leather-wrapped book. The rich scent of old leather and decaying vegetation filled the room. The girl left to get Blackmole.

"Oh my God! That's eighteenth century," said Ingrid, who had noiselessly approached the table and was gently turning the pages.

Blackmole stood momentarily at the doorway. His expression of cool arrogance acquired a patina of gloating self-satisfaction. He had been right—right in the manuscript's location and right in his method of finding it. Ingrid backed away from the table, and he strode confidently forward to claim his prize.

Margaret, who had just emerged from a backroom, approached the table as if she were in a trance. "Where did that come from?"

Blackmole didn't answer her. He paged through the book, stopping at the final page to look at the water lily. "My company will, of course, make a sizable donation to the…Herbarium," he said.

The color drained from Ingrid's face and her brow furrowed.

With effort, Margaret drew her gaze from the manuscript to look at Derrick, who gave her a little shrug that he instantly regretted.

There was a knock at the door. Carol motioned to Margaret that she would get it and returned a few moments later with a man of medium height wearing a crisp white shirt that contrasted with the soft roses of his cheeks. His black hair that was pulled back into a ponytail flecked with silver, and his eyes were surrounded by abundant crow's feet.

"This is Mr. Flores," said Carol. "The archivist from the Pokagon Band of Potawatomi."

"Sorry, have I walked in on a meeting?" he asked. "Carol called me about a Native American manuscript?"

Everyone looked at Carol. "Yes, it's an ethnobotanical manuscript." She gestured towards the table. "Take a look. It's a Medéwewen book…"

Blackmole was standing directly in front of the manuscript.

"Sorry," Flores said.

Grudgingly, Blackmole moved a few steps away as Flores extracted his reading glasses from his shirt pocket. The others gathered around, while the newcomer gently and reverently turned the pages.

Despite her disappointment that the manuscript had been discovered, Carol felt parental pride as they all circled the table lost in admiration.

"If this is the book I think it is, it's been missing since the 1830s," said Flores, taking off his reading glasses and looking at Carol, "even before the tribe was removed to Kansas." He pointed to the edge of the page. "These are words from the wiigwaasabak, the birch bark scrolls. Where was this found?"

"In the basement of the Rare Books Room," said Carol, feeling the color rising to her cheeks. "But it came from Nieuwland Hall. It must have belonged to Father Nieuwland. I realize I should have told my supervisor immediately about the manuscript, but I wanted a chance to study it first," Carol said, shrugged slightly, and continued, "My graduate work was focused on the Jesuits and Native American tribes in New France. I hoped that the manuscript could provide the dissertation topic I was looking for."

"If Ms. Bouchard had come to me with this," Ingrid said peevishly. "I can assure you I would have immediately contacted representatives from the tribe." The air reverberated for several seconds with the falseness of her words.

"Well, it sounds as though Ms. Bouchard has made herself an expert on the manuscript, which is just what is needed," said Mr. Flores, looking at Ingrid. "This is an amazing find. The next step is consulting with the tribal community."

"Before we make plans for that, I have something here that might be of interest," said Blackmole snapping his briefcase open and pulling out a piece of paper. "It's dated January 8, 1917." He began to read. "I, Julius Aloysius Arthur Nieuwland of South Bend, Indiana have been paid the sum of two hundred dollars by the pharmaceutical company Park, Davis & Company for the manuscript entitled: *Plants of North America and their Medicinal Use*. The receipt of the two hundred dollars in hereby acknowledged, and I do covenant to and with said party that I am the owner and have the right to sell or transfer the said property and will defend the right against any persons whomever."

He dropped the letter for an instant to enjoy the look of discomfiture on his listeners' faces then continued, "Nieuwland goes on to say that the two hundred dollars from the manuscript's sale will be used by the Brothers of the Holy Cross to purchase Liberty Bonds for the war effort. He writes that he is 'very thankful'." He then put the letter back into his tidy briefcase.

"Why was the manuscript never sent to Park-Davis, if they were the rightful owners?" Ingrid asked Blackmole.

"Nieuwland never sent the manuscript because Park-Davis never requested it," Carol answered. All turned to look at her. "The company already had the information it needed from the manuscript. One of Nieuwland's students, Jeremy Thorton, had provided it. He gave them a compound from a local water lily—now, sadly, extinct in the wild—that he hoped would be an effective pain killer. After Park-Davis started selling the drug, they found that it was causing suicides and schizophrenia." She paused; her voice grew stronger. "I know this because I found a series of newspaper articles from the 1920s and 30s connecting your company's drug, 'Soothing Lily,' to several bizarre, unexplained deaths—murder, suicides, mostly drownings."

Blackmole looked as though his patience were being tried.

"Mr. Blackmole's company continued to claim the drug was a cure-all—sleep aid, anxiety reducer, pain reliever. It did it all." Carol paused and looked at Blackmole. "It was mostly women who took the drug, so their suicides were chalked up to hysteria. Morphine was considered the big threat in those days, since it killed so many more. Nobody paid much attention to the deaths caused by the 'Soothing Lily.'"

Blackmole's face relaxed into what could have been a smile. "You're talking about something that *may* have happened eighty to ninety years ago. No one cares about that now."

Carol furrowed her brow. "Not exactly a great legacy though, is it? You took information from a Native American sacred book to make a drug that you didn't test properly, and it killed people, particularly psychologically vulnerable women. Doesn't sound like great PR, even if it did happen a long time ago."

Unmoved, Blackmole stood stiffly with his briefcase firmly gripped in his hand. "People die from drugs they don't take properly all the time. It's not the fault of the manufacturer." He turned toward Margaret. "Our company will be back in touch about the manuscript and…their donation to the Herbarium."

He turned to Carol. "I think you should know that the water lily is not extinct." He pulled from his pocket a teardrop-shaped glass vial and held it up. "A young woman by the river sold me this." Inhaling rapidly as if out of breath, he added, "She said she made it from local water lilies; she called it, nabagûck."

He smiled quietly to himself, turning the vial over in his hand and caressing it. "She told me to come back tonight for more."

Returning the vial carefully to his pocket, he patted it gently and left the room.

Ingrid, who was determined not to make eye-contact with Carol, apologized to Margaret for any "inconvenience" their morning visit might have caused.

"Carol, could I speak to you for a minute," said Flores. Carol looked at him warily—he didn't look angry. No, definitely not.

Flores pulled up a chair and Carol sat down across from him. "This is huge," he said, holding both his hands up. "We've known about this manuscript for hundreds of years, but we started doubting what we knew because no one had seen it—or even knew someone who had." He put his elbows on the desk, put his fingertips together, and continued.

"So, clearly you know, from the way this meeting has played out," he waved his right hand vaguely around the room. "Ownership of this manuscript is a contentious issue. This book is filled with wisdom from our people—*peoples*, to be more precise, but it was written by a White man. Not just any White man but one who was part of an occupying force hostile to Indigenous people."

"However,"—Flores tapped his heart with his right hand—"in my view, and I'm expressing *my* views here not necessarily those of the tribe, things are not black and white. What do you see when you look at the manuscript's drawings?"

Carol smiled, "Beauty."

"I see love," Flores shrugged. "The artist had no commercial motives. Who would have paid him to create this capturing all the beauty of the wilderness, collecting all the Medéwewen secrets about their medicines and their uses? The man who put this together was someone who felt great reverence—if not great love—for our people."

He leaned back in his chair. "So, what I'm saying is that I don't think we should see the manuscript like a child in a custody battle, and I don't want to see the manuscript used as a proxy for bigger fights over imperialism and conquest. Those are legitimate issues, but what we're dealing with here," he said, pointing to the manuscript, "is *world* culture—nobody should own it; everyone should have access to it."

"Mr. Flores, you speak of beauty and world culture, but I'm afraid guys like Blackmole aren't interested in all that high-minded stuff. He's thinking about how much money his company will make if it gets exclusive rights to the manuscript's secrets. He's thinking about all the cool new drugs they'll have that their rivals won't, and what sort of mansion he's going to buy for himself after his next big promotion."

Flores smiled and rubbed his forehead with the back of his hand. "There will always be Blackmoles." He looked suddenly thoughtful and cocked his head sideways. "You know, it just occurred to me that some of these ownership issues might be moot. We just hired a digital archivist. If we could make a digital copy of the manuscript, then we can share it with whomever we want."

Carol looked suddenly grave. "I'm not sure everyone should have access to it, Mr. Flores."

He looked, confused.

"I found a note in the Archives testifying to one of the medicine's, the water lily's, prophetic powers. I feel strongly that…" Her voice became suddenly stronger, more insistent, "there is some knowledge that does not belong to mortals." She locked him in her gaze. "There is some wisdom that belongs only to the gods…and goddesses."

Flores eyes widened, and he drew back. "Yes, yes, I see that."

Carol wasn't sure what had come over her. She smiled and quickly softened her tone. "Perhaps a digital copy could be made that excluded certain pages."

Flores nodded. "Yes, certainly."

The room was clearing. Margaret was back at her desk typing on her laptop. Derrick was waiting for her by the door with his head propped in his hand.

Flores took his card out of his wallet and handed it to Carol. "Let's continue our conversation, Ms. …Bouchard. I have some documents at the tribal archives I'd like to show you."

"Thank you," said Carol reaching out to shake his hand. "I'll look forward to that."

Flores went to talk to Margaret. Ingrid was long gone.

A wave of relief washed over Carol followed by an even bigger wave of exhaustion. Her knees felt as though they might buckle.

Derrick's eyes were closed when she stopped at the door and looked at him. There was something transcendently sweet about him. He opened his eyes and stretched.

"Ready?" he asked.

She nodded.

The rain had finally stopped, and, as they left the building, a patch of yellow light was warming up the silver clouds in the east.

"It looks as though our adventure in the tunnel, though fun, was entirely unnecessary," Derrick said, inspecting a small hole he had just found in his jeans. "We would have had the same results had we just walked the manuscript to the Herbarium in broad daylight."

"I'm sorry, I know it was for you," Carol said, suddenly serious. "But I had the strangest experience down there. I've had recurrent dreams where I'm swimming in the river—always with someone, someone who looks like me." Carol looked at Derrick out of the corner of her eye to see his response. He looked attentive. "Tonight, when we were in the tunnels, I was there again—the place that appears in my dreams. I could smell it, taste it even. And I realized that it was in *our* river, the St. Joe, and it felt like…well, it felt like home."

A gust of wind blew Carol's black hair into her face. When she pushed it back behind an ear, she turned and smiled at him. He gave her a quizzical look.

"What?"

"Your eyes. It must have been a reflection from somewhere. They flashed red."

She smiled and took his arm as they walked through the parking lot, and into the endless, dark, whispering forest that had suddenly opened before them.

AFTERWORD

THE KING'S MAN IN THE WILDERNESS

~ 1766 ~

Schlosser secured his canoe and walked up the embankment to look at the ruins of the fort. His memory preserved this place intact despite what the fire and the passage of time had done to erase it.

There's where the trading post had been. Here were the trails leading to the trillium, bloodroot, and morel. They'd seen the fox kits playing over there where the choke cherries now grew. Across the river next to the sumacs was where Marguerite's village had been. That flat river rock had been the step to his cabin, and their lumpy straw bed had been where the patch of burdock now grew.

He did not really remember the men—"his" men. He remembered the blacksmith's bad teeth; the young man from Austria who never shut up about his village; the old cook whose bones stuck out at odd angles beneath his shirt. Even when they'd been flesh and blood, they had occupied only the very periphery of his consciousness. Now their bones were moldering in the damp earth. As much as he wished to return to the life that he had had here, he did not want to be the same man.

The generals hadn't censored him after the attack for being unprepared. Michilimackinac had fallen too. Lack of vigilance in both cases. There, the Ojibwas had staged a game of lacrosse, hurling a ball on cue through the Fort's open doors. Their need to retrieve it was then the pretext for passing through the unguarded gate. A year and a half ago, he would have said that the attack was unprovoked. Now, he knew that wasn't true.

He shielded his eyes from the setting sun as he looked across the river to what had been Marguerite's village. There'd be no point in seeking her out. Bodwéwadmi women he'd met when he pulled his boat ashore a day ago said that Marguerite had married one of the tribal chieftains who was ten years her senior.

He walked closer to the river, and a cool breeze drifted toward him. It felt like a soothing compress on his aching head. How strange, he thought, the whole improbability of their love. Despite all their outward differences, the very architecture of their hearts and minds had been the same. Tribal lines had inevitably reasserted themselves, and now he had to figure out what to do with the years that lay before him.

Schlosser took one last look around him, saying a silent farewell to the man he had been here and the dream that had brought him back. He pushed his canoe into the river, through a cluster of water lilies, which he recognized immediately. It was the last plant he had entered in the manuscript. Their pods were just opening in the twilight. He plucked a blood-red blossom: nymphaea odorata, nabagûck, vision flower.

As darkness fell, he knew its inflorescence would be perfected. Its red-velvet petals would open, and it would float in its full glory through the night. Seen by no one. Then, imperceptibly, the petals would begin to close. By morning, it would be once again a plain, green pod. As the days shortened and the cold weather arrived, the decaying pod would sink beneath the water to await the arrival of spring. He tossed the blossom he had plucked back into the water, then sought the river's fastest current to take him north.

Mishipeshu saw that one of her water lily blossoms had been rudely torn off. She rose to the surface to claim it, placing it carefully behind one ear before returning to the lower depths.

She had felt such despair when her sister had not recognized her. After all her searching, to finally find her and then be treated like a stranger. But one moonlit night, Meswake returned to the river bank, knowing at last who she was. It was then that she swam with Mishipeshu, even returning with her to their cave at the river's bend. What a happy homecoming they had with Muskrat and Namé!

But her sister had lived for too long among the two-leggeds to give them up. One night, Meswake brought to the river a two-legged man. Muskrat taught him how to eat pondweed, which he tolerated far better than the man with the torch.

Harnessing Namé once again, Mishipeshu time traveled, but now they searched for seeds. The magic book showed them the plants that grew in Manitou's first garden, and Mishipeshu returned there to gently shake seeds from pods, uproot tubers, and collect leaves and spores. She brought back the animals, fungi, bacteria, even the slime molds.

Meswake, her two-legged, and their many friends planted the wild plants. They brought back Manitou's garden.

Yet all was not as it should be. Thunderbird had flown to far off wintering grounds and not returned. And Mishipeshu, her long black hair, a thundercloud above her head, still dreamed of the two-legged beyond her reach in the Sanctuary of the Dead.

Mishipeshu leaned against a rock and watched the catkins, loosened by spring winds from the river birch, fall gently on the surface. The doe, black bear, and cougar dipped their faces into the crystal water to quench their thirst, and, when raindrops fell, they traveled north, following the river's serpentine path to the mouth of Gitche Manitou.

Glossary

Preface

Senathëwen Zibé
St. Joseph River in northwestern Indiana

Theatiki
Kankakee River, originating in northwestern Indiana and merging with the
Des Plaines River in Illinois

Chapter 1

Illiniwek
Native American tribe called the Illinois by White settlers

Zhagnashêk
The English

Fort Pontchartrain
Fort Detroit

Chapter 2

Wgema
Leader

Medéwewen
Native American medicine society

Wiigwaasabak
Native American ethno-botanical manuscript written on birch bark

Nabagûck
water lily

Chapter 3

Myaamia
Miami People

Chapter 4

Mchëzibe

Mississippi River

Mishigami
Lake Michigan

Chapter 6

Nadwék
Iroquoi People

Afterword

King's Man
A supporter of the British during the American Revolution

Historical Notes

Chapter 1

Father Jacques Marquette, a French Jesuit missionary, explored the Great Lakes region and the Mississippi River from 1669 until his death in 1675. Born in Laon, France to a wealthy family, he arrived in what was then New France in 1666. He learned Native American languages and founded the Mission of St. Ignace, which still stands in St. Ignace, Michigan. In 1674, on a trip south to evangelize the people of the Illinois River Valley, Marquette began to suffer from dysentery while wintering over in the site that would become Chicago. He continued south in the hopes his health would improve. After an abbreviated stay among the Illinois, he set off on a return trip north to St. Ignace, accompanied by two Illinois companions. He died before reaching his destination near what is today Ludington, Michigan. He was 37.

Chapter 2

Fort St. Joseph was built by the French in 1691 to protect a newly-established Catholic mission and an important portage between the St. Joseph and Kankakee Rivers. The British won the fort from the French during the Seven Years War (1756-1763), and it was under the command of Lieutenant Francis Schlosser when it was attacked and burned during Pontiac's Rebellion on May 23, 1763. The fort is currently an archeological site in Niles, Michigan. The medallion described, along with several other artifacts from the fort, are on display at the Niles Fort St. Joseph Museum.

Chapter 3

Spanish soldiers under the command of Captain Eugene Pouré attacked and captured Fort St. Joseph in 1781. The Spaniards occupied the fort for two days before making the long trek back to St. Louis in the snow. Louis Chevalier was chief interpreter. Don Carlos Tayon was a sub lieutenant of the militia. Siggenauk (also known as el Heturno) led the Native American soldiers who had been recruited by the Spaniards to participate in the attack. Siggenauk was an anti-British Potawatomi who migrated to northern Illinois and the Milwaukee area after the failure of Pontiac's Rebellion. The term Midewiwin is used to describe a Native American society dedicated to the use of plants for medicinal purposes and spiritual ceremonies.

CHAPTER 4

In 1822, Baptist missionary Isaac McCoy established the Carey Mission close to the St. Joseph River near present day Niles, Michigan. McCoy led a number of the Potawatomi to a new mission in Kansas in 1831. The story about Christian ladies from Boston sponsoring a Native American child on the condition the child take the name of one of their friends was taken from McCoy's extensive autobiographical writings. McCoy's views on the value of dreams were expressed in his autobiographical writings as well.

CHAPTERS 5-6

Alexis Coquillard was an agent for John Jacob Astor's American Fur Company and is considered to be one of the founders of the city of South Bend. He tried unsuccessfully to create the Kankakee Mill Race, a waterway connecting the St. Joseph and Kankakee Rivers. The story of Coquillard taking Chief Peepenawah's necklace can be found in Chapman's History of St. Joseph County. As mentioned in the story, Coquillard had a licensed ferry service across the St. Joseph River. He died following a head injury from a beam falling during a fire at his mill on January 6, 1855. Chief Menominee's village was outside today's Plymouth, Indiana. Bartlett's Bakery was on 124 Washington Street.

CHAPTER 7

Pierre Navarre was the first White settler in St. Joseph County. He trapped and traded furs among the Native Americans who lived in the area and married a Potawatomi woman named Angelique (Kechoueckquay) with whom he had six children. When the Potawatomi were forcibly removed from their homeland in the 1840s, he traveled west with the tribe, returning home after his wife's death. Pierre's son Anthony became an active member of the Mormon Church but later drifted away from the church and pursued real estate. By the spring of 1831, keelboat service for general freighting was initiated on the St. Joseph River. Pierre Navarre died on December 27, 1864 in his daughter's home. Isaac McCoy's son Josephus did become a doctor, but he died 33 years before the time of the story.

CHAPTER 8

The death of Henry Porter is documented in Chapman's History of St. Joseph County (pp. 592-593). The reason for his death is unknown. Porter's employer, the Studebaker Company, founded in 1852, originally built wagons, buggies, carriages and harnesses before becoming an automobile manufacturer in 1904.

230

The "Haymarket Affair" was the aftermath of a bombing that took place at a labor demonstration in Chicago on May 4, 1886. The bombing caused the deaths of seven police officers and led to the hanging of four protestors, despite the fact that none of them was charged with actually throwing the bomb.

CHAPTER 9

Father Julius Nieuwland was a Holy Cross priest and professor of chemistry and botany at the University of Notre Dame, Indiana. Although best known as the inventor of a type of synthetic rubber, he also discovered the chemical compound lewisite, a chemical warfare agent. Nieuwland was the student of Edward Greene, an American botanist, who was an associate in botany at the Smithsonian Institution. Nieuwland, like the character patterned after him, was known to shoot leaves off of trees for botanical samples. Green's herbarium is now at the University of Notre Dame as part of the Greene-Nieuwland Herbarium. The lab assistant named Knute who appears in the story is Knute Rockne, the legendary Notre Dame football coach, who was one of Nieuwland's students and served as his lab assistant. Greene died at Catholic University before he could start his professorship at Notre Dame.

CHAPTER 10

The Grand Kankakee Marsh originally encompassed 5,300 square miles and was part of the Kankakee River's floodplain (for comparison, the Florida Everglades cover 2,357 square miles) It was one of the largest marsh wetlands in the United States and was an important Native American hunting ground. By the nineteenth century, it had become a favorite hunting destination for tycoons, celebrities, and political leaders including, it is believed, Theodore Roosevelt. Collier's Lodge, now an archeological site, was a popular destination. Evidence of a sweat lodge was found during an excavation of the lodge site. Although there are conflicting stories about the origin of Dunn's Bridge, it was believed to have been constructed in the mid-1890s, using steel beams salvaged from the Ferris wheel built for the 1893 Columbian World's Fair in Chicago. Quentin Roosevelt, the former president's youngest son, was killed in aerial combat over France, July 14, 1918. The State of Indiana passed the Swamp Act in 1852, which initiated the draining of the Kankakee wetlands to create farmland.

CHAPTER 11

The story of Katy McQuillan was based on an incident described in Chapman's History of St. Joseph County (pp. 594-95) of a murder-suicide that took place in 1876 and involved a Kate Fleck. After her sister died in childbirth, Fleck came to live with her sister's husband to take care of the infant. After a dispute over pay, Kate left a note for her brother-in-law which said: "Charley: Hunt me and your baby on the other side of the railroad bridge in the river." The bodies of Kate and the infant were found in the river several days later. The railroad bridge referenced in Kate's note is now a pedestrian walkway near Western Avenue. Zell's Funeral Parlor, Hudson Lake Casino, City Wide Liquor (still in operation), Robertson's were all businesses operating in South Bend in the 1930's. The Shadow was an American radio show that ran from 1937 to 1954. Lost Horizon was an adventure fantasy movie released in 1937 that was based on a novel by James Hilton.

Chapter 12

Anne Raven Wilkinson was the first African-American ballerina to dance for a major classical ballet company. She danced with the Ballet Russe de Monte Carlo, a company that performed in South Bend in 1952. Alicia Alonso danced the role of enchanted princess in Swan Lake at the Palace Theatre, and Igor Yousekevitch danced the part of Prince Siegfried. Nina Novak danced Columbine. Despite the company's efforts to protect her, Raven experienced discrimination, especially when the company toured the South. Ultimately, she moved to the Netherlands where she joined the National Ballet for seven years and performed Swan Lake many times.

Chapter 13

The Century Center Convention Center in South Bend was designed by architects Philip Johnson and John Burgee and was completed in 1977. The center, built on the banks of the West Race canal, overlooks the St. Joseph River and includes a two-story high glass wall. The historian's comments about the city's relationship with the Potawatomi can be found in the South Bend History Museum Archives. The old hydroelectric plant described in the story was built by James Oliver in 1905 to power the Oliver Hotel and Opera House. The foundation of the Oliver powerhouse still stands in the St. Joseph River, though the building was destroyed in the 1980s. Kubiak's Tavern opened in 1933 and is still in operation.

Chapter 14

Schlosser and two other soldiers were exchanged for two Native captives at Fort Detroit. He was later assigned to Fort Stanwix in Syracuse, New York.

According to the British Annual Register (1768), an "Indian slave" shot Schlosser dead; his remains and possessions were sent to Montreal, which was then under British control. The botanist mentioned by the character Derrick Fischer was Christian Gottlieb Ludwig (1709 – 1773), a professor in Leipzig.

Afterward

As part of the coordinated attacks against the British in Pontiac's Rebellion, a group of Ojibwe, Ottawa, Wyandot, and Potawatomi warriors stormed the British Fort Michilimackinac on June 2, 1763. Native Americans staged a game of baaga adowe (similar to modern day lacrosse) to distract the British and gain entry to the fort.

Selected Bibliography

Chapter 1

Edmunds, David. (1978). *The Potawatomi—Keepers of the Fire*. Norman: Oklahoma: University of Oklahoma Press.

Thwaites, Reuben Gold (Ed.). (1927). *The Indians of North America: from "The Jesuit Relations and Allied Documents: Travels and Explorations of the Jesuit Missionaries in New France."* New York (State): Harcourt, Brace & Co.

Chapter 2

Harburn, Dr. Todd E. *(2002).*"British Folly on the St. Joseph: Ensign Francis Schlösser of the 60th Regiment and the Massacre at Fort St. Joseph During Pontiac's Uprising, May 25, 1763." The Michilimackinac Society Press: Publication No. 4, pp. 1-12.

Nassaney, Michael S. (Ed.) (2019) *Fort St. Joseph Revealed: The Historical Archaeology of a Fur Trading Post*. University Press of Florida.

Nassaney, Michael S. et al. (Fall, 2003). "The Search for Fort St. Joseph (1691-1781) in Niles, Michigan." *Midcontinental Journal of Archaeology*. Vol. 28, No. 2, pp. 107-144.

Peyser, Joseph L. (1988). *Letters from New France: Selected Translations and Readings on the Pays d'en haut 1686-1783 (revised edition)*. Indiana University at South Bend.

Chapter 3

Clifton, James A. (1977). *The prairie people: continuity and change in Potawatomi Indian culture, 1665-1965*. Lawrence: Kansas: Regents Press of Kansas.

Emery, Frank B. (1931). *The passing of the mission and Fort St. Joseph, 1686-1781*. Michigan: Old Forts and Historic Memorial Association.

Mason, Edward G. (1886). *The March of the Spaniards across Illinois*. New York (State): Historical Publishing Co.

Nasatir, A. P. (1928). *"The Anglo-Spanish Frontier in the Illinois Country during the American Revolution 1779-1783."* Journal of the Illinois State Historical Society. Springfield: Illinois State Historical Society, Vol.21 (3), pp. 291-358.

Chapter 4

McCoy, M. Isaac. *History of the Baptist Indian Missions: Embracing Remarks on the Former and Present Condition of the Aboriginal Tribes; their settlement within the Indian Territory and Their Future Prospects*. (1840) District of Columbia: W. M. Morrison; H. and S. Raynor.

Chapter 5

Alex Coquillard. (1890). "Family Papers" (1833-1879). Collection code CZEB. University of Notre Dame Archives.

History of St. Joseph County, Indiana. A; Together with sketches of its cities, villages and townships, educational, religious, civil, military, and political history; portraits of prominent persons, and biographies of representative citizens. (1880) Chicago: Chas C. Chapman & Co. pp. 462-467.

Chapter 6

Schmal, Richard. (2011). *Tales of the People and Places of the Olde Kankakee River.*

Bartlett, Charles Henry. (2009). *Tales of Kankakee Land.* Kessinger Publishing. Written in 1904.

"The First Settlers: Pierre Navarre." https://www.historymuseumsb.org/the-first-settlers/

"The Navarre Cabin." https://www.historymuseumsb.org/see-do/the-navarre-cabin/

Chapter 7

History of St. Joseph County, Indiana. pp. 592-593.

Miceli, Stephen R. (2009) *Industrialization and Immigration: Labor at the River's Bend.* University of Toledo. Dissertation.

Chapter 8

Nieuwland's letters to E.L. Greene, 1910-1. University of Notre Dame Archives.

"Father Nieuwland and the 'Dew of Death,'" Joel L. Vilensky, Notre Dame Magazine, Winter 2002-03.

Chapter 9

Folder on the Kankakee River, Local & Family History Room, St. Joseph County Library, South Bend, IN.

Bartlett, Charles Henry. (2009). *Tales of Kankakee Land.* Kessinger Publishing. Written in 1904.

Chapter 10

Chapman's History of St. Joseph County. pp. 594-95.
South Bend Tribunes, 1930s.

CHAPTER 11

"A Conversation with Raven Wilkinson," Michael Langlois, *Ballet Review*, Fall 2007.
South Bend Tribune, December 9, December 16, 1956.

CHAPTER 12

South Bend Tribune, January 17, 1975.
History Museum Archives. South Bend hydroelectric power plants.

CHAPTER 13

Harburn, Dr. Todd E. *(2002)*."British Folly on the St. Joseph: Ensign Francis Schlösser of the 60th Regiment and the Massacre at Fort St. Joseph During Pontiac's Uprising, May 25, 1763." The Michilimackinac Society Press: Publication No. 4, pp. 1-12.

ABOUT THE AUTHOR

Karla Cruise is a historical fiction author focusing on the Great Lakes region, known for her debut novel, *The Water Lilies of Mishipeshu,* which won a silver medal from the UK's Historical Novel Society in 2024. She holds a PhD in Russian literature and language from the University of Chicago and has contributed to publications such as Russian Life and the Slavic and East European Journal. Karla also translates works on diverse topics, including Russian art and AI. Additionally, she writes on science and engineering, with articles featured in *Futurity, Science Digest,* and *RealClear Science.*

About HTF Publishing

Founded in 2023 as an imprint of History Through Fiction, HTF Publishing is hybrid publisher of compelling, high-quality historical novels. Following in the tradition of History Through Fiction, HTF Publishing seeks to provide readers with engaging historical narratives that are rooted in detailed and accurate historical research. As a hybrid press, we want to work with authors who are serious about their craft and aspire to share imaginative, important, and well-researched, historical narratives with the world.

If you enjoyed this novel, please consider leaving a review. It's the best way to support us and our authors. Plus, you'll be helping other readers discover this great story.

Thank you!

www.HistoryThroughFiction.com